Lost Souls of Paradise

Ian Ritchie Stewart

Published by Ian Ritchie Stewart, 2020.

This is a work of fiction. Similarities to real people, places, or events are entirely coincidental.

LOST SOULS OF PARADISE

First edition. October 15, 2020.

Written by Ian Ritchie Stewart.

Table of Contents

For Sunshine, and all the lost souls who find themselves at the end of the road, and for the people who see themselves when they look in their eyes, then cry.

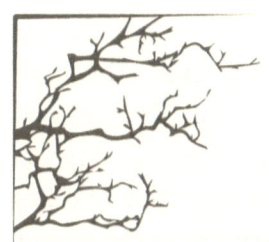

1. Amelia Calling

Dr. **Walter Arlin Colburn** had been a prominent and popular Chicago psychiatrist for more than thirty years. As he approached his sixty-first birthday, he was finding himself less and less willing to tolerate the selfish indulgences of his wealthy executive clients and their overly shallow and excessively extravagant wives. He had grown increasingly aloof and disinterested, unable to control his daydreaming as his clients settled into the deep leather chair and revealed their secrets. He drifted off to times in his past when his wife was still alive and his life was full of purpose, compassion, satisfaction, and love.

He had developed the uncanny skill of being in two places at one time. He became increasingly anxious for his clients to arrive for their appointments, anxious to escape into his dream world. He became agitated if they failed to fully use their allotted fifty-minute session or tried to manipulate him into allowing it to dissolve into friendly chit-chat, cheating him out of precious moments of personal bliss.

His ability to remain perfectly 'in the moment' and focused on his client had evolved into an involuntary reflex. His congenial responses to their prompting remained appropriate and caring, even though he was completely, 'out of town'. Cloaked in his reputation as one of the most sought-after psychiatrists by the Chicago elite, he had full command of his practice.

He was the captain of his ship.

He sat alone in his upscale downtown apartment surrounded by memories of his past. Photos of his two sons, his three grandchildren, and his mother and father stood sentry on every tabletop. Pictures of him and his beautiful wife of thirty-six years, Amelia, posing with friends on the slopes of Colorado's finest winter resorts, sipping wine in a Bordeaux café, and riding the rapids on the Rio Grande, decorated the hallway walls from end to end. Every corner of his fourteenth-floor flat gave him reason to smile. Or, so it seemed.

Sitting in his grand recliner he sipped his favorite Spanish brandy from a cut crystal glass. His eye traveled slowly around the room and back to the glass in his hand. Lost for a moment in a thoughtless stare, he sighed deeply. Bending down, he reached into the open black bag on the floor by his side and picked up the camera that he and Amelia had used on their last vacation together. He opened the tiny access door on its side and sat staring at the memory card contemplating the potential flood of emotion that might be unleashed if the hidden images were released.

Distracted by the ringing of his telephone, he shut the camera and answered, "Hello!"

His son Daniel was calling to remind him of the birthday dinner for his grandson on the following Thursday night. The conversation was short and after he mounted the phone back on its cradle, he turned his stare once again toward the camera. Silent pain and yearning brought him to tears as he submitted to the calling of the images trapped within. Holding the camera in both his hands he pressed it against his forehead. The faint sounds of laughter rang in his ears. He rocked back and forth in agony as the tears poured from his eyes. Then, sometime later, his head dropped to his chest, and he slept away the pain for another day.

The next morning, he sat in his office chair staring out the window at the clouds drifting over the Chicago skyline.

"Dr. Colburn, Dorothy McClain is here for her ten-thirty appointment," sounded out the announcement from the intercom on his desk.

"Thank you, Jennifer, please have her wait. I'll be just a moment!" He remained locked in his stare at the gray sky outside his twentiethfloor window.

After a moment, he pushed himself out of his leather chair and gently pulled the curtain closed. He removed his overcoat from the rack and dropped it over his arm, then, he opened his office door and walked through the reception area, and out the front door. Mrs. McClain looked at Jennifer, jumped to her feet and anxiously asked, "What about my appointment?"

As the doctor walked across the street the sounds of happier times were faintly resounding in his ear. He walked up to the teller's window at the New Commerce Bank and Trust and slid a withdrawal slip across the cold granite counter as Marjorie greeted him like an old friend.

"Hi Doctor C.!" she said cheerfully.

"Getting hotter outside?" she asked as she began processing his transaction.

"Not much we can do about that Margie." He smiled as he wiped the beads of sweat from his brow. Her eyelids rose as she read the amount on the withdrawal slip.

"Gee Dr C., how do you want this? "Hundreds, please!" the doctor responded.

She opened her drawer and began counting out one-hundred-dollar bills into stacks of one hundred until there were five stacks on the counter.

"Fifty thousand, now let me just put these in envelopes, and there you go Dr. C . . . I sure hope you don't have far to go with all that cash."

He slid the envelopes across the counter, then into his coat pockets. "My grandson's birthday is Thursday. He's going to be six," he said with a smile.

"Ooh, lucky boy!" she exclaimed as he turned and walked toward the exit. As he pushed through the revolving door his cell phone rang. He pulled it out of his pocket to see who was calling and recognized his office number. He opened the phone with his thumb and then let it snap closed as he hailed a cab.

"Good morning, sir!" the driver greeted him as he pulled the door closed and straightened his glasses, "where to?"

As the doctor settled into the back seat he asked, "Do you know if the Lord and Taylor store is still open in the Water Tower Place building?"

"Oh, yeah, Oprah's got a penthouse up there ya' know. My brother's wife works at the Wow Bao restaurant on the ground floor where she eats sometimes. According to what I've heard Lord's isn't supposed to be closing until next spring," the driver explained.

"Great! Take me there first and then any chance you could wait while I pick up a gift for my grandson?" the doctor asked.

"I'm all yours, bud!" the driver responded as he flipped his meter to hourly.

After a short drive through town, the cab turned left onto North Michigan Avenue and pulled over in front of the Water Tower Place, just beyond Macy's front door. He slipped the car into park and turned to look over the seat at his passenger, then said, "I'll be watching for you from over there when you come out," pointing toward the cab stand across the street next to Borders Book Store.

Dr. Colburn stepped out of the cab and headed toward the expanse of doors which led into the mall. Once in the main lobby, the very object of his intent was immediately in view. Through the Lord and Taylor store's tall glass entrance, he could see his prize, mounted artfully atop the cabinet halfway down the aisle on the right. His eyes were glued on a meticulously detailed model of a wooden schooner in full sail. He had admired it a year earlier while shopping in the store for a new briefcase. It was still there, waiting for him to claim for his favorite grandson.

The clerk went to get a ladder from the storage room in the back. Within minutes the doctor was hurrying out the front door and across the avenue to the waiting cab. Back on North Michigan Avenue, he asked the driver's name.

"Leo," the driver answered.

As Dr. C. passed a crisp one-hundred-dollar bill over the front seat, he asked, "Leo, what would you say to three hours of helping me for say, one hundred dollars an hour?"

"Hey, if it's legal, and I can tell the story to my wife when I get home without bein' whacked in the head, I'm good to go," Leo answered with a laugh. The doctor directed him to his apartment building and told him to wait at the front door for twenty minutes. As he opened the side door and stepped out onto the sidewalk, he handed a second hundred to the driver as a deposit. He entered his access code and proceeded to the elevator. The doors opened and out stepped Dr. Colburn's neighbor Mrs. Elliaser and her new Pomeranian, Shootsie.

"Oh, Dr. Colburn, what are you doing home in the middle of the day?" she nosily asked.

"Forgetful me, I left some letters that need mailing. How is Shootsie adjusting to high rise life?" he asked.

"Oh, Dr. Colburn, I would have never thought any dog could ever replace my little Poppie, but Shootsie is even sweeter than Poppie ever was, and he never has to . . . ," she kept talking as the elevator door closed and the doctor headed up to his fourteenth floor flat.

The telephone was ringing as he entered the room. He walked to his desk where he checked the caller I.D. Again, his office was trying to find him. He left the phone ringing and crossed the carpet to the huge leather recliner where he had fallen asleep the night before. On the floor was the camera. Just thirteen hours earlier it had driven him into a painful abyss of memories.

He slowly picked up the camera and flipped open the side access door. Out popped the memory card and with it the sounds of a crowded bar full of happy people flooded his thoughts. He plucked out the card, closed the access door, set the camera on the chair, and dropped the card into his pocket. As he locked the front door, he turned to take one last look at the room, as if he might never return.

With the telephone still ringing he whispered through his tears, "I'm coming sweetheart."

He slid back into the cab and shut the door. "To the airport if you please Leo," he instructed the portly driver.

As they pulled into traffic the doctor took out a business card and wrote something on the back. "Leo, what's your wife's name?" he asked.

"Oh, you don't want to hear this," Leo laughingly answered.

"Cleo!" "You're kidding me, aren't you?" asked the doctor in good-humored disbelief.

"No sir, there ain't no kidding when it comes to that big mama, we're Leo and Cleo Rabonnavich," the cabbie laughingly answered.

"Is Cleo any good at wrapping birthday gifts?"

"After six kids, I guess so, why you askin that?" Leo curiously returned. The doctor slid forward on the back seat and handed the card to the giant of a man behind the wheel. Held to the underside of the card was another onehundred-dollar bill. "Here," he said. "Have her wrap this boat and put a big bow on top, then you drop it off at my office and tell my secretary to put a card to my grandson on it. The address is on the back of the card. Tell her to take it to the party on Thursday night. If she asks where I am, just tell her you were only hired to deliver the gift. You don't know me and have no idea where I am, savvy?" "Well sir, that won't be any stretch for me, 'cause unless your name is on this card, and I choose to look, I won't know who you are, or where you went after you got out of my cab. So, whatever secret you want to keep, sits in your back pocket, not mine," Leo explained as he turned onto West Kennedy Expressway and negotiated the cab into the center lane.

"You can just count on that Mr. Whoeveryouare. This fat boy don't know nothin' bout nothin', but he and his fat mama goin' out for Tbones in this windy city tonight," he added.

Doctor C. smiled as he watched a plane lift above the airport fence. "It all changes in a breath Leo. You only get so many. Don't waste a one my friend! Not a one!"

Walking into the terminal he pulled his silk tie from his collar and wadded it into a ball, then tossed it into the trash can that stood beside the escalator as he stepped onboard. He locked his eyes on the outbound marquee that hung above the upper landing. He glanced down at his watch; it was six minutes shy of noon.

He was studying the departure time listings when his phone rang again. Jennifer was making one more frantic attempt to find out what to do with his patients. He looked around the huge lobby and saw a fountain at the entrance to the airport food court. He headed to the bubbling water and dropped his cell phone in. It sank slowly to the bottom where it rested among hundreds of coins and ten times as many soggy wishes.

The renegade doctor took a deep breath as he contemplated the consequence of his next move. He reached into his left pocket and turned the memory card over three times with his thumb. He listened to the sounds of a distant ocean. He heard seagulls and laughter. He heard someone far off calling to him. He felt pulled. There was no way to resist. He was already gone. Standing with his ticket in hand, he had a little time to kill before boarding. He wandered into the gift shop, hoping to find a book worth reading. He glanced at the titles and was disappointed to find so many books that he had already read. He looked through the self-help titles, but nothing caught his fancy. Then he glanced up at the magazine rack on the back wall of the shop. One magazine came into focus. He frowned and tried to clear his vision as he realized that his eyes could see none of the other magazines, only the one. He dropped his glasses from his eyes and strained to clear the view, still only one magazine in a blur of color. He was scared for a moment as he approached the rack.

"Excuse me!" he said after bumping into a lady on his way down the narrow aisle. He moved slowly toward the mirage with apprehension and reached out his hand to see if it was real.

"SAILING WORLD Magazine"!

Why was this magazine calling to him? He stared at the cover straining to understand what message he might be meant to receive from it. He studied the photograph of the beautiful white sailboat cutting through a sea of blue. The couple at the helm seemed distantly familiar but he was unable to make the connection. He looked at each feature title to see if perhaps there was some hidden explanation. Nothing seemed to click into place. He was aware that he was being pulled into some hole by some power he had never known existed.

In less than one second, he consciously decided to yield completely to whatever destiny lay before him. As he took the magazine from the rack, his vision returned to normal and he nervously straightened his glasses to their proper position. He proceeded to the checkout counter and tendered payment for the first boat magazine he had ever purchased.

"Sir, sir, excuse me, sir, we'll be landing in Atlanta shortly. You'll need to put your seat in the upright position."

The doctor awakened to the flight attendant's instructions and adjusted his seat. He yawned and stretched as best he could in the cramped space, then leaned toward the oval portside window to catch the view. He watched as the city lights rose to meet the landing jet. He walked down the ramp and into the giant terminal. He asked the attendant where the next gate was located. She looked at his ticket and gestured down the long corridor, "All the way at the end, then take a right."

She reminded him that he needed to be in the loading area in ten minutes and that he should not delay. He expressed appreciation for her directions and set out down the long hallway.

"Walter!" He heard someone call out from the crowd of people passing by in the opposite direction

"Hey, Walter," someone had apparently recognized him.

There he was, in the Atlanta International Airport, far from Chicago, and someone had recognized him. Was it a colleague, or perhaps a patient? It didn't matter. He kept walking without paying the least attention to whoever it was. If he didn't respond to his own name, well then, it must not have been him. That was his hope, at least. He moved on toward the next boarding station and didn't even want to know who had seen him. It was behind him. Not even a part of him. A mistaken identity. It happens all the time.

His next stop was the Miami International Airport where he had a three-hour layover. There was quite a difference between the July air of Chicago and the salt-soaked tropical air of Miami. He yearned to smell the beach, the coconuts, the Cuban, coffee, and that fabulous Caribbean cuisine as it gets served up heartily on the roadside tables at those quaint little South Beach cafes. Walking out the front door, he looked toward the east, then, he crossed the footbridge, to the top of the parking garage and gazed toward the distant glowing lights of downtown Miami bouncing off the underside of the low-hanging clouds.

He was taken back thirty years, to the week that he had taken the family with him to a psychiatric symposium at the beautiful Fontainebleau Oceanfront Resort in Miami Beach. Amelia and the boys spent their days swimming in the glass bottom pool, diving down to wave to the tourists that watched from the other side of the thick glass, and playing on the beach while he attended workshops and lectures. He remembered the wonderful Cuban restaurant on South Beach and Joe's Crab House. The boys wanted to see an alligator so they stayed an extra day and drove west on the Tamiami Trail to watch a Seminole Indian chief wrestle a giant alligator named "The Boss."

The roar of a jet plane taking off shook him back to the moment and he walked back down the long hall to gate 23 at the end of the corridor.

A small two-engine puddle jumper taxied up to the end of the tarmac and after a dozen or so commuters unloaded, the attendant announced it was ready to board. There were only three people, other than Dr. C., being picked up in Miami that evening; one businessman and a very amorous young couple, full of anticipation and affection. The doctor handed his ticket to the flight attendant as he approached the bottom of the boarding ramp.

"No luggage, Mr. Colburn?" she asked, handing back the ticket.

"I've got everything I need waiting for me," he answered with a gentle grin. He smiled as he pushed himself into his seat. He overheard the pretty girl whisper to her boyfriend something about, "doing it" over Key Largo as he snapped his seatbelt closed and tugged it tight.

The plane was less than half full that night. The pilot and copilot carried on conversations from the cockpit with the passengers in the forward section. It was very relaxing. Dr. C. was feeling more than just melancholic, more like he was in his "perfect" place. The plane rose through the wispy clouds and into the darkening sky. He watched the colored lights of Miami Beach fade as they banked to the left, then to the right, then followed the shoreline of Biscayne Bay and off toward the Florida Keys. Leaning his head back on the headrest, he recalled a conversation he once had with a colleague and good friend at a dinner party many years ago. The two psychiatrists were sharing cigars in the night air on a patio overlooking a golf course. Dr. Juan Miller was originally from Venezuela and had come to Chicago to complete his doctorate and establish his practice. Juan had presented an interesting approach to the issue of purposeful living and existential intervention. It seemed very simple and somewhat profound, but Dr. C. never really grasped just how profound. He could hear Juan's broken English as he closed his eyes. He could taste the cigar and smell the grass of the golf course as he mulled over his deceased friend's words.

"You know, when I want to consider if I am in the right place, I simply look at my feet and accept that at this particular moment, this is where I am, and this is what I am doing, and if I am treating people right, and my conscience is clear, then this must be where I am supposed to be."

If this philosophy never seemed applicable in his life before, Dr. C. was ready to embrace it now. It allowed him to temporarily justify the place in which he was currently sitting, on a little plane, over a big ocean, headed back. Back to Old Key West.

2. The Haunting of Jillian

Jillian Bethany Dougherty, or Jill as she was fondly known by friends and family, was the daughter of Bill and Dolores Dougherty from Gloucester, Massachusetts. The oldest of three children, Jillian was the jewel of her family. As a young girl, she tended to her responsibilities working in her parents' ice cream store, doing her chores, babysitting her brother and sister, keeping up with her school assignments, and flirting with boys. She had loads of friends and was full of promise.

As she grew through her teen years, she became known as a girl well-skilled at taking advantage of every opportunity to promote her best attributes in a favorable light. Her accolades were celebrated at almost every Friday morning school assembly. Awards and recognition for her achievements of excellence were held as a standard that few other students could hope to match. In tenth grade, she was the president of the drama club. In the eleventh grade, she was the top performer in the debate club, the point guard on the girls' basketball team, and president of the student council. As a senior, every dream she had ever imagined was exceeded when she was elected the Gloucester High School homecoming queen.

Yes, everyone in town felt that she was destined to become a Washington politician, a Wall Street legend, or a Hollywood movie starlet. Somehow, her path had already been laid by some distant planning board, and after spending two summers as a Candy Striper at the Addison Gilbert Medical Center, she made a decision that would carve her destiny into Pennsylvania granite.

In hind sight, everyone should have seen it coming. Her compassion and love for life, her amazing capacity to be sympathetic to the suffering of others, her unending generosity and her absolute dedication to finding solutions to others' problems; the signs were abundant. How could anyone have been surprised when she announced she was entering the nursing program at Boston College?

In 1997, Jillian's father and mother had taken the children on a vacation, camping in the Florida Keys. They closed the ice cream shop for two weeks and had driven the long stretch south, down I95, in three days. Jillian was eleven at the time and she and her younger sister Katrina, Trina for short, and little brother Bo, had the time of their lives. Bo and his dad fished while the girls hunted for sand dollars in the clear shallow waters. Their mother sat on the sand in the sun, looking up from her magazine to monitor the family's whereabouts and calling out if they wandered too far down the beach. The girls chased the sandpipers and laughed at the crabs and the colorful parrot fish nibbling on the rocks along the seawall. They imagined them telling each other stories about the people watching from above. "That one can't swim, and that one can't hold its breath for even one whole minute."

They gathered coconuts and struggled for hours trying to find new ways of breaking them open to eat the hidden flesh of the sweet meat. They caught fiddler crabs as they scampered from hole to hole trying to beat the gentle wash of the incoming waves and ran to give them to Bo and their father to use as bait. Hiding in the mangroves, they spied on lovers that lay on blankets in the sand, soaking in the rays and making their romantic plans of marriage and spending a lifetime in each other's arms. They pretended they were shipwrecked children of a king from a faraway land, hiding from pirates who sought to capture them and sell them as slaves or hold them for ransom. They laid out shells in the sand in the shape of a hull from a Spanish galleon that had sunk to the bottom on a reef, and pretended they were scuba divers on a treasure hunt. By the end of each day, they were exhausted and so sunburned that they couldn't sleep.

Their father had borrowed a huge umbrella tent from his cousin Mort whose sons had been Boy Scouts. Mort had loaded them up with all the sleeping bags and cooking gear they would need for the trip. They had a Coleman lantern and a green two-burner cook stove so most of their meals were prepared right there at the campsite. Bill budgeted enough extra money into the trip to be able to take two jaunts to town where they could enjoy the sunset fanfare and try some of the famous Key West cuisine. On the last afternoon before their scheduled departure, they loaded into the station wagon and headed down the Overseas Highway toward Key West. During the thirty-five-mile drive, Jillian's blistered nose was glued to the window, watching as the evening sun sank lower and lower over the Gulf of Mexico. Trina entertained herself with keeping count of the number of bridges they crossed while Bo remained asleep, slumped over with his head against her arm.

Bill parked the car in the Old Town section of the city where every house reminded him of his great-grandmother's home in Salem. The slatted shutters and the huge front porches and the beveled glass windows brought back all those long-lost childhood memories when his brothers and cousins, and he, gathered to celebrate the holidays. He could almost smell the cinnamon from Gammie's sugar cookies as he climbed out of the front seat and turned to lock the car door. He just wanted to take one last walk through the Old Town section before ending their vacation and heading home. Just one last visit with a feeling he thought had died, many years ago.

They took their time walking as Bill pointed out the curious architectural nuances that make Key West such a unique and quaint island town. The gingerbread filigree that hung from the soffits above the porches, the fancy scrollwork that flanked the ends and corners of the eaves and tops of the columns, the ancient glasswork that rippled and flowed like honey under the gravity of antiquity, and the wreckers' watch towers that were mounted on the roofs, where old-time captains of wrecker boats watched the reef for the next claimable cargo ship to fall victim to the treacherous tides as they attempted to navigate the southernmost point of a young America.

Before long they came to the Pirate's well, historically known as the only freshwater source on the island, and the destination of every thirsty pirate and seagoing man that drifted within one hundred miles of its location. Legend has it that many a bad man lost his life fighting over the precious water that lay at the bottom of that well. The kids huddled together as their mother read the plaque that marked the spot. When she got to the part about dead pirates Trina started crying, so they moved on.

THEY CAME UPON AN OLD building constructed of quarry stone. It was a theatre house with a tin roof and a huge ficus tree growing out of its side. The quarry stones bulged from the expansion of the tree roots, leaving gaps in the wall where they could see into the darkness of the building. A dim light illuminated the green curtains that hung over the stage, making the room look like a dungeon. Wild chickens were roosting in the limbs of the tree and started cackling as the family approached. There was a wrought iron gate and a stone wall that wrapped around both sides of the building and the place looked like a set from a movie scene.

An old man with a brown leather vest and long thin hair was sitting on the lower section of the stone wall smoking a cigarette. Next to him were two huge green lizards with pink rhinestone encrusted cat collars around their necks. Leashes kept them next to him as he sat there waiting for the tourists to walk by. The man was very dirty and smelled like a dock piling at low tide. The girls began screaming and stomping their feet wildly when they saw the lizards. This angered the old man who then yelled at them to get away from his lizards before they got loose and escaped. Bill herded the family out of the area, apologizing to him as they left. Bo thought the iguanas were "cool" and wanted to go back to pet them, but Jill and Trina were scared and wanted to leave. Bill and Dolores kept them moving until they were safely around the corner.

They moved down the brick-paved street until it opened onto a wide pavilion overlooking the water. They could see the lights shining in the homes on Tank Island just offshore, across the fastmoving channel. A second island was further to their right. Wisteria Island, or more popularly known as Christmas Tree Island, was a completely uninhabited dredge site that had become seeded and overrun with nonindigenous and intrusive Australian pine trees. The dark forest silhouette covered it from end to end. Sailboats, with tiny flickering lights, were anchored all around it, bobbing up and down in the waves.

As they stepped out into the crowded boardwalk they felt as though they had entered another world. There were gypsies and tightrope walkers, fire eaters, magicians, fortune tellers, jugglers, animal trainers and musicians everywhere. It was very exciting! Like stepping right into a circus! They felt as though they were a part of some great parade. Trina was so excited that she wet her panties, which was not unusual for her; she would never in her life use a public bathroom.

The fiery orange sun was sinking low in the sky over the western horizon, casting a blaze of colors from pink to purple into the darkening sky above the crowd. There were all kinds of boats parading by the pier, some going one way, some going the other, all of them were loaded with people drinking and having a grand time. Every boat was decorated with strings of outdoor Christmas lights. Sailboats with tall masts had lights strung all the way to the top, and people were climbing up the wires on the sides, waving at the crowd up on the pier. Just as the family made their way over to the water, a huge two masted sailboat went by. Every single person on board had turned their backside toward the crowd and in unison bent over, then dropped their drawers. The crowd roared with laughter and applause while Bill and Dolores nervously shaded the children's eyes and turned them one by one away from the water. To say the least, the event had quite an impact on all three of them, especially little brother Bo.

They meandered through the crowd, stopping periodically to listen to a tightrope walker shout out a joke to his audience, or sniff the aroma of freshly made scented candles, or enjoy the carnies performing their awe-inspiring antics. One funny fellow had a red dog named Mo that wore a pair of baggy shorts and sunglasses. The man played a banjo and sang a funny song while the dog walked through the crowd gathering dollar bills from people and dropping them in a silver bucket that sat next to the man. Next, he had the dog climb a tall metal tower, walk across a tightrope to a second tower, then turn and come back. It was great fun and the kids insisted on watching the whole show a second time.

At the far end of the wooden wharf, there was a small crowd listening to three musicians that were sitting on stools. The family drifted over and was intrigued by the enchanting sounds of mountain dulcimers being played by a young man dressed in overalls and a red cowboy shirt, and a girl wearing a plaid cotton dress. Another fellow stood over them playing an accompaniment on a mandolin. They sang a charming old-time mountain lullaby.

What'll I do with the baby-o;
What'll I do with the baby-o;
What'll I do with the baby-o;
When he won't go to sleepy-o.

It was a magical night for everyone. They left the square and walked up Green Street to a little gift and treats shop where they ordered frozen Key Lime Pie bars and sat out front in chairs painted with monkeys and pink flamingos as they enjoyed their creamy delights. A very funny fellow walked down the sidewalk and stopped in front of them. He was dressed in the most fanciful white jumpsuit covered in sequins and shiny bric-a-brac. He had huge sideburns and wore dark sunglasses. After striking a pose he turned toward them and started singing and playing on his whimsical white guitar which was covered in feathers. Tourists from up and down the street gathered to dance and sing with the funny Key West Elvis, aka 'Quelvis'. When everyone had finished their treats, they headed back up Green Street toward the spot where Bill had parked their car.

As they approached Duval Street two drunken men fell from the doorway of a yellow saloon with a big pink fish over the doorway and landed in the middle of the street. One man was falling backward and hanging on to the shirtsleeves of the other, trying not to hit the pavement with his head. The other man was throwing punches toward his face, yelling at him as he threw blow after blow, his fist connecting with the poor fellow's face on several occasions. It looked just like a scene from an Old West cowboy movie. Bill gathered the family close to his side and led them safely across the street. They reached their car and began piling in. Jillian held the back door while Trina and Bo climbed up onto the vinyl seat.

Just as she was stepping from the curb, she heard a moan from a dark place under a bush on the edge of the sidewalk. She turned and looked but could not make out what had made the sound. Her curiosity outweighed her fear and for another second, she strained to make out the image. It was just at that moment that her father turned the key and the red taillights blinked on. She gasped as she caught the image of a bearded man, lying in the darkness squinting into the bright red tail light, holding his dirty arm up to block the painful flash. She jumped into her seat and slammed the door shut. She hit the lock button and glued her body onto the cold plastic seat.

"Go! Daddy let's go! Go! Move! Now, Daddy!"

She choked out the commands.

"OK, hold on! What's the matter with you Jillian?" her dad asked as he maneuvered out of the parking place.

"Please, can we just pull out of here?"

Tears were flowing down her face as she cried out. She didn't make a sound for the rest of the ride. When they pulled into the campsite, she stormed into the tent and hid under her sleeping bag.

She never told a soul what had scared her so.

The man in the shadows would haunt her forever, and somehow, she knew it.

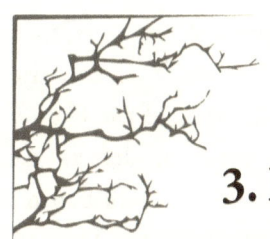

3. Destination Paradise

Jill's eyes blinked twice, then opened. She squinted to see the green numbers on the clock as the ceiling fan spun linen dust into their barely opened corners. At about five a.m. she had fallen asleep to the sound of a gentle rain that had moved in over the Florida Straits. The cooling Caribbean showers wash over the island several times a day this time of year and come as a welcome relief to everyone from the free roaming chickens to the beach-bound tourists. She sat up and stretched her arms one after the other and yawned so loudly that she surprised herself. Hesitating for a moment to consider if she might capture another hour of sleep, she quickly decided that she had too much to do in the short time before her next shift began at three p.m. and climbed out of bed.

Seven weeks earlier, she had applied for the job at the Lower Keys Medical Center online from a computer in the job development center at Boston College. She had never seriously considered working in Florida but, while reviewing the nationwide nursing vacancy listings, she had come across a posting of nine open positions at the Key West facility. She immediately envisioned herself scuba diving on the reef, being courted by rich young doctors, dining at fine oceanfront restaurants, and walking the moonlit beaches. She felt a flood of excitement and romance as she crystallized her plan.

After completing the application, she hit "SEND" and called her sister Trina to tell her what she had done. Trina was of course completely supportive of the idea and reminded her of the wonderful time they had had as children, swimming and playing on the tropical beaches and laughing at the comical people they saw in Key West.

Jill had left the Chestnut Hill campus and stopped off at the Office Depot in Woburn to make copies of her transcripts, driver's license, the letter of recommendation she had received from the director of the Candy Stripers, her high school diploma, and three personal letters of recommendation, then she handed the stack of papers to the clerk behind the service counter, along with the fax number to the Lower Keys Medical Center human resource department and stepped off to one side to wait. Five minutes later, she was out the door with her fax confirmation and receipt in hand.

Under normal conditions, it took Jill about one hour and fifteen minutes to drive the fifty miles from Boston College back home to Gloucester. Lunchtime traffic was light that day and by the time she left Woburn and pulled back up on Yankee Division Highway her little yellow VW Bug was pedal to the metal and damning all torpedoes. If she hadn't been banging her head wildly to Green Day's song *Basket Case*, she might have noticed that she was three lanes too far over to safely make the I95 on-ramp at the Peabody/Portsmouth exchange. And, if she hadn't decided at the last minute to go ahead and risk her life and the lives of seventeen other mid-day commuters, and cut dangerously across traffic to get on that ramp, she wouldn't have been pulled over by the state trooper who was just finishing his lunch when the call came over his radio. "All units in the vicinity of 95 and 128 North be on the lookout for a northbound late model yellow VW Beetle license number RY327LU. Suspect is a white female reported to be under the influence and driving erratically."

After a pathetic display of begging and a convincing story of moving to the Florida Keys to start her first nursing job, the understanding officer re-leased her with a stern warning and a wish of good luck. Grateful to have successfully skirted a well-deserved ticket, she turned off the CD player and proceeded north toward Gloucester. Pulling up the driveway to the family home, she noticed her mother looking out the window while holding the phone to her ear. Jill gathered her purse and papers from the side seat and climbed out of the car. Her mother met her on the sidewalk, halfway to the

front door. Handing Jill the telephone her mom exclaimed, "It's a lady from a hospital in Florida! This is the third time she's called in thirty minutes. Take it!"

Her mother pushed the cordless phone into Jill's hand and gave it an anxious shove toward her ear. Jill frowned at her as she took hold of the phone and answered the call.

"Hello? Yes, this is Jillian Dougherty. Oh no, that's fine. I just walked through the door. Ok! No, that will be fine. Great, eight-fifteen, yes ma'am, this number is fine. Thank You!"

Jill handed the phone back to her mother who stood waiting anxiously beside her, waiting to hear the details of the call. Jill was numbed by what the woman had said. She turned to look into her mother's eyes, grabbed her by her cheeks, and screamed into her face, "I'm gonna be a nurse!"

Locked in each other's arms, the two began jumping up and down with excitement. After a minute, Jill's mother's enthusiasm faded and a perplexed look came over her face.

"Wait, wait, she was calling from Florida!" her mother said. "I know," Jill excitedly responded, "the Key West Hospital!" "Oh Jill, you're not thinking of moving to Key West, are you?" her mother asked, hoping to interject some rationality into her daughter's obviously impulsive consideration of moving so far from home.

"Well, it sure looks like I am!" Jill exclaimed with exuberance as she grabbed a bottle of water from the refrigerator and headed toward her room.

"They've set up a conference call for tomorrow morning. I just sent in the application and they're already calling me." She was in tears over the prospect of rising so quickly into the professional ranks.

Her mother was fighting to level her thinking on the matter and followed her down the hall and into her bedroom.

"Sweetheart, you don't want to go all the way to Florida for a job you may not even stay with," she tried to reason with her.

"Oh Mother, don't you do that to me. Don't you try to take this from me! You just wish this had happened to you twenty-three years ago. Instead, you choose to marry Daddy and have us. If it hadn't been for that, I know you would have been on the next train out of here. Well, leave my life alone! You had your chance and you gave it up for Daddy."

She slammed her door closed as she scolded, never giving her mother a chance to respond. That evening the family gathered in the living room. Through tears and hugs, they shared their fears as well as their joys. They hashed out as many concerns as they could. In the end, if hired, they were all behind her.

Jill didn't sleep at all that night. Her mind was racing through all the exciting prospects that might be coming her way. She was on the phone with her girlfriends until dawn. The rest of the morning she sorted through everything she owned, picking out all her favorite summer clothes, stuffing them in suitcases, emptying her drawers, sorting her underwear, socks, jewelry, frantically packing for her anticipated new life in paradise.

The closer that the clock on her dresser got to eight-fifteen, the more frantic she became. By seven-forty-five, she was all packed and ready to go. In her mind, there was absolutely no possibility that the interview might not go her way. It seemed ordained by a higher power and she was ready to hit the road.

She answered the phone on the extension in her room. After a fortyminute interview, the head nurse in Key West asked her when she would be able to start work, and Jill said she could be on the road in one hour. The nurse put her on hold, a minute passed, and when she punched back in she said, "Ms. Dougherty, thank you for waiting," then added, "Please drive safely and call us as soon as you arrive in Key West."

"Really?" Jill squealed.

"Yes, really! We are so shorthanded that if you were here right now, I'd put you out on the floor immediately. Do you have any questions?" the nurse asked.

"No ma'am! I guess it'll take me a day or two to get there from here," she said.

"Just drive carefully!" the nurse instructed. "Especially through Miami, if you stay on the turnpike, it'll go a lot smoother but you've got to pay tolls. Hang on to your receipts. I may be able to get you reimbursed."

Then she explained, "We've got a lot of papers to sign when you get here. The hospital has a condo where you can stay for up to fourteen days while you settle in and there are plenty of ads on the bulletin board of other nurses seeking roommates so if you are comfortable with all this, welcome aboard". Jillian left that day about eleven a.m., stopping off at the ice cream shop to say goodbye to her sister, Bo, and her dad, who had left the house while she was still on the phone. She drove to the bank to withdraw the last of her savings and then over to the hospital to tell all of her Candy Striper friends the news. With great expectations, three sleeves of her favorite CDs, and a four-pack of Starbucks Frappuccinos on the floorboard, she headed for the on-ramp to Interstate Highway 95 South, and her awaiting island destiny.

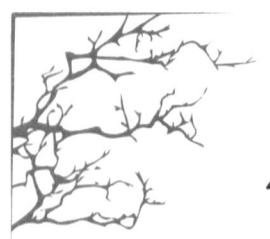

4. Farewell Amelia

"**H**ey Marty, I didn't know you were on tonight," Jillian called across the nursing station counter as she closed the night shift log book and returned it to its position on the desk. Marty stepped into the kitchenette behind the station to put a Tupperware dish in the fridge and answered as she slid a chair across the floor.

"Well, it's not my choice. You can bet on that. I'm being punished by Nurse Ratchetass for getting caught with Dr. Bowen at Smathers Beach last Tuesday. I mean, really! How can she get away with this? We were both off duty, and we weren't even doing anything. I mean, come on. Who the hell does she think she is anyway?" Jill finished loading the patient charts onto the rounds cart and pushed it around the end of the nursing station and into the hallway.

"Come on, Marty, you know she wouldn't risk another EEO complaint. I think, considering all the staff shortages we've got, she does a pretty good job. My bet is she couldn't care less about what we do on the beach when we're off duty," Jill explained.

She listened as Marty mumbled her disdain for the head nurse under her breath.

Two patient alarms sounded on the wall behind the desk.

"318 and 307," Marty announced as she turned off the switches.

I'll take 307," Jill called out. "Mrs. Colburn probably needs a reset on her O2," she continued, "You want to drop these down the laundry chute when you go by?"

"Got-ch!" Marty answered as she headed down the hall, grabbing the sack of dirty sheets and pillowcases from Jill as she passed.

Jill glanced at the clock as she turned to enter the room. 1:07 a.m. Mrs. Colburn had been brought up from intensive care earlier the previous day and this was the third time Jill had actually seen her. As she pulled back the curtain, she sensed there was something different. Mrs. Colburn's husband had been in the chair beside the bed since she had arrived and Jill expected to find him still there, but he was gone. Mrs. Colburn had not moved since the 11:23 p.m. reset. She was still in the exact position as before. The expectations for her recovery seemed poor. The doctors had not yet determined a formal prognosis, it was a wait-and-see kind of time. She was just hanging, hanging in limbo.

Jill reached across the bed and pushed the blinking red button on the nebulizer, then lifted the access flap on the clear plastic tent and checked the position of Mrs. Colburn's nasal cannula. The saline bag hung from above, slowly dripping the fluids through the tubing down to her motion-less arm, then into her vein. As Jill rose back to a full standing position, she was overtaken by some unexpected impulse to stroke Mrs. Colburn's beautiful hair. Just then the bathroom door opened and she turned to see Dr. Colburn step into the room. He tossed a paper towel into the trash can and slipped back into the chair by the bed. His eyes were red and swollen as he forced a smile in her direction, then gazed longingly back at his motionless wife. Jill sensed that he was precariously teetering on the edge of a break-down and though she was inclined to comfort him, she feared that she might be drawn over the edge herself. She returned his smile and sympathetically touched his shoulder, then left the room, closing the door behind her.

Returning to the nursing station she sat at the desk reviewing Mrs. Colburn's chart. For over fifteen minutes she sat there flipping pages, reading test results, and thinking aloud, but her questions could not be answered. Sometimes, the light just burns out. It's a part of life! People just break! Sometimes they can be fixed, sometimes they can't. It's just another reality to accept.

"It's an aneurysm. Cerebral aneurysm I'll bet," Marty said as she leaned over the front of the counter to grab a pen off the desk. "Read the intake notes from the paramedic report. He nailed it in the first five minutes."

Jill flipped through the papers for the patient identification number and entered it into the computer. She scrolled through the pages until reaching the initial assessment entered by the attending emergency room nurse. Then she paged down to the PPR, *Patient Pickup Report*, and read the paramedic's account of the incident that led to her being admitted.

"Key West Emergency Medical Services Mobile Unit 14 responded to a 911 call for medical support rescue dockside at the Key West Bight at 4:17 p.m. The initial call for service was called in by the captain of the Yankee Freedom on its way back to port from the Fort Jefferson National Monument in the Dry Tortugas. The victim was a white female approximately fortynine years old and was reported to have been unconscious since halfway back to port, approximately one hour. Upon arrival, the paramedics took her vitals and stabilized her for transport. Attempts to revive the patient had been unsuccessful and she was accompanied by her husband en route for delivery at Lower Keys Medical Center Key West."

Jill looked up at Marty who was still standing above her at the counter making notes in a file. Marty pointed the pen at the computer screen and said, "You won't run across this kinda stuff at the Boston College of Nursing!"

Jill grinned and returned to her review.

The patient's husband, Dr. Walter A. Colburn, had provided the following assessment information to the E.R. intake nurse. Jill read it out loud, "The patient had been snorkeling among the shallow reef outcroppings and dock pilings at the Fort Jefferson landing for approximately twenty minutes when she stood up and became disoriented. The husband was on the pier and not participating in the activity. He reported that his wife made her way to shallow water and leaned over to shake water from her ear canal at which time she fell into the water and was unable to recover her footing. The husband reports that she was underwater for no more than twenty seconds when he and other swimmers rescued her and carried her back onto the boat where she partially recovered."

Jill paused while taking a sip of her coffee, then continued reading, "Dr. Colburn reports that Mrs. Colburn complained of sensitivity to the sunlight and remained on the boat for two hours while the tour continued. During this period, adequate hydration was administered and her vital signs were taken. All findings were within normal ranges. The patient remained seated and on two occasions expelled the contents of her stomach, after which she complained of blurred vision and severe pain behind her eyes. Dr. Colburn reported that while returning to Key West the patient's head pain increased and her pupils became dilated. He reported that her cognitive ability diminished and she suffered a noticeable change in her speech functions. It was at this point that she lost consciousness. Her breathing was determined also to be diminished but not limiting for the sustaining of life."

Jill sat back in her chair as Marty walked out of the staff lounge behind her and asked, "Have you seen the C.A.T. scan results?"

Marty slipped the last bite of a cherry Popsicle off its stick and tossed the wrapper in the can under the desk as she sat down in the next chair over and answered, "Yeah! It was negative."

She rolled the chair to the back wall and grabbed the clipboard for room 321, then slid back over to the desk and continued, "They did a lumbar puncture at lunchtime today. I haven't checked to see if the results have shown up."

She opened the metal lid to the case file on the desk, then without looking at Jill said, "She's your patient, the only reason I even know this much is because I heard Luanne and Carol talking about it downstairs in the cafeteria."

Jill frowned at what seemed to be a rude thing for Marty to say, then turned back to the computer screen and searched for the puncture results to see if the doctor found blood in Mrs. Colburn's cerebrospinal fluid (CSF). There it was. The report revealed that a massive intrusion of blood had flooded her brain. They had not yet recorded the diagnosis, but it all seemed to point to an aneurysm.

"Ya know," Jill said after exiting the system and rolling back from the desk to stretch her legs, "It seems to me that if that boat captain had called the Coast Guard or asked for Trauma Star to be sent, we could have flown her in and gotten to her quicker. Maybe she could have made it. Now, she hasn't got a chance."

Marty answered without looking up, "By the time she was unconscious she was halfway here. They couldn't have gotten her any quicker than they did. That's it, she's toast! Sayonara! End of chatter! Good night!"

Marty slapped the lid closed on her case file then threw it down on the desk and stretched her arms as she stood up. She walked out of the cubicle and down the hall toward the elevator.

"I'm on break!" she snarled as she rounded the corner.

Jill got off duty at three a.m. After she clocked out, she poked her head through the door of 307 and quietly choked on her tears from what she saw. The man was clutching his dying wife's hand as he knelt by her bedside. She could hear his whimpers as he rocked gently back and forth, tapping his temple gently against the bed rail, softly calling to his beautiful wife.

"Amelia, please don't leave me," he cried.

"Please, don't go."

By the time Jill reached her car she was precariously teetering on an emotionally unstable edge. Through swollen eyes she fumbled with her keys and fought to hold back her tears. The door finally opened and she slipped into the driver's seat. Then, the rains came.

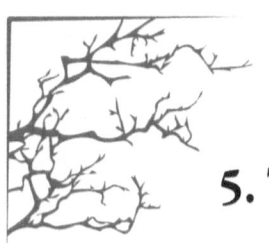

5. The Ride of Her Life

Five hours of sleep seemed better than no hours of sleep. She stepped into the living room where the bright morning light poured in off Higgs Beach through the sliding glass doors. She squinted from the pain as she shuffled across the cold tile floor and into the kitchen. Her new roommate, Canyon, had been considerate enough to leave the coffee pot on, but dumb enough to not add water. She wasn't sure how long this living arrangement would last, but, since they worked opposite shifts, she figured there might be potential. Besides, at fourteen hundred dollars per month for her half of the rent, there was no way she could ever afford a view like this on her own. Not yet, anyway!

She set the coffee carafe in the sink and ran a little warm water in it to soften the sludge. Checking the fridge, she felt lucky to find an unopened Frappuccino hiding behind a halfeaten cantaloupe and commanded it to, "Come to mama!" She scooped up her mail from the coffee table, slipped her glasses on, and pulled hard on the sliding glass door handle. Leaning out over the railing, she took a deep breath of the salty Atlantic air.

Two shrimp boats were dragging the bottom about a mile offshore and a cloud of seagulls trailed behind them, diving into the frothy prop wash to scoop up their crustaceous breakfast. Jill could smell the sweet aroma of coconut palm blowing in from the south across the rows of trees that line the beachfront highway below. She scanned the waterline behind the historic West Martello Fort where the Key West Garden Club is housed, and watched a group of seniors practicing Tai Chi on the sea wall. A little further down the beach was the dog park. There were several large dogs running in the open field while their owners sat in the shade of some palm trees talking about politics, prices of real estate, and crime. It was so not Massachusetts! It was so Jillian!

She smiled as she thought about how free she was.

So, in control of her own life! Grown up!

So, on her own!

After a few minutes of basking in the morning sun, she sat down in the plastic chair next to the little patio table on the balcony, set her coffee down, and looked at the three envelopes in her hand. There was another letter from her mother, an advertisement for an upgrade to the cable TV subscription, and her third paycheck. She ripped open the paycheck envelope, pulled the check out into the sunlight, gave it a kiss, and took another swig of her coffee.

Pushing herself up from her chair, she turned to open the glass door and heard a voice shouting from down by the beach. She looked over the railing just in time to see a half-naked man angrily pulling another man off of a bicycle. He was screaming profanity while pounding on the bike rider with his fists. A short distance down the sandy sidewalk there were some covered picnic tables where a group of other men and two women were watching the pummeling. Several of the men approached the two brawlers. Jill thought they might help the man on the bicycle, but to her surprise, the entire crowd started yelling at him. The closer they got, the louder and angrier they became. He dropped the bicycle and fell into the sand, spilling all of his belongings onto the sidewalk. He curled up to protect himself while three or four of the men took turns hitting and kicking him. They finally finished, and one by one, returned to the picnic table. The man that had started the altercation picked up the bike and pushed it over to the table, then came back to spit at the guy on the ground and kicked him one last time.

Jill watched as the poor fellow rolled back and forth in the sand, obviously in severe pain. He pushed himself up and staggered over to the outer brick wall of the old fort. He stood there leaning against it for support, spitting on the ground, then stretched his arms and rubbed his bruises. He finally limped back to the sidewalk, looked toward the picnic table, and threw his fist in the air, and screamed something unintelligible. Several of the other men stepped toward him from the table area and returned angry threats, but didn't go after him.

About that time a police car pulled up and they all started yelling about who did what. Jill thought it was so sad at first, but soon figured that the bicycle was probably stolen and though she wanted to tend to the man's need for medical attention, she wasn't about to inject herself into such a dangerous situation. She went back inside, set up the ironing board, and watched the noon news while she prepared for her three o'clock shift.

It's only a seven-minute drive from her apartment on Higgs Beach to the Lower Keys Medical Center. Jill never went anywhere in what others might call a 'straight shot'. Back home in Gloucester, she always defended herself by insisting that exploration broadens a driver's experience and helps lower the chances of having a wreck. At least that's how she always explained her joyriding when she was caught by her dad.

In Key West, there is ample opportunity for 'exploration'. Though the island is a mere two miles by four, she could take a different route to work every day for three years and never follow the same route. There is something of interest down every street. Between the funky houses, the quirky people, the crazy chickens, the beautiful tropical plants and trees, the ocean, and the everchanging sky, one is never without something new to see or experience.

By the time she pulled out of the parking garage and drove to the gate at the front of her apartment complex, the police had already cleared up the mess across the street. Jill took a right turn on South Roosevelt Boulevard and drove past the picnic tables to see if the man that had been beaten up was still hanging around. She passed by the crowd of people that had been sitting and lounging on the picnic tables. They apparently were not a working class of people and appeared to have lots of personal belongings in bags and backpacks leaning up against the concrete seats and trees. Jill tried not to appear to be gawking as she drove by, but she was curious to try to figure out how they took care of their personal needs if they weren't working.

She circled Old Town and pulled back on Roosevelt, heading north this time to take a second look at the haggard crowd. There were older men, younger men, and now, several more women. Everyone appeared to be of a working age and one of the older women looked much more like a man than a woman. Jill felt that every one of them needed a shower and a haircut. On the way to work, she was wondering, "Where do they go to the bathroom? Where do they shower? Where do they sleep? And, how do they buy food without a job?"

She turned into the parking lot of the Oceanside Bank and pulled up to the drive-through window, then shoved her check and the deposit slip into the tube and pushed SEND.

"Afternoon, Ms. Dougherty, how are you doing today?" the teller called out through the intercom.

"Just fine, thanks!" she answered as she took her receipt from the tube.

"Have a nice day!" the teller added.

Jill waved goodbye to her as she pulled out and headed back toward the highway. Having worked for years at her parents' ice cream shop, she had learned a certain set of principles that few twenty-one-year-olds ever acquire with regard to work ethics. One is, if your sign says "We open at ten a.m.", you better be at the door with your key in the lock by nine fifty-nine.

She checked the clock as she unloaded a banana, strawberry yogurt and a box of raisins from her satchel and shoved them into the staff fridge in the lounge behind the thirdfloor nurses' station. Two fiftyfive p.m., just how she liked it. Jill just couldn't live with herself if she was ever found to be a second late.

She proceeded to the rack of patient files and reached for the one for room 307. It was gone. She hesitated for a moment and considered why it might be gone. She couldn't remember the name of the patient whom she had checked on just twelve hours earlier, but hoped that a move toward recovery had brought about a positive discharge or perhaps a transfer to a mainland facility that might offer better care.

She walked down the hall to the room and looked in. The sheets were wrinkle-free. It was ready for the next patient to arrive and that was already in progress. As Jill turned back toward the nurses' station the elevator door opened and a gurney was unloaded with a little girl on board. Her mother was anxiously trailing on one side, a nurse and staffer on the other, followed by what appeared to be a social worker with an arm full of files tucked under her arm. The social worker was glued to her cell phone as they passed by.

"Listen, Lewis, you're not telling me anything I don't already know. That injunction has been in place for over six months and somebody needs to step up to the plate and come clean on this now," Jill heard her say. She gave an assuring smile to the child as she was rolled past, but though their eyes connected, the little girl was too weak to respond.

Jill was surprised that there were no other nurses on the floor. She grabbed the duty roster off the hook on the wall and read that Crystal was supposed to have reported in at three o'clock and Rosa Sanchez was supposed to still be on until six. Three patient call buttons were blinking and the phone was ringing.

"Third-floor nursing, this is Jillian, may I help you?" she called into the receiver.

"Jill, I'm pulling into the parking lot now, I'll be right there." It was Crystal. Late again!

This was the second time she had pulled this trick in a week. Jill turned off the blinking lights and proceeded toward the first of the three patient's rooms. After stepping from behind the nurses' station, she saw Rosanna coming out of room 318 with a load of soiled sheets in hand.

"Thank you, Jesus!" Rosanna called out toward the ceiling after seeing Jill rounding the corner.

"I thought I was on my own and gonna be runnin' another back-to-back. That surely would have put me in the grave," Rosanna said as she pushed the linens down the laundry chute.

"We've got calls from 301, 309 and 323," Jill announced as she passed by the portly Puerto Rican and headed for the highest room number.

"What, no hello Rosanna? How are you this fine day Miss Rosanna? Just, I get two while you get one, Miss New Girl in Charge?"

Rosanna complained as she lowered her face to toss a condescending glance. After two weeks of sharing this shift, Jill was getting used to her style of banter and returned with, "You look fabulous darling!"

Rosanna responded with her pink tongue stuck out toward her petite coworker, then chuckled as she disappeared into room 301.

Jill heard the elevator chime as she entered room 323 but didn't turn to see who would be getting off. Exiting the room a moment later with a lunch tray in hand, she saw Crystal heading down the hall toward the nursing station. Beside her was the head nurse, Beth O'Neal. Behind them was the administrator for the emergency room, and a tall girl in a nurse's uniform that Jill had not seen before. She arrived at the nursing station at the same time as the others.

"Good afternoon, Mrs. O'Neal." Jill offered a friendly greeting.

"Hi, Jillian," the head nurse returned.

Rosanna stepped out of room 309 and Mrs. O'Neal called to her to join them at the station, and then addressed the group. "Ladies, this is Tunisia Jameson. She just got picked up to help ease some of the pressure around here."

She turned to Tunisia and continued, "Tunisia, I need you to shadow Rosanna until she signs off, and then if I'm not back up here, switch to Crystal." Then the head nurse turned to Crystal and sternly directed, "Crystal, straighten up! Stay focused on the priorities. We can't afford to lose anyone right now! Am I making myself clear or do we need to have a session?" "No, Mrs. O'Neal. I'm good to go." Crystal answered.

She then turned to Jillian and said, "Jill, I need you to gather any personal items you have up here and follow me."

"Yes ma'am!" Jill said as she quickly grabbed for her purse and retrieved her lunch from the next room. She caught up with them as they reached the elevator. The two ladies were discussing the workforce issue that plagued the Florida Keys while they waited for the door to open. Jill stood to the side, listening.

"This housing thing is killing us!" she heard Beth exclaim.

"How are we going to be able to provide adequate care for people if we can't afford to pay employees enough to live here?" she vented.

The elevator door opened and, as they stepped in, the administrator said, "I suppose you heard that Dr. Larkin accepted that position in Milwaukee." "Oh no! He's the only one in E.R. that's worth a damn. Couldn't we match their offer?" Beth asked.

"It's not the money," the administrator explained. "It's too much overtime and working with, uh, you know."

She raised her eyebrow and looked over at Beth. The head nurse understood clearly that she was referring to their constant turnover of nurses and technical staff. Jill fought the urge to turn her head to see if Mrs. O'Neal would acknowledge with a nod toward her. She felt awkward but could not help assuming they were referring to the new "green" nurses that were fast-tracked in from all over the world. Jill wanted to be assertive and inject her opinion. Maybe say something like, "Listen, ladies, I am not like all the rest of those lightweights, I make commitments! I stay in the battle! You're going to soon see that I am a woman of the highest caliber who doesn't know how to say, 'I quit.'" It took a lot of discipline but she wisely kept her thoughts to herself. The doors opened on the second floor and a utility worker from the maintenance department rolled a cart full of tools and broken electrical parts onto the elevator. The three ladies crowded to one side of the car to make room. The emergency room administrator reached her hand over to Jill and said, "I'm sorry Jillian, I'm Candice Monahan. We haven't met but I've heard good things about you."

The doors opened again on the first floor and she continued as they stepped out into the hallway, "Beth and I need you to help out in the E.R. for a while. Have you had any emergency room experience?"

"Oh, I actually love E.R." Jill said. "I used to candy stripe there all the time and know a lot about protocol from two years of watching everything they did." She then added, "In school, anytime we were working E.R. was when I got my highest grades. I've always felt that it's where a nurse can best develop her skills."

"I'm glad to hear you say that," Mrs. Monahan responded, "but, a Key West E.R. is not like any other E.R. We get lots of nasty stuff in here. People get hit by boat propellers, plane propellers, fall off hotel balconies. Hell, one time a lady almost got torn in half by a parachute rope while she was being pulled behind a parasail boat. We get lots of drunken stabbings, broken bottle fights, and people hit by cars and buses. We even had a child mauled by a Key deer. It really is messy in here sometimes. Do you think you could deal with this kind of stuff day in and day out?"

"Oh, yes ma'am!" Jill proudly proclaimed. "I really think you'll find that I can rise to any occasion, whatever it is."

They continued down the long corridor toward the east end of the hospital. The double doors ahead of them opened and Jill could see the Trauma Star helicopter docked on the heliport outside in the hot sun. Her heart skipped a beat as she pictured herself scrambling into the medical officer's seat, flying over the water to rescue an unconscious diver suffering from a case of the bends on a ship ten miles offshore. She smiled as the fantasy started to take a hold on her imagination. Then the automatic doors closed and she snapped back into reality. She had already signed on for the ride of her life.

6. The Devil

As **Jillian followed** the two ladies through the next set of double doors, she was struck by how hot it was in the emergency room waiting area. It seemed unusually muggy and oppressive, uncomfortable beyond what might be considered humane. She was sure that if there was a thermometer it would read over one hundred. The front doors were blocked open with concrete cigarette butt stands and a slight breeze was blowing some pieces of dried palm fronds through the threshold and dust was everywhere.

There were about a dozen people sitting around the room in metal chairs waiting to be called to the front desk. Jill's overall impression was that there must be some third-world triage unit that proudly claims to have been used as the model for this waiting room. Beth reached toward a keypad on a side door as she turned to Jill and said, "I'll check on you in a couple of hours. If you need help with anything, just get with Ms. Monahan or someone on her staff and they can see to it that you get what you need. OK?"

Jill acknowledged she understood as she followed Ms. Monahan toward the 'staff only' entrance of the emergency room.

"Thanks, Beth, I'll talk to you later," Ms. Monahan said as the head nurse disappeared through the door.

"Just hang in there the best you can," she responded as the door closed on her words.

Jill was led behind the intake counter and into the operating area of the emergency room. She had been walked through the area six weeks earlier on her first day orientation. At that time everything was clean and seemed completely functional, a far cry from today's dismal presentation. Her new supervisor led her through the room introducing her to her new coworkers. Everyone seemed engaged in attending to patients or preparing to receive the next one brought in.

There was one doctor moving from station to station and then to the central desk to make his entries on the computer and write prescriptions before moving on to the next patient. Ms. Monahan told Jill that she would be able to meet Dr. Larkin later in the day. As they proceeded toward the back of the room, they passed by a gurney pushed against the wall. Lying on it was a contorted little gentleman in a fetal position struggling to find a comfortable position.

He was moaning and calling out, "Oh God, somebody help me, please, somebody please have mercy here. Please!"

His cries for help grew louder, then softer, and then became louder again. Jill felt driven to attend to his needs. Her eyes were fixed on the man when Ms. Monahan stopped at the employee lounge door and looked straight into Jill's eyes and said, "Do not let him suck you into his scam."

Jill was completely caught off guard by this, and listened intently while she explained.

"That's Paddy, aka Patrick Oran Broslen. He practically lives here. He is disgusting and the more we do for him, the more problems he makes for us." She seemed very animated as she talked.

"I would suggest you avoid him as best you can or he will lock in on you and suck the life out of you."

Then she added, "I don't know what else to say about Paddy, just be careful!"

Jill listened and decided to chance one question, "What's wrong with him?" she asked.

Ms. Monahan shifted her weight onto one hip, dropped the files on the table by the door, put both hands on her hips and gritted her teeth. As she glared over at Paddy she said, "He's the #!**!*# Devil!"

She snapped her head back toward Jill, pushed her face forward and stared with her eyebrows raised as high as they could stretch. Then she added, "Certiflukinfiably!" She then picked up the files and led Jill into the lounge. After pointing out the amenities, she directed Jill to blend in for the rest of her shift and shadow anybody she felt might seem willing to show her the ropes. She then offered, "If you need me, take a number! Any questions, sweetie?" Jill was so taken aback she could hardly mutter anything more than, "Ah, I guess, no ma'am."

"Great! Go get 'em, Tarzana," Ms. Monahan said as she turned and headed back toward the front of the E.R.

"I hope you can handle it better than the rest of 'em!"

The springs on the double doors seemed to slip into slow motion and her voice spiraled morbidly to a crawl as Jill tried to recharge with a deep breath. One of the nurses passed by on her way into the lounge and smiled at poor Jill as she stood in the doorway, numbed by the supervisor's pessimistic attitude.

"She hits like a hurricane, doesn't she?" the nurse grinned as she said the words.

"My God, what was all that?" Jill turned and followed the girl into the staff lounge where she was shoving a Turkey Hot Pocket into the microwave.

"Oh, she just wants you ready for it when it hits. And count on it, it will hit," she said.

"I'm Danna." The girl offered her hand as she introduced herself. "Jillian, Jill Dougherty," Jill responded with a smile. "Is it OK if I work with you for a while when you go back out on the floor?" she asked.

"Baby, you can shadow me till three a.m. as far as I'm concerned. We're gonna be slammed all night and I'm gonna lean on you all the way," Danna explained with surety.

"Why are we going to be slammed?" Jill asked.

"Have you seen all the trucks rolling into town, pulling the speed boats behind them?" Danna asked.

"Oh yeah, I saw a couple blocking traffic at the light on my way in today. What are they doing here?" Jill asked.

"Oh, my God! There's going to be serious brain damage for the next week. Party on! Party on! Party on party! Non-stop! Powerboat races are big stuff down here. We're gonna see it all this week." She rolled her Hot Pocket from its sleeve and sliced a small bite from the corner. The steam was a warning she took to heart as she gently cooled it with her breath, then continued her explanation.

"Last year we had a guy in a spectator boat get impaled on a fish gaff after his boat got hit by a wave. It threw him up in the air so high that he got hooked right under his shoulder blade. There's a picture on the board over there if you wanna see it," she said as she took her first bite and pointed to the corkboard on the back wall.

"That's why you got pulled in. It's four-thirty now. We're all hoping that by seven p.m. you'll be ready to take it all on," she said as she took another bite of her lunch.

"What about the guy on the gurney? Aren't we going to do anything for him?" Jill asked.

"Paddy, asshole," Danna said. "He deserves everything he gets. Trust me! He's in here probably twenty times a week, him and his homeless buddies. Unlike most of them, he doesn't like the food over at the jail so he pulls his scams to get sent over here where we end up babysitting him. He thinks all the police officers wanna kill him. The thing is, they all do. You'll see! It doesn't take long for Paddy to show what he's made of." She went on to offer, "Help yourself, you're gonna have to deal with him eventually. You might as well hit it now, before we're swamped."

Jill cautiously approached the man on the gurney. She lifted the chart off the hook on the side of the bed. Reading through the vitals she saw that there was a mixed bag of high and low readings. Looking over the complaint, she noted he had rated his pain level as twelve on a scale of one to ten.

"Mr. Broslen, sir, my name is Jillian. I'm going to be your nurse. I need to ask you a few questions so I can better assess your needs." As she spoke, she scanned his emaciated arms and frail bony legs for any obvious wounds that might be in need of immediate attention. She took note of several scars and contusions that seemed consistent with the descriptions she had previously received from her new coworkers. This was clearly a man who was intimate with an injurious lifestyle. The signs were everywhere.

"What seems to be the problem today?" she asked as she leaned over his fetid body.

"I'm *%$#@*ing dyin' here, can't you see that?" he yelled between his bogus moans.

Jill stepped back two feet to catch her breath. It was immediately apparent to her that Paddy may have a drinking issue. After surveying his physical condition, she recognized him as the victim that she had seen being pummeled on the sidewalk across the street from her apartment building.

"Mr. Broslen, where specifically is your pain?" she asked.

"Just get me some medicine. I'll be all right. Just go get me something for the pain. Maybe some Percocet or Percodan, any of that Perky stuff. Anything, it don't matter to me." Paddy barked out his request as he rolled back and forth on the gurney as if he was about to die.

Jill spent another thirty minutes trying to get his cooperation but he seemed more interested in keeping her attention on his manipulative guise than actually gaining progress toward his medical needs. She brought him a Coke. She bought him a bag of Cheetos from the lobby vending machine. She got him a wheelchair and wheeled him out the front door and waited while he smoked a cigarette. Every time she thought he was going to let her tend to his cuts and bruises he started his nasty attacks, lashing out at the doctor, the nurses, and the hospital. He was an incredibly angry and miserable little man. Danna passed by several times with a 'told ya so' grin on her face.

She finally could no longer resist, "I tried to warn you," she said. Jill rolled him to the men's bathroom and waited for probably twenty minutes while he took care of "business".

When he came out it was apparent, he had smuggled in some whisky. He was now not only a pain, he was a drunken pain. She got lucky when Paddy caught sight of one of his road buddies that had drifted into the lobby, and bolted from the wheelchair to join him. When the two of them disappeared through the open front doors, Jill grabbed his chart and entered a note that said he had refused treatment for his medical condition and voluntarily self-discharged.

Danna led a staff-wide round of applause for Jill's success in getting rid of Paddy. Jill laughed so hard she thought she was going to fall over. Danna showed her how to enter the discharge on the computer and it was completed at six fortyseven p.m. This left her exactly thirteen minutes to nail everything else down tight before she hit the four-hour point in her shift.

Danna was setting up a drip line for a diabetic woman that had been brought in by her daughter. She had almost completely stabilized and Dana was monitoring her glucose level every thirty minutes.

Jill slipped through the curtain and asked, "Got something for me to do?" Danna opened the inline clamp and the fluids began to flow down the long clear tube and into the lady's arm. She leaned over to view the setting on the pump one last time, then she smiled at the old woman and said, "Queenie, hang in there just a little longer. I'm sending you home as soon as the numbers look right." As Danna pulled the curtain closed, she asked Jill, "How are you on intake?"

"Totally up on intake!" she responded with enthusiasm. "Good! Check with the front desk and tell them to feed you whatever they've got waiting in the chute. They can get you anything you need tools-wise." Danna said.

"Excellent!" Jill responded as she headed out to the front office. Nonstop for the next six hours, she handled case after case with the finesse of a master puppeteer. Her assessments were accurate and concise. Her data entry was impeccable. Her recommendations were perfect. She resolved more than half of the cases without the need to engage second-level treatment. She moved patients smoothly through the system like a seasoned pro.

As staff members got off duty, they stuck their heads into Jill's doorway to introduce themselves and give compliments to her for a job well done. Dr. Larkin checked out at eleven p.m. and stopped in to thank her for her efforts. She periodically was called out front to assist with unloading Trauma Star patients, and took to it with the confidence of a veteran nurse.

Danna grabbed her by the arm at one a.m. and insisted she take a dinner break. Reluctantly, Jill passed her duties over to another girl who had reported in at midnight and headed for the lounge and a well-deserved breather. She was in her stride, in the right place, at the right time, and felt like a hero! She was floating on pride!

She walked through the E.R. feeling like a rock star. With each staff member, whose eye caught her passing, there was a smile or a wave, one thumb up, and several outcries of "You da man, new girl."

Smiling from eartoear as she stepped into the lounge, she reached into the fridge to grab her yogurt, her banana, and the box of raisins she had brought for dinner. She hadn't even met most of the E.R. staff but she felt as if she had no further need to prove herself to anyone. As she slipped into the chair at the table and pulled off the top of the yogurt container a very immaculately dressed woman stepped into the room and introduced herself.

"Hi Jillian," she said. "I'm Mrs. Sessions. I'm the emergency room night supervisor. I just wanted to tell you how pleased we are that you're going to be a part of our team and see how things are going so far."

Jill was flattered by her positive tone and remarked that she had always hoped to someday work in a busy emergency room. She told the supervisor that, so far, everything was fine and that she felt that she would be able to get up to speed in no time at all. Then the supervisor went on to address another issue.

"I know that you are scheduled to have the next three days off, but I needed to check with you and see, if we get into a pinch with all these boat races going on, would you be opposed to maybe giving us, oh, six hours or so if we need some relief?"

Jill was flattered to be considered so valuable on her first day as an E.R. nurse and answered, "Oh, absolutely! Call me day or night! Nothing I'd rather do! Besides, the sooner I get the experience, the easier the job will be." "Great," supervisor Sessions exclaimed with enthusiasm. "Hopefully, everybody will show and we'll be OK, but, I just need to know who I can lean on."

She stopped at the door and turned back toward Jill and said, "Thank you, and if I don't see you again for three days you can consider the E.R. as your new assignment." She smiled and added, "I hope you'll find it to be exciting enough to stay."

"Yes ma'am, nice to meet you," Jill answered. She was too excited to eat, and a moment later tossed her dinner in the trash and walked back out to the emergency room floor. She was walking on cloud nine without a net.

7. Harmless Little Fishes

Three a.m. was like crossing the finish line of a New York City marathon. Boot Camp was completed. Jill had her wings and was ready to fly. As she walked out the front door and into the brightly lit parking lot she felt as if she had somehow matured beyond her age. She could feel a power growing within.

She was two different people at the same time. One, the greenhorn nursing student on her very first professional job assignment, and two, a future head nurse supervisor of a busy emergency room on an island between two vast oceans. Full of aspiration, confident beyond hope, she felt like a boat in a slack tide and the powerful flow would soon shift in a new direction, carrying her farther than her imagination could ever conceive.

She slipped her key into the door lock of her little yellow VW Bug. The moon was huge that morning. It hung low in the southwestern sky. Its brightness laid the shadows of the palm trees like printed silhouettes across the pavement throughout the almost empty lot. Everything on the island seemed artistic! Poetic! Infused with inspiration! Living here was like walking down a long corporate corridor lined with motivational posters. Everywhere she looked were images that made her want to breathe deeper, sing louder, climb higher. Jill was filled with purpose, but her feet were numb.

She slid into the front seat and turned the key. The engine sluggishly turned over and started. Two weeks earlier she had to call AAA for a jump start in a grocery store parking lot. She knew she needed a new battery but had not yet committed to parting with the fifty dollars it would cost. This episode was the necessary impetus for that commitment. She determined she would be at Sears sometime that afternoon.

College Road runs around the Key West Municipal Golf Club in a half-mile loop. The hospital is in the middle of the loop. The Florida Keys Community College is directly across the road and the college property is on the waterfront, with a billion-dollar view of the Gulf of Mexico. She could not see the ocean from the road but thought that the view of the moon setting over the Gulf waters would be a fabulous way to end her work week and begin her three-day, much deserved respite. As she drove over the Cow Key Bridge, she considered which of her favorite scenic stops might lend the best advantage for viewing the moonset. "Spotswood Park!" she thought. "Oh yes!" A quaint little neighborhood park nestled between the beautiful Casa Marina Hotel and The Coconut Beach Resort. What a view!

She turned west onto Flagler Avenue, named to commemorate the work of the great railroad developer and real estate tycoon Henry Flagler. He had built the overseas rail system of train trestles and causeways to make Key West accessible by locomotive and later by automobile. Jill had stumbled into the little oceanside park on her first day of exploration after coming to Key West. It was the place from which she watched her first waterspout as it formed many miles offshore and meandered on the surface sucking up torrents of water from the warm Atlantic Ocean. That same day she had seen her first cruise ship coming into sight with its plume of diesel smoke shadowing its route, as it approached the outer channel to the island. "Yes," she decided, Spotswood Park would be a magnificent place to unwind and say good day to the moon.

She drove past the Key West High School and under the blinking yellow caution light that hung from the wires above the intersection. There were no other vehicles on the road. The block beyond the high school was taken up completely by the Salvation Army Outlet Store and administrative offices. She was in no hurry and drove past at a speed that may have seemed more appropriate for a time of day when the school crossing guards would be on duty to applaud her attention to the 'Go Slow' signs.

Her eyes were exploring the stacks of furniture, clothing, yard tools, and boxes which had been generously placed along the front of the building by residents that had cleaned out their garages that day or wrapped up their weekend garage sale endeavors after something less than fulfilling their hope to "get rid of all their junk". As she scanned the scene she realized that there was a man sleeping on top of a stack of large plastic bags. In the bright moonlight, she could see him clearly. He was wrapped in a child's blanket with his feet sticking out from one end. He was wearing a huge pair of army boots.

It seemed so sad that someone would have to sleep on top of a pile of stuff that someone else, who was probably sleeping in a cozy bed, had just hours before, basically, thrown out as trash.

Her car was now at a complete standstill in the middle of the moonlit road as she studied the scene in amazement. Oblivious to the consequence that any other time of day might cause a crash and leave her trapped in a mesh of metal and flames, she sat watching as another human form began to take shape in the pile of discards. Then a third man sat up and repositioned himself. She was utterly astounded at her discovery. Probably since she had subsisted on five or less hours of sleep per day for the past seven weeks, she remained emotionally paralyzed.

Her jaw dropped open, "OH MY GOD!"

"I can't believe this." She spoke the words as if she was giving a narrative of what she was watching. "Who are these people?" she asked herself.

"Look, that guy is so dirty. How could he let himself go like that?" she asked. The third man sat up and pushed against the concrete divider between the large glass windows and struggled to get to his feet.

No one noticed that she was out there in the road, watching, as if she had pulled up on wildlife. The dark figure stood scratching himself, then turned toward the far end of the walkway. He hesitated, swaying in a circle, and almost fell over twice. He locked his stare on the frangipani tree at the corner of the building and shuffled over to it. He fumbled to free himself from his belt. His pants dropped and he swayed in the moonlight, like a willow in the wind, as he relieved himself, missing the bushes completely but successfully meeting his needs and drenching the sidewalk.

"Jesus!" she said aloud. "Look at this guy!"

She was still watching, with her head turned to look through the driver's side window. The man recovered his trousers with much difficulty and returned to the pile of household discards. She watched as he tore open a bag and began rummaging through old clothes and children's toys.

"What the hell is he doing now?" she asked as if someone was there to answer. Her nose was still glued to the glass as she scanned the shadows.

Suddenly, as if someone had thrown a hand grenade into her face, a blast of blue light filled her eyes and scared her out of her skin. Her heart pounded as she heard the chirp, chirp of the police cruiser's loudspeaker.

"Ma'am, please move along!" the officer called out in what Jill felt could have been as loud as the voice of God telling Moses to, "Let his people go." She lifted her foot cautiously off the brake and her car slowly moved forward.

At the next corner, she sat under the red light, hoping the officer had already run her tag number and seen that she was not a terrorist, or a night stalker, or a thief casing out the local businesses for vulnerabilities in their security systems. Her mind and heart were in a race with each other. The heart pulled ahead only to be left in the dust by the mind.

"Nope, she's just a little nursey from a little bitty town in Massachusetts. Came to Key West to be a big nursey."

She pushed the words through puckered lips as if she was talking to a little tree frog caught in the hands of a child.

She kept glancing in her rearview mirror to see if the officer was listening to her.

"That's right, leave the pretty little girly alone. Leave her little yellow bug to fly away."

She started whispering now, "That's right Mr. Policeman, she means you no harm. She does not look good in handy cuffys.

"Now softly whispering, "That's right, good boy, let her go. Let herrrrrrrrrr . . .

"The light turned to green and she saw the cruiser turn right as she drove straight ahead.

"Go!!!"

"Yes!" She exclaimed loudly.

"The little yellow butterfly has spoken!"

Smiling wildly, she said, "Now watch her fly, fly away to the moon."

At the very end of Flagler Avenue was the historical Casa Marina Hotel and Resort. It was originally built by Mr. Flagler for the wealthy northern visitors who rode his southbound overseas railway to Key West to avoid the cold harsh winter weather of the north. After surviving years of neglect, several serious hurricanes, and extensive renovation, it is still an award-winning piece of real estate. Its five-star accommodations are said to be well worth the price of a stay. Jill didn't care about that though. It was the little neighbor next door that she came to visit, the Spotswood Oceanside Park.

"There you are my pretty!" Jill said as she pulled up to the park. She had her choice of parking places at this early time of day, and, after a quick but exceptionally well executed Uturn, she docked her little magical yellow submarine perfectly, right in front of the cute little red capped thingy on the sidewalk.

She climbed out through the driver's window and skipped to the front of her bug, singing gaily, "We all live in a yellow kinda thing, a yellow kinda thing, a yellow kinda thing."

Her sister Trina and she had christened the bug, "The Yellow Kinda Thing", on the day her father presented it to her for her seventeenth birthday. She and her yellow submarine had become somewhat of a celebrity couple in Gloucester. She and all her friends would climb out the windows pre-tending they were exiting a submarine. It was cute then, but now it looked a little strange to the night guard that was watching from the pool area on the other side of the fence.

It was threethirty a.m. and sunrise was probably two hours away, but she was not here to see a sunrise. Jillian was here for the moonset. And the view was absolutely spectacular. A trillion stars sparkled in the sky. The night air was as still as if God and all his angels were holding their breath. Jill skipped through the park like a Tinker Bell fairy. She jumped into the air and landed on the seawall. Wrapping her arms around herself, she swayed back and forth gazing at the moon.

"Oh, aren't you beautiful tonight!" she romantically offered to the sky. There were two sailboats anchored a mile offshore and the mast lights softly rocked in the tide. She slipped off her shoes and stretched out on the sea wall. "Well," she said.

"And who might you be?" She was apparently lost in a dialogue with the universe.

She went on, "Mr. Mars, Mr. Saturn, and Mr. Pluto"

She slipped off to sleep right there, on top of the wet, stone seawall. When she awoke, she was in so much pain she couldn't bend over to put her shoes back on. She pulled her watch out of her pocket and was surprised to see that it was eightfifteen. The sea gulls were soaring over the water, diving for breakfast, and shaking the salt water off their catch as they returned to the sky. Guests from the hotel were already sitting in the lounge chairs on the beach while their children played in the crystal-clear water of the shallow lagoon. She sat for a short time gathering her thoughts and planning her day. When she got back to her car, she found that a parking ticket was clipped behind the wiper blade.

"One hundred and fiftyfive dollars!"

She read the note at the bottom where the officer wrote, 'Vehicle towed if not removed before eight a.m.'.

She realized she was on borrowed time and opened the door. Out of time is not quite the same as out of juice, but, she was out of both. Her battery was completely dead. She just knew that any minute a tow truck would be coming around the corner. She thought she may be able to push the car beyond the fire hydrant and out of the no-parking zone. She turned the key, set the shifter in neutral, climbed out and placed her hands on the back bumper. Barefooted, she slipped on the sandy pavement, but soon she had moved the bug the necessary distance to clear the zone. She opened the engine compartment hatch and stood on the sidewalk trying to look as helpless as possible.

"Hey, what's the matter with it?" a construction worker on a scaffolding two houses up and across the street called out to her.

"It's the battery; I'm gonna get a new one today," Jill called back to the gallant young hunk that was now swaggering across the street headed her way. He was pulling off his gloves as he approached and asked, "Are you sure it's the battery?" He continued smiling as he inspected the engine compartment on the back of her little bug.

"Yeah, this is the second time this week I've needed a jump," she said. "Well, let me go get my truck and we can get you back on your way," he offered.

"Thanks!" Jill nervously said in his direction as he turned around and headed back across the street. She was never a girl who fell for men quickly.

They had to prove themselves trustworthy before she would ever allow herself to be swooned in a boy's direction. But! This boy was an ordained knight of the roundest of tables, personally christened by King Richard, and dedicated to the safekeeping of the chastity of the queen's handmaidens. If she couldn't trust a knight in shining armor, where was the hope for the world?

Seconds later a huge Dodge Ram on steroids pulled across the street and towered over the back end of her little yellow thinga-mobile. Climbing down from the roaring dragon, he wiped his hands with a greasy towel and said, "They're cute, but if they don't turn over that's all they'll ever be, cute!"

His sparkling white teeth and cowboy grin won Jill over on the spot. She nervously smiled and tucked her chin down and felt she had been roped, hogtied, branded and ready to turn over at his will. It was scary and she liked it. He went on talking as he opened the diamond-cut toolbox in the back of his truck and hooked up the cables. His armor shone in the bright morning sun as he set up for the final slaying.

"Yeah, I thought it might have been your car. I got here at seven and Stookey was just finishin' writin' up the ticket. I grew up with him and we all knew he was gonna be a cop someday. Kinda an asshole when he's in uniform but on the football field he was always the guy to team up with. Son of bitch just has to make that quota though," he said as he lifted his head back out of the engine compartment.

He reached through the driver's window, turned the key, and the little bug flipped over and started purring like a kitten. Jill was trying to keep her internal thermostat from setting off alarms while she pushed the butterflies out of the way and said, "Oh, my God! I am so in debt to you. Thank you so much."

"No sweat! Maybe we can hook up sometime and go fishin' or something. You like to fish?" he asked with a boyish hope that she might say, "Hell yes, and swiggin' down beers behind Kmart, too."

Instead, she said, "Not really but I like the coconut shrimp at Schooners." He grinned, ear to ear, and said, "I'm ready when you are. I'm gonna be working this job here for at least three weeks so just come on over anytime and we'll set it up."

Jill surprised herself with her next remark. "I'm off for three days." And then she shut up, ashamed that she had acted so forward, like a desperate teenager.

"Well, OK then. I'm Timmy Vassar. I'm a conch. You know, born and raised here on the island. What's your name?" he asked as he shook her hand.

"I'm Jill. Jillian. I'm a nurse at the hospital. I just moved here a couple of months ago. Do you want me to meet you here?" she asked.

"Yeah, that'll be great. I'll see you about five o'clock." He walked backward till he got to the cab of his truck, and then swung himself into the seat like a cowboy mounting his steed. He slammed the door shut, leaned his sun-burned bulging arm out the window, pointed his finger at her and said with a big southern smile, "Don't park in front of the fire hydrant!"

She laughed and said, "You better get back to work." He peeled off leaving two black streaks in the pavement. Jill was laughing as she honked her horn and waved her hand in the air goodbye.

"Beep! Beep!"

She left the engine running, pulled the emergency brake handle up and walked through the glass door of the Sears Automotive Service Center.

"Yes Ma'am, how can I help you?" the service manager behind the counter asked as she approached. "Would I be able to have a new battery put in my car if I wait here till it's done?" Jill asked.

"Oh, yes ma'am. I've only got two cars on the racks right now and as soon as one of my men gets freed up, I can get that for you," he said as he laid out the paperwork. "It will take maybe an hour to an hour and a half. If you want to shop in the store I can page you when it's ready."

She signed the work order, retrieved the keys from the ignition, dropped them on the desk and headed across the parking lot toward the garden shop next to the back entrance of the main building.

The hot morning sun was now starting to make her sweat. She was still wearing her pink smock with its Lower Keys Medical Center emblem embossed on the left front panel, and her blue, cotton V- neck pullover. She liked the look of an offduty nurse at that time of day. It said to the world, "I am good enough at what I do to handle the night shift!"

Whether anybody would have thought that or not, she still liked the look. It was like hanging her stethoscope from her rear-view mirror. A visual badge, signifying she was in a 'special' occupation. Same reason young cops and cop wannabes always hang their handcuffs on their rearview mirror. Little do they know that it screams out, "I'm so insecure! Please approve of me!"

As Jill approached the open gate to the plant cage, she watched a girl wearing shorts and a vest and covered with colorful tattoos on her arms and legs, moving potted plants to the outside displays.

"Oh, these are so pretty," she said as she walked up to a rack of pink flowers in hanging baskets. "Bogainvillea?" she read the floral I.D. tag on the basket.

"Bougainvillea," the girl pronounced.

"Watch out, the thorns have a bite like a baby rattlesnake. It'll hurt for a week I guarantee." She continued, "They climb a trellis or wall like a climbing rose but don't need nearly as much care. You do have to keep them trimmed back from sidewalks or some asshole could sue ya for getting bit. It's like having a pit bull you don't have to pick up after or feed, protects your house from the freaks that try to sleep on your porch."

"I live in a condo," Jill said.

"Yeah, well they're great on a balcony, too," the girl added as she returned to tending her stock. Jill slowly meandered through the meticulously kept garden.

"You really do a great job of keeping these plants looking good," Jill said after walking the length of the plant cage.

"You must really love working out here." She was interested in connecting further with the tattooed girl. There was something intriguing about her.

"Yeah! As long as the suits stay out of my hair, there's nothing I'd rather do. I worked for the county for nine years. Hated that though! Too many snow birds that wanna bitch about code enforcement. When people cut the trees and plants down here without a permit, they can get huge fines. Almost everything is endangered or protected and I was an 'in the field' officer. They all hated my guts." She apparently was a woman of both strong opinions and many words. Jill asked, "Who, your bosses?"

"Hell no! Casey and I still live together. Shit, I'm the one who got him that job. It was the sons of bitches that own all the houses down here now. They live up north and come here for the winter and think they can do things like they do back home."

She continued moving between her plants as she smoked a cigarette and kept talking. She turned on a watering hose and stretched it down the aisle.

"So, you work for a doctor?" the girl asked, glancing over at Jill's white shoes and pant.

"No, I'm an E.R. nurse at Lower Keys Medical," she said with pride. It sounded so good to hear the words spoken in her own voice.

"Cool! You work with Crystal the Pistol?" the girl asked as she took another long drag from her cigarette.

"I did when I first started there, but I've moved over to the emergency room. Is Crystal a friend of yours?" Jill asked.

"Naw! Everybody knows Crazy Crystal the Pistol. She's tha 'fruit' at the Garden of Eden. You haven't been up there?" the girl asked.

"No, what's the Garden of Eden?" Jill asked.

"Oh, my God girl, you gotta see this place. It's an openair bar on the roof of the Bull on Duval Street. At night, they have a disc jockey and it gets packed, mostly with tourists and gold diggers like Crystal. By midnight, about half the people are dancing completely in the buff. Girl, it's wild! Your girl Crystal always shows up in a cowgirl costume and strips down to nothin' but a gun belt and two water pistols. So, Crystal the Pistol, get it?"

She lit another cigarette and was laughing as she continued watering the plants and talking.

"She gets all her drinks paid for and more sex than a pretty boy in prison, if ya know what I mean. She's only there when she's off duty but most of the daytime she's working the tourists for picture money of her in her short cowgirl skirt showin' her tight little ass to beerbellied old guys. She's pinching in the bucks! Man, she's gotta be sleepin' on a bed of cash. And that's on top of the nursing gig."

Jill was amazed to hear this and even grateful to now have ammo in her arsenal if Crystal should ever be assigned to the emergency room.

"WOW!" she exclaimed. "That's amazing! I never would have guessed all that. She seems so straight."

"Well, I don't think I'd go as far as thinking she was 'straight' if ya know what I mean."

She laughed while her cigarette hung from one side of her wrinkled mouth. Her voice broke up from the years of congestion that someday would read as C.O.P.D. in the box labeled Cause of Death. The girl coughed up the blockage and swallowed before continuing.

"Yeah, she ain't straight! I'd put a guarantee on that." She raised her eyebrows as high as possible as she said it.

The girl had a funny mannerism when she was trying to make a point. Jill had never seen it before. She would lean to one side in the direction of the person she was talking to and bounce her body like she was on a pogo stick. It was funny, quirky, and, Jill was beginning to realize, typical behavior on this weird little island. Jill picked out a beautiful bougainvillea that was in full bloom and the two headed for the cash register at the other gate.

"I'm Jillian by the way."

Jill offered her hand to the girl that looked sixty but was probably not older than forty-four.

"Oh, pleased to meet you, I'm Marty," the girl said, fighting to keep from launching into a coughing spell.

"I'm here all the time."

Jill asked, "Is it okay to pick this up when I come back out?" Marty assured her it would not be moved. After offering her thanks Jill walked out the open gate and through the back door of the Sears store.

She had time to kill and didn't need a thing. She walked past the rows of lawnmowers and yard tools and into the electronics section of the store. All the TVs were locked in unison to the same video. Jill stood staring in amazement at the wall of big screens. Vivid images of tropical fish were darting in and out of a coral reef in front of an underwater camera. They were so fabulous! She had never known that fish could be so colorful, that water could be so clear, or, that a TV could be so expensive.

"May I help you, Miss?" a voice crashed into her trance.

A tall young man in a white shirt and tie was trying to break into her world but he had little chance. With her eyes glued to the T.V. screen, she leaned slightly toward him and with one finger pressed to her lips quietly said, "Shh! There's a huge shark right over there."

She slowly pointed her finger toward the screen and sure enough, there was a shark, a nurse shark. It was wedged under a huge ledge of coral. Its gills were pulsing as it filtered the oxygen from the clear water. It was sleeping. The young man turned his head toward the TV then looked back at Jill. She was paralyzed.

"Ma'am, it's a nurse shark," he said. "It works parttime over in the shoe department! It's harmless! If you need any help I'll be right over here." With that, he walked away leaving Jill standing in the showroom with her eyes wide open, making a breathing sound as she sucked air slowly in and out through her teeth. She was one hundred and fifty feet down and almost out of air.

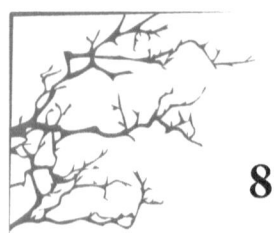

8. Paddy's Irish Way

There were very few customers in Sears on that Monday morning. It was almost ten o'clock when Jill said goodbye to the fishes on the reef and walked back to the service center to check on her car. She had forgotten to pick up her new plant from the plant cage just outside the back door and had to backtrack to get it. Her car was still parked in the same spot where she had left it and had not yet been touched but the service manager promised it would be ready within the hour. She told him she was going to walk over to the phone center across the parking lot and would be back when she finished. After placing her new plant on the back floorboard, she began the long hot walk across the blistering pavement toward the phone store.

Upon entering the store, she caught the eye of the man who had written the repair ticket on her cell phone one week earlier. He was engaged with an older woman and called out as the door closed behind her, "I'll be with you in a moment."

Several of the functions on her phone were failing and had been causing her to lose pictures, text messages and voicemail. The man had promised it would be ready for pickup that past Saturday and Jill was anxious to have it back so she could catch up with family and friends.

"May I help you?" the manager asked after he completed his previous transaction.

"Yes," she replied. "I'm here for my phone."

"Do you have your slip?" he asked.

"It's somewhere in my car," she answered.

"By chance could you come back with it?" he firmly asked, as he leaned into a large box on the floor and started pulling out boxes of new cell phones and stacking them on the countertop.

Jill felt she deserved closer attention from him and leaned halfway over the counter and loudly said to him, "The slip is in my car. My car is in the shop. You have my phone and I need it now!"

The busy store manager was keenly aware that he may be on the edge of a difficult encounter and he hoped he could defuse her before the spark reached the rocket. He stopped unloading the box, and stepped to his computer and said, "I'm sorry, could you give me your cell number so I can pull up your account?"

A local real estate broker came through the door with her daughter and a box to be shipped with U.P.S. and said, "Hey Thomas, I've got two more the same size in the car."

Jill spun around and glared at the well-dressed lady, then spun back to face the store manager.

"My phone, I need my phone!" she growled at the poor fellow.

He was obviously becoming increasingly nervous and responded accommodatingly, "Ma'am, I've really got to have your number to access the account so I can find out where it is."

He leaned back from the counter in case she decided to get physical. She slowly scanned the counter where the cases of new phones had just been stacked. She looked back at the manager then, with her left arm, knocked the entire stack off the counter and across the lobby. The child behind her shouted to her mother and ran to her side. Jill turned around and threw her shoulders back before stepping toward the door.

"THREE, 0, FIVE, FIVE, FIVE, FIVE, ONE, FOUR, ONE, EIGHT."

She called out each number as she stomped her feet in cadence and marched out the door. Once she had left, the store the manager scrambled to enter the numbers into his system. In a moment, he had retrieved the status on Jill's phone; 'irreparable due to water damage'; 'insurance coverage: policy expired'. He was relieved that he had not had to deliver the bad news.

Jill was furious that she had not been able to retrieve her phone! She stepped off the curb without checking for cars and was almost run over by a delivery truck. The driver hit his brakes and tapped his horn but she didn't even look as she stomped across the road. His window was down and he called out to her, "Hey, wake up, lady."

She stopped then, like a Gestapo foot soldier, spun and shot her arm out toward him with her palm facing inward. She dropped all fingers but the middle one, then turned around and marched across the long parking lot and back toward the Sears store.

Halfway across the lot she began to realize that she may have been acting out of character. She slowed her pace as she tried to gain perspective on the recent events. She felt a little lightheaded and instead of attributing it to the last seven weeks of inadequate nutrition and a serious deficit of sleep, she determined all she needed was a cup of coffee. It seems reasonable to hope that someone who had been trained to recognize such indicators of impending trouble might be able to see the red flags flying. Apparently, when the red flags are flown too close to home, they fade to green and signal the horses to take off running.

She walked into the Publix grocery store to pick up a bottle of Frappuccino. Waiting in the express line she spotted the display rack of a product she had never seen before. She reached over and grabbed one of the tall narrow cans. Red Bull! She began reading the print on the back of the can. Wow, she thought, this may be even better than a Frappuccino. She purchased both and headed out the door and down the front stairs. She opened the can and took her first sip. She gagged a little but it made her curious enough to finish reading the ingredients. A city bus pulled past her and stopped at the far end of the Publix store.

"Hey, hey, there's my nurse. Hey, come here, I wanna talk to you darlin'." It was Paddy. He climbed down from the bus and spun around to shout something vulgar to the driver. Then he turned and headed toward Jill, falling forward into every step he took, staggering along the sidewalk with one hand reaching toward her as if he was stretching to catch a dollar in the wind.

"Come here, you beautiful angel from God. You saved my life.

"His crumpled hat was pulled down over the top of his flyaway white hair, which was completely a mess. He rambled on. She thought it was wonderful that anyone was recognizing her in public. She felt like a celebrity. It didn't matter who it was. It was a welcome affirmation of her newly acquired identity.

"There she is, my beautiful private nurse." His drunken spit sprayed from his mouth as he spoke each word.

Once he reached her, he grabbed the no parking sign for support and said, "Hey, where'd you go? I was lookin all over for you. I'm a Marine you know!"

She laughed and switched her drink to her other hand. Paddy took notice of the can and said, "Oh, those are good stuffs!"

He smelled like a rum barrel, but her ability to smell had obviously gone out with her ability to use good judgment.

She found Paddy's Irish way charming and somewhat flattering.

"Say, what do ya say? Can I have a little taste of the Bull?"

He twisted his wrinkled little head to one side and raised his eyebrow as he gave her a wink. She leaned the can back and took one great swig then handed the can over to him.

"Polish it off!" she directed him with a smile.

Paddy chugged down the sludge and wiped his slobbered mouth on his freckled, hairy arm.

"Ah!" was the sound he made as he finished the last of the brew, then smacked his lips in ecstasy. They stood there smiling at one another, nothing said, just standing, smiling.

Paddy wore a baggy tank top that appeared to be meant for a man three times his weight. The bottom two feet of it had been cut off which left his shrunken waistline indecently exposed. He was a haggard lost soul of an old man. Best guess, seventythree years. He wore a pair of denim shorts low on his bony hips. The style would have been in vogue on an eighteen-yearold female gogo dancer in 1966. On Paddy, they looked disgustingly brave at best.

He kept his legs shaved. His bony ankles were shoved into black army boots left untied and flared open at the top. He was a flaming spectacle to behold. His appearance, coupled with his aggressive and obnoxious behavior, left no wonder why he was so often attended to in the emergency room. His mug was often found deeply imprinted on the knuckles of the fists of others. It was a fame he held as an honor; that, and having at one time been a U.S. Marine, were the two things he bragged on most.

Often heard to report, "I got hit by another car last night."

Or, "You know, I was a United States Marine."

Or when asked, "God, Paddy, what happened to your face?" His response was usually, "Two guys beat me up."

That was life for Paddy, repeatedly stumbling into a bus here, a car there, or some guy's fist. The twisted little fellow needed an angel. Just maybe he had finally found one.

9. The Driftwood Resort

When a hurricane is born off of the coast of Africa, it starts as a small storm, that's all, just a breeze. Maybe some rain to go along for the ride. In its earliest stages, someone watches, waits, ready to scream, "Here it comes! Run for your life." Unfortunately, no one had the necessary vantage point from which to yell, as tropical storm Jillian began to build.

Paddy insisted on tagging along with his unwitting personal nurse, to act as her "protector." She offered no resistance to his incessant nattering and seemed completely unbothered by the obnoxious chatter. The wiry little imp followed her across the Sears Town parking lot and through the door of the automotive service center like a six-year-old following his mother as she ran her morning errands. Jill put her hands up on the counter and Paddy did the same. He stared at her lips as she talked and hung on her every word.

The service manager met them at the counter and tried to ignore the surly little man. After the transaction was completed, he handed Jill the receipt and passed her the keys to her car. Paddy held out his hand and said, "You better let me see that. These sonsofbitches would rob their own sister for a dollar."

He held the paper close to his face and pretended to scan it for mathematical errors. He snarled unintelligibly as he moved the paper in a circle like a magician performing the setup for a trick.

"Yeah well, add this here. Go here, too much this, add this, tax, tax." He handed the receipt back to Jill and followed her out the door and over to her little yellow VW bug. "Say missy, I'm awfully thirsty; what say we stop off and get us something to drink?" He was surprised to hear her response.

"OK!"

He threw a high-five to heaven behind her back as he ran to open her door. When she reached over and unlocked the passenger side he almost passed out, dumfounded at the ease with which she had fallen into his clutches. He looked like a little child as he struggled to pull the door open. Once he had settled into the seat he crossed his bony legs and scooted as far forward as he could. He was as proud as an Irish leprechaun that had just bagged his first mortal. Unable to see over the dashboard, he stretched to look out the side window as they pulled out of the parking lot and joined the eastbound traffic.

The sun was burning brightly, directly overhead. The temperature flashed 101 degrees on the sign in front of the Oceanside Bank as they passed by. Jill was enjoying the breeze as the unlikely pair drove past the shops at Sears Town and the many high-rise hotels lining the bayside highway. She was driving much slower than her fellow commuters and traffic was backing up as cars took turns passing her. Horns blew and fists shook as the cars sped past. Each was met with a friendly smile and wave. It was a parade! Her parade! She just knew that the morning paper had proclaimed that this day would be forever known as Jillian Day and no longer referred to as Monday. As she passed people on the sidewalks and waiting on benches for buses she raised her hands to the left, then the right, and smilingly nodded her head in their direction, waving to their cheers. She listened to the crowd chanting her name from bandstands that didn't exist. She began looking for the turn into the city hall parking lot where she just knew that the mayor was preparing a speech on her behalf. She would be given the keys to the city and, when asked what her plans were for this wonderful holiday, she could hear herself shouting out, "Everybody to the beach!"

Paddy watched, smiling! Rocking merrily on the passenger seat like a proud puppeteer watching his handiwork cut free from its strings to perform his bidding. One thing was constantly on his mind. Whether in the form of beer, wine, whisky or cough medicine, he had to get some alcohol. The parade was lots of fun but he was starting to reach that tipping point that always made him uncomfortable. He was getting a little too close to sobriety for his liking.

"Oh," he moaned miserably with one eye closed. "I haven't had a thing to eat in three days," he lied as he bent further forward on the seat, holding his belly with both hands.

"Please, please help me ease this pain before I dry up and blow away." He continued to nail the scheme down with, "Do you think you could buy me a big cold bottle of water?"

Jill was so upset that he had not asked earlier she sped up like a race car driver pulling out of the pit. "Hold on!" she said. "You'll make it."

Paddy was thrown backward and so startled that he started grabbing for the seat belt. With much fumbling to lock it in place, he calmed himself and suggested, "A very dear friend of mine owns a grocery store just past the Cow Key Bridge." He then added, "I think he's open today." He directed her into the parking lot of Bone Island Liquors and excitedly hopped out. Jill followed him like a personal servant to a crowned prince.

He grabbed a cart and flew to the cooler in the back of the store where he loaded it with four sixpacks of Miller Premium Gold, several bottles of cheap wine, and two fourpacks of Bacardi Breezers. Then, as he pushed it toward the checkout counter, he grabbed two gift boxes of Absolut Swedish Vodka. He arrived at the counter where Jill was enjoying playing with all the colorful gift items, fake jewelry, cheap watches, novelty lighters, naked lady pens, etc. She was completely mesmerized, lost in wonder. Grabbing a handful of Slim Jims and a bag of corn chips off the rack, Paddy turned to Jill and asked, "Excuse me, Angel, would you like me to get you a bottle of water or two?"

She turned and said, "Hey! Let's get some Bull."

It was like hearing the three bells hit on a Vegas slot machine.

"Yes dear, anything you like my darling," the twisted old conniving bum said. On the inside, he was jumping in air, thinking his numbers had finally hit. He retrieved two fourpacks from the cooler and set them on the counter.

"Hello Roger. A carton of Salem 100's if you please."

He greeted the clerk who was eyeing him with disgust as he rang up the load.

Roger asked, "Anything else you need lady?" Jill was rocking side to side with a teddy bear key chain between her fingers. She held it close to her nose, watching it twirl, mesmerized as it flipped back and forth.

"This!" she called out and tossed it at the clerk, laughing as it hit him in the chest. He was startled and missed catching it by a few inches. Untrusting as he bent to retrieve it from the floor, he kept his eye locked on the duo the whole time.

"How do you want to pay for this?" he asked glancing between Paddy and Jill. She reached in her pocket and threw her ATM card at him, laughing as he jumped. He shook his head as he searched for it on the floor and rang up the sale. Paddy snatched the receipt and the card and shoved it into the back pocket of his tight short shorts. Roger gave a disapproving glare at Paddy as he placed the cigarettes in the cart and left the store.

After popping open the latch on the front of the bug, Paddy began loading up the booty. He stopped when Jill approached him from behind. She stood there, drenched in sweat, with a most distant and melancholic grin on her face, still flipping her new teddy keychain from side to side in her hand as she squinted to bring the diabolical little man into focus. Paddy grabbed a Red Bull and snapped off the tab. He took a generous swig then held the can high toward her face and insisted, "Here my sweet little flower, you need to be lubricated in this hot sun."

She took the can of super fuel in both hands and as he tilted it into her mouth, she gulped it down. He kept his hand on the bottom to ensure she emptied the can. He was grooming her for his introduction of future and more potent libations. He was improvising as his plan unfolded. They laughed together as she wiped her mouth of the spillage. She spun around in the pearock gravel parking lot and shouted to the sky, "I want a suntan!"

Paddy liked the sound of that and answered, "And so ye shall have, for I control the sun and a wonderful beach awaits you."

They laughed as Paddy held her door open like a carriage master for a princess. She curtseyed and he bowed and then slammed her door closed. She started the car and off they went, Paddy in the passenger seat, his lap loaded with Bacardi Breezers, and a beer in each hand. It was just like Christmas Day. At least for him!

Poor Jillian, if only there was someone who could have warned her. The turbid waters that lay before her were full of eyes, hungry for a fresh kill, ready for a feast. Little Jillian was being led blindly to the table. Delivered by a masterful hunter who had smelled the blood and taken his first taste! Merely eight hours of deep sleep and one good breakfast could have bridged the river and delivered her safely across this evil pool.

On that very morning, her mother and father had been voicing their concern that she had not communicated with them in over a week. They were aware that she had been having difficulty with her cell phone after being drenched by a tropical rain. They were comforted by reminding each other how resourceful and capable she was. The letter mailed by her mother on the previous Thursday had offered their willingness to cover the expense of a new phone, if it was necessary to replace her old one. That letter remained unopened, wedged in the visor above her head. If only she would pull over and open it now. Perhaps it would shake her back into reality. Maybe some unsuspected word would be the trigger that would wake her from this dream.

She had lost her sunglasses on her last three days off and had not yet replaced them. She squinted as she reached up and pulled down the visor to block the blinding glare. Jill didn't notice when the letter from home floated down to the center console. Paddy grabbed it and read the name on the envelope. If she had earlier introduced herself to him that memory had dissolved upon entering his drunken brain. He now locked it into his memory as if it was a combination to a vault. And it may well have been, as far as he was concerned! Paddy was always looking for opportunities for easy pickings. His motto was, "If God lets it fall off the tree and it don't knock you out, then shut up and drink it! Praise his Holy Name!"

"What's this?" he asked as he held the letter up for her to see.

"I don't know; bills, I guess."

She was clueless to just how far from home this journey was about to take her. Paddy immediately changed the subject as he shoved the letter into his side pocket.

"Ya know, I have a dear friend who has built the most wonderful seaside resort. It's very private but he has hidden a key just for me and we can have the entire run of the property." He went on weaving his tale as he glanced over to see if he was hitting the right nerve.

"He named it *The Driftwood Beachfront Resort and Hacienda*, and its beaches are the envy from here to Jamaica."

Jill was listening with elated interest and when he had finished his dissertation of bullcrap she squealed with excitement, "Ooh, I wanna see it! Can we go now?"

"My darling nurse Dougherty, you are almost there," he said, as he glanced to check on how deeply his hook had penetrated her lip.

"Take the next right." He directed her onto Boca Chica Road which follows the chainlink fence at the east end of the Naval Air Field and along the blacktop runways where the F15s scream as they launch into the air, deafening any unfortunate sightseers that might happen to be exploring the area with their top down. Today, they were lucky! The pilots were all over at the officer's club enjoying their lunch break while their fiery jet engines cooled down before the next training run.

Jill never noticed Paddy glowing with pride after remembering her name from the envelope and creatively incorporating it into his diabolical scheme. He was even more proud that his pickled brain was able to pronounce it correctly. She followed his instructions and turned onto the two-lane road at the next corner.

The shallow waters along this low caprock covered land are fed by tributaries cut through the coral in the 1920s and had originally been expected to be developed further into deep water canals with large homes built on stilts on each side. When the Navy later contracted to build their base there, all residential plans screeched to a halt. Now, the long ride out to the desolate stretch of neglected Boca Chica Beach was littered with old mobile homes and abandoned boat trailers.

The road followed the shoreline until the new highway located further inland was completed, Boca Chica Road was known as the original Overseas Highway. Hurricanes and tectonic shifts have left it vulnerable to high tide washouts, and neglect by the D.O.T. has turned it into little more than an unkept fishing trail that ends where the water swallows up the pavement. The beach is a seaweed covered smelly, buggy, littered stretch of about one mile, with barely a single sixfoot square that's appropriate for sunbathing. The area is generally visited by people who wish to get away from anyone who might be suspicious of their activities, and that made Paddy feel right at home!

There were fewer than ten cars in the parking area. Two ratty vans, several rusty pickup trucks, a motorcycle, and an old orange Datsun station wagon were parked on the sides of the road. Where the pavement ended, there were three huge limestone boulders that had been dropped in place to block vehicles from driving into the washout just fifty yards beyond. At that point, the road becomes a walking trail with the Atlantic Ocean on one side and an eightfoot barrier fence on the other.

The U.S. Navy owned the beach, the road, and everything connected to the property. The fence was to keep people off the airstrips and marked the boundary that the public was expected to honor. The rest of the area was offered for public access and was generally unpatrolled by authorities. Anything anyone wanted to do could be done out there and potentially never be discovered. It was the *"Badlands of Paradise!"*

Jillian loved it! Paddy clicked the trunk latch open and loaded his favorite beverages into a doubled plastic bag while she explored the beach by the water. He shoved the packs of Salem into his beltless waistband and threw the empty carton over his shoulder toward the chainlink fence. Next, he opened the first bottle of Vodka, leaned his head back, and downed half of the venomous poison in one long swig. His hat slid off his tiny, bald head and landed on the pavement behind him. After securing the cap back on the vodka bottle, he ripped open the remaining bags and boxes, and threw the packaging on the ground.

"Aha!" he exclaimed loudly toward the water.

"We are almost there my dear," he announced as he gathered up his belongings and headed down the broken road, leaving behind the pile of trash on the ground, a six-pack of beer hidden under the seat, and the trunk lid wide open. Jill was spinning round and round, breathing in the putrid air as if it were holiday potpourri. Piles and piles of wavewashed seaweed lay decaying on the sand and the water was clogged with more, waiting to be deposited by the next incoming tide. Dead fish and crustaceans, trapped in the seaweed, were everywhere, rotting in the sun. The smell would have rendered a flock of vultures nauseous. Neither Paddy nor Jill was the least bit affected.

Paddy was almost out of view when Jill turned and headed his way. She skipped like a schoolgirl and threw herself against him from behind when she caught up. There were clusters of purple flowers growing on crawling vines all over the cracked and crumbling asphalt road. The sea was eating the land, grain by grain! The vines were the first soldiers of its reclamation.

Jill grabbed the vodka bottle from Paddy's gnarly knuckles and held it to her lips. Tilting it back like a pro, she chugged the poison down as if it were a harmless cream soda that she had pulled from the cooler at her father's ice cream shop. Her throat wrenched from the burn but her brain gave it a much more palatable interpretation.

"Ummm, banana!" she announced with glee.

They walked together along the narrowing road. Several washouts had caused the pavement to completely cave in. They jumped across the fast-moving tidal runs and waded across others. Jill laughed like a child with every stumble. More trips were made to the well of poison and before long they were completely out of sight of the little yellow bug.

Wet now from the waist down, her thin white pants were clinging to her legs and buttocks, allowing full view of her lacy red thong.

"Ooh, very nice!" the drunken old man pointed at her crotch as he laughed. Jill surveyed the damage and looked up surprised and announced, "Well, Mrs. Dougherty, I believe it's a baby girl!"

She cracked up as Paddy reached down to help her out of the water and up onto the next chunk of broken asphalt.

The afternoon sun was blistering and no shade would be available for another three hundred yards. Paddy pointed to a section of the tall fence fifty feet ahead.

"Look!" he said. "There's the Wall of Lost Soles."

"Jill was in the middle of another swig of banana soda (aka vodka) and laughed so hard that she lost her lip lock, spraying Paddy with his favorite flavor. When she realized what was before her, she started crying. Her tears flowed down her cheeks as she pushed her way through the seagrass and weeds and closer to the colorful montage that hung from the tall fence. She broke into a slow trot and dropped to her knees on the hard, hot, broken pavement in front of the grand display. Paddy caught up to her and stood over her, drinking from the plastic vodka bottle. She stopped crying and softly spoke the words, "The Wall of Lost Soles."

After a pause, she asked him, "Whose, are they?"

Paddy answered, "Hell, who knows? Yours, mine, the Cubans are just ninety miles that way." He turned and pointed directly offshore at the southern horizon.

"They might be Osama Ben Pluckin' Laden's for all I care."

He braced himself with one leg on each side of her and placed the lip of the bottle to her mouth. Jill offered no resistance as he poured the poison down her throat. He stood over her, dripping sweat from the tip of his crooked nose, wavering in the heat. Then he wiped the sides of her mouth dry with his nicotinestained thumbs. After licking the vodka from his fingers, he moved back to her side and faced the sculpture, and exclaimed, "Well I'll be damned! There's my shoe! I've been lookin' for that Goddamn shoe for seventeen years."

He handed her the bottle and staggered the rest of the distance to the tall fence. He ripped a pink flipflop from its wedged position among probably two hundred shoes and sandals that someone had carefully stuffed into the holes of the chain link fence.

"Finally, I got my soul back!" he said coughing and spitting through the laughter. Jill rolled on the rocks hysterically over the spectacle. After a few minutes, they gathered their belongings and returned to the trail and their westbound trek.

Shortly, they saw a man walking in the shallows coming their way. He was a handsome man with dark skin and black wavy hair. He had a bohemian look about him and carried a bag over his shoulder. He was completely without clothing and his manhood bounced as he walked. Jill held out both hands in his direction as if she could embrace him over the one-hundred-foot span between them as he passed. He tried to look away and seemed uninterested in the beautiful girl. She stopped in her tracks and stood watching him as he passed by. She ran to rejoin Paddy who had continued up the trail.

"He's a fag! He's fishin' for men," Paddy growled out of the side of his mouth. Jill was lost in the beauty of the place and offered no emotion other than bliss. Soon, they came in view of the Driftwood Hacienda.

"There it is!"

He held out his free hand toward the amazing structure, then added, "It's all yours!"

Wedged into the mangroves between the pavement and the fence, an enormous castle had been constructed out of chunks of lime rock and driftwood. It rose through the trees with grand appendages that anchored the rocks and wood together. There was an old fishing boat, probably placed by a hurricane, thirty feet above the main structure in a most creative position. There were meandering walkways that led to hidden caverns and rooms, porches and courtyards. A stone stairway led to an open rooftop over the main room with a wonderful view of the ocean. It had a look of perhaps being built by island aborigines thousands of years ago.

Jill ran from room to room howling like a wild dog. There were shelves in all the rooms. The place was stocked with supplies that had been delivered by the tide. There was soap, toilet paper, china, cups, glasses, candle holders, flashlights, and matches. There was a room full of fishing gear and another with yard tools. The whole place was constructed of things washed up on the shore or pulled out of the surrounding trees. It was fabulous!

Paddy caught up with her on the rooftop solarium and set his bag of bottles in the corner. Jillian was up on the wall looking out at the sea.

"Look!" she shouted, pointing down to the beach. Two young men were just beyond the first line of waves swimming in the crystal waters. A wave passed by as they stood adjusting their face masks and Jill saw that they were both naked. She watched them in the water and turned to dismount from the high wall. She leaned against the rocks and pulled her shoes and socks from her feet, then unhooked her waist snap and shed her pants. She shed her pink smock, then peeled off her pullover and threw them both into the trees beyond the wall.

Paddy was more interested in choosing which beverage was to be served next than enjoying the show of a twentyoneyearold female stripped of her clothes and spiraling out of control toward a mental breakdown. He pulled two Bacardi Breezers from the bag, opened both, and took one over to Jill. She reached behind her back and popped the hook on her bra. After firing it off into the trees, she took the bottle and guzzled down the hot, fruity elixir. Paddy watched with relative disinterest as her subtle breasts swayed with her movements. She ripped off her tiny lace thong and trotted off down the staircase toward the refreshing water.

By the time she was knee-deep in the surf, the two men had seen her coming toward them and nervously turned to leave the area. They briskly waded through the water toward their towels hidden in the mangroves. Jill was intent on meeting them and gained on them as they reached shallow water. She ran up to them without a word and stood on the beach before them, smiling. If she had said anything they wouldn't have understood a word. They were new arrivals from Cuba, close to Jill's age.

The threesome stood looking at each other for a moment. One boy nervously said something in Spanish to the other then offered her his face mask. She took it in her hands and put her arms around the two boys, gently pulling them toward her. They tentatively accepted her gesture but quickly pulled away. She gave them both a kiss on the cheek, then skipped back through the waves swinging the mask in the air above her head, like a rodeo cowboy twirling a lasso. The two young lovers held hands as they returned to their privacy under the shade of the trees.

Paddy finished arranging his collection of bottles on the shelves of the solarium and looked over the wall to see where his little angel might have floated off to. He saw her drifting in the water over the reef and was less concerned for her than the protection of his hooch from thieves. He counted the bottles and rearranged their positions again. Experience had taught him, many years ago, that a corkscrew is sometimes harder to put your hands on than getting your hands around a bottle cap you could unscrew. Paddy was married to that wisdom and always purchased his wine in bottles with screw-on caps. He selected a Brazilian Sangria and twisted off its top. Then he downed its entire content. Barely able to stand at this point, he decided to make a crutch from a piece of driftwood. Upon its completion, the old man put a Red Bull into the now empty plastic bag and hobbled toward the shore. After relieving himself in the sand, the old drunk kicked off his black army boots and stepped out of his shorts. He threw the crutch down and waded out to the reef where Jillian was enjoying watching the tropical fish.

"Oh, the little fishes love me!" she exclaimed as he approached with her drink. He popped the top and after taking a gulp handed it to her. She drank it down and handed him back the empty can which he discarded across a wave. She readjusted the face mask and returned to her underwater discoveries. Paddy fought the current to stay upright and determined it was taking much more energy to stay on his feet than he was willing to exert, so he turned and struggled to make his way back to shore. After retrieving a fresh bottle from his stash, he proceeded to stumble down the beach to visit the new neighbors. Jillian was lost in joyous wonderment of the sea life on the reef below her. Afraid only of blinking, and the possibility of missing an opportunity to make a new aquatic friend, she melted into the water. She became the reef. She felt her body morphing into coral. She looked at her hands. Her fingers had already completed their transformation. She tucked her face to look down the front of her body as it floated in the water. Her breasts had become pink fire coral. The skin on her smooth white thighs formed polyps as she watched. Starfish, sea horses, and tiny clownfish took shelter in the shadow underneath her. Crustaceans were gathering below her for protection. And the parrot fish nibbled softly on her toes, tickling her playfully as she continued her change.

An hour later she was unaware that she was drifting farther and farther out on the reef. She had no idea that the area where she was now floating was within three hundred feet of a deep drop-off and that the cold water beyond was a favorite hunting area for adult bull sharks.

No one was looking after her as she floated over the reef. She was so far stretched from conscious concern for her own safety that she was perilously without hope if she should need a rescue. She was haplessly drifting away when something bumped her leg. She turned to the left and there was one of the Cuban boys, treading water beside her. The water was over fifteen feet deep and he was struggling to keep his head high enough to signal to her that she needed to swim in. As her hallucinations sank away she turned to swim with him back to shore. The boys gathered their belongings and the four of them walked naked along the beach and back up to the Hacienda.

The afternoon light was waning in the western sky as they gathered on the wall of the rooftop solarium. The boys talked sweetly to each other in their native tongue and seemed completely comfortable with their nudity in the company of their newfound friends. Jill stretched out on the stone wall and soon drifted off into exhausted sleep. Paddy was surveying his supply of hooch and tasting one and then the other. After about fifteen minutes the two gay boys from Cuba put their clothes on and offered their gratitude to Paddy. When they motioned in Jill's direction Paddy held his finger to his lips and shook his head indicating they should not wake her. The boys left and Paddy continued nursing on his bottles and smoking cigarettes.

Jill had not moved on the wall in over two hours. The evening air was still warm and luckily the bugs were not flying high that night. Paddy passed out several times and finally ran out of hooch. He retrieved his pants from the sandy beach and put on his gritfilled boots. It took him forty minutes to navigate his way back to the car. He left without the least bit of regard for Jill's safety. He loaded up the last cans and bottles and started his journey back to the Driftwood, stopping several times to sit in the moonlight, tasting from one bottle, then another. He passed out again after a difficult passage through a fastflowing outwash of tidal water. Luckily, he had not lost any of his supplies, or his life.

Jillian awoke to the sound of a bottle being broken against a rock not ten feet from her head. The moon was halfway up its climb in the sky. She turned in time to see two ravenous animals snarling in the corner then disappear over the stone wall. She had no idea where she was or how much danger she was in. She felt a breeze brush across her skin and realized she was naked. The short nap had been enough to bring her back to reality and she was scared. Scared with good reason!

She looked around the unfamiliar structure and soon became oriented to the darkness and shadows. Her hand felt a loose rock in the wall and she tightened her grip on it. She ran her other hand across her body to deter-mine its condition. She felt her private area and was shocked to find herself so vulnerable and compromised. She searched for indications of injury.

First things first, she decided to challenge her most immediate threat. She jumped to a seated position and shouted, "Agggggh," and threw the rock. She immediately realized the intruders were raccoons and she could still hear them moving on the other side of the wall. They scampered off through the bushes as she continued to survey her surroundings. In the dim light, she looked for her clothes and tried to determine if she was in some dungeon or holding pen. Without clothing, she felt extremely vulnerable and much more defenseless.

She looked over the wall toward the ocean and thought that she may have been kidnapped and taken to an uninhabited island possibly in swimming distance to Key West. There was no movement on the beach. She hoped at worst that the damage had been done and she was just abandoned. She tilted her head, listening for voices but only heard the breeze and the gentle lapping of the waves against the rocks on the shore. She looked through the bottles and cans but no clues were revealed.

Poor Jillian's head felt like concrete and her back as if she had been tortured. She was still in fear that whatever had earlier befallen her may only have reached a lull. She had questions she wanted answered. The pile of cigarette butts on the flooring assured her that she had not ventured here alone. She found her wet shoes and socks and rushed to get them on. Then, at least she could run if needed. She was scared that she may have been raped. The pain that was running through her body was mostly in her back and head. She was relieved to have not found any suspicious sites of trauma when she scanned her body. She ran her hands over her skull for possible contusions. All clear! She inspected her vagina for indications of any damage to her sexual organs. Thank God, she seemed intact.

With her initial assessment completed, she felt a little relieved, and turned her attention to her search for her clothing. She circled the patio looking down over the outside of the wall as she went. Luckily, her bra had not traveled far on its projection. It was caught on a piece of driftwood just three feet out. This discovery led to her pants and then to her top which, unfortunately, someone had apparently thrown with greater fervor than the rest of the articles because it was far beyond her grasp. She never saw her smock hanging in the mangroves. It had dropped halfway to the ground and was hidden by the shadows of the building. She explored the first level for a long pole and successfully returned to the roof where she quickly retrieved the shirt.

She finished dressing and bolted toward the water to get away from the strange and scary structure. She had no idea where she was or how to get home. Her belly hurt, her back felt broken, she had a migraine, and she could feel a bad case of diarrhea coming on, but, she was alive, and apparently, had escaped being raped and tortured.

She climbed up on a large rock by the water and looked one way, then the other down the cluttered beach. The sky in one direction was very bright, which she thought may be an indication of a town where she might find help. In the other direction, the sky was a little bright but the moon was rising from that direction and she couldn't tell if the light was a reflection of the moon on the water or manmade.

With much deliberation, she determined her greatest promise was to walk toward what she felt was most likely manmade light. Unfortunately for Jill, it would take her three hours to realize she had made the wrong decision.

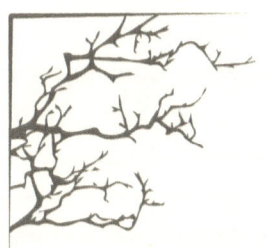

10. Still Alive

Jill stepped down from the rock and considered the dangers that might be waiting for her in the shadows of the dark beach. She determined that humans posed the greatest threat. Luckily the moon was going to be joining her on her walk tonight. She picked up four fistsized rocks and pushed them into her pockets. She walked to the tree line to try to find a piece of driftwood that she could use as a club if needed. There were a lot to choose from and she found the perfect piece. She felt empowered again, in control of her situation, and ready to solve her problem.

Still in pain, she pushed it to the side as she focused on the task of getting home. She could see that the terrain was extremely cluttered near the water and very dangerous near the trees. Large boulders and rocks were everywhere. She started her venture near the water line. She could feel the shells and crustaceans crunch under each step. The seaweed stuck to her shoes and threatened to trip her as she maneuvered across the hazardous terrain.

She climbed up, over, down, and around the giant flattopped boulders with razor-sharp edges. She soon began to wonder if the danger may lie in being sliced open and found days later, eaten by crabs. She made her way cautiously along the ocean's edge. Her concentration remained on traversing the difficult threatening landscape and soon she had forgotten her pain. She did feel a growing need to relieve herself but determined she would solve that problem when it became an emergency.

She pushed on through several tidal streams that were flowing briskly from what appeared to be a marsh behind the trees. While studying one fast-moving tributary for the safest approach, she was startled by a flock of wood storks that were roosting in the twisted mangroves. Hundreds of birds broke into deafening squawks, alarmed apparently, by her unexpected intrusion of their private and very remote rookery. As she squinted to look into the trees, she became aware of a flashing blue light reflecting into the air some distance beyond the marsh.

A little further up the beach she came upon a break in the tree line and could see that the blinking light was the reflection from the strobe lights lining the landing strip of the Boca Chica Naval Air Station. She could just make out the top of the tall control tower and sat down on the edge of a large flat rock to catch her breath and reflect on her predicament. She had enjoyed viewing the satellite images on her laptop while researching the islands on Google Earth and felt sure she could orient herself with this new-found information.

Though she was tired and hungry and not feeling well, she thought hard about the satellite pictures she had seen just weeks before. She realized some important elements of her predicament needed to be considered before moving on. If she were to keep walking toward the first lights she saw, which she knew now really were the city lights of Key West, she would never get there. From the east end of Key West to the west edge of the Navy base she would have to walk about three more treacherous miles through jungle growth and bad road, and then find the energy to swim at least two and maybe three deepwater channels, which she imagined were, most likely, full of bull sharks. Hungry bull sharks! Bull sharks that feed at night!

OK, this was good information! She was clear about it! Now, what about walking back the way she came? She looked to the east, toward the weird castle where she had no idea what had happened to her. If there was any alternative to going back in that direction, she would have taken it. But, nobody trespasses on the Navy base property unless they're crazy. Especially at night! She pushed herself off the rock and started walking, up through the marsh, and into the mercy of the U.S. Navy. There were dead trees and twisted limbs everywhere. Climbing over one and under the next was a workout that any athlete would be challenged to complete. It was just like the scene after that Malaysian tsunami, after the water subsided, leaving all kinds of junk piled up. She made her way, climbing through broken lobster traps washed in by storms with miles of tangled rope still trailing their floatation buoys, boat parts, an old mast with its guy lines hung up in the trees, broken glass, rocks, coral, old plastic coolers, fishing line with hooks still tied on, twisted bushes, lots of coconuts, and more dead trees. She heard rats, raccoons, and crabs scattering in the darkness as she climbed through the mountain of rubbish. She forced herself to keep the thought of snakes out of her mind. It was a gauntlet of a climb just to get past the first tree line.

Next, she stood before what appeared to be a shallow salt marsh lagoon. Thanks to the assistance of the moon, which now had risen high in the eastern sky, she could see how far across it was to the other side. There she would reach a wall of dense mangrove growth which she thought she would be able to traverse without much trouble. That would prove to be another misjudgment by the time the sun came up. For now, she had to wade across the muddy lagoon.

She thought she had understood that alligators don't live this far down in the Keys. She probably had not been advised about the three hundred or so endangered American crocodiles that were living in the lagoons of Key Largo just seventy-five miles up the keys from where she was standing. She probably, like so many other Keys transplants, didn't know that the American crocodile is much more aggressive and territorial than his cousin the Florida alligator. She most likely had not taken the opportunity to visit the Florida Alligator Farm, just nine miles west of the turnpike and outside the city limits of Miami. If she had, she could have watched as Seminole Indian Chief Billy desensitized 'Gomeck', the eighteenfoot gator, by smacking his snoot several times before sticking his head in its mouth. If she had stopped by for the show, she might have remembered that Chief Billy always advises the crowd not to try this at home and that the Florida alligator has a biting strength of threethousand pounds per square inch. Of course, that really didn't matter to Jill. It was information that she had not learned! She was right about the Florida alligator though, they don't usually venture this far from the mainland. Not usually!

So, in the dim light of the eastern moon, Jillian Bethany Dougherty took her first steps into the mangrove marsh. Her feet sank into the white lime-stone silt just about high enough to fill her tennis shoes with muck. She thought to herself that maybe she should have tightened and double-tied the laces before she made this move.

Too late! The very next step left her digging into the slimy silt for her left Reebok. She pulled herself back to the hard sand and after cleaning her shoes and shaking out her socks, she tried again. This time she had taken her own advice and tied the laces twice.

'Oh God', she thought as she stepped further and further out into the marsh. She was right. It was shallow. There was only about ten inches of water out there and well supported by, oh, about two feet of marsh silt. She made it twentyfive more feet and found herself stuck up to her waist. She fought for another hour and was still in the same place. She was tired, hungry, filthy, sunburned, lost, and now, her headache was back, stronger than before.

Her situation could have only been worse if the trouble she was having with her stomach revisited. It did! After a long battle to fight it off, she surrendered. Now, not only was she tired, hungry, filthy, sunburned, lost, and headachy, she stunk, too. Still in a daze as to how she found herself in this condition, she remained hopeful that if she was unable to save herself, someone would surely come to her rescue. After all, it wasn't like she was on a lost island in Indonesia. People don't die from being stuck hip deep in mud flats. Hell, it was Key West, not the back side of Borneo.

From half a mile away, on the other side of the navy base, she could hear trucks on U.S. Highway One as they raced to make their daily deliveries of beer and bread to the island bars and stores. She was probably just two hundred yards from the end of the landing strip where, at some point, F16s would be flying over, and if she still remained stuck, surely a pilot could call to the tower for someone to come rescue her. No one could die like this, she hoped, so close to a United States naval airfield. She looked around the shadowed marsh and prayed an idea would soon come to mind.

Alas, she was out of ideas.

Good ones and bad ones.

She could smell only the stench of her miserable predicament. At least she was alive. At least for now!

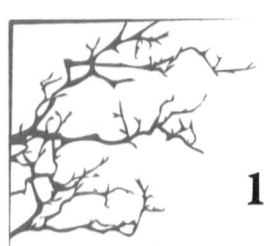

11. Stuck in the Mud

Jillian struggled frantically to free herself from the sticky mud. She made little progress over the course of the next hour. She pulled her watch from her pants pocket and wiped the crystal clean. Midnight had passed.

Exhausted from the ordeals she had thus far survived, she broke down and cried, softly at first, mournfully sobbing into her hands. She felt beaten to a pulp. She hurt from head to toe. Tortured by her own misfortune, she racked her brain to find an image hidden somewhere in her memory of the past twentyone hours. Some glimpse of a face of someone to blame. It was then that a vague recollection of a sandyhaired carpenter pierced briefly into her memory and then drove off in a pickup truck. She wondered if she had been carjacked. Maybe she had been brought to this place by boat. There were so many unanswered questions. She lay back and fell asleep in the warm mud.

She awoke to the sound of anhinga, screaming their celebration of the sun's glorious rising. They dove from their roosts in the mangrove trees and headed toward the ocean to perform their aerial ballet, diving for fish. They were followed immediately by the wood storks and other sea birds that had watched over Jill through the night. Sand gnats were swarming all around and biting her skin. She swatted wildly in her misery as she was being eaten alive. She had welts on her arms and neck from the stings of mosquitoes that had been sampling her blood while she slept. She fought to free herself from the bed of silt only to find that she had lost ground as the tides had risen and retreated again.

She screamed for help as she swatted at the feasting, winged creatures. Hundreds of fiddler crabs were watching as she struggled to fight off her impending doom, positioning themselves in the drying silt, staking claim to the juiciest parts of her flesh. She had lost the feeling in her feet and lower back. She thought now that she would have been better off being eaten by the sharks than to be nibbled to death by these tiny, bloodsucking devils. The more she swung her arms, the more their numbers increased. Screaming and crying was only getting in the way of battling the bugs. She smeared mud thickly on her head and face. She packed it in her ears and on her neck. Then she burrowed down until she was nothing more than a lump of mud with two eyes and a mouth. Still, she could not get relief from their incessant biting at the edges of the exposed areas. Her tears were further refreshment to the tiny beasts. Every few minutes she cried out as loud as she could.

"Help! Anybody, help!"

She continued her calls for the next two hours. She was almost ready to give up. She had cried herself dry. She felt like a dying bird, trapped in a tar pit. She was sure her bones would never be found. She offered up her final goodbyes to her loved ones and friends. She apologized to everyone she had ever taken for granted, and then she prayed.

Though Jill had spent her earliest six years of her life attending a small Episcopal church that was about a mile from the family home, she had never actively developed an interest in continuing. Her father and her mother periodically prayed with the children at home but did not encourage them in any particular spiritual direction.

Her prayers were for a speedy death. She had suffered enough. Her pain and inescapable fate were turning to the final page of her short life.

She whimpered her last goodbye. "Thank you, God, for all of the wonderful people you brought into my life," she softly cried, then listened for his voice to answer. She believed it soon would come. She shut her eyes to wait.

"Hey! Hang on! We'll get you out of there! Hang on!"

A woman's voice was calling to her from the mangroves that stood between the mud flats and the beach.

"Dillon! Dillon! Hurry up! There's a girl stuck in the mud over here!" she called out to a second person who came running up from the beach and pushed through the bushes.

"My God!" the man screamed with surprise as he climbed through the stand of mangroves and saw Jill's exhausted body covered in the bone-white mud.

"Just hang on now! I'll have you out in a minute," the man said as he worked his way out to Jill and wrapped his arms around her from behind. He pulled slowly and she began to dislodge. It took him another few pulls before she was free and he carried her back to the beach and down to the water. Jill was unable to speak she was crying so violently. Dehydrated and weak, she could barely move.

Jill lay crying in the salty water while the man and his companion splashed her clean. They had arrived on the beach in kayaks. The woman retrieved a bottle of drinking water from a cooler on the back of one of the kayaks and held it for Jill to drink. Once cleaned off and refreshed, Jill was able to communicate her appreciation but she was far too weak to explain how she had come to be in such a dismal situation and graciously submitted to their offer of assistance in getting out of there. As the man lifted her onto his kayak he asked if she was the owner of the yellow VW bug that they had seen back up on the car park where the road ends. Jill excitedly exclaimed, "You found my car!" He said that he and his wife had parked their jeep right behind her car and unloaded their gear. He felt it strange that someone would leave their car out there with the windows down, one door left open, and the trunk lid up. He also was concerned because they are regulars at that beach and didn't recognize the car as one that they had seen there before.

As they paddled Jill back to her car she made up a story of how she and friends had been out the night before for a beach party and after drinking too much she got lost and trapped in the mud. They talked about Jill's life in Gloucester and her new nursing position. Dillon told her that he was a retired structural engineer and his wife Kitty was a Key West artist. Kitty told her that they kayak over to that spot in the mornings to shoot pictures of the birds which she uses in her artwork and that they had almost canceled their trip that day due to the heat.

Upon their arrival, back at the parking area, they traded phone numbers and planned to get together soon. Jill looked through her car and determined everything of value was gone. On the floor was a parking ticket that she had no explanation for. She studied the time and date issued and the location, but no lights came on so she added it to her mystery file. On the back floorboard was a pile of dirt. A thorny plant with withered pink flowers was lying on the other side with its bare roots drying in the heat. The glove box was open and all that was left were old maintenance records and the original VW owner's manual. Dillon and Kitty retrieved two more bottles of cold water from the cooler in the back of their Jeep and gave them to Jill. They waited while she searched under the rear bumper for her magnetic hidden key box. The bug started on its first turn and they exchanged their goodbyes.

She took slow deep breaths as she made her way back to the main road. She still had no recollection of driving so far out of town. The last thing she thought she remembered was driving home from work on Monday morning, taking a shower, and climbing into bed. It was almost thirteen miles back to her condo.

She parked in the covered garage and before locking the car door she took a closer look from one end to the other. She found a receipt from the Key West Sears store dated the same day that she had gotten off from work and started her threeday weekend. At this point she realized she had no clue as to the current date or how long she had been gone. She could have been out in the woods for a week for all she knew. It was all very disturbing and she was sure she had been the victim of a kidnapping. The time that she picked up her car at Sears was recorded as ten fortynine a.m. This may be helpful. She checked the engine and confirmed there was a new battery. She checked the trunk and found a torn plastic bag from the Bone Island Liquor Store and a crumpled Salem cigarette package. Also, there was an empty Salem carton stuck in the center of the spare wheel as if it had been forced there by someone.

The whole car stunk! Cigarettes and booze!

Jill was in pain and a total mess and hoped to get upstairs without being seen by her neighbors or roommate. She judged the time to be about nine a.m. She hit the elevator button and waited for the car to arrive. It did, and unfortunately, it was occupied. "Holy crap Jill! What the hell happened to you?" As Jill's luck would have it, her roommate had the day off.

"My car broke down last night and I tried to cut through the mangroves to get to a phone. I fell in a bunch of mud in the salt flats."

She was barely sharp enough to cover her tracks, but it seemed like a workable alibi for now.

"My God girl, you better hit the shower. You stink! Maybe we can hook up later and you can tell me the whole story. I'll call you this afternoon. Good luck." Canyon headed out the door and Jill slipped into the elevator. She pushed the UP button and headed for the third floor. She felt like she had been hit by a freight train. She just wanted to take a bath and go to bed. After a piece of toast and a bowl of cornflakes, that's what she did. The alarm clock read [Tuesday 10:37 a.m.] as she closed her eyes.

She slept all day. Canyon stopped back at the apartment in the afternoon to change clothes and stuck her head into Jill's room to check on her. She quietly closed the door and left her sleeping. She returned at ten p.m. and again checked on Jill. When the light pierced the opening door, Jill opened her eyes.

"You OK?" Canyon whispered into the darkness of the room.

"Yeah, thanks though for asking," Jill mumbled.

"I've got over half a pizza left from New York Pasta if you want."

The New York Pasta is a trendy Italian restaurant that offers far more than your typical pizzeria. They make a great pizza but their Italian sausage rigatoni is right out of Little Italy. You can dine in their elegant interior dining room or sit outside under the giant Royal Poinciana tree and watch the owners' two scarlet macaws chatter about there being too many chickens running around in the courtyard, begging for cracker crumbs from the patrons, and stealing their show.

"That sounds great," Jill said as she yawned and slid her feet out from under the covers then into her slippers.

She followed Canyon to the living room. The open pizza box was on the glass coffee table. Canyon had been watching TV and was about to turn in but wanted to make sure her roommate was OK. After all, she had looked horrible the last time she had seen her. Jill sat down on the couch, grimacing from her sunburn pain.

"Man, I need to get something on this burn before I go back to bed."

Canyon offered, "I've got a fantastic product that will kick the sting right out of there." She headed down the hall to her room and returned with a tube of Burnsetic. "We just started selling this at the cabana and everybody is raving about it. Take your shirt off and I'll fix you up."

Jill was still partially sleeping or she would have seen what was coming.

"Geez girlfriend, you were neckid!" What did you do yesterday and I mean all the details?"

Jill was stuck for an answer. She had no clue what had happened. This was the first time she had had a chance to even think about why she was completely sunburned. There was only one way to go with it. She reached into the pizza box and pulled out a piece of pie hoping to buy enough time to come up with something believable. She filled her mouth with the still slightly warm delight and began to chew. Canyon's imagination was willing to contribute with a starting point. As she applied the first of the soothing cream to Jill's back she offered, "You went skinny dipping on the beach, didn't you?"

Jill felt a twofold relief. The ointment was performing as advertised and instantly yielded relief everywhere it touched. She was even more relieved that she didn't have to come up with an elaborate tale that might lead from answer to question and more neverending questions.

"None of your business, nosy!" she answered faking to be playful and coy. Canyon moved from Jill's shoulders and had her turn around. She squirted more of the lotion into her hands and spread it on Jill's neck and chest. After wiping her hands clean, she grabbed the remote and muted the TV.

"So, come on you nasty girl, who'd you do it with? One of those hot young interns from the hospital I'll bet."

Canyon was excited that for the first time since knowing Jill she was possibly going to hear that she had hooked up with a man.

"Leave me alone!"

"There were a bunch of people; we went out in two boats. Yes, I met a guy, and no, he's not a doctor. His name is Dillon and 'yes' we had a blast, and 'no' I'm not telling you anything more, so leave me alone."

She grinned like a teenager at a slumber party, telling about her first time she let a boy feel her up. She thought she had done a pretty good job of walking the fence without falling. She wanted to give a 'tada' on the dismount but grabbed the TV remote and brought back the sound instead.

"You got laid, didn't you?" Canyon just had to push for more. She was a woman who didn't turn loose till she had her fill.

"No!" Jill shoved her to the side and reached for her cotton nightshirt. "I don't think so," she added with a devilish grin.

That did the trick. They laughed while Canyon wiped down the kitchen counter and Jill grabbed another piece of the pie.

"I'm hitting the sack. This was fun, just you and me hangin' out," Canyon said. "Maybe we can do it more often."

"Yeah, I've got one more day off. Gotta run some errands and do laundry but I'll be in and out," Jill said. "Night!"

She stayed up and watched her favorite late-night show, David Letterman, then put the last of the pizza in the fridge and went back to bed. Sleep was now a reacquainted lover. It embraced her as soon as her eyes were closed. It healingly nursed her all through the night.

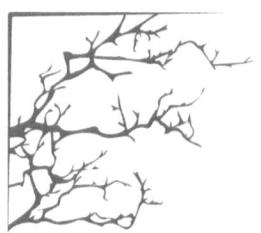

12. Smile Paddy

Barbara Dixon had managed the small Oceanside Bank in Key West since it opened in 1983. It was the first branch to be opened and three more would follow as their patronage grew. She loved her work, she loved her co-workers, she loved her customers, and she loved to gossip.

This was an attribute that the whole town knew well. Several times over the past few years, that very quality was used by local political factions to promote certain interests regarding acquisitions of property. The most recent elaborate scheme had been masterminded by the city attorney and the head of code enforcement. Barbara's involvement was merely to be played as a patsy, to compromise some proprietary legal information regarding the change of some building zones from residential to commercial. Without the opportunity for the public to contest the changes, the projects at hand would have sailed through unopposed, and allowed to bypass the normally rigorous and lengthy city council fair ruling procedures.

The necessary information was leaked to Barbara and the rest is history. Both the city attorney and the chief of code enforcement are currently training canaries in a ten-by-ten Okaloosa Correctional Institution prison cell twenty-four-seven, at taxpayer expense, of course.

Barbara would never discover just how critically her love of gossip had played a part in exposing the scheme, nor would she ever find out just how appreciated it was by the fathers of city government. She just did what came naturally, leak what she thought was truth into thirsty ears.

"Good morning Jillian, are you all settled into your new job at the hospital?" Barbara greeted the young nurse as she stepped into the lobby of the bank and approached her glass office. She enjoyed being able to watch everything that went on in the lobby and especially being able to greet customers that appeared to be looking for her personally. The only drawbacks were the times that bank robbers stormed through the front door, intending to make withdrawals. She was an easy target with nowhere to hide.

The most memorable suspect entered the bank with a metal yard rake under his coat. He was one of the local homeless fellows and made no attempt to conceal his identity. Under full surveillance, from the time he hit the front door to the time he walked out, he was destined to become a star on the Florida Department of Law Enforcement's Funniest Homeless Criminals show, in which Barbara was proud to have costarred. The old fool was captured counting the stash while sitting against the wall on the side of the bank building. The rake was impounded as evidence.

"Well, things are going great. Thank you! I have just been assigned to the E.R. and it's really where I think I belong."

Jill couldn't resist projecting her future hopes by saying, "I'm hoping to work my way into the Trauma Star medical officer's seat someday."

"Oh, wouldn't that be exciting? I think you would do fine at that. I heard that Millie Comstock had qualified for that position but couldn't make it because she got airsick every time they took off. Poor girl! It got so bad that she now has dizzy spells all the time and nightmares that she is falling from the sky. She's a dear, have you met her yet?"

"No ma'am, but I have heard that she is now working in the records department," Jill answered.

"Oh, you don't say. That must be because of her condition. So, she doesn't work with patients anymore?" Barbara asked hoping to add to her quiver of arrows about Millie.

"Well, I don't really know anything about all that, but, I need to talk to you about my ATM card missing, and see if I can get a new one."

"Sure sweetie, come on in, and let's get right to work on that."

Barbara pumped everybody for as much information as she could about everyone. And she couldn't help but pass it right back out the door in the next person's ear. The good thing is that she was usually true to the original tale. Usually! She had no real interest in putting her own spin on anything. She just harbored this uncontrollable need to fulfill some communication track. She was happy to be a cog, a cog in the Coconut Telegraph.

"When did you lose it?" Barb asked as she logged into the Accounts program on her new Dell computer.

"Well, it had to have been sometime since Sunday, about two p.m. I had it when I was at Starbucks downtown when I went for coffee before work. My shift is three to three."

Barbara asked for her account number and pulled up the information. "Oh! Oh My!" she exclaimed as she reviewed the screens. "This card was stolen for sure." She spun the screen around to share the information with Jill and the two ladies stared intently into the cyber world as it rolled out the data.

"Look here, this is your transaction report from Starbucks on Sunday for a total of $6.52. Next, you made a purchase Monday morning at nine fourteen a.m. at the Sears store on Roosevelt for $11.87. That's right up the street from here. Then you made . . ."

Jill cut her off. She was frantic, "Oh my God!" she said. "No, I was home asleep Monday morning. It must have been my roommate, Canyon. She stole my card. She's got all my IDs and everything. I can't believe it!" Jill was standing next to Barbara's desk digging nervously in her pockets and scratching the mosquito bites on her neck.

"Now, Jillian, you need to calm down and stay with me for a minute. There is information here that may lead us to who is trying to use your card. Come on dear, sit with me and let's go through this together. There appear to be more transactions worth taking a look at."

Barbara directed Jill's attention back to the screen. Jill sat anxiously scratching the swollen welts and her sunburned skin. The two leaned into the computer screen and Barbara calmly continued.

"Now, look right here! There was a purchase made in the amount of, $4.78 at nine thirty-nine a.m. at the Publix store on Roosevelt, also in the same shopping place as Sears."

"No, I was never there on Monday! I was sound asleep. I was completely out of it after work. Monday was my Saturday! My God," she said, "what has she done to me?"

"Stay with me Jillian!" Barbara calmly encouraged as Jill was rubbing her legs frantically. She continued, "At nine fifty-one a.m. it appears a purchase was made for $56.17 at the Sears Automotive center."

Jill turned white as she sat back in shock. It was as if Barbara had stood up, slapped her in the face and said, "You listen to me, you little twerp! I'm running this show and you will sit there and quit scratching till I say it's OK! Do you understand me?" Jill was temporarily lost in a search for answers. She had found the crumpled-up Sears receipt. She recognized her own signature, but wondered, could it have been forged? She would take a closer look when she got home. She leaned forward again to pay attention as Barbara led her further down the dark trail toward more of the blinking lights.

"Then there was a purchase of $89.01 at ten twentythree a.m. Monday. This is strange though." Barbara sat back in her chair and swiveled it slightly toward Jill. She had a confused look on her face as she announced the location of the next transaction as, "ABC Island Liquor, on Overseas Highway." Jillian was completely without a response as the two turned once again to the data on the screen. Barbara read on.

"That is all the activity on this card for Monday. Then, on Tuesday afternoon there seems to begin a flurry of attempts to access your account from ATM machines all over town." Barbara picked out a yellow #2 pencil from the glass vase decorated with colorful fish that was on the edge of her desk, and turned the eraser toward the screen. She began counting carefully out loud. After reaching eleven she picked up her phone and dialed four numbers. As she put the receiver to her ear she held up a finger to Jill and whispered, "Just a minute!" Someone answered at the other extension and Barbara said, "Hey Deb, I'm in here with Jillian Dougherty, one of our customers." She pushed the button for speakerphone and recradled the receiver then continued, "Can you hear me all right?"

"Yes, I can hear you fine." the teller on the other line answered. Barbara began, "It appears that her card has fallen into some unscrupulous individual's hands and I need you to take a look at all ATM and retail transactions from ten twentythree a.m. Monday till now and then pull up the citywide current activities on your 700-system and watch it for any activity."

Barbara called out the account number and Debbie instantly responded with, "I think you're right Barb; I'm looking at a total count of one hundred and fifteen PIN attempts at twentyeight different ATMs around the city."

"And, are we still allowing for the seven attempts on the first failure before dropping to four?" Barbara asked.

"Oh yes, the new system will soon be in place to recover the card after only four failed attempts even on the first try. We hope to have that program online by the end of this month," Deb explained.

"Read me the 700-system profile report if you've got it up yet," Barbara requested.

Jill's attention was split between the information being divulged and her agony from the burn and bites. Barbara reached into her bottom drawer and pulled out a box of first aid supplies she had customized over the years. She handed three Benadryl tablets to Jill and pointed her finger at Jill's nose and then firmly toward the water cooler. Jill motioned an appreciative "Thank you" with silent lips, and then left the room to down the three pills. The phone conversation had already resumed as she slipped back into the chair by the desk.

"OK, got it! Boy, somebody is out there digging for gold with this card. Whoever it is seems experienced and determined." Deb goes on to interpret the 700system data.

"The first readout is at the ATM inside the Circle K gas and grocery store at the corner of Boca Chica and Overseas yesterday, Tuesday morning at eight-seventeen a.m. seven initial attempts, then, it stopped. The perp obviously knew the seventime rule." Jill looked a little confused and Barbara explained to her, "Your particular style of debit card triggers a program in every ATM that will tell the machine to 'Eat' the card if, on the first attempt to use it in a twenty-four-hour period, which begins at midnight, the user enters seven incorrect PINs. On the eighth attempt the machine will not give back the card and our security system puts out a worldwide alert on that account." Jill seemed to follow this explanation and Barbara continued.

"If the user retrieved the card after seven PIN error attempts, all subsequent attempts for that twentyfourhour period drop to just four tries before the card is held. Debbie is analyzing the report on a live system so we will know every activity as it happens. Does all this make sense?"

Barbara wanted to feel assured that Jill was with them before moving any further. Jill acknowledged she understood and was now feeling the effects of the Benadryl as they moved on.

"Go ahead Deb, we're with you," Barbara said into the speaker.

"The next hit is at the Flagler Avenue Bank of America ATM. Now we know it's a pro. He's trying only four PINs this time," Deb's voice sounded from the speakerphone.

Barbara knew exactly what to do next. "Give us the time differential on the two hits and email all the PIN entries used so far."

She drew a map of Key West on a piece of printer paper to show Jill the route that the card was taking as it made its way around the city. She accessed the email and printed the list of PINs that the perp was entering. They were in a long list of groups of four numbers. The first group had seven groups of four, and then the rest had only four groups of four.

0317—7130—3170—1703—7031—1987—7891
And the next list:
9871—8719—7198, etc.

This was the Bank of America attempt. The list went on for two pages with only one more set of seven attempts at one ATM which represented the midnight system reset effect. The time of each attempt was recorded on another page. Barbara pulled up Google Maps and entered the address for the Circle K store, where the first try had been attempted, and then the Bank of America address on Flagler Avenue where the second attempt was made. The total distance was 14.7 miles from one ATM to the next.

She grabbed her calculator and plugged in the figures that would give her the time that elapsed between the two attempted transactions; 8:17 a.m. to 1:39 p.m. meant that it took someone five hours and twenty-two minutes to get from one site to the next. After dividing 322 minutes by 14.7 miles, Barbara estimated that the perp had traveled at an average speed of 2.74mph to go from one stop to the next. She continued these calculations respectively through the next six stops and turned to Jill and said, "This guy is really thirsty."

"Why would you think that?" Jill asked.

"Because, it's over one hundred degrees out there, and he's walking. Now give me your date of birth and social security numbers."

Jill called out the numbers and Barbara wrote them down on a postit slip. She stuck the postit above the listing of PIN numbers and spun the page around for Jill to see.

"This jerk has your driver's license and your social security card, too," Barbara said as she circled certain random groupings of the four-digit entries and drew a line from them to the individual numbers within her date of birth and social security number.

"See, he is systematically walking the city stopping at every ATM and trying the next four consecutive numbers. He apparently believes that someday, if he never quits, he'll hit the jackpot." Barbara sat back and smiled with pride.

"You're kidding!" Jill exclaimed, dumbfounded that anyone would try such a foolish scheme.

"Oh no, sweetie, the pitiful thing is that, most times, within the first five tries it works," Barbara quipped.

Jill responded matter-of-factly, "Well, not this time, I use the day and month I graduated from nursing school for my PIN number." She continued with the thought, "Can we find out from cameras or something who it is?" Debbie was still on speaker phone and spoke up, "I'm already closing in on him. He made his way through Old Town area hitting all the banks and independents yesterday. This morning his last try was over at the Waterfront Market. That was thirty minutes ago. He should be across the street near Harpoon Harry's restaurant any minute. He apparently knows where every ATM in town is. He hasn't missed a one on this route."

Barbara finished drawing out the sites on the city map and showed it to Jill while she directed Debbie in the next part of the plan. "Deb, give a call to Leon Daniels over at Harpoon Harry's and have him call my number as soon as he sees the next person using the ATM at the corner across the street. He'll know what to do." Debbie acknowledged as Barbara grabbed her cell phone from her purse and pushed the quick call button for the cell number of her husband, Carl.

"Hey Sugar, what's up?"

Carl was a sergeant for the city police and was permanently assigned to the highly desirable day shift. After many years of working the drunks and wild nightlife, he was proud to be able to claim that his dues had been paid in full. He was the shift supervisor for twenty day-shift officers including the equestrian and bike patrols. He was good at everything there was about police work and nothing scared this guy.

"I've got a stolen card about to be used at the corner of Caroline and Margaret." Barbara never needed to give much information. They had been married twenty-six years and she was his right hand in everything. There was no room for questioning the dedication to each other in this peapod. It went beyond trust. When it came to criminal activity, they took personal pride. "I'm almost there," he said. "Stay on the line a minute. Let me get situated and I'll give you a play-by-play."

Carl parked his blue, unmarked Crown Victoria behind the Caroline Street Music Shop and watched the approach to the Nine To Nine store hidden from sight. The ATM stood just inside the front door. One lone individual staggered into the intersection, a man with whom Carl and Leon were both intimately acquainted.

Carl heard Barbara's desk phone ring through her cell phone as she sat waiting for information from her second source.

"Barbara, this is Leon. I think I've got my eye on what you want." He continued before she could respond, "Carl's already on top of him."

She laughed into the phone, "Thanks anyway, Leon. We'll see you on Sunday." Every Sunday she and Carl have breakfast at Harpoon Harry's. That is, unless there's a hurricane.

Carl entered the Nine To Nine directly behind the wiry little drunk in the short shorts and the tattered tank top. Carl was a huge man and the little imp didn't even see that the giant that had entered behind him was a cop in full blues. The little bugger staggered up to the ATM and stood there, swaying like a willow in a soft wind. He was a sight to behold. Anchored to the ground by two untied oversized black army boots, the skinny little Irishman reached into his back pocket and pulled out an ink pen and a white piece of lined paper. While he studied the markings on the paper he reached his free hand into his other back pocket and retrieved a stack of cards which he dropped onto the floor.

The clerk behind the counter watched and shook his head at the spectacle, then looked up at Officer Dixon who was standing halfway down the chip and candy aisle with his huge arms crossed across his monstrous chest, rocking up and down from heel to toe as the pickled little leprechaun attended to his crime. Carl smiled and placed a finger over his lip to signal the clerk to hold his laughter.

It was all so very comical. The little imp retrieved the cards from the floor and struggled to resituate himself in front of the machine. After several tries, he was able to insert the card properly into the slot and began studying his list of numbers. If he was unable to effectively manage anything else in his life it sure didn't show when he was in pursuit of a source of procuring his whisky. There, this guy excelled! Carl watched as long as he could stand it then spoke into his cell phone.

"Hang on honey, I gotta show you this." He closed his phone, pushed the tiny button on the right side, held it high in the air over the little man and said, "Smile, Paddy!"

The drunken little criminal slowly turned his upper body around toward the officer as if he expected to greet one of his good-time buddies. "POP", the flash bulb illuminated his dilated little eyes and he fell back against the ATM as if he had been shot by the officer's 9mm Glock. The clerk joined Carl in a hearty laugh while Carl sent the picture to Barbara's inbox.

"Oh, good shot!" Barbara exclaimed as she opened the attached picture file, then turned her computer screen fully toward Jill and asked, "Do you know who this is?" Jill's mouth dropped open and hung frozen for a moment as she studied the face on the screen.

"That's a patient I tried to work with in the E.R. Sunday night. How the hell did he get my things?"

Barbara answered her cell phone laughing, "Yeah, she says Paddy was in the E.R. the other day. She's a nurse. He probably lifted her purse and took off. Great! Love you, too!"

"Well, I've got some good news to tell you." Barbara said thanks to Debbie and pushed the speaker button as she stood up and motioned for Jill to join her in the lobby.

"Our little friend Paddy is now in custody and your cards and driver's license will meet you at the front door as you leave."

Jill could not believe that in just one hour Barbara had managed to bring her life back into somewhat of an acceptable degree of alignment.

"I am so indebted to you!" she said. "How can I ever make this up to you?" Barbara gave Jill a hug and a pat on the shoulder and said, "Oh, maybe someday I'll need a good nurse to fly me to one of those big hospitals up in Miami." As they walked to the front door a dark blue police cruiser pulled up to the front door. The huge handsome officer climbed out of the front seat and gave his wife a sweet kiss as he handed a stack of cards to Jill.

"Hang on to these now!" he ordered with a smile. Jill blushed and gave them each hugs as she fought to keep from crying.

Paddy was in the back seat of the patrol car watching. When Jill's eyes turned his way, he started waving with excitement as though he had already forgotten he had stolen her life. For now, she had it back.

Jill had other matters to resolve on her last day off. She was almost to the cell phone repair shop where she hoped her phone was ready for pick up. She was mulling over the information she had learned from Barbara and was applying it to the timetable of the past two days, trying to plug some holes. There was one gap she could not explain! If Paddy had lifted her purse at the hospital, how were the Sears and Publix grocery store purchases made? Something just did not fit! She still wanted to get a closer look at the signature on the Sears receipt back at home.

As she parked her car and headed toward the front door of the phone store, she set her mind on more tangible issues and solvable problems, like getting her phone back, and new sunglasses.

13. Island Air Surf Shop

The Phone Store was a franchise and Thomas had purchased it eight months earlier from an older husband and wife team, Marjory and Bob Herndon. They had operated it for six years. In that time, it had been robbed five times and completely flooded twice by hurricanes. It had originally been referred to as their retirement nest egg, but they decided they had made more money from it than expected and wanted to cash in and enjoy life. At least that was what they had told their realtor when they listed it with him. The truth is, they were running for their lives.

The financial records supported its stability and promise as a viable income producer, and Thomas still held the seed money needed for the purchase after his great aunt Helen Boyd had died the previous year.

Mrs. Boyd was unfortunately without the necessary female plumbing to exercise her natural maternal favor, widely rumored to be due to the error of one drunken Key West doctor, Gomez Waldo Conception. Gomez had been forced into early retirement after being found unconscious in his secret backyard distillery/operating room with his neighbors' fourteenyear-old daughter bleeding to death after a similar botched attempt to erase a young promiscuous girl's unfortunate romantic consequence. Mrs. Boyd had left Thomas the sole heir to her estate. Said estate included a dilapidated historical Old Town residence and trust holdings from the sale of the cigar factory which her first husband had owned. The cigar factory had been sold years before to the city of Key West and converted into a beautiful municipal government office.

Thomas had just handed over the cashier's check for fifty thousand dollars and all the necessary signatures were in place. As they shook hands the couple came clean and made clear the real reason, they were selling the shop and heading back to Milwaukee. Marjory started with, "I just hope you understand, we're getting old and can't take all the abuse."

Thomas was a little nervous as he listened; after all, he had just stepped into the driver's seat. He was worried that they were about to advise him that the brake line was cut, and a downhill run was coming up fast.

Bob offered further reason for concern when he added, "Just keep your eyes open! Watch the front door and always know who's coming through it." Then Marjory laid down her strongest advice with, "I always keep one phone in my pocket with the sheriff's emergency number plugged in and ready, then all I need to do is push 'SEND'. They can hear every word you say and within seconds you'll see an army of blues with guns drawn and ready."

Thomas was in shock as he listened.

She added, "That's when you need to hit the ground just in case the perp has a gun; you don't want to get hit by friendly fire."

Thomas listened to the old girl and watched her face grow wildly excited as she gave her instructions. She reminded him of Granny from the Beverly Hillbillies show. He imagined that if he looked outside, he might see Jethro and Ellie Mae sitting in the old truck with Jed and Duke, the family blood-hound, waiting out in the parking lot. They handed over the keys and he was on his own.

In the eight months of operating the little store at the end of the strip mall, Thomas had only called for police assistance three times. Once when the alarm system malfunctioned during a power outage, once to have a pan-handler removed from the front sidewalk, and once when three teenagers had run out the door with some of his display phones.

He had, up until the past month, remained keenly vigilant with regard to Marjorie's warnings, and kept one phone preprogrammed to the police number in his left front pants pocket. In the event that he might need to summon help, he knew he could initiate the call by hitting 'SEND' while appearing to be scratching his thigh. He had practiced the move many times in the first month of business and felt quite sure he could successfully pull it off without the least notice.

Unfortunately, for Thomas, the lack of necessity had caused him to grow lax, and more and more, he was leaving the designated safety phone on his desk in the back office. Today was one of those 'lax' days. There it was, sitting on his desk in the back room. He realized it as soon as he saw Jill put her hand on the front door and pull. Oh! Oh! He thought. Trouble was coming his way. He was in the middle of a demonstration with another customer and nervously continued his dialogue as he watched Jill's every move.

"I'll be with you in just a minute," he called out to her as the door alarm chimed to announce her arrival.

Jill smiled and to his surprise seemed quite congenial as she responded with, "That's fine. I can wait."

Thomas was expecting her to become hostile as she had two days earlier, especially after he told her that her phone was not repairable. He finished his demonstration for the girl he had been helping, then said to her, "You know, I think I may have this in other colors in the back," and slipped into the stock room where he situated his emergency phone in his pants before returning.

"No, I'm sorry, this is the only one left." Realizing this customer could be used as a witness if Jill were to stab him, poke his eyes out, or detonate a bomb, he said to her, "Just take your time; I'll be right over here with this lady."

He made his way around the corner of the glass counter and approached Jill with apprehension. Surprisingly, she was still smiling and though she was sunburned to a crisp, seemed normal in demeanor.

"Yes, Miss, I believe I have the response here from the repairman." Thomas wanted to get the bad information out of the way quickly so he could hit the floor, or run if needed. He lifted an open box from beneath the counter and slid it across to Jill, explaining, "Unfortunately, it appears moisture has gotten into the interior through the charging slot and corroded the diodes and capacitors, leaving your phone," he looked up into her seconddegree sun-burned face and finished with, "fried."

He flinched slightly and leaned away as if he expected something to hit him across his cheek. He kept one hand wrapped around the open-faced phone in his pocket. He was perfectly poised to execute the call while falling to the ground to dodge the shrapnel.

Then Jill spoke, "Oh no!" she whimpered. "Can I get another one just like it?" Thomas was more than relieved by her response. Not only had he averted being tortured, maimed, or killed, he was going to sell another phone. Oh, life was dealing aces to him today!

After he finished with the first girl's business, he took the SIM card out of Jill's old phone and inserted it into a new one, allowing her to keep her original phone number. Once it was successfully activated, he advised her that due to the moisture in her old phone, her contact data had been lost and she would need to enter that information manually on the new phone. He proceeded to walk her through the usual new phone technical checks and then set up her preferred functions. Jill made pleasant conversation as she considered adding a Bluetooth device. She happened to mention how lucky she was to have been able to retrieve her credit cards and driver's license after a homeless man had stolen them.

"Oh, man," Thomas asked, "Did they catch whoever took them?"

"Yeah!" Jill said. "Some older fellow named Paddy. He said he found them on the beach but we think he took them from the hospital E.R. when I was on duty the other night. He's on his way to jail right now."

"I think I know the guy," the young man said. "Wears short shorts and a white wife beater tank top and shaves his legs?"

"Yeah, that's him!" Jill exclaimed. "You know him?"

"Oh, yeah! I get nothing but trouble from that little dirtbag. Run like hell when you see him coming! He's got only one way of doing things, his way, and he has absolutely no consideration for who gets hurt."

Thomas dialed Jill's cell phone number from his phone and set her new one, ringing, on the counter in front of her. He motioned that it was all set and she picked it up.

"Hello!" she answered.

Across the counter from her, Thomas started the conversation with, "Hey, Ms. Dougherty, this is Paddy. Say, could you come bail me out of jail? The food down here stinks!"

They both hung up laughing and the test was determined to have been a great success.

Thomas completed the sale and offered his further assistance if needed. As he handed her the receipt and the box with her old phone in it, he remarked, "I half expected you to cause me a little trouble after Monday's episode."

Jill looked up at him in total confusion. "What episode?" she asked.

"Monday, when you were here, and threw all my phones on the floor, you really scared the crap out of Mrs. Weinstein and her daughter," he said.

Jill had no recollection of being there on Monday but was supremely appreciative that another tidbit of information had found its way back to her. She planned at some point to plug it into the larger picture which might answer for the lost day.

She apologized by saying, "Oh, I'm sorry about Monday, I was so wigged out. Thanks!" She hoped this would cover the damages and left the store with her new phone.

Back out in the bright sun, Jill painfully squinted to see her way. She placed her right hand over her eyes while she scanned the shopping center for a good place to buy a replacement pair of sunglasses. Looking down the sidewalk, she read the shop signs out loud, "Naomi's Nails, Island Pawn and Jewelry", Island Air Surf Shop." There, only three storefronts down! She headed for the door. Jill was thrilled to find that the cute little shop was full of beachwear, dive equipment, surfboards, bathing suits and, oh, sunglasses.

"Hi, I'm Salvia," the girl said. She spoke with a beautiful accent and Jillian thought she may be from a mountaintop village in Sweden. Her English was quite good and she was obviously well educated. She continued with her greeting by saying, "Is there anything in particular I can help you with?"

Jill was immediately attracted to this Scandinavian beauty and thought that she might be a perfect prospect as a future friend. "I need to replace a pair of sunglasses and maybe pick up a new bikini," Jill said as they walked through the shop. She was impressed with everything she saw and knew she had stumbled into her newest, "favorite" boutique. "Your accent is so sexy," Jill said. "Is it Swedish?"

"Oh no, I'm Polish." The stylish yet unpretentious girl responded, "I came here with my friend Tasha four years ago to work and meet the handsome American boys." She continued, "Now we both have babies and no boyfriends. We share an apartment and everything we make goes to paying the bills."

The girls had a wonderful time chatting about their lives and Salvia invited Jill to come to her home and meet her son some evening. They traded phone numbers and planned to meet at Starbucks for coffee the next morning.

Jill settled on a pair of stylish Costa wraparound glasses and a fabulously sexy new swimsuit.

As she returned to her car, she was pleased to feel that she was beginning to establish herself as an accepted member of the island community, and, hopeful that her Monday mystery might soon be solved.

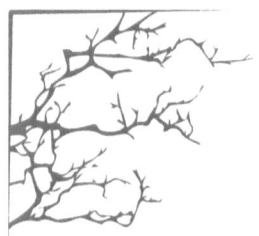

14. People to Fix

Jillian's new phone chimed to signal she had messages in her voicemail. She turned the car on and set the A/C blower on high then dialed in her access code. Sitting there in the parking lot she waited to see who had called. "Your voicemail is full."

The familiar voice was like a friend she had not seen in a week or more.

She put the car into drive and waited for the first message.

"Ms. Dougherty, this is Susan Sessions. I met you Monday morning. I'm the night shift supervisor in the E.R. at Lower Keys. It's 11:15 a.m. Wednesday and I am at my home. I've been trying for two days to get hold of you. We've been hoping to get a call back from you but you obviously have not been answering your phone nor checking your voicemail. Please call the E.R. as soon as you get this message, and, in the future, don't say you'll be available if you're not going to be. Thank you, and have a nice day!" Jill felt nauseous as she punched the "7" button to erase the message. She knew this was not a good thing.

Dependability was one of her most highly cherished attributes. It always had been! She was raised to regard her word as a sacred trust; to break it was a taboo that she could not tolerate in herself. She wanted to throw the phone into the water, off of the next bridge down the road. After all, if she had never picked it up from the repair shop, she would not have heard the damning message and would have reported to work on Thursday with a clean conscience. It was too late now! The next fourteen messages took her to tears.

"Jill, it's me again." Danna's voice seemed tired and strained. "They told me to make one last stab at getting you to answer." The voice hesitated in case she happened to pick up, and then continued, We really need you over here! Try to get back to me on my cell. Come on girl! Get dressed and get over here!" In the background Jill could hear the sounds of the busy emergency room. She wished so badly that she had picked up her new phone on Monday. Now, her credibility was in question. She knew she would never live this down.

She raced back to the condo, punching through each message on her phone. On the elevator, she listened to the first two messages that had been left. Both messages were from her new supervisor, Ms. Sessions. The second call had seemed more desperate than the first. In the background, she could hear a man screaming in pain. Behind Ms. Sessions' voice, there was a room in total chaos. Oh, she felt badly! She was so disappointed in herself for not being there when they needed her.

She hastily dialed the main hospital phone number as she darted through her bedroom door and pulled a clean uniform from the closet. "Emergency Room, please!" she directed the operator. "Emergency room, may I help you?" Jill did not recognize the voice but asked her for the E.R. shift supervisor. She was put on hold and as she waited to be connected, she set her phone to speaker mode and set it on the bed.

She ripped off her civilian clothes and downed a wrinkled smock and some clean white work pants. She had not yet cleaned her only pair of white sneakers from the muddy Monday night fiasco, and rushed to the balcony to slap them against the railing. As the dirt drifted to the balcony below a man's voice shouted out angrily in her direction, "Hey, what the hell do you think you're doing?"

She apologized and ran back to her room. The music playing on her phone let her know that she was still on hold. She hung up and dialed the number a second time as she hit the elevator button and started down. Again, she was put on hold and she waited till she was half a mile down the road before she hung up. One last try yielded the same failed result.

After parking on the grass as close to the emergency room entrance as she could without blocking Trauma Star staff, she walked briskly into the waiting room and through the "Staff Only" door. She looked around for a face she could recognize. Every staff member she saw was engaged in servicing patients. All four of the operating bays were full. There didn't seem to be anything unusual, but she was aware of a level of stress that could only be explained as a lull after a harrowing storm. This was the day shift. She recognized two of the nurses only because she had passed them in the hall or sat next to them in the cafeteria, but no one she had yet met. No one acknowledged her standing there by the central desk. She went over to the back entrance to the admissions office and interrupted one of the clerks who was in the middle of an intake interview.

"Excuse me, who is the shift supervisor?" she asked.

"There isn't one!" the clerk flippantly answered. "She walked out!" then she added, "If you want the job, it's yours!" Next, the girl stood up and threw her hands in the air wildly announcing, "And if I don't get some help with this crap, you can have mine, too!"

Jill was embarrassed by the attention that the girl's loud response had brought and drifted out of the cubical, quietly closing the door behind her.

She had no idea what to do. She had not clocked in, so she really didn't know if she would be disciplined for being there. She surveyed the room for clues as to how she could help out and possibly begin rebuilding her soiled reputation. All of the wastebaskets were overflowing. The lids on all the Bio-waste cans were propped open and bloody cotton pads and swabs were lying on the floor around them. The nurses' station desk was a mess with clipboards and papers. A large plastic tub full of open medication bottles sat teetering precariously on the upper console ledge, waiting to snag a passing sheet and disburse the pills across the dirty floor.

She heard a voice from behind the last curtain call out, "I need a swab in four."

It was Dr. Larkin. Jill slipped the curtain open and said, "Yes doctor, I can get that for you."

She moved to the sink to scrub up and then arranged the prep tray per standard ER setup. The patient was an older black man dressed in blood-soaked overalls. He had sliced across the end of his thumb and fully through the bone on his adjacent finger. Dr. Larkin looked up at Jill for a second but offered no noticeable acknowledgment that her presence was appreciated. He had already stitched the nub of the old man's thumb and was on his fifth stitch of the finger.

Jill wanted to run away in shame for not being there when they needed her earlier. She thought that she should just quietly tend to every possible duty that she found and draw the least amount of attention to herself as she could. She swabbed the man's wounds and gathered the bloody rags for disposal as the doctor tied the last stitch and moved out of the cubical. After cleaning the dried blood off his hand and arm with a warm Betadine solution, she carefully wrapped the injuries and prepared a removable sling to cradle his arm until he could have it seen by his primary care physician.

Doctor Larkin stuck his head back in and dropped three prescriptions on the side table without saying a word. Jill picked them up and directed the old man to have them filled as soon as possible and to make an appointment with his regular doctor. She helped the old black gentleman swing his heavy legs around to the side of the bed as she handed him the prescriptions. He was weeping so gently, something she had not noticed before.

"I know this must be difficult for you but at least you still have the rest of your fingers." Jill hoped to cheer him up as well as lead him into a more positive approach to his grief.

He hung his head and cried quietly as he explained, "Yes ma'am! You don't understand though. I don't got no way to get dis here medication. The only way I can eat is to use these here hands. If I cants do no work, I cants eat!" Jill was moved deeply as she listened. She was torn between the need for her to expedite his discharge and her desire to console his grief.

"What about your wife, is she able to work?" Jill had no way to know that this question would lead him into further despair.

"She dead!" He muttered in his low swollen voice. "She been dead twenty-year dis November. All my peoples' been dead fo a long time now. I got nobody!"

Jill was fighting for an idea of how to help this fellow without getting emotionally involved. She was losing ground. "Do you have anyone where you live that can help you?" she asked.

"I lives in a shed behind Ms. Albright's house on United Street. She been letting me sleep there for the past couple of months." He wiped his runny nose on his dirty blue shirt and Jill grabbed him a box of tissues from the cabinet beside the gurney. When he was better composed, he added, "Ma'am, I cain't eat if I cain't work." Jill was now gripped by his sad, and despairing story.

At twentyone years, old, this was a new and foreign reality for her to face. How does a person survive when they have reached such a point? Where do they turn? Who could she refer him to, and her immediate concern, how could she discharge this dear fragile man with nothing out there for him to grasp hold of? "Do you have any money?" she asked.

"No ma'am, not a penny if I cain't work," he answered.

She thought for a minute and smiled as she said, "I'm going to finish your discharge paperwork and then I'll need you to sign it. I want you to go out to the front of the building and sit down on the bench that's there by the door. Give me fifteen minutes and I'll meet you out there with something to help you. Does that sound good?"

"Oh, yes ma'am! That sounds real good. Thank you, ma'am, God bless you!" Jill printed his discharge papers and he signed his name. She directed him to the corridor that would lead him to the front entrance of the hospital, and then she headed to the ATM machine on the second floor by the cafeteria. After withdrawing two hundred dollars she rushed out to meet the old man at the front door. In the fifteen minutes, it took for her to make it to the front door, he had gone.

She walked out into the burning sun and caught the last glimpse of him across the parking lot as he disappeared down the road. She sadly turned and walked back toward the emergency room. She could not convince herself that she had done all that she could have done. She felt as though she had failed him.

Jill had always struggled with the understanding of sympathy and the role that it played in the development of a successful nurse. As a student, she was never able to experience it to a degree that satisfied her thirst for it. As she crossed the threshold to the emergency room, she entered with a brand new and clearer understanding of just how it makes one feel. It would remain with her for life. It would mold her into a nurse among nurses.

She faced the coming tasks with a new outlook. She regained lost status. She now knew that she had missed the phone calls for a reason. If she had not arrived when she had, she would have missed the lesson she had just learned. She was right where she belonged, or, so she thought.

"Well! Well! If it ain't the super nurse! Look at you all sunburned and sandyassed. Must be nice to just slide on down to the beach while everybody else has to drag the chain."

Danna was just showing up after being called in three hours earlier than her scheduled start time. She was obviously upset that Jill had failed to answer their earlier calls for her assistance. She had been impressed with Jill's performance on Monday, as was everyone else that had worked with her in the ER that day. Her outstanding performance was now null and void as far as Danna was concerned. She had not only been called in early on Tuesday, she had stayed until six a.m. today. After four hours of sleep, she was back at work and low on reserve for doling out sympathy for someone who obviously had spent the past two days lying on the beach.

"My phone was in the shop for a week, I had to buy a new one and . . ." Jill started to explain.

"Just stop it!" Danna cut her off.

"Don't even think you can come up with anything that we haven't all heard a dozen times before." She added, "Hell, you think I haven't used that broken phone crap?" As Danna loaded her dinner into the refrigerator, she threw out one last quip toward Jill. "Just get some of this work done and help carry out some of the crap that no one else seems to want to pick up."

Jill followed Danna to the human resource office where they both clocked in. On the way back to the emergency room Danna told her some of what had befallen them on Monday afternoon.

"Did you see the news about the boat crash?" she asked.

"No, what happened?" Jill replied as they climbed into the empty elevator. "Well, you knew that the boat race trials started on Monday morning, right?" asked Danna.

"Yeah, I remember they were supposed to," Jill answered.

Danna continued, "Well, at about four-thirty in the afternoon, one of the lead boats went into a turn one mile off of Fort Zack Taylor Beach and had just straightened out for the stretch back when it apparently caught some wind and flipped. It broke up and within seconds one of the next boats slammed right into the center of it. The second boat went completely airborne and came down nose first and flew into pieces. A third boat tried to miss the debris field but went over a piece of fiberglass and knocked off all three of its outdrives, then, with no control or power, that boat slid straight into a private yacht that was anchored in the spectator area. It started sinking and had to be pulled to shore after the passengers were all rescued. Everybody involved ended up with us."

The two girls exited the elevator and crossed the emergency room lobby as Danna continued, "Anyway, total count was one DOA, one in a coma, one amputation on the scene and eleven triage cases all at once. We started calling you as soon as the first medevac pulled in."

Danna pushed open the "staff only" door and they entered the operating area.

"OK, let's get this place cleaned up, and then we've got people to fix." Danna was ready to forgive Jill for not being there when they needed her, but she wanted her to taste her shame for a while.

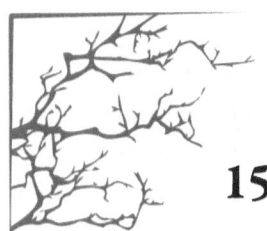

15. The Cuban Passage

Doctor Larkin was sitting at the center desk, entering his case notes on the computer as the two nurses stepped through the door. His concentration was obviously intense and he looked like he had been run through the wringer as he finished fortyeight grueling hours of triage. He was due to be relieved at noon by Dr. Emilio Cardinaello, a retired surgeon from Miami who owned a condominium on the seventh floor of the Galleon on Front Street overlooking the Gulf of Mexico.

The two doctors had been neighbors for the past three years after Dr. Cardinaello and his wife Angelica had purchased a unit as their weekend getaway and winter retreat. They usually stayed at the Galleon for four or five months in the winter but had come down this month for the boat race.

Emilio was one-third owner of a forty-seven-foot Fountain Super Vee Class Racer named the *Tight Stitch*. He and two other Miami doctors had purchased the boat to use as a tax shelter ten years earlier. They began the project with an initial investment of $150,000.00 each. They now had a team of three mechanics, one primary and one secondary driver, one throttle man, one overtheroad driver, and two mates. Two general clean and set-up crewmen rounded out the team. The Tight Stitch was pulled by a brand-new Volvo VN series 780 hauler with a 77inch sleeper. The guys had just taken delivery of the huge rig two weeks before leaving for Key West. With only 833 miles on the odometer, it wasn't even close to being broken in. The rig was color coordinated with the same motif as the boat. When they travel, the big rig chases behind a 44foot Monarch Motor Coach and a 30-foot tool and crew sleeper truck follows at the rear. There is an 8-foot trailer pulled by the motor coach that opens into a class "A" portable barbeque station. It is a site to behold when their colorful caravan flies by.

After ten years on the racing circuit, the corporation held physical assets worth eleven million dollars plus, and pulled in annual sponsorship contributions of just shy of six million twohundred thousand dollars. Their list of sponsors reads like a who's who of Fortune 500 medical services and equipment corporations. Sporting an impressive track record of world-class performances afforded the trio of owners a lifestyle far beyond their dreams. Still, Dr. Cardinaello was always happy to contribute his services to the little Key West hospital, and relieve his friend for a twelvehour shift. It fit his image to be the hot shot, big-time surgeon from Miami who comes south to save the day.

"Hello everyone!" Dr. Cardinaello announced as he entered the room. "So nice to see you all again!"

"Emilio, I am so glad you made it!" Doctor Larkin said as he stood up and shook his friend's hand.

"I guess you had it pretty rough over the past two days." Dr. Cardinaello was referring to the boat wreck that had happened two days before.

"Did the throttle man come out of his coma yet?" Doctor Larkin asked as he sat back down to finish his entries on the computer.

Danna had just finished discharging her last patient and had overheard the two doctors talking. After dropping a bag of trash into a large mobile bin, she offered, "I'll check that out! I did his transfer work to I.C.U." She stepped over to the second computer at the central desk and pulled up his name.

"Pouigdonavitch," she said.

"Uh! He still is not responding." She read the notes from I.C.U. and continued to relay the patient's status.

"Ventilation is at full low and the neurosurgeons have already done their assessment. He was scheduled for an M.R.I. this morning at eight. Give me a second, yep, the radiologist has already sent the results to neurology. And, here they are working out the details to have him flown to Jackson Memorial if he doesn't snap back by tomorrow."

"Oh, that's great!" Doctor Cardinaello was pleased to know that the man would be cared for at the larger Miami hospital. His chances for recovery would be far greater as Jackson Memorial has one of the top neurosurgery departments in America. It is the teaching hospital that works in conjunction with the University of Miami Medical School and the service hospital for the Miami VA facility which is right next door. Doctor Cardinaello had been a resident at Jackson for eighteen years as well as Director of Emergency Services for another four years before retiring to pursue his passion for racing powerboats. "You know, I've known Colt and his brother Shawn for ten years. They are good men! My wife and I will be flying to San Diego for the funeral as soon as a date is announced," he said sadly.

Jill had not read the news in *The Citizen* that had reported on the fatal crash. She was only familiar with the outcome from the briefing that Danna had given her a few moments earlier. She finished emptying the trash cans and rolled the heavy mobile catcher unit out to the pickup station for the maintenance people to get rid of. As she re-entered the E.R., she listened as Dr. Larkin, who had apparently just asked Dr. Cardinaello how well he knew the two brothers. The doctor was describing them as one of the best cockpit teams in the business.

"Shawn was a world-renowned driver with a wall full of trophies," he said. "I've never beaten him but have come close three times. We used to have him and his wife Gina as guests at our home in Coconut Grove when the Fort Lauderdale International races were on. They stayed with us last February when the Miami Boat Show came to town. Great guy! One in a million!"

The stocky greyhaired Cuban doctor was obviously emotionally affected by the loss of his friend and wiped his eyes as he said his last words.

"We're all gonna' miss him."

There were patients backing up in the lobby and two in beds waiting for services. Dr. Larkin finished his duties and bid everyone goodbye. Until three p.m. the emergency room would be manned by one doctor, three nurses, one nursing assistant, and one intake clerk. As far as Jill knew, there was no staff supervisor, and, according to the earlier blowup she had had with the intake clerk, there may not be a supervisor. She stepped into the cubicle where Danna was taking vitals on her first patient of the day. "Should I be here?" she whispered to Danna.

"I don't know what to tell you!" Danna said. "We needed you really bad for the past two days. I'm on now, but Kat and Tanissia are due to leave at three. Somebody's probably scheduled to come on then. Around here, people quit or don't show up for all kinds of reasons. I'm runnin' on empty and could pass out anytime, so, I'd say, dig in. Just be ready to be chewed out when a supervisor shows up." Danna gave her the best advice she could considering the staffing problems they were prone to.

"The worst that could happen is they tell you to leave, but that's a rare event around here!"

Jillian took this as good reason to stay and try to recover some of the reliability she had lost over her failure to show up when she was needed.

She stepped into cubical number two and grabbed the clipboard from the end of the bed. The gentleman lying under the sheet seemed relaxed and happily content.

"Good afternoon," she greeted him as she read over the original complaint. She noticed first that his assessment had been performed by supervisor Susan Sessions at 8:46 a.m.

"How long have you been waiting here?" she asked with a frown on her face.

"I think it's been about four or five hours," the man replied.

"No one has checked in on you in four or five hours?" she asked with surprise.

"No ma'am!" he said.

"Why didn't you tell someone you were in here?" Jill was hoping there was a reasonable explanation for having the patient wait that long to be seen. His response was a surprise to her.

"Well, I got to the E.R. about four a.m. and it took till almost nine to be brought back here. I've been listening to everything that you folks have been talking about and I could tell that everybody was stressed. I just didn't want to make you guys think that I was being demanding so I have just been waiting till you got back around to me." He kept his hands crossed across his chest as he lay there. Jill set up her equipment and started taking his vitals.

"On a scale of one to ten what is your pain level now?" she asked.

"Oh, about a three I guess," he answered.

She continued with her exam and asked him why he had reported his pain level to Ms. Sessions at a seven almost five hours earlier and he answered, "Cause, I can't feel much from my waist down now. Earlier, I could feel all the way to my toes. Now, it just tingles. That's not really pain, it's just uncomfortable."

This made sense to Jill, but gave her greater reason for concern and supported her opinion that his waiting time was completely unacceptable. As she read through his initial complaint, she asked him to tell her just how he had come into his current predicament.

"Well, about two a.m., I drove over to the grocery store to pick up some ice cream. I parked my car and walked into the store. I grabbed one of those little carry baskets because I wanted to get some pineapple topping and chocolate sauce. After I picked up the ice cream, I headed down the middle aisle and turned right to head for the condiments section. Two men were heading toward me with push carts so I stepped to the center of the aisle to go between them. The next thing I knew, my feet were up in the air and I was flat on my back looking in the faces of these two guys trying to pick me up off the floor. My back was soaking wet and I was so embarrassed I thought maybe I had wet my pants. When they got me up I turned around and looked at the floor and saw a puddle of water flowing out from under the freezer skirting."

Jill stopped him and asked if he was in pain at that time and he said, "I was shook-up, but not in pain. I just wanted to get out of there. When I got to my car, I noticed I felt shaky. I was nauseous and went home. I was in pain by the time I went to bed though, and even after two Tylenol PM's I couldn't get to sleep. So, I'm here to see what you think I need to do."

Jill felt sure that she knew what the course of action should be and told the gentleman, "Let me get the doctor to take a look at you and we'll probably need to send you down the hall for a CAT scan."

She told him to sit tight until the doctor could see him and went to enter her notes and advise Dr. Cardinaello.

As she pulled the curtain closed behind her, she noticed Dr. Cardinaello leaning against the back doorway to the intake cubical. He was carrying on a conversation in Spanish with the clerk in the little room. They were both laughing but it appeared that he was doing most of the talking. His voice would drop very low and as it did, he would bend his body down toward the girl. Jill could not see her but could hear her squeal and giggle in a way that seemed inappropriate. She had the feeling that the doctor was being flirtatious and that the clerk was encouraging the behavior.

She sat down at the nursing station and entered her notes into the computer. The printer rolled off the report and she clipped it to the top of the patient record and returned it to the hook, on bed #2.

As she turned toward the doctor, she watched his eyes travel the length of her body. He seemed to enjoy watching Jill grow increasingly uncomfortable as he slowly scanned her as she walked. He continued joking with the clerk as his devilish black eyes returned to meet Jill's.

Embarrassed, she turned away and approached the nursing desk. She fumbled with a cup of pens and turned again toward the doctor. She needed to tell him that the patient in #2 was ready to be seen. She was awkwardly intimidated by the Latin monster of a man and could still feel his eyes scrutinizing her every move. She felt like a fly being stalked by a highly skilled predator. She dug deep to find the courage to speak.

"Doctor," she called out across the room, "#2 is ready to be seen."

Dr. Cardinaello did not respond and continued to direct his attention toward the clerk. Jill tried to keep from appearing to be listening, but, having taken two years of Spanish in high school, she recognized a few of his words. She knew enough to know that the doctor was displaying sexual overtones which, in Jill's mind, had no place in the ER.

She didn't like this doctor, and, she didn't trust him. He seemed to her to be egocentric and interested only in promoting himself as a ladies' man. Her biggest concern though, was whether, or not, he was going to help the patients. She wished there was a supervisor on duty that might influence the situation in a more professional direction. This doctor was loud, arrogant, flirtatious, and wore way, too much cologne. Jill wished he was gone before he had even gotten started.

The nursing assistant was setting up #4 for the next patient and Jill grabbed the intake list off the front wall. She walked through one of the three doors to the assessment offices where she would meet her next patient.

"Enrique Valero!" she called out into the waiting area. As the young boy and his portly mother rose from their chairs and headed toward her, Jill surveyed the room to determine if there were any serious problems that needed immediate attention. This duty would normally fall to the intake clerk but, the only intake clerk was still engaged in her infatuation with Dr. Cardinaello and was apparently intentionally neglecting the patients. There were approximately ten people in the waiting area but only three names remaining on the list. All the people were in various stages of expectation and several appeared to be in discomfort, but none seemed to need critical attention. There were two people sitting in seats at the closest proximity to the intake window and both looked at Jill hoping for her assistance.

"The intake clerk will be with you in just a moment."

She said it loud enough for the clerk and the doctor to hear and then escorted the boy and his mother into the assessment room. As she closed the door behind them, she heard the clerk and the cocky Latino doctor laughing. Jill was quickly becoming furious and had to take a deep breath before beginning her assessment.

"*Buenas tardes, cómo le puedo ayudar yo?*" she greeted the lady and her son and then asked if she understood English.

"*Hágale comprende inglés?*"

"*Sí, si usted habla lentamente.*" The woman said that she understood English when it is spoken slowly.

"Is this your little boy?" Jill asked as she gestured toward the six-yearold leaning against the woman's huge thigh. His head was down and his thumb was stuck in his mouth. He tugged away from the woman when Jill lifted her hand in his direction. His eyes were sunken and swollen, obviously from crying. He was a small boy for his age and Jill was genuinely concerned that he may be the victim of abuse. It was too early in the assessment to allow that possibility to hamper her gathering of the facts.

"No!" the woman responded softly.

Jill was puzzled that she didn't continue and explain the relationship. After a minute, she asked, "Whose little boy is he?"

The woman turned her head toward the boy and then back toward Jill. She never reached out to touch the child and Jill remembered that as they had gotten up from the lobby chair there had been no indication made by the woman that the child was even present. There seemed to be a strained relationship between the pair. They had moved across the floor separate, but, as one.

Jill's instincts were telling her to tread lightly to avoid scaring the duo away. After a minute of silence, she realized that the woman was not ready to answer the question of maternity so she directed her attention to the child's needs.

"Well, Enrique, what seems to be the problem today?" The little boy tightened his body as he held his clenched hands tightly to his chest. His bony shoulders pulled forward and his mouth puckered up. Jill immediately thought to herself that he had suffered abuse and he was angry. His t-shirt was two sizes too big, and as he rocked from side-to-side Jill caught quick glimpses of his emaciated rib cage. On Monday, she had discovered that the hospital keeps bags of candy in the desk drawers of the intake offices and she took a quick look.

"Oops, look what I found!" she said smiling as she took a purple sucker from the bag and held it up for the boy to see. He quickly grabbed the candy and ripped off the wrapper. Throwing the paper on the floor he turned to the woman and defiantly said in Spanish, "*Esto es toda mina y nadie tendrá de ello!*"

Jill understood him to be saying, 'this is all mine and no one will have any of it.' The boy turned toward the back door to the interview room and listened intently to the voices that could be heard through the closed door. The voices of the Cuban doctor and staff could be heard as they attended to patients and occasionally, the doctor could be heard speaking in Spanish. The boy appeared to be curious about what was happening behind the door. As he now began rocking back and forth Jill noticed that he was holding his left arm tighter to his chest than his right.

Though she had offered the sucker to him from his left side, he had reached across with his right hand to grab it. He never unclasped his left fist even as he had approached her in the lobby. She felt sure that whatever injury he had sustained was either on his left inner arm, or his left chest. Until she could gain his trust, the mystery would remain unsolved.

"Would you like a piece of candy, too?" she asked the woman. She interpreted the smile as a positive response and felt she was making headway as she took a red sucker from the bag and extended it toward the lady. "*No, no! Estos son míos! Toda mina!*"

The boy screamed as he grabbed the red lollipop from Jill's hand and then turned toward the woman scolding her in Spanish. The back door opened and Dr. Cardinaello's head appeared.

"Hey, Hey! What's all this yelling in here?"

The boy began screaming like a wild wolf caught in a trap. He fought to cross over the woman's lap, reaching frantically for the front door. He was crying frantically and calling out, "*La mami, la mami, yo deseo a mi mami no, no, la mami, la mami.*" He was scared and wanted his mommy. As he slid across the big woman's lap his left arm lifted from its retracted position for just a second or two and Jill caught a look at his injury. Hidden by his shirt was a bandage made of cardboard and duct tape. The tape had come loose just enough to reveal to Jill an infected burn at least three inches long. The skin was bright red and pus was oozing from the entire perimeter. Jill understood the severity of the injury immediately and held her hand against the door as the boy frantically pulled on the knob. He finally slid down to the floor in bitter despair.

"*La mami, la mami, yo deseo a mi mami, la mami, la mami,*" he cried out as his face pressed against the tile. Dr. Cardinaello called out to him firmly, "*Oye mi hombre pequeño, viene a aquí a mí. Aquí está a su mami. Permite ver esos ojos secos y mostrar a mami lo que un hombre usted es.*"

"Hey my little man, come here to me. Here is your mommy. Let's see those dry eyes and show mommy what a man you are."

Jill squinched her face and whispered to the doctor as she shook her head, "This isn't his mommy. We don't know where she is yet."

The doctor stood up and asked the woman, "Who is this little boy?" The woman in the chair turned toward the doctor but didn't raise her head high enough for him to see her tears. She spoke in Spanish and Jill was unable to follow the story due to the speed with which she spoke. She explained to him that on the previous Thursday night, she and sixteen other Cuban dissidents from a little town east of Havana had climbed into a homemade boat with a motor from an old rusty truck. They had read that there was going to be a boat race in Key West so they thought that if they tried to cross the Florida Straits while the race was going on, then all the police and Coast Guard would be tied up, and they might have a better chance of not being seen. The boy and his mother were on the boat but she had never met them before. They had come from another town near the foot of the mountains.

She went on to explain that all the people on board the boat had to pay money to the man that built it. He would not be coming with them, though. She said she found out later that some of the people paid him more than others and that some of the men, and the boys' mothers, had paid him with sex. She said that everything seemed to be going well for most of the night and the waves were not very high. The engine had stopped several times but one man was a self-taught mechanic and was able to get it going again. She told them that at times the diesel smoke choked them until they thought they would pass out. It was close to dawn and they could see America just at the horizon. It seemed to get farther away at times but they kept going.

The boat was made of rebar covered in scrap sheet metal from the siding of an old storage shed. The builder had mounted the engine and all the hoses inside the rebar then he sprayed cans of expandable foam inside the frame. He had covered the floor with ragged sheets of fiberglass that were pulled from a wrecked fishing boat. There was an exhaust pipe that came up from the engine underneath the floor and they were told to stay away from it or they could be burned.

She said that one of the bad men on the boat kept trying to get Enrique's mother to show him her breasts. Enrique had tried to fight the man and fell across the hot pipe, burning his chest. The other men had beaten the man up for being so mean. The poor child suffered unbearably with the pain.

Then there was the fuel pipe that came up on the railing. The builder had fashioned a gas cap out of wood so that if it rained the fuel would not be contaminated. She said they were told they had plenty of fuel to get to America but that was not so. The engine died and they drifted all that Friday in the hot sun.

The tides took them for many hours, first north, and then back south. All the time, she said, they could see America, in the distance. They floated past Miami two different times, once in the day, and once in the night. She said they ran out of food on Saturday. The bottles of water were all gone, too. They were caught in a terribly fast current and on Monday a wind blew all day from the north. She said they watched sharks and stingrays circle the boat and, on several occasions, they were slammed from underneath by them. They all thought they would die.

They waved and yelled at boats and planes but no one came to their rescue. After four days at sea, the men began to drink the saltwater. That night they were all sick and crazy. There were only three women; one older lady whom she had known since childhood, herself, and Enrique's mother. There were two storms that last night and everyone had their fill of water. It satisfied their thirst and most of them fell asleep. The boat was flooded and sat low in the ocean. The foam started to get soggy and big pieces began to float away.

She told them that when they saw the bright lights of Key West most of the men decided they could swim to shore. They thought they would not be seen in the darkness and be free men by sun up. There were waves and lots of wind, but they believed they could make it. Everyone went in the water but the two older men, the three women, and Enrique. She told the doctor that on Tuesday morning the speed boats could be heard in the distance and they were afraid they would be picked up by the Coast Guard and returned to Cuba, so she and Enrique's mother fashioned a piece of the foam into a raft. They put the boy on top of it and began kicking toward the shore.

The older woman and the two older men remained with the flooded boat. She described how difficult the passage was and how they were both ready to die. Several times the waves hit hard against the tiny raft and Enrique's mother lost her grip. Finally, she was washed away by a wave, and never came up again.

The woman collapsed as she finished her story. Enrique had passed out on the floor. Dr. Cardinaello looked at Jill and the two were locked in disbelief. "*Bien*," he said as he turned his head to the woman. "*Me Dispensa un mo-mento mientras discutimos lo que podemos hacer para usted.*"

He signaled to Jill to follow him into the back. She caught up with him at the desk as he sat down and flipped open his cell phone. As he punched in a phone number he said to Jill, "There are several things I would like for us to do for these poor souls and I will need your help."

She was attending to his every word as he spoke into the phone.

"Yes, Julian, this is Emilio . . . yes, I know . . . we are down here in Key West for the races . . . Oh yes, listen Julian, I have a very serious dry foot issue that needs your intervention as soon as you can . . . no, no, it is a woman, oh, possibly fortysomething, and a young boy. One day, yes just one day. No papers, no family, no nothing. No, no contact with immigrations. Yes, well I'm at the Lower Keys Hospital right now and I'm expecting to leave here in about eight hours or so. Yes, yes, thank you my friend, just a moment."

The doctor asked Jill for her name and returned to the phone.

"Nurse Jill will have them ready and I have a little medical work to perform on the boy but they will be ready when your people get here. Thank you my friend and we will get together for dinner when I get back. Yes, you too! Thank You!" The doctor leaned back in the chair and crossed his arms as he explained his plan to Jill.

"OK, we need to move on a few things here for these people. I have arranged for their transportation to a facility in Miami where they will have all their needs met. My friend is the C.E.O. of a nonprofit organization in Miami that helps in these kinds of situations. He is arranging for a van to come here today to pick these people up and transport them back up there. I will tend to the boy's chest and put together a bag of medications and bandages for them to take with them. I want you to go immediately up to the cafeteria and purchase enough food to fill the both of them." He reached in his pocket and took three $100 bills out of his wallet. He handed the money to Jill and continued, "I want you to go to the gift shop and buy the boy new clothes and some books and toys. And if you see some nice clothes for the woman, also. I want you to take care of all of that, right away. Can you do this for me?"

Jill was numbed by the sincerity in his voice. She felt embarrassed that she had earlier thought him to be a shallow, uncaring ogre, bending everything to his own will.

"Absolutely, Doctor, I'll get right on it." She turned and exited the double door with a mission. It felt good to be Jillian. Damn good!

Lost Souls of Paradise Photo Gallery

The Wall of Lost Soles See Chapter 9 & 27

Jillian's Mom visiting the Driftwood Oceanfront Resort and Spa
See Chapter 9 & 27

The Driftwood Resort and Spa

Boca Chica Mangrove and Buttonwood Beach area where Jillian got lost in the darkness See Chapter 10

The "Lucky" ones!

Waterspout behind the Dock Master's office at the Key West Bight.

Harold's Pet Bird "Yella Top" See Chapter 21

Harold and Jo's Boat 'KOKOMO JOE' See Chapter 21

Jillian's "Yellow Submarine" still sits in the impound lot covered in sea grass and salt.

Left: *The author Ian Ritchie Stewart and wolf-dog Java.*
Right: *Ian, playing his mountain dulcimer at the Key West Turtle Museum.*

Christmas Tree Island as seen from the Key West Bight See Chapter 3

The Landing on St. John U.S.V.I. See Chapter 31, 36 &37

Ethan's boat 'The Canadian Soul' currently registered to Jillian's dad, William Dougherty, Key West, Florida. Docked and maintained at the K.W. Bight. See chapter 31, 36, &37. Also, see Epilogue

Ethan was a master carpenter. He remodeled old houses in Key West.

Ethan hand-carved these sculptured stanchions out of Key West mahogany. The tree was knocked down during Hurricane Dennis.

Krismas Chastity Hall See Chapter 34 & 35

Jillian's dad and mom now own the Key West Ice Cream shop on Duval Street. Bill stays on the Canadian Soul while he is working in Key West and Jill's mom and sister are running the operation back home in Gloucester.

16. The Cow Key Bridge

Jillian was pushing a cart down the second-floor hall on her way back to the ER when her cell phone rang. She recognized the voice as soon as she heard it.

"Ms. Dougherty, this is Officer Carl Dixon with the Monroe County Sheriff's Office; I met you earlier this morning at the bank."

"Oh, yes sir, thank you again for all your help." She had no idea why he would be calling her.

The officer then explained, "Ma'am, we have a little problem over here and I'm hoping you can help solve it."

Jill kept walking down the hall as she asked, "Yes sir, what can I do for you?" "Ma'am, the man we picked up with your credit cards and ID says that you gave him your cards. Can you give us any good reason why you would have done that?"

Jill went blank and exclaimed, "That's absolutely ridiculous!" She slammed her fist against the metal service cart angrily as she insisted, "He stole them from my purse on Monday morning while I was trying to help him in the ER. Why would I do a stupid thing like that, anyway?"

"Well, you see, he says that you and he had an allday beach party and that you had gotten so inebriated that you asked him to hold onto your cards and that he was to take care of you. He went on to describe the situation as uncomfortable for him and that you had insisted on him purchasing liquor at the Bone Island Liquor Store on Stock Island. Can you shine any light on why this would have taken place?" the officer asked in his authoritative yet compelling manner.

"Absolutely not!" Jill told the officer. "I did no such thing."

"Well ma'am, I thought you may say that so I took the initiative to go over to the liquor store and talk to Roger, the manager of the store. Now, he has a story that, frankly, I find hard to believe, but I've got to admit there is some reason to question you on it. He said that you came in his store Monday morning with Paddy and that you appeared to be, as he put it, looped. Is there anything missing here that might help me get this story unraveled?" he asked.

"He's lying! He is a thief and needs to stay in jail. I've never been to a liquor store. I rarely even drink alcohol." Jill was beginning to move from concerned to angry.

"Yes ma'am! One last thing if you don't mind, are you driving a yellow Volkswagen Beetle?" The officer already knew the answer to his question.

"Yes! Why?" Jill asked.

"Well ma'am, Roger gave us a statement that says that you and Paddy left together in a yellow VW Bug. He also said that the car had an upside-down *PEACE* sign in the lower right corner of the back window. By chance, does your car display this sort of decal?"

"Yes!" Jill answered. "But it couldn't have been me."

"Yes ma'am, I thought that might be your answer, so I've asked Roger to bring me a copy of his security disc for Monday morning. I'd like to have you come over and take a look at it and see if we can wrap this thing up. I'm sure you realize we can't keep a man in jail if we can't prove a crime was committed," the officer explained.

"When would you need me to come over?" Jill asked. She had no idea if she would remain on duty for the rest of the day. She was at the mercy of the supervisor, if she even had one. She felt sure that she would be getting off at the regular time of 3 a.m. that night.

"Would tomorrow morning be alright?"

Officer Dixon responded, "Yes ma'am, I should be able to get the video this afternoon and have it ready by tomorrow morning. How does 8:30 a.m. sound to you?"

Jill was rolling the cart off of the elevator as she finished up the call confirming the appointment. "Yes sir, that will be perfect!"

He gave her directions to the police station, which happened to be just up the road from the hospital, and how to negotiate the building to find his office. As she pushed through the doors into the emergency room, she noticed that the gentleman that had previously been waiting in room #2 was nowhere to be seen. Dr. Cardinaello was working with the little boy in room #1. Room #3 was empty and the nurse that Jill had not yet met was in room #4 with an older woman and her husband. Jill parked the cart out of the way, against the back wall, and picked up a tray of hot food. She carried it over to the Cuban woman that she had met earlier. The woman was more than appreciative and sat in the corner of the little room as she surveyed the offerings and began eating.

Dr. Cardinaello had apparently built a strong rapport with the little boy and as he cleaned the burn they talked back and forth in Spanish. Jill brought a second tray to the bedside table and the boy sat up to eat. Danna returned from the pharmacy with a bag of antibiotics and tubes of Neosporin. The doctor's tray had two syringes which had apparently already been administered and several soiled swabs. Jill picked up the tray and, as she turned to dispose of it, said to the doctor, "Doctor, I have your care packages ready to go and your change is on the desk."

"Thank you, nurse!" he responded with a respectful acknowledgment, and then asked, "I don't believe we have been formally introduced. You are?" Jillian was pleasantly encouraged to see the possibility of developing a comfortable working relationship with him and told him her full name. "It's a pleasure to be working with such a charming and obviously well-trained nurse." He turned back to the boy for the final application of salve and said, "Where did you study?"

She was halfway into her exit from the cubical and turned back to answer. "I just finished my two years at Connell School of Nursing at Boston College three months ago."

"Gloucester is in Massachusetts, near the coast, isn't it?" the doctor asked. "Yes, that's right!" Jill answered. "I lived about sixty miles from the campus." She felt a need to assure the doctor that she was qualified to assist him in spite of her recent graduation, and added, "I worked as a candy striper for almost four years before I entered the nursing program."

She was looking at his face hoping for assurance that he was impressed but he gave her no clue.

"Did you find the boy some nice clothes?" he asked her as he finished wrapping the boy's chest.

"Oh, yes. I think you will be pleased with everything," Jill answered.

"I want you to stay with the boy until the driver arrives from Miami. Make sure you keep him entertained. Try to make him and the woman comfortable and if they need anything at all come find me."

He turned and said to the boy, "*Allí mi amigo pequeño, como nuevo! Ahora, permanece con esta hermosa señora. Ella le ha traído nueva ropa. Pronto usted estará bien! Chico bueno!*"

He had told the boy that everything was going to be just fine and that Jillian had some gifts for him. With this the doctor directed his attention toward the Cuban woman and explained the arrangements he had made for the two of them. He assured her that he would rendezvous with them in Miami and assured her that their future in America would be well provided for.

"*Ah, gracias! Gracias! Dios le Bendice para su porción nosotros! Gracias!*" She kissed his hands as her tears washed over them. Little Enrique was only interested in the cup of butterscotch pudding, which he was carving into with a spoon. The doctor left the cubical and joined Danna in room #2. She had just returned from radiology with the gentleman that had been waiting all morning to see a doctor. Jill listened as she rolled the cart of new clothes into the room where Enrique and the woman were waiting anxiously.

Doctor Cardinaello was examining the man in the cubical next door. Jill overheard Danna explaining that the results of the CT scan would not be available until the radiologist filed his findings sometime later that afternoon. After a thorough physical exam, the doctor wrote the man a prescription for a muscle relaxer and Percocet for his pain. He was advised to make an appointment right away with his private doctor and that he would probably be looking at further attention with a neurosurgeon. Danna escorted the man to the lobby and completed his discharge.

The emergency room remained busy for the rest of the afternoon. Jill watched the activities through the open curtain, wishing that she could be in the center of it all. She played games with Enrique until he fell asleep. She folded his clothes and gathered his new toys for the trip to Miami. It was almost three p.m. when the driver was led into the room by the intake clerk.

Dr. Cardinaello broke away from the patient he was attending and carried the little boy out to the van while Jillian pushed the cart full of supplies and gifts. He set the boy into the back seat and snapped his seatbelt in place, then pulled his wallet from his back pocket and put three one-hundred-dollar bills into the woman's hand as she cried out her blessings upon him. He then gave another one hundred to the driver and directed that he stop for dinner at the new Cracker Barrel Restaurant when they got to Florida City. Jill was struck with awe over the degree of compassion exhibited by the doctor. It was as if he was saying goodbye to someone in his own family. It was a deeply pleasant feeling she had not felt before and hoped that she would experience again. After hugs were exchanged with the departing duo, she and the Cuban doctor stood in the hot sun waving as the van pulled out of the parking lot.

"I want to thank you for being so attentive to these people," he said to Jill as they turned and walked back to the main emergency room entrance.

"My brother and his family arrived on a makeshift boat two years ago. Luckily for them they were able to make the passage without incident. Unfortunately, this little boy will have a difficult time growing up. If he were turned over to the authorities, he would probably be sent back to Cuba."

"Why would they send him back?" Jill asked.

"Well, with no family members and no sponsor here in America, temporary custody is awarded to the state until his next of kin is located. Then, the I.N.S. must try to reunite him with a grandmother, uncle, or anyone else willing to assume responsibility for him." The doctor held the door open as Jill stepped back into the E.R.

"What about the group that your friend manages? What can they do?" Jill asked.

"Well, we can only do so much. The laws are very clearly defined on such matters."

The doctor hesitated before proceeding to his waiting patient. He placed his hand gently on Jill's shoulder as he winked and said, "Maybe my friend Julian can pull some strings."

It was now three twentynine p.m. and the second tour had taken over the operations. Danna was in a cubical attending to a man with a pulled groin muscle. Two other nurses and three nursing assistants were engaged in various duties. Patients were being escorted into the examination rooms and Jill felt as though she may be just extra baggage. She recognized most of the staff members as she had passed them in the halls and break rooms throughout the hospital over the past seven weeks, but none seemed to connect with her, face to face. She felt awkward, intentionally avoided.

She struggled to find a way to casually inject herself into the activities. All bases seemed to be covered and she wanted to just disappear, unseen, out the back door. Aware that she was not really authorized to have assumed any duties for today, she walked out to the lobby, intending to slip into the elevator and head for the time clock in the human resource office.

"Excuse me," a voice called out to her. "Aren't you Jillian Dougherty?" Jill turned to acknowledge the inquiry and before she could open her mouth to answer, the lady had turned away from her and headed toward the staffonly door to the E.R. "You can go clock out!" she directed as she walked away.

"We've got everything covered."

Jill felt like a kindergarten child being sent home for misbehaving. She was crushed. Her self-esteem balloon had been hit dead on by a flying dart. As the elevator door closed, she wiped her tears. Full of self-doubt she considered whether she was really meant to be working in the profession. Maybe she was just too sensitive. She clocked out at 4:06 p.m. and headed for her little yellow bug.

As she pulled out of the parking lot onto College Road she remembered that she would be meeting with Officer Dixon the following morning and decided to do a little reconnaissance. Just up the road on the right she saw the sign announcing the entrance to the Monroe County Sheriffs' Office and she turned in. A police car pulled in behind her and followed her up the winding road, then, as they approached the huge complex, the car pulled into the parking lot under the building and disappeared in the dark shadow of the threestory detention center. There was a marina on the righthand side of the road and, beyond the buildings, the open water of the Gulf of Mexico. As she continued along her way, she passed by groups of haggardly dressed people headed in the same direction. Some of the people were pushing heavilyladen bicycles, carrying knapsacks, dragging carts, or just shuffling along as if they had heavy weights in their shoes.

There were old men, young men, even a few women. It seemed as though they were all headed to some event at the sheriff's office. She had no clue as to their intended destination. There were more than two dozen of them. One man was walking alone and as she approached him from behind she watched curiously as he made his way on the narrow grass patch beside the road. He would stop after a few steps and turn toward the building. Throwing his arms into the air, shaking his fists and shouting toward the uninterested building; he cussed up a storm, then turned and stood there, yelling at his feet as if they were responsible for some malady in his life. After a few moments, he would turn back to his original posture, and allow them to carry him a little farther down the road. Jill slowed as she passed him and was unable to make out anything intelligible from his ramblings.

A sign on the left side of the road said, 'Sheriff's Zoo'. Looking over through the chain link fence, she saw a huge pig lying on the side of a muddy pool of water. Three ducks were in the little pond and she thought she saw a large turtle in a pile of dust along the fence line. She strained her eyes to see deeper into the pen but could not make out any other images. She chuckled out loud as she slowly drove by. "Not much of a zoo if you ask me!"

The afternoon sun had fallen deeper into the western sky, blanketing this side of the building in shade. Jill continued exploring the area as she drove further along the narrow road. The next sign announced 'K.O.T.S.' (*Keys Overnight Temporary Shelter*). Three tall, white tents towered over an eightfoothigh security fence. It looked like a prisoner-holding compound but Jill soon realized that it was a shelter for the homeless.

"Well, well!" she squeaked as she ducked her head to take in the full view of the high fence. The entrance was a wide gate locked from the outside and a guard station just to the right on the inside. A sign hung on the chain link fence advising that the check-in time was at 6 p.m. and no alcohol or drugs were allowed on the property. As she passed by the gate, she slowed enough to read all the signs. Showers and bedding would be available on a first-come, first-served basis. No food or beverages were allowed inside the tents, all radios and electrical devices were to be turned off by 10 p.m., and all men were to remain fifteen feet away from the women's facilities. All guests must vacate the premises by 7:30 a.m. Jill had always wondered where all of the people she passed on the streets and along the beach slept every night. Now she knew.

THE ROAD ENDED IN A wide circle between the detention center and the sheriff's office building. As she made the circle and headed back out toward College Road, she rolled her window down about three inches. She could hear the prisoners on the upper floor of the jail playing basketball. Their voices echoed loudly off of the concrete enclosure, then fell to the ground below. The homeless people were now on her left. As she rounded the last bend before hitting the main road, a police car blocking the roadway came into view. The officer had jumped out of his cruiser and left the driver's door open. He had his hand on his holstered gun as he confronted two men that were walking on the road. Jill stopped her car and watched the confrontation from a safe distance.

The two men were arguing with the officer and becoming very agitated. The policeman was a short stocky fellow built like a football linebacker and appeared to be antagonizing the men. Jill couldn't hear what he was shouting but she felt that he was trying to get one of them to make a move on him. He stuck his face right up to one of the men as he shouted. They were nose to nose. The two fellows seemed to be willing to get physical but after a moment more of the officer's threatening behavior, they both backed down. Jill was captivated by the scene as it played out before her. She half expected the officer to pull his gun and start shooting.

A second police car arrived and two more officers stepped into the street. One of the officers approached Jill's car and motioned her to proceed toward him. He signaled her to roll her window down and as she put her foot on the brake he leaned against her door.

"I'm sorry miss; this will just take a second more," he told her as he glanced back at the scene. Jill was nervous but curious enough to ask him what had happened. "Oh, same old stuff! These two allegedly assaulted a tourist that was fishing off of the Cow Key Bridge. They supposedly stole his wallet and threw his fishing gear in the canal. We'll get them out of here in just a minute."

"Did they hurt him?" she asked.

"Who, the tourist? Yeah, well, they cut him up bad enough that we had to send him to the E.R." the officer explained. Jill could hear an ambulance coming up College Road as they spoke. A third police car pulled up with its emergency lights blinking. There were now four officers combing through the two men's pockets and belongings. They were put into the back seats of separate cars, and then all three cruisers sped off toward the jail.

On her way, back out to the main highway she passed more and more people making their way toward the shelter. They all looked like they needed a shower after spending the day in the blistering sun. Jill fantasized what it may feel like to be dependent upon the charity of others to maintain your hygiene.

First come, first served! It rang in her head. What germs would you find growing in a public shower for the homeless? She began to imagine the danger that each person might be exposed to if the facility wasn't disinfected properly. Head lice, scabies, impetigo, staphylococcal and streptococcal bacteria, as well as many other airborne pathogens, were some of her main concerns.

As her mind combed over these thoughts her face tensed up. Her eyes were squinting from the disgusting image. In the tropical heat and humidity, infections could rapidly develop strains that might become immune to conventional antibiotics. An island like this, she thought, could suffer a pandemic that could eventually spread to the whole continent. She struggled to pull her attention away from this obsessive thought, and back to her driving.

Jillian had once again been neglecting her nutritional needs. Her last food was the pizza that she had barely touched the night before. The fibers of good judgment and reason were beginning to stretch dangerously toward their limits and she could not see what was happening as her mind began to race. Thought upon thought marched into her consciousness like Nazi soldiers on parade. She began talking out loud as each new idea hit her gray matter.

"Ooh, this red light, so pretty! This green light, so bright! This fisherman, so silly!" And as she pulled out onto the Cow Key Bridge, "Those bad boys, they fight!" Driving slowly over the Cow Key Bridge, she scanned carefully along the concrete wall for blood stains. She saw a spot that she thought might be the site where the man was beaten. Traffic was coming up fast from behind but she didn't care. She was on a mission. A string of cars were backed up as she crawled across the bridge. Horns were honking as the five o'clock rush hour launched into its daily freeforall.

She pulled off of the highway and onto the grass as soon as she cleared the guard rail. She climbed out of her car, leaving the engine on and the driver's door open, then started walking back to the sidewalk that crosses the water. The Cow Key Bridge had been built in the 1930's, high on a raised berm, to allow for the storm surge to clear underneath during hurricanes. Even during normal tide levels, the current under the bridge is ferocious. This canal was the east end of the island of Key West and the Gulf of Mexico was always in a race against the Atlantic Ocean to see which could unload its waters into the other the fastest. It is a treacherous passage for even the most stable of boats.

The earthworks that had been built up on both sides of the bridge provided a twentyfivedegree incline at the approach to the road, and then tapered down to the water. Jill had parked her car at the highest point of this berm and forgotten to pull the parking brake up. She was fifty feet behind and facing the other way when she realized that all the people that were honking and yelling were trying to tell her that her car was fast on its way toward the canal. She turned and watched as her bug rolled below the bridge, hit the rocks on the erosion bank, and launched itself three feet into the air. It landed upright in the fast-moving current, and then quickly leaned to the left as the rushing water poured in through the open door. Jill stood on the bridge waving goodbye as it disappeared into the turbid abyss.

"We all live in a yellow kinda' thing!"

"A yellow kinda' thing!"

"A yellow kinda' thing!"

"We all live in a . . ."

She began softly singing the anthem that had so well reflected her imagination and her love for the little bug. Now it had become what she always knew it was supposed to be, a yellow submarine. She changed the verses of the song as the tears began to flow.

"In the land, where I was born, lived a man, who sailed the sea

We all live in a yellow submarine . . ."

She watched as her little yellow car tumbled in the rushing water, disappeared, broke the surface further down the canal, then surfaced no more. It was headed out to the vast, blue waters of the Gulf of Mexico. She smiled as she imagined herself in the front seat, driving past coral reefs, sunken ships, and across the sandy ocean bottom. She leaned against the side of the bridge and forgot all about the man that had been beaten there just thirty minutes earlier. She had no concern that her purse was on the front seat of her car, now providing entertainment for the curious little fishes of the sea. Her key to the apartment was on the key chain that was probably still locked in the ignition slot. And, her new phone, receipt and all, washed out to sea.

Poor Jillian! She didn't care at all. She was completely oblivious to the seriousness of her condition and clueless to the dangers at hand. Once again, she stood knocking on the door of sanity. Unfortunately, it was the exit door

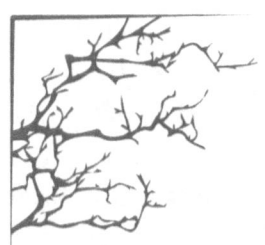

17. The Feral Man

"**H**ey lady, was that your car?" someone shouted from under the bridge. Jill was still standing there, waving goodbye to her little yellow bug. She leaned out over the concrete railing and looked to see who had called out. Directly below her, she saw six men standing in the mud. On the other side of the canal, she saw two more men standing on the other bank, and one old woman. They were all looking at her, waiting to see if she would answer and confirm their suspicion.

"It's not a car!" she yelled back to the crowd. She was laughing so hard she almost fell over the railing.

"It's a submarine!" She could barely get the words out she was laughing so hard.

Once the derelict crowd weighed her answer, they began laughing and singing the famous Beatles' song,

We all live in a yellow submarine,

a yellow submarine, a yellow submarine . . .

They were all dancing and howling with joy after witnessing such a comical event. Their laughter echoed off of the pilings and the bridge's concrete understructure from both sides of the waterway. They sounded like cavemen celebrating from the mouth of some huge cave after a successful kill. Jill watched smiling from above as the men sat in the mud below her, passing their bottles of liquor from one to another. One of the drunken men fell into the rushing water. Two others fought to pull him back to shore. Soaking wet, they laughed and cussed and drank themselves a toast over their friend's rescue. They seemingly had not a care in the world.

Several street people passed behind Jill as she leaned out over the rail watching the comical little band of gypsies under the bridge. They were making their daily pilgrimage to the shelter beside the sheriff's office. The sun was dropping lower in the west as Jill straightened up and turned to look toward the city and into the faces of what seemed to be a multitude of hopeless souls. She smiled at everyone as they passed but was disturbed to find that almost none of them made eye contact with her. More people were making their way up the sidewalk toward the bridge. Jill stood to the side with her back to the water as each person approached.

"How do you do, my friend?" she bowed and curtsied to a young man pushing a bicycle up the bridge. He smiled but dropped his eyes back to the sidewalk to avoid connecting with hers. His long dirty hair looked as if he had not bathed in weeks. His beard was knotted and full of food drippings. He looked to be in his forties but, truth be known, he had just passed twenty-nine. His shirt was stained with food and generally filthy. Jill returned to an upright position and watched him limp down the sidewalk. The baskets on the front and back of his bicycle were overflowing with crushed aluminum cans and bags of trash. The back of his khaki trousers were dark brown from his seat to the cuffs. He wore a pair of torn, black canvas deck shoes. The sole of his left shoe was held in place by duct tape that had almost given up its ability to restrain. Periodically he would knock it on its side against the other shoe to reattach the tape. In most people's eyes, he would have been a sad spectacle of human neglect.

Jill called out cheerfully to him as he passed by: "I like your shoes!" The poor man was so lonely. He spent most of his days pushing his bicycle around the island, picking up aluminum cans, digging through trash barrels for discarded lottery tickets that the tourists had scratched off while too drunk to add up their winnings, oh, and avoiding making eye contact. That was always his most demanding priority. Everyone he passed looked the other way. He had lived so low for so long that he was afraid he couldn't reach high enough, over the pain, to look into anyone's eyes. So, he just quit trying. He had become a feral man.

He spoke to no one, and no one spoke to him. Every day he stood in the soup kitchen line, waiting for his once-a-day, 4 o'clock meal. The only three words that were ever passed his way were, 'God Bless You'. He graciously took his plate from the little lady and sat alone under the tin roof of the pavilion. No one knew his name and no one asked. No one knows where he came from. No one really cared! He was just another pilgrim, trying to survive another searing, hot day in paradise.

"I really do!" she tried again to make a friend of the stranger.

As he reached the other side of the bridge, he stopped. Jill felt her heart pounding with hope that he would come back and join her. He turned his upper body halfway around but left his feet where they were. For almost two full minutes he stared into the pavement adjacent to the bridge. He didn't move. One car after another passed by. His eyes were fixed at tire level. He looked as if he was listening to sounds that might be coming from below the pavement or perhaps he was deaf and thought he heard a voice. He slowly turned back and resumed his trek eastward toward the shelter.

"Well, you must be a nurse!" Jill was leaning against the bridge with her arms crossed across her chest when she heard a most delightful and charming voice. She turned her head away from watching the young man and looked into the eyes of one of the most wonderful faces she had ever chanced to see.

"Oh, do you mind if I just catch my breath?" The beautiful whitehaired granny set her large quilted bag down on the dirty sidewalk and leaned against the railing next to Jill. In broken breaths she said, "You won't believe it, but, in my younger day, I actually used to climb mountains in North Carolina."

She was breathing heavily and waving a folded knitting pamphlet to cool her flushed cheeks. Jill was lost in the marvelous discovery of such a beautiful face. She studied every eyelash and wrinkle, every gentle curve, every fold. She looked like a portrait in a fine art gallery. She just couldn't be real. Jill lifted her hand and slowly brushed the lady's cheek with the back side of her fingers. The woman leaned away slightly but realized that Jill meant no harm and trustingly allowed her to continue. Jill leaned her nose close to the woman's neck and filled her lungs with air, then leaned back and said, "You smell so wonderful."

"Oh Lord, child, I am covered in sweat and haven't bathed since yesterday. You have got to be joking!" the woman embarrassingly replied.

She forced herself off of the railing and back to her feet as she chuckled at her comment. Jill watched as the lady straightened her cotton summer dress and stretched out her arms. The woman reached deep into her large side pocket and took out a pink handkerchief. Unfolding the kerchief, she wiped the sweat from her brow and said, "Are you a nurse?"

Jill lurched forward to free herself from the gravitational pull of the bridge railing and regained her footing on the sidewalk. She fought the inertia to keep from falling too far forward and into the oncoming traffic. She dropped her chin to her chest and looked at her feet for a second. Realizing she was dressed in a nurse's uniform she looked up at the lady and answered, "I guess I am."

The lady looked puzzled by Jill's answer. She was well experienced in dealing with people in various conditions of mental distress and recognized immediately that Jill may be suffering from some psychiatric disorder.

"I was a nursing assistant at the convalescent center around the corner up until three months ago when they closed it." She leaned toward Jill and set the back side of her hand against the corner of her mouth as if to frame a secret and whispered, "One of the good ones."

Jill just stood, grinning and glassyeyed, hanging on her every word, but not really listening. The lady held out her right hand and offered a friendly, "I'm Gamelady! Well, that's what my bingo friends call me. Most other folks call me Mama C. for Cheryl." Jill's focus was on the movement of Cheryl's mouth as the words rolled off her tongue. She was copying Cheryl's lip movements with her own and exaggerating each syllable. She sucked in her cheeks as she moved her lips open and closed. It was a comical face. She looked like a fish.

Cheryl laughed out loud as she picked up her bag. "You are so funny, what's your name?"

Jill once again dropped her chin to her chest and contemplated her answer. She snapped her head back up and barked out the name of the family dog that had passed away six years earlier.

"Chester! What's yours?" Jill asked.

"I just told you, Cheryl. Aren't you listening?" Jill laughed again as she answered.

"I think I've got bugs in my ear. All I hear is bugs buzzing in there. I hope they find their way out soon."

Poor Jillian was beginning to show the early symptoms of what might later prove to be a lot more serious than bugs. Cheryl sensed there was something wrong but was far removed from being able to offer anything more than comfort and advice.

"Do you have some place you need to go?" Cheryl asked Jill in a calming tone. Jill looked out toward the darkening sky over the Gulf and seemed to linger awkwardly without answering.

"Chester dear, look at me." Cheryl knew just how to talk to someone that was out on a ledge. She had always been the one they called when one of the Alzheimer's patients had failed to return from never-never land. They might be five feet from their own bed but lost hundreds of miles away. Cheryl had a gift for leading them back. She had already tuned into Jill's frequency, and was ready to answer the call. She took Jill's left hand and placed it between her own. They were soft and warm. The day's sweat had left them slightly sticky. They had a healing effect on her. When Jill turned back to face Cheryl, her eyes were thick with tears. Cheryl melted into a puddle of sympathy though she had no idea of where Jills' sadness had come from. So young! So innocent! So beautiful! Cheryl began to pray for guidance as she sought the best way to help her.

"Sweetie, let me help you," she gently suggested.

Together, they turned toward the other end of the bridge. Darkness was rapidly falling and the automobiles had turned on their lights. As the oncoming bright beams flashed into their eyes Jill turned her head and buried her face into Cheryl's shoulder. She held Jill safely to her side as they walked the long mile to the shelter gate. Like the rescuer of an injured sparrow, Cheryl would see to it that Jill was kept safe, at least for tonight.

18. Shelter for the Night

"**O**k, who's next?" Ronnie's voice bounced off of the concession overhang, through the chain link fence, and into the ears of the waiting crowd. Everyone in line shuffled their feet one step closer to the open gate.

Ronnie, or formally Ronda Helena Bozeman, is the sister of Thomas Bozeman. Tom had been hired into the directorship of the Keys Overnight Temporary Shelter, like many others in the Keys workforce, over the phone. He had accepted the position without ever putting a foot on the island. His was another successful 'hook line and sinker' story from the internet employee recruitment website of, www.snaggedwhilesurfingthenet4agoodjobinparadise.com.

He had applied online, eighteen months earlier, from his apartment in Yonkers, New York, where he had managed a private not-for-profit homeless men's shelter and soup kitchen. At fiftyfour years, old and after twentytwo years of working with the New York homeless, three stab wounds, one bullet in the chest, several broken noses and one broken rib, he felt he deserved a "vacation" job.

The ad posted on Craigslist.com looked so benign. Working in the tropics, sipping on a rum and Coke, watching the girls on the beach, it sounded so right to Tom. He could hear Jimmy Buffett singing, "All of the tourists are covered with oil," as he emailed his resume to the human resource department of The Florida Keys Outreach Coalition. Two weeks later he was driving down Highway A-1A, completely oblivious to the trap he was already caught in. He was still clueless as he toured the facility. By the end of his first night on the job, he was ready to run for his life.

Three days later, his sister Ronnie arrived after receiving his call for help. She also worked at the Yonkers shelter. Tom had hired her as the intake clerk and bookkeeper for the facility. She had not been interested in moving to Florida with him, but had never been able to say 'no' to her big brother. Besides, she owed him her life. He had rescued her from her heroin and alcohol addictions after fourteen years of dragging her out of every pit the devil sucked her into. She had been clean for almost a year when he left. On one hand, she felt precariously vulnerable, on the other, she felt free. Still, her mentor was in need and she hit the road.

That was eighteen months ago. Not only was Ronnie still clean, no small miracle on an island that financially stays afloat due to the consumption of spirits, but she was now making more money than she had ever made in her life.

"All right, I said who's next?" she shouted out again with a little more attitude. "Oh God, they haven't figured you out yet?" she joked as she took his identification card and pulled him up on the computer.

"Julius Michael Rosenthal," she read from the screen. Jules had drifted to Key West from Memphis, Tennessee when he was in his forties. Now, standing hunched over, on the back side of seventy, he was as familiar an island fixture as the sunset off Mallory Square. His skin was dissolving off of his sundried face. Thirty years of sleeping on the beach and canvassing the island streets for lost change had left this worn-out old fellow with barely the energy to dig up anything heavier than a smile. But, tonight, he got lucky. After a minute of fighting with his COPD for a half breath, he coughed up something into a dirty blue mechanic's rag, wiped his mouth, and there it was, a wee little smile.

"Thanks, Ms. Ronnie!" His voice was hardly audible but Ronnie knew his heart was in it.

"You sleep well now, Jules," she said in a friendly voice.

In her years of shelter work, she had lost two homeless men. One was on a cold New York morning in December. Heavy snows had left many of their regulars unable to traverse the distance from the city to the suburban neighborhood where the mission property was located. About four in the morning, she checked the front door to see if the snow had built up too deep for it to be pushed open. Ronnie was a big woman, weighing close to 180 lbs., and had leaned her body into the large steel door. It budged about an inch but the weight of the snow pushed it right back. Two hours later, when several of the men had awakened and gathered at the door to go out for a morning smoke, they found the man frozen on the stoop. He was one of the regulars.

That afternoon, six more homeless men were found around town. Most of them were out in the open, assumingly, trying to make their way to the shelter. Tom and Ronnie both found a deeper purpose that day. That's what it takes to work with these people, a feeling of purpose.

The second man died on a cot in the back of the Keys shelter about one year earlier. He had checked in the night before, feeling sick. He had been up almost all night in the men's room. The next morning one of the other guests alerted Ronnie that the toilet was full of blood and it had been tracked all over the floor. She figured that one of the men probably had a hemorrhoid fissure break. This was a common health issue in homeless shelters. The guys mopped it up and disinfected the bathroom and then left for the day.

At seven-thirty Ronnie had locked the gate and began her daily inspection of the tents. Everything seemed copasetic as she entered the men's #2 tent. She started pulling the bedding off of the cots. When she got to #38 she saw that the sheets were soaked in blood. On the floor, between the cot and the canvas wall, she found him. The man was tightly balled up in a fetal position. A stream of blood had flowed from his groin area onto the floor and followed the seam of the canvas to a low area in the concrete floor. There it had trailed out to the gravel behind the slab. He wasn't breathing. He wasn't moving either. There was no pulse to check. Ronnie ran back to the office and in three minutes the tent was swarming with officers and detectives.

Ronnie was always cognizant of those episodes whenever she checked in a guest that seemed ill. It wasn't an experience you wash away easily. She hoped Jules would not be found like that. Not by her at least.

"Ok, let's move! I haven't got all night," she barked out her call for the next person. As the fellow handed his card through the raised window Ronnie leaned forward and took it in her hand, then she stuck her head out through the upper opening and called out, "Well, wait a minute, yes, I do have all night. Never mind, take all the time you want!"

The crowd was used to her Yankee banter. She may have had a bull dog bark, but she had the heart of Mother Teresa.

Cheryl and Jill were in the middle of the line. The last few stragglers were dragging up and it looked like the crowd was settling in at around sixty or so. Cheryl knew several of the people and made conversation with those that she had previously been acquainted with. Many of the men were drunk and loud. Jill stood close to her new guardian, taking in all the activity as though she was at the county fair with her mother. A police car was parked directly across the parking lot facing the crowd. Its engine was running and the parking lights were on. In the front seat everyone could see the young officer's face illuminated by the light from his computer screen. Every now and then, when someone in the line got too unruly, the officer would turn on his loudspeaker and call out, "All right gentlemen, let's remember where we are. If you want to go upstairs, just keep it up." He was targeting the problem people in the crowd.

Most of the regulars had long arrest records for disorderly conduct or assault, trespassing, open containers or worse and the police seemed to know every one of them. What the people waiting in line didn't know was that the officer was monitoring the nightly registry as they were being checked in by Ronnie. This helped them to be better prepared to intervene if they had to respond to a 911 call. Or at least, that was their reasoning when the live link was proposed to the shelter's board of directors. The full reasoning behind the proposal remained only in the hands of the Sheriff's Office.

As the officer read the entries online, he was running a program set up by FDLE, *Florida Department of Law Enforcement*, called The Predator Finder or TPF for short. This very high-tech and useful diagnostic tool takes the demographics right off of any highlighted digital document and runs searches through specified national databases, checking for inconsistencies of information.

It also validates whether the information is accurate. Each search is posted with a color tag that indicates the degree of validity or the lack of validity of the information entered. A red tag would indicate that the information is highly suspect. Also, a second national search will identify if the subject has outstanding warrants or is an unregistered sex crime offender.

The bottom line, as far as the island police are concerned, is that the sheriff wants his officers to protect the tourists, as best they can, from the threat of being affected by crime. Crime is bad for a tourism-based economy. He has dedicated his forces to this purpose. All in all, most residents say he has done an outstanding job. But, security doesn't come easily in a town this small.

The officer in the car was watching each registration with his finely-honed senses. He expertly scanned reports and arrest records from databases all over the United States. If he determined there might be good reason, he could refer suspect information for an international criminal search through the Interpol database in Paris, France. All from the front seat of his cruiser.

Unfortunately, when he finds a registrant that warrants apprehension, he cannot make a move on the subject until he or she leaves the shelter. If the general homeless population knew that they may be arrested while seeking shelter through the various homeless service providers on the island, the ones that knew they had good reason to be arrested, would try to stay under the radar and avoid those service providers. Also, they would probably rely more on criminal activity to provide for their needs. For the police, having the knowledge that a criminal is in the shelter is a twoedged sword. They want to do something about it, but they can't do anything about it. One bust could take years to overcome.

As a suspect's information alerts the officer to the need for intervention, he enters a destination code that delivers the file electronically to the Monroe County Sheriff's Office, Warrants Division, for priority attention. The next morning the suspect will be observed as he leaves the property. Once he has reached a place where his apprehension will go unnoticed by others from the homeless population, a team of undercover officers will discretely remove him from the streets and detain him at the jail. In its clandestine way, it's an unprecedentedly successful system. Unfortunately, it must remain clandestine if it is to continue being effective.

"Next!" Ronnie's voice bounded off the Coke machine and ricocheted back toward the waiting crowd. "Hey Cheryl, how's it going?"

Cheryl handed over her social security card and her Florida ID as she greeted Ronnie.

"I'm just fine. A little tired but, all in all, I'm fine." Cheryl was no complainer. She was always prepared to consider that someone other than she might have greater problems than hers.

"Listen, Ronnie, I need to ask if there is something you can do for a friend of mine." She turned and gestured toward Jill who was now entertaining several of the homeless men in the concessions area.

"This is Chessy. She got here yesterday and last night somebody stole her purse. She has no money! Nothing! Her driver's license, credit cards, everything gone. Is there any chance that she could stay tonight and have her parents fax her information tomorrow?"

"Yeah, no problem," Ronnie answered. "As long as she's eighteen!" Cheryl assured her that the girl was twenty-one and waited nervously with her fingers crossed behind her back.

"Let me get you checked in, then we'll fix her up." A minute later she ripped the bedding voucher from the printer and passed it to Cheryl.

"Ok, give me her full name."

Jill had drifted away from the concessions area and over to the entrance to the men's bathroom. She was watching the other guests as they gathered around the picnic tables smoking cigarettes and talking. Cheryl leaned into the window and spelled out a fictitious name.

"Chastity A. Marrow," she spelled out as Ronnie made the entry.

Cheryl quickly went to rescue Jill. She took her by the hand and pulled her gently away from the bathroom door. After pointing her back toward the concession tables, she stepped back to the window.

"Do you know her D.O.B.?" Ronnie asked.

"December fourteenth, 1981," Cheryl responded. "Social?"

"023-66-XXXX." Cheryl avoided looking at Ronnie as she delivered the fictitious information. She was just trying to buy time for Jill and was counting on being able to help her put her pieces back in place after a good night's sleep.

"Address?" Ronnie continued as she typed the data into the computer beside the window.

"3498 Paiute Drive, Provo, Utah 84604," Cheryl answered without hesitation. Cheryl had not seen the Paiute Drive house since before her parents moved the family from there to Raleigh, North Carolina back in 1947. Her sister had heard that the little wood-framed white house had burned down in the seventies and had been replaced with a huge two-story. Cheryl had hoped she could go visit the old neighborhood and perhaps jog her mind back to the memories of growing up in such a wonderful place.

The little white house was at the end of a gravel cul-desac. Paiute Drive followed the base of a mountain and theirs was the first house on the right where the turnaround began. The girls and their friends used to hike up the old Indian trail that was directly behind the house. It led far up the mountain to an enchanting place they called Hanging Lake.

It was a flat clearing in the rocky woods, less than seventy feet across, where the snowmelt had long ago backed up just enough to form a crystal-clear lake. There was a waterfall feeding it from above and a gently flowing stream that ran all the way down to the culvert that led under Paiute Drive, then off to a bigger creek behind the high school three streets farther down the hill.

So many wonderful childhood memories were hidden there, just waiting to be uncovered. Cheryl had suffered a series of strokes in recent years. They blanketed her past in a fog of forgetfulness. It wasn't unusual for her to stop in the middle of a conversation and just draw a blank. She had pretty much accepted the condition as something to be expected considering the closeness with which she had danced with death. She kept it secret from no one. She felt that by refusing to feel ashamed or embarrassed by her loss of connectivity, she could help others prepare for the possibilities of dealing with their own maladies. That was Cheryl, seeing everything in her life as an opportunity to help others. She liked to jokingly reference her memory loss by saying things like, "Ya know, if it weren't for what's missing, it wouldn't be Swiss cheese."

"Next of kin?" Ronnie asked.

"James and Caroline Marrow!"

The Marrow family had lived directly across the culdesac from Cheryl's house in Provo. As she tested her recollection of these bits of information, visual images began streaming back from her childhood. She felt a hopeful excitement as she considered that the memories she had thought had been lost forever, might find their way back. Some magical trigger had launched a free fall of data. Cheryl was more than pleased with herself for accomplishing the task at hand without going blank. Now, maybe she could enjoy the evening reacquainting herself with old friends she thought had abandoned her. Ronnie handed her a bedding voucher for Jill and wished her a pleasant evening.

"Hey, Carter!" Cheryl greeted as she and Jill stepped over to the window to the laundry room where Carter, one of the regular shelter guests, assisted with the disbursement of toiletry needs, bedding, hygiene kits, first aid kits, and reading material.

"Well, who's this pretty lady, Mama C.?" Carter asked in his usual friendly manner.

"We haven't seen anything as beautiful as this in town since this morning's sunrise."

Carter seemed to be a harmless fellow of probably fifty years. Well educated and quite nicely groomed for someone who would be hard-pressed to rub the buffalo off a nickel. He had come to the island years ago after being fired in Atlantic City, New Jersey where he claims he had been a blackjack dealer at Harrah's Resort Casino. After a few years of working odd jobs and panning handouts from tourists, he ingratiated himself into the shelter's operations as a volunteer. This tactic had served him well at the Daily Bread Soup Kitchen, the Good Sheppard's Breakfast for the Homeless and the Saint Theodore's Thrift Shop on Petronia, Street. His dependability and sobriety secured him a ring of keys that guaranteed him almost an unlimited access to the top shelf of any of their pantries and supply rooms. He had first pick of everything. He needed nothing! Nothing, save for the pleasures that fed the vice which had forced his leaving Atlantic City. Carter was a sexual predator. His victims of preference were prepubescent boys. Released from supervision only on the condition that he leave the State of New Jersey, he, like so many before him, found his way to the city at the end of the road, where he believed he could spend the rest of his days, hiding out, under the radar.

Tom and his sister Ronnie were well aware of Carter's criminal history and the information was kept confidential. Since the shelter housed only adults, Carter was allowed to sleep there. He was one of many known offenders who showed up at the gate for a free cot and a cover. There were probably many more unknown offenders standing in line each night, hiding their shame in the comfort of numbers.

"This is Chastity Marrow. She just got here from Provo, Utah."

"Cheryl gathered up the two stacks of sheets and towels as Carter slid two Red Cross toiletry bags across the counter. Jillian wasn't paying attention when Carter reached out to shake her hand. Cheryl interceded by turning her around and directing her toward the man in the brightly-lit booth. Jill squinted her dilated eyes until they were almost closed.

"Utah!" Jill was hiding her face from the lights with her hands.

Cheryl explained, "I'm sorry, Carter! Let me get her bedded down. She isn't feeling very well right now."

Cheryl balanced the bags on top of the towels and sheets and took Jill by the hand and headed for the women's tent entrance. There were sixty beds in three rows of twenty, set up from the front of the tent to the back. Cheryl explained that sleeping in the back was quieter and led her down the side aisle. Jill sat on a thin grey and black striped prison mattress and watched as Cheryl made up two of the beds. When she finished, she led Jill into the women's showers and chattered about shelter rules as she disrobed. Jill sat on the wooden bench and watched as Cheryl pulled her tired body into the stall. From behind the closed curtain, she continued instructing Jill in issues of safety and hygiene.

"Make sure you keep clean!" she directed as she lathered up. "These men are nasty with their nose blowing everywhere, so don't touch anything. Wash your hands every time you see soap; if you don't, you'll surely get sick." Cheryl realized that no other shower was running and pulled back the curtain to find that no one was there.

"Oh Lord, where is she now?" She rinsed off the soap and rushed to put her night clothes on. Jillian's blouse lay in the water on the floor.

"Hello, is this girl with you?" Benita, or Beni, as she was known by most people, was walking behind Jill, guiding her back into the women's shower room. Jill's bra was unsnapped and her pants were halfway unzipped.

"I can't tell if she's on something or if we need to call 911, but she needs to stay in here and get her shit together before the idiots out there get hold of her."

Jill weighed in at just shy of onetwenty but Beni was lucky to knock off at eighty pounds on a wet day. All of her days were wet! If not soaked in sweat from swimming with crystal meth, or half drowned in a bottle of vodka, she was hanging with the winos under the bridge, sharing the last drops from a stolen bottle of Mogen David. If it made it up her nose, into a vein, or down her throat, and didn't kill her, it probably left her a pound lighter on the fly. Her frail, tortured, and heavily tattooed body barely kept her clothes from falling to the ground. The hand-rolled cigarette that hung from the side of her mouth lent support to those wondering if she were a man or a woman.

"Oh, thank you, Beni," Cheryl offered graciously as she took Jill's hand. "She's my friend's daughter from back in Utah. I'm helping her get settled in. Thanks! I can take it from here."

Beni was happy to be free of the responsibility for the girl and was now able to resume her freedom from responsibility for her own self-induced problems. There were fourteen women that reported into the shelter that hot summer night. A wind was threatening to unleash a thunderstorm. The salty island air was taking on a refreshing ozone feel. Anyone that didn't make it through the gate by ten p.m. would have to face a night of storms under a bridge or beneath one of the overhangs behind Sears Town.

Sometimes the men would break into the drydocked boats at the marina next door to escape the bad weather. Once, after a hurricane, two homeless men were found trapped inside a flipped sailboat. Cleanup crews got to them a week after the storm. They were both dead. Now, the police keep a closer eye on the marina. They shine their bright lights over the hedges that separate the sheriff's property from theirs, but rarely do they ever actually push through the bushes and patrol the property. On a stormy night like this one, lots of people will probably end up sleeping over there. Any damage they do will fall on tomorrow's call sheet and be investigated by the day shift. No one needed to be concerned tonight except the boat owners.

Several of the women made their way into the shower and started disrobing. The chatter was mostly about how bad the food was tonight at the soup kitchen or how long a wait it was to get checked into the shelter. The shower room smells changed, from fresh and clean, to low tide on the shrimp docks of Stock Island. Lots of the shelter people pop shrimp heads at the fish house this time of year for cash. A sixhour day can net about forty dollars if they hustle. Their arms and legs get covered in shrimp guts and by the time they drink two sixpacks and walk the mile and a half from the docks to the shelter, the hot sun leaves them stinking to high heaven. From that time on, the room would smell like a fishmeal factory. Cheryl hurried to get Jill undressed and clean before the stench took over.

Back in the tent, the girls bedded down. Jill flipped through the copy of the *All Hands Navy Magazine* she had picked up out front while Cheryl read from a book. The sounds of smokers talking loud by the picnic table outside the tent made concentration impossible. Cheryl took a pair of orange earplugs out of a small plastic bottle and bid goodnight to her newfound friend. When the lights went off at ten-thirty, Cheryl was already sleeping like a rock. Jill, on the other hand, was ready to roll.

19. Comme Ci, Comme Ca!

The wind was blowing fresh gusts of salty air into the huge tent. The walls stretched and swayed like sails on a ship heaving to as it raced across the roof and through the compound. The heavy canvas snapped as it pushed the limits of its restraints. The sounds grew louder as the storm moved across the island. Thunder was roaring in the distance and lightning was setting the sky on fire as it cracked. Jillian watched the blazes dance across the tent ceiling above as she lay on her sweatsoaked cot. She counted the seconds, waiting for the thunder. She imagined great wooden ships loaded with bronze cannons battling over newfound treasure stolen from Indians in the mountains of Peru.

Across the parking lot, another battle was taking place. "Where the hell is my attorney?" a snarling voice bit the silence of the dimly lit hall.

When Paddy had been arrested earlier that day, he had not had a drink since approximately 4:30 a.m. He had walked almost ten miles from the Driftwood Oceanfront Resort out on Boca Chica Road back to town, and had circled across the island as he ran his route of ATM scams. Now, at 11 p.m. Wednesday night, while all the other inmates were trying to sleep off their day's troubles, Paddy was as sober as a sober judge and mad as hell about it. He had no intention of sleeping, and in true Paddy nature, ready to be a problem to those in charge.

"Goddamn it, she gave me every one of those cards," he announced to the second-floor night shift guards.

"I want my phone call you sonofabitch!" Paddy shouted through the slot in the cell door.

The two corrections officers were growing tired of his constant badgering. They had heard it all many times before. Every time Paddy goes to jail, he unloads this same old detox poison on the corrections officers. "I'm a goddamn United States Marine! You can't just lock me up without charging me. I've got rights, goddamn it!" Paddy continued to shout through the door.

His favorite claim had always been that he had once served in the U.S. Marine Corps. He announced it to everyone he met. It was hard to tell if perhaps he felt this claim may gain him some particularly patriotic sympathy as he worked his scams on unsuspecting victims, or he actually had served in the Marines and proud to boldly proclaim it to the world. One thing you could bet on though, the U.S. Marine Corps surely wasn't out there telling everybody it met, "Hey, you know Paddy used to be one of us!" Nope, not in a long shot.

His claim seemed so impossible to imagine. This pathetic lightweight of a man, to have ever qualified as an American fighting machine, stretched one's gullibility beyond reason. With his rancid disposition and despicable personality, how could he have ever evolved from one of America's favorite sons into this? It was just too hard to believe. Wherever he was, whatever he was up to, Paddy always displayed the same hideous behavior, unless there was a beautiful female in the picture. That's when he turned on all the impish charm of a bridge troll.

"Hello, my sweet angel. Would you like me to sing you a little song? I wrote this for a beautiful girl I was once in love with. You remind me so much of her. It goes like this . . ."

He would then improvise a few unrhyming verses of immature mush, and when he sensed the attention fading, he would take a bow and announce a pathetically executed and overly theatrical, "Thank you!"

Tonight, there was no charm on display. Paddy would rely on other fine attributes to persuade his will be done. Relentless demand, mixed with screaming and lots of spitting! Every time the guards came near the cell door to apply control over him, Paddy would launch a ball of sputum through the narrow feeding slot in the door. This seemed an appropriate modus operandi until the door flew open and he found himself struggling against four corrections officers as he was buckled into a straightjacket and a spit hood was secured over his head. As the door locked shut, one of the offices capped the door slot with a thick rubber, magnetic seal. Paddy could spend the remainder of the night employing any tactic of manipulation he liked. Soon, the sounds of the storm faded over the dark horizon, and the jailhouse was quiet.

Ronnie looked up from her computer screen and over at the office clock. "Damn, it's almost three," she called out to her brother Tom who was reading the paper in the adjacent office.

"No kidding!" he remarked.

"How 'bout you put on a fresh pot of coffee and I'll make rounds?" she suggested.

Tom folded the paper closed and laid it on his desk as he stood up and stretched his arms.

"Naw, I'll do the coffee and the rounds, you stay put," he said as he walked into the front room.

Ronnie was engaged in a game of computer solitaire and happy to oblige. A moment later, she looked up when Tom exclaimed, "Oh, oh!" He was looking out the window toward the covered picnic tables.

"I think you need to handle this one!" He bent over the counter to get a better view of the dimly lit concession area. Ronnie slid her chair back and joined him at the window.

"Oh man, we've got trouble!" she said. "You better stay inside, I'll get it!" She grabbed a stack of clean towels off the chair by the door and the keys to the storage room from the hook on the wall as she flew through the office door and out toward Jill.

"OK sweetie, let's get you cleaned up and back to bed before the bad boys get wind of all this."

Poor Jill was a bloody mess. She apparently had started her menstrual period and ruined her pants and blouse. She had blood on both hands and was standing in front of the Coke machine running her fingers along the back-lighted graphics. She had outlined the picture of the soda cup and several of the words in blood.

Ronnie led her into the shower room and turned the hot water on.

"So, Cheryl says you're from Provo, Utah. Pretty country out there I guess."

Jill smiled and squirted the water into the air with her mouth as Ronnie gently washed and then dried her off. She took her into the storage room where she picked out clean underwear, blue jeans, and a tropical shirt with pink flamingos and a coconut palm print. Before putting on the clothes, Ronnie gave her a box of tampons. Jill seemed confused so Ronnie helped her with the applicator. After she was dressed, Ronnie led her back to her cot and had her lie down.

"OK Sugar, now you stay in bed till wakeup or I'll have to kick you out of here." Ronnie had not tried to make much conversation with Jill while she attended to her problem. She could tell there was something missing. She had learned over the years not to get too involved with the clients, otherwise, they become dependent. After scrubbing down the Coke machine, she re-joined Tom who handed her a cup of coffee as she came through the door.

"Man, I'm glad you're here," he confessed as she sat back down to her card game.

"Yeah well, how 'bout a raise?" she joked as she threw her leg up on the corner of the desk and lit a cigarette.

"I'm not that glad!" he responded with a laugh.

Several of the guests were already dressed and gathering around the tables when Tom came out of the office and flipped the lights on and called out, "OK guys, have a nice day." He unlocked the padlock on the gate and kicked it open for them to head out. He didn't recognize Jill as she passed by him and exited the compound. He had not been able to get a good view of her face in the darkness earlier and was not on the property when she had checked in the night before. She left with the first crowd and seemed to blend in as the shadows of the night lingered.

The full moon was hanging in the morning sky and the stars were still blinking brightly. The storms had passed into the west and puddles of water filled the road. The drains from the roof of the jail were pouring into the parking lot. As the morning lights came up, you could hear the clanging of cell doors and the shouts of inmates as they rushed to their showers. A dark blue Crown Victoria turned up the winding drive from College Road, headed toward the sheriff's office. The windows were blackened out and a tiny antenna at the top of the rear window identified it as an unmarked police car. Officer Dixon always reported to the office at six a.m. Muster was at seven and he usually had lots of preparation to do before addressing the day's assignments with his men. As he rounded the second bend in the road the first group of shelter guests walking toward town passed by. Jill was walking alone between the first and the second group. She watched the car pass but kept walking. Officer Dixon was lost in planning his day as he pulled under the building, grabbed his briefcase, and headed for his office on the second floor of building number two.

Jill followed the group of men as they made a right turn at the end of the road and headed across the Cow Key Bridge. She seemed completely oblivious to the events of the day before, when she lost her little yellow car to the outgoing tide. She had slept less than two hours but felt fully rejuvenated and infused with energy as she stared out across the Gulf of Mexico and felt the breeze kiss her on the cheek.

"Have you seen Chastity?" Cheryl asked Ronnie when she found her loading the washer with its second load of last night's dirty sheets.

"Yeah well, let me tell you 'bout your friend Chastity." Ronnie grumbled as she poured in a scoop of soap powder. "Don't bring her back here until she gets straightened out. I don't have the time to babysit these people."

Cheryl had slept through the night's episode and had no clue as to why Ronnie had reached this decision. She felt no authority to address the issue further and simply asked, "Have you seen her?"

She had already searched every corner of the shelter and had come up with nothing. She was concerned for her newfound stray and genuinely worried about her safety.

"She left with the first batch about a half hour ago," Ronnie barked the answer with enough attitude to tell Cheryl she was not interested in addressing the issue further. Cheryl quietly shrunk two sizes in her dress as she turned back toward the tent.

"I'm sorry, Ronnie," she offered as she headed to retrieve her personal belongings and head out for the day. As she stepped through the gate, she said a silent prayer that maybe today would be the day her new apartment would be ready to move into. She was so tired of this homeless thing. It was almost too much for her to bear.

"Hi, what can I get for you this morning?" the girl in the green apron cheerfully greeted Salvia from across the counter.

"I'll have a cinnamon dolce latte and chocolate biscotti please." Salvia turned her head and scanned the little Starbucks coffee shop to see if Jill had shown up and was already waiting for her at a table.

"That will be four eightyseven."

Salvia handed the girl a five-dollar bill and tossed another single in the tip jug. A minute later she took her drink and headed over to a table for two by the front window. She pulled back the clear plastic wrapper of the biscotti and grabbed her phone from her purse. The girls had traded numbers at the surf shop the day before and Salvia had already recorded Jill's first name as the contact.

The phone rang four times. "I'm sorry; the Verizon Wireless customer you are trying to reach is unavailable at this time. If you would like to leave a message please push 'one.'"

Salvia pushed 'one' and listened to the announcement. "I'm sorry, but the mailbox for (305) 5552778 is full. Please try your call at a later time. Thank you!" She slipped her phone back into her purse and took a bite of her biscotti. Her latte was still too hot to sip so she dipped the cracker into the cup and blew on it before putting it in her mouth.

She soon resolved herself to the reality that Jill was not going to show and started watching the people on the sidewalk as they strolled by. It was almost seven thirty a.m. when she finished her coffee and headed out the door for work. She was disappointed that Jill had not recognized the value of developing a new friendship with someone like herself, someone so sincere, so honest, and so dependable when needed by a friend. It had happened before, it would probably happen again.

Comme ci, Comme ca!

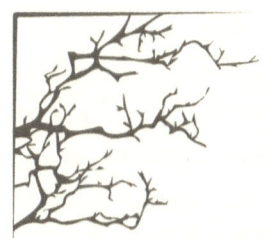

20. Cut 'Im Loose

Sergeant Dixon stepped out of the elevator and rounded the corner as he headed for his office. He could hear his desk phone ringing through the closed door. Inside, he dropped his briefcase in the chair by the wall and hung his holster on the hat rack as he answered, "Dixon!" He recognized the corrections officer's voice and felt sure the call was related to the recently arrested Patrick Oran Broslen (aka Paddy).

"Good morning, serge! We need to do something about your boy, Paddy." Omar Townsend was on the line.

He was calling from the second floor of the jail across the parking lot. Sergeant Dixon turned and stood behind his desk looking out his window as he listened to the C.O.'s complaint.

"He's in serious detox and I've got half my staff tied up keeping him from killing himself. I just wondered if you've got a plan in the making for this guy."

In the corner of Officer Dixon's office was an A/V cart with a TV and a VCR loaded and ready to play for Jill at her 8:30 appointment. Officer Dixon had already viewed the security footage of her and Paddy loading a yellow Volkswagen trunk with liquor on Monday morning and he concluded that there was no reason to believe that Paddy had committed a crime against the girl. On the grounds that she seemed under no duress throughout the entire shopping spree, and that she appeared to be a willing participant, and that there had been no formal filing of a complaint, he gave Omar his answer.

"Cut 'im loose," he said. "I'll fax the release papers over in just a minute." Then he added, "Emphasize that he needs to cut back on the drinking. He won't even remember why we picked him up."

Omar had worked under Sergeant Dixon's supervision as a patrolman for almost two years and had an unending respect for the man. After taking a fourinch blade into his upper right arm during an arrest, he had lost all feeling in his hand and was temporarily assigned as the detention center's Inmate Logistics Coordinator. Thanks to weekly physical therapy sessions, his progress gave him the hope that he might soon return to his regular duty assignment.

"You got it, Serge! Thanks!"

Officer Dixon glanced at his watch as he finished up the final minutes of the Thursday morning briefing with his men. He had spent more time than usual due to an announcement and subsequent questions concerning necessary reassignments due to the wrapping up of the annual speedboat race. His past experience gave him a much-warranted reason to expect an increase in crime as the celebratory partying got underway, and he knew he could depend on his men to remain flexible and ready for anything.

At 8:27 he walked out the briefing room door and headed toward the front of the building. The sheriff's office, like the jail across the parking lot, is appropriately built to accommodate the storm surges that frequently wash over the island after hurricanes. There are no facilities on the ground floor other than egress enclosures that protect the stairwells and elevator shafts. In the event of a serious washout, the entire complex could survive for weeks as a waterbound island of concrete and steel. The floor to the first level was twenty feet above, and parking under the building offered protection from the hot sun.

To enter the building, a visitor must ride the elevator or climb the stairs. Entering the receiving area for the sheriff's office is sometimes a startling experience. The elevator doors open into a very small room, delivering the visitors directly in front of a thick, bulletproof, Plexiglas booth. Security cameras scrutinize from every angle. Solid steel doors with electronic coding access panels and small reinforced viewing windows stand on each side of the booth. The receptionist sits safely behind the counter and communication to the lobby is facilitated through an intercom system. The building is a modern-day fortress designed to protect and defend the people who are sworn to protect and defend.

"Rita, I'm expecting a Jillian Dougherty any minute."

Officer Dixon always prepped Reception if he expected visitors. He felt it was a security issue as well as a courtesy that should be employed by everyone in the office. Awareness of the environment removes the element of surprise. It was a fundamental principle he had always taught to his recruits at the academy.

"Thank you, sir, I'll buzz you as soon as she gets here." Rita knew every angle of the business. She was the hub of the wheel as far as the sergeant was concerned. After twelve years of dedicated service, she had given notice that she and her husband were selling their home and moving back to the hills of Tennessee. They had purchased a beautiful parcel of land in the foothills of the Smoky Mountains where they planned to build their dream home. The guys in the office had already thrown her a retirement party and hired a local artist to construct a comical shadowbox commemorating the fun times they had working together. The box hung on the wall in the hall directly behind her desk and was often the subject of reflection and laughter as the officers and staffers gathered to enjoy the montage of memorabilia overlaid with photos of each of them in funny poses.

The good memories ran deep; she would be heartily missed by all. Officer Dixon stood at his window looking down over the turnaround

between the two buildings as he sipped coffee from his academy instructor's mug. He watched Paddy exit the jail elevator and stumble down the sidewalk toward the quarry stone memorial fountain that had been erected in dedication of past fallen Monroe County police officers. He studied the little imp's antics as he struggled to step over the curbs without falling face-first onto the pavement. There was no mistaking it, Paddy was full of fury. With fists raised high in the air, he turned toward the jail building and yelled defiantly toward the second floor.

Walking backwards across the pavement, he fell into the grass when he backed into the curb. Officer Dixon shook his head in disgust as he watched Paddy straighten himself and reseat his pink straw hat on his head. He sat pathetically swaying from side to side, checking periodically to see if anyone might be passing by from whom he might bum a cigarette.

Disappointed to find no prospects, he got up and climbed over the curb. Once fully erect he found himself looking up into the face of the towering bronze police officer that stood guard over the lost officers' memorial pond. After a moment of maniacal deliberation, he unzipped his zipper and fished for his man part. After a lengthy discharge of fluid, he upzipped his pants, stepped back one step, brought his scraggily body to as proper a military attention as possible, and ripped a salute to the looming monument. Officer Dixon grinned as he heard the other officers and detectives cheering, and laughing at the pitiful spectacle from their office windows. He sat back down and began prioritizing the mounds of paperwork and files on his desk. He loved his job, but hated the work.

"Hey pal, you wanna go get a bite to eat?" Tripp Hughes stuck his head into the doorway and asked.

The two men had worked together for almost ten years and periodically lunched together at the local spots.

Tripp was a retired U.S. Coast Guard criminal investigator who had moved down to remodel his family summer house on No Name Key. He and his longtime girlfriend, Maggie, had teamed up when they were both stationed in Miami. Now, they were each working on their second career at the Sheriff's Office. Tripp had always been a whiz with computers. He had established a repair service, working from his home when he first relocated to the Keys. Somehow, he screwed up. His reputation for solving the most difficult of I.T. problems landed him a referral to the Monroe County Sheriff where he now manages approximately two million dollars' worth of hardware and software.

Officer Dixon glanced at his watch and frowned as he answered, "It's almost two o'clock! Man, I'd love to, but I'm buried here for another hour. You better go without me this time. Thanks, though!"

"Did that video I set up for you yesterday work out OK?" Tripp asked. The day before he had directed one of his technicians in the A/V department to transfer the VHS surveillance tape from Bone Island Liquor to a digital disk so Carl could show it to Jill.

"Oh yeah, I checked it out last night. It was perfect! Thanks!"

"So, what'd the girl say?" Tripp asked.

"What, you saw the clip?" Carl asked with surprise.

"Damn right! I always go over my boys' work before you guys get it. What? You think I wanna catch the blame if the chief sits down to a blank screen? How long do you think they'd keep me around if that was the quality of work I put out?" Tripp was proud of his work. He had a right to be. It was good!

"She was a no-show. I figured she would be though. Nobody wants to face up when they know they've been caught in a lie," advised the officer.

"Yeah! Amen to that." Tripp added, "I'll catch you later, buddy."

"Hey, how 'bout pulling my door for me, will ya?" Carl asked his friend as he left the office.

"You bet! Don't work too hard now." Tripp left his friend to his demanding responsibilities and headed off down the corridor.

After a few more minutes of reviewing work schedules, Officer Dixon leaned back in his leather chair, locked his hands behind his head, and stared at his favorite mentor. The second ceiling tile from the corner was about to speak and Carl was ready to listen.

"Ok, give it up! What's not right here?" The officer mentally cleared his desk and imagined a paper roadmap stretched out across it from edge to edge. On the left edge of the map he envisioned the words, START HERE. A small red circle encapsulated the little liquor store. A tiny toy yellow VW bug was parked at the front door. The hood was up. Three people were inside the store; Roger, Jillian Dougherty, and Paddy. The day was Monday, three days ago.

The officer reached his right hand into his side desk drawer and pulled out two remote controls. He pushed the red button on the Panasonic control, the TV gave out a click, then powered up. He pointed the second remote a little lower and pushed the other red button. The DVD player powered up and on the green screen he read the words, DISK READY FOR VIEWING. He pushed the PLAY button and set the remotes on the desktop.

Returning his hands to their previous interlocking position behind his head, he lifted his feet over the edge of his desk and crossed them, left shin over right as he reviewed the video again. This time, he was looking for clues. Somehow, he felt Paddy had to be up to something. The question that was eating at him was what? Almost every day, if he had not done so before noon,

Sergeant Dixon tried to be in the field by three p.m. He would cruise the island listening to the service calls on his police radio and pull up alongside his patrol officers as they responded. This raised the communities' impression that the police had a cohesive and well supported system in place to defend them against crime. The patrolmen were always happy to see their boss on the scene. It yielded substance to their fraternal order and trust that they could depend on his support.

As the sergeant came to the stop sign at the end of the drive, he could see the edge of the hospital building and the Trauma Star Helicopter on its pad. He could see the entrance to the emergency room but the rest of the building was obscured by mangrove trees. He thought for a second, then, turned toward the hospital.

"May I help you officer?" the intake clerk at the E.R. window asked. "Yes please, I believe you have a nurse named Jillian Dougherty working somewhere in the hospital?" he asked.

"Let me get you a supervisor, just one minute." The girl walked through the door behind her desk and as she returned, the supervisor entered the lobby through the employee's only door and introduced herself as she offered him her hand.

"Hi, I'm Susan Sessions. I'm the night shift supervisor and I believe you and I have met. Aren't you Barbara Dixon's husband Carl?" The nurse was absolutely, charming as she greeted the officer.

"Oh yes," Officer Dixon returned with a smile."We sat with you and your husband at the Children's Relief banquet last year. George, isn't that your husband's name?"

"That's right, good memory." The nurse wrapped her arms across her clipboard and leaned against the door frame as she offered, "What can I help you with?"

"I need to get in touch with a nurse that I believe is on staff here," he explained.

"What's her name?" asked Mrs. Sessions.

"Jillian Dougherty," he answered.

"Oh yes, she's been with us about two months and was just assigned to the emergency unit on Monday. She was supposed to be here by now. No one's seen her and I haven't gotten a call. Is there something we need to know about?"

"Nothing I'm aware of," he said.

"I had recovered her bank cards and just had a question or two for her." He reached into his top shirt pocket and retrieved a business card. He held it out for her to grasp and as she did, he asked, "When you see her could you ask her to give me a call?"

"Absolutely, but, between you, me, and the clock on the wall, I'm not so sure that she's going to last here much longer," the supervisor offered her opinion.

"Why's that?" The officer asked.

"Oh, I think she may be flying back to 'The Nest' if you catch my drift," she answered.

"Well, if by chance you see her would you give her my card?"

She took the card and ran her thumb over the raised gold badge in the corner then responded, "Of course, I'll be happy to." She lifted her hand for him to shake and smiled as she added, "It's so nice to see you again, Carl. Please tell Barb I'll be in touch real soon."

"You bet! Thank you!" he said as he turned and waved across the lobby to a young mother with two little boys. One of the boys had his hand wrapped in a bloody white towel and his eyes were red and swollen. Both boys lit up with excitement as the monster of a man finished his wave and walked out of the building through the double doors. It's not every day that a superhero walks by, and a day to remember if he throws you a high five.

It had been almost two weeks since Jill last returned a call to her mother. The phone connection had been terrible and Jill had told her mother that she was about to put her phone in the shop to see if it could be tweaked for a better signal. Mrs. Dougherty wasn't particularly concerned that Jill had not responded to the letter she had mailed one week earlier. The last she knew, Jill was working the night shift and assumed she was sleeping in the daytime. Still, she made regular calls to Jill's phone number to see if the problem had been solved. She had left one message on Sunday morning but ever since then, the recording had said Jill's voicemail box was full.

Everything was going well back in Gloucester. Jillian's sister Katrina was working hard at the ice cream shop every day with her dad. Bo was in summer school for the second year. At sixteen, he was into everything that causes a parent to lose sleep. If not for his love of sports, he probably would have been a dropout by now. If the Dougherty's could hang in there for two more years without choking him to death, they hoped he would get his bearings and maybe a scholarship to boot.

Still, there was no need to be worried about their loving joychild Jill. She was on her own and flying high. At least, that's what everyone back in Gloucester, Massachusetts thought.

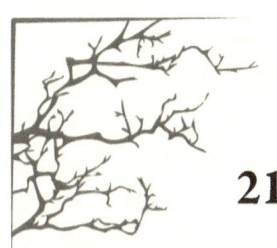

21. Yellow Submarine

"**T**yson!" **Gilbert Conrad Haley** called out to his son from up on his boat's flying bridge where he was securing the outriggers to the mounts on each side of the cabin roof.

"Yeah Dad?" came the response from inside the dockside utility shed behind the house.

"Grab the old blue sled off the top shelf over the dryer. If the new one snaps we can use it as a backup."

"Got it Dad!" Tyson's voice boomed from the open shed door.

The two-day sport lobster season would be starting in twentynine more days and every bug chaser from Key West to Coconut Grove would be scouting out their favorite hunting grounds. Tyson was home for the summer after completing his third year at Stanford. Following in his father's footsteps as a trial lawyer seemed a lifetime away as the two prepared for a day on the water. The dive tanks sported the green and yellow labels, '*NITROX*', the fishing poles were secured in the gunnels rod holders, the spear guns were hanging in the overhead rack, the gas tanks were full, and the beer and sandwiches were in the cooler. They were ready to shove off.

The engine exhaust boiled up through the emerald green water as Tyson threw the line over the transom and jumped on board. He retrieved the two white fenders that hung from the port side and pushed against the wooden dock until the heavy boat was clear.

"Ok, Dad!" he called out to his father who was at the controls up on the flying bridge. He grabbed the stainlesssteel ladder rails and pulled himself up. Seconds later, the two suntanned men were cutting through the canal headed for the pass that would lead them out to their favorite dive spot. A perfect day! No storms, no wind, no women, and visibility as high as it gets.

Gil's eyes were glued to his Garmin depth finder's screen, watching the profile of the bottom as it rose and fell across the reef below. "We're coming up on the humps in just a minute," he announced. "Go get ready to drop anchor when I tell you." Tyson launched himself from the bridge and hit the lower deck. In a flash, he was standing at the bow with the anchor in one hand and the rope coiled in the other.

"Can you see 'em?" his dad called out from topside as the boat slowly drifted forward across the glassy water.

Tyson lifted his glasses from over his eyes to try to get a better view, and then dropped them back in place.

"Just off to the right."

"There they are!" Tyson excitedly announced. He leaned over the railing and gently lowered the anchor to the sandy bottom.

The ancient coral heads had formed hundreds of thousands of years ago. They were originally attached to the huge colony of coral that now forms the bedrock of the islands that lie off the southern tip of Florida. The men were exactly one-mile due north of the Cow Key Channel and from the boat they could see the cars on U.S. 1, passing over the bridge and heading into Key West. A short look to their left and they could see the sheriff's office and the jail that towered over the mangrove trees along the shore. These veteran divers always went to great lengths to protect the coral heads from being damaged by an illplaced anchor. Gil killed the engines and joined his son at the bow where they surveyed the area for the best approach to the humps below. At a depth of twentyfive feet, visibility was the best it could be. The tide was slack and they both quivered with anticipation. Among the rocks below they saw the familiar hordes of tropical fish. Though these particular, coral heads had been dead since the midnineties, they still provided safe-haven to the many species of fish and crustaceans that these two avid sportsmen loved to hunt.

As they donned their dive gear and purged their regulators, they discussed their dive plan. Gil grabbed the clear watertight bag that kept the diver down records. He had already drawn a map of the area and together the two men discussed which heads they would explore and in which order. As the decisions were made, Gil recorded the path on the map. He slipped the plan into the watertight bag and clipped it to the steering wheel at the helm. If they were separated from their boat, this would lead rescuers toward their possible location.

Tyson raised the dive flag while Gil set his new Sea View digital camera over the side and checked his spear gun to assure it was not loaded. Tyson checked his spear gun and over the side they went. Face to face, they checked their airflow and gear. Once satisfied, they each signaled thumbs up, blew out their buoyancy bladders, and disappeared into the silent world below. Their first order of business was to survey the best lobster hideouts so that on day one of open season they could be ready to beat the crowds. Gil had mounted his camera housing on an extendable handle that gave him an extra thirtysix inches of reach. This would prove to be an invaluable decision. While Tyson rounded the huge coral head chasing after a twentyinch hog snapper, Gil studied the bottom edge for access points to the inside.

Caribbean spiny lobsters are vulnerable night travelers. They sneak along the dark ocean floor feeling their way with their two long sensitive antennas, searching for anything to lock their jaws around. A favorite delight of the stingray, the bonnet head shark, and the nurse shark, they seek refuge during the daylight hours underneath the seemingly impregnable coral heads. From the outside, no one could see that the oldest of the dead coral heads, or 'Dead Heads' as they are called by divers who wish to identify themselves with a reference to the famous rock band *The Grateful Dead*, have dissolved from the inside, to create a dome where the lobster hide in great numbers. If a diver is able to find an access point large enough to inject one arm, a flashlight and his head under the edge of the coral, he will be amazed to find sometimes dozens of lobsters clinging to the ceiling like cave bats. Many a dive boat has met its catch limit by shoving a cotton floor mop under such a head, and waiting for the long threads to entangle themselves around the spiny creatures' antenna, then extracting as many as eight or ten with one smooth pull. In past years, this technique of catching lobster was a well-practiced technique. Now, if caught employing such a practice, a diver can win a thirty-night stay in the big house on College Road and a hefty fine to boot.

Gil found the cave entrance he was looking for and flipped his camera upside down. He carefully stabilized himself on his knees and took the remote cable in his free hand. He gently slipped the camera under the edge of the coral far enough to assure it was halfway through and in the middle. He pushed the trigger with his thumb and a flash of light burst from the edge of the coral head. Two more shots to be sure and he moved off to the next head. Later, on his laptop, he would record the picture numbers on the map of the dive so they would know which heads housed the greatest number of mature lobster.

He retrieved his gear from the underwater cave and proceeded to head #2. Tyson passed his dad on his way back to the boat. As he glided past, he tapped on his air tank with the butt of his spear gun to get his father's attention. Gil looked up and tucked his index finger under his upturned thumb as a signal of approval for the beautiful hogfish with the steel rod through its side. A few minutes later as he was setting up his camera, Tyson passed by on his way toward a second kill.

The cooler now held two black grouper and four hog snapper. The two divers sat in the fighting chairs on the back of the boat enjoying their turkey sandwiches and cold beer. The afternoon sun was leaning to the west and the sky was beginning to change its colors from frosted blues to tangerine. Gil had removed his camera from its protective acrylic case and was paging through the shots.

"Oh man!" he said as he handed the camera over to his son. "This is gonna be a great year."

The two men relaxed for a while, passing the camera between them. There were several shots of Tyson with fish on the end of his spear and lots and lots of pictures of lobsters. They reminisced of summers past when they would come down to the family summer home to fish. Tyson would someday inherit the house and continue the tradition with his sons. Each year in October, Gil's mom and dad come down from Cincinnati to escape the cold weather and then return home the first week of April. There was nothing they didn't love about life. They were a family surrounded by blessings and they appreciated every one of them.

"You ready to skid?"

Gil asked his son. "You bet! Let her fly!" Tyson reached into the storage box under the transom and retrieved his father's newly constructed toy. Unlike the old sleds that were made of wood or fiberglass, Gil cut this one out of a scrap piece of one-inch thick Corian left over from when his dad had the kitchen rebuilt. It was wider than others and instead of the ski rope being tied to a hole in the front; he cut a trough halfway through the board and mounted a stainless 'O' ring that had a clip connected to it. The Corian was more flexible than other materials and Gil hoped that this design might be much more maneuverable.

The engines rumbled as Tyson pulled in the anchor and stored it under the hatch. Gil idled out into deeper water and knocked the engines into neutral.

"Ok, you know the routine," he called out to Tyson who was situating his mask and snorkel for a tight seal. The young athlete picked up the skid and dropped off the transom with a huge splash then turned around and faced the back of the boat as he uncoiled the ski rope. Kicking forward with his flippers he stretched the rope until he was fifty feet behind the boat. One last check of his mask and he raised his right fist into the air over his head. He kicked his thumb out to signal he was ready and, as his dad put the boat in gear, Tyson disappeared below the surface of the water.

Many a bloody face has been treated in the emergency room as a result of this undersea sport. Grossly disfigured teenagers spend the rest of their lives hiding their scars after meeting hidden coral heads face-first in the murky waters. It's like flying underwater. You lean the skid in whichever direction you want to go. Up, down, lean out hard left and hard right, it turns you in that direction. The fish fly by and sometimes the tarpon and dolphin try to race with you. You can do a rollover and fly upside-down. The faster the boat goes, the more responsive the skid is. It's not a game for kids though. Extremely dangerous! But, in the hands of a skilled diver being pulled by an experienced captain on a beautiful day in July, with visibility of over eighty feet and a cooler full of fish, it was a great way to cap off a day on the water with dad.

Gil stood at the controls on the flying bridge where he had a perfect view and solid command of the boat if an emergency should arise. As they sliced through the clear water, he could see the rock piles and coral heads long before Tyson was close enough to collide. He maneuvered the boat between the obstacles with masterful finesse then turned to watch Tyson mimic the maneuver on the skid. It was poetic art, an experience to cherish for a lifetime.

Gil was proud of his son and the relationship they had built was so like his and his father's. He wished these summer days could go on forever. He turned again to watch Tyson burn a bubble trail through the water. They were a little over one mile offshore in the Gulf. The depth finder on the console read twentysix feet. Gil was making a quick scan of the shoreline and had taken his eyes off the water for only a second. He never saw it as the hull of the boat passed directly over. If his eyes had been on the fishfinder he would have noticed the anomaly and changed his path. If he had been scanning the waters in front of the boat, it would have been obvious, but, he missed it. His only son was rapidly bearing down on what would soon become the most bizarre dive story of the summer.

Tyson hit the surface screaming his lungs out:

"Dad!"

"Dad!"

"Dad!"

Gil looked back to see the young man waving his arms frantically above his head. He threw the wheel to the left and made a wide circle, pulling the skid and the ski rope clear of the propellers on his way back to where Tyson was treading water. As he knocked the engines into neutral, he saw Tyson's flippers kicking the surface of the water as they propelled him toward the bottom. The boat drifted over the site and Gill leaned across the guardrail of the flying bridge to get a better view. He watched as Tyson placed his hands firmly on the window frame of a yellow Volkswagen Beetle, and pushed his head into the cab. Gil hurried to the bow and dropped the anchor. By the time that he got to the back of the boat, Tyson was climbing over the transom gabbing a mile a minute.

"Damn, Dad! It's a V.W. Bug!" His words were broken by gasps for air. "It's full of sand up to the seats."

He leaned against the gunwale as he slipped off his flippers and dropped them on the deck next to his mask. He supported his upper body with his hands on his thighs while he bent his head low toward his knees.

"Breathe son!" his dad calmly directed him.

Tyson was too excited. He kept breaking through his breaths with more descriptive explanations of what he had seen. "It looks like the strap of a purse." He again was gasping for air.

"Take a minute son, there's no hurry. Just breathe," his dad continued to encourage.

"OK, I'm OK!" Tyson was gaining on himself and sitting up more comfortably.

When he recovered, he laughed loudly and said, "Oh, man that was such a rush! I never expected to come up on a 'bug' like that. I mean, really, here we are hunting for bugs and what do we find? A Bug! A yellow one, too!"

The irony of the discovery brought them both to hysterics. Gil opened two Coronas and handed one to his son. They moved into the fighting chairs and laughed as they mulled over the events of the day. Tyson wanted to have a picture taken of him sitting in the driver's seat so, after they rested for a few more minutes, they put on their dive gear and descended on the mysterious discovery. Tyson had to take off his tank to squeeze through the open window, but after several tries, they got a series of shots that they felt captured the moment, and returned to the boat.

When they got back to the house Tyson started setting up the gear while his dad went into the shed and rolled out the pressure washer. After a thorough freshwater washdown, the two men stood side by side filleting the days catch and tossing the scraps to the pelicans that hung out in numbers around the tethered boats.

"Hey, how 'bout throwing the good pieces over here!" Harold and his wife Joanne, "Jo" for short, had lived across the canal from Gil's father's house since they had retired thirty years before. His old boat *The KoKoMo Joe* was a fortyfoot motor yacht built in 1937 and meticulously restored. It was Harold's pride and joy. It was a favorite at all the boat parades and an award winner in the Christmas parade at least seven times over the years.

"Now you quit feeding those damn birds or I'll have to get out my twelve-gauge and pepper your ass with some of my special salt and jalapeño recipe," Harold jokingly called out across the canal.

The guys laughed. They'd heard the same threat for years and knew Harold had been feeding those same birds since they hatched. Hell, they were his birds, according to Gil's dad. Besides, when the bird crap built up thick enough to stink, Harold had the keys to their shed and used their pressure washer to clear the mess. The friendly banter was merely the mortar that bound the neighborhood together; that and the hurricane parties. After dinner, Tyson removed the SanDisk from his dad's camera and loaded the pictures onto his laptop. They picked through the thumbnails and deleted the darkest copies. They corrected the orientations and loaded the pictures into a slide show, then set the laptop on top of the barbeque grill and smoked cigars as they enjoyed the presentation.

"Hey," Tyson said to his dad. "I think I'll email the pictures of me in the Bug to Mandy and see if she can get them in the *Mast Head*."

Mandy Bolen was an old family friend who had been hired as a circulation desk clerk for the local paper, *The Key West Citizen*. She and Tyson had met when he was a high school senior and worked there as an editor's assistant. The *Mast Head* is a popular department at *The Citizen* that offers local residents the opportunity to submit their photographs to be considered for publication as the '*Mast Head*' at the top of the front page of the paper. Many of the photos selected are comical in nature and Tyson felt sure Mandy, who was now a staff writer, could get his pictures through to the right people in charge of the selection process. It was close to midnight when he sent a note to Mandy and attached the pictures.

Officer Dixon had just finished the morning briefing and returned to his desk. He sifted through the stacks of papers to find the fifteen time sheets clipped together by a purple paperclip and slid the clip from the top. Upon his completion of review, he signed the bottom approval and moved to the next stack.

"Hey bud, you doin' lunch today?" Tripp was making his morning rounds of the office.

Carl leaned back and stretched as he said, "If I can catch up on some of this paperwork I'm supposed to meet Barb and drive her up to the *Rain Barrel* to shop for Christmas gifts."

"Man, she sure likes to get the jump on that stuff." Tripp grinned as he said, "By the way, don't you get the electronic version of *The Citizen*?"

"Yeah! Why?" Carl curiously answered

"Pull it up! You gotta see this!" Tripp moved to the side of Carl's desk and the two men watched the screen as the front page of the paper came up. Once the full page finished loading Carl asked, "What am I looking for?"

"Hang on! Just keep watching."

Tripp raised his hand toward the top of the screen and waited as the digital images in the upper right-hand corner scrolled through the day's *Mast Head* entries.

Several scenic beach shots, a picture of two wild iguanas, some birds in a banana tree, then, "There!"

Tripp flicked his finger at the picture of the diver sitting in the driver's seat of a yellow V.W. Bug. Underwater!

A sobering thought blanketed the officer's mind. The sight shocked him deeply as he considered the possibility. He looked up at Tripp who stood grinning at the discovery.

"Ya think?" Tripp asked as he stood with his hands in his pockets, proudly smiling that his investigative juices were always ready to turn over anything suspicious he uncovered. Years of case work with the Miami Coast Guard taught him that mystery hides in the most obscure places.

"I don't know. This is weird. Can we get a closer look at it?" Officer Dixon and Tripp were both exploring the possibility that this submerged car may be the same car they had been viewing for the past two days on the video.

"Let me get in here a minute," Tripp said as Carl slid out of his chair and Tripp sat down. Seconds later, Tripp had followed the link to the photo gallery section and pulled up the submissions for the past week.

"There, three pix, submitted by Tyson J. Haley." Tripp read aloud the inscription text.

"Big Bug Ready For Takin."

"Can you get me a bigger view of this one here?" Carl pointed to the last picture in the group. The photographer had moved to the front of the vehicle and the shot had been taken through the windshield. Tripp pulled his flash drive from his pocket and popped the clip off the top. He plugged it into the USB slot and sent a copy of the picture to the drive unit. He closed the *Citizen* link and transferred the photo into the PhotoSmart file. Once it finished loading he clicked on *TOOLS* and a little magnifying glass cursor appeared.

"Have at it!" Tripp exclaimed as he slid out of the chair.

Carl situated himself to study the screen closely. He adjusted his eyeglasses and leaned forward in the chair. He hoped that what he was looking for was not there. He was afraid to think that it might be. As he slid the cursor across the image, a large bubble followed the movement, magnifying it enough to count the fibers on the front seat upholstery. There, in the righthand corner of the rear window, the faintest image of an upsidedown peace sign.

"Oh, God!" He fell back into his chair and took his glasses off his tired eyes. "It's the same car," he said as he adjusted his stare beyond Tripp's face and upon ceiling tile #2.

"This had to have been taken since Monday." He looked at Tripp as he lifted his finger and pointed at the image on the screen.

"I need to find that car!" he exclaimed.

Tripp unplugged his flash drive and stuck it back in his pocket, then turned toward the door. Before exiting he turned and leaned in toward his friend and said, "Shoot, that's the easy part. The car ain't goin anywhere!"

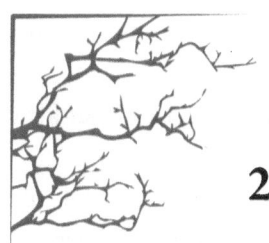

22. Tag It and Bag It

"**G**ood morning! How may I help you?" the Lower Keys Hospital receptionist cheerfully offered.

"Emergency Room, please." Officer Dixon pulled out a fresh legal pad and slipped it into his leather field notebook as he balanced the phone against his left ear with his shoulder.

"Emergency Room, may I help you?"

"Susan Sessions, please!" he requested.

"I'm sorry sir, Ms. Sessions reports in at three. Is there someone else that can help you?" the girl asked.

"Could you transfer me over to the personnel department please?" Officer Dixon asked the girl.

"Yes sir, transferring you now. Have a nice day!"

He began scribbling names, phone numbers, and notes on the yellow pad. Off to the right side, he recorded the time each contact was made. When he connected with the hospital personnel director, she verified that the last time Jillian had clocked in or out was two days earlier, Wednesday. She left at 4:06 p.m., and had failed to clock in for work on Thursday. Officer Dixon understood that if he was unable to find anyone who could verify that Jillian had been seen after 4:06 p.m. Wednesday, then after 4:06 p.m. today, she could be reported as missing.

"Hey, Babe, I hate to have to tell you this, but, I'm gonna have to put off our shopping trip until next week." He held his cell phone to his ear and felt the disappointment in his wife's voice as he gave her the news. They talked for another moment then he was hit with an idea.

"Say," he said, "have you got any information on that girl that lost her credit cards the other day, Jillian Dougherty?"

"Yeah, right here!" Barb answered as she accessed Jillian's account information.

"Is there a problem?" She was always interested in being at the start of a good scandal or news story.

"Probably not, but, I need to ask her a few questions concerning her little episode with Paddy."

He knew she was going to fish it out of him so he went ahead and told her the basics of his concern. He didn't even bother to advise her to keep the info under hat. Years of marriage taught him that would be like asking the moon to get lost. It wasn't gonna happen. She read off the phone numbers Jillian had provided in her application. Her parents' names, numbers, and address, her own address, etc.

"When was the last account transaction?" he asked.

Barbara pulled up the two accounts and read off the most recent info.

"She pulled $200.00 out of her savings account on an ATM withdrawal transaction at 12:36 p.m. Wednesday." She went on reading from her computer. "Before that, she had a debit transaction for $193.14 at 10:21 a.m. the same day."

"Where were they from?" Carl asked.

"The last was at the hospital ATM on the second floor and the debit transaction was over at the Verizon Wireless store." She once again probed for tidbits of juicy info that she could pass to her friends.

"Is she in trouble?"

"No, darling!" he said with a certain expectation that she wouldn't believe him.

"She just missed her followup appointment yesterday and I need to wrap up the case against Paddy."

He really wanted to get back to his preliminary investigation and he was wasting time with Barbara.

"I'll tell you everything tonight over a glass of wine. It's nothing to be worried about."

Barb had already dialed Susan Session's home phone number on her desk phone as she was stuffing her cell in her purse.

Carl was scanning his 911 master matrix screens for an address for Tyson J. Haley. As he was copying the name 'Gilbert Conrad Haley' into his notebook, his cell phone rang.

"Hey doll, what's up?" he greeted his wife.

"She didn't report for work yesterday and she never called in," replied Barb. He wasn't surprised that she had followed up so quickly. "And, they haven't seen her since four p.m. Wednesday when she was sent home." Barbara was animated as she conveyed the information. "Susan said they're probably going to fire her since she is still on probation."

There was nothing else to tell him and she hung up without giving him a chance to tell her 'Thanks'. He laughed as he clipped his phone back on his belt. Grabbing his desk phone, he dialed the local number listed for Gilbert Haley and listened to it ring.

"Hello!" Gil answered.

"Good morning, this is Officer Carl Dixon with the Monroe County Sheriff's Office. Is this Mr. Tyson Haley?"

"That's my son." Gil answered. "Is there something I can help you with?" he asked.

Carl had an intuitive feeling that the father may have the answers he needed and he explained, "I'm calling in regard to some photographs of a yellow Volkswagen that were posted in this morning's edition of *The Citizen*. Is there any chance that you might be able to tell me the location of that vehicle?"

"Absolutely!" the man answered. "Are you calling from the office on Stock Island?" Gil asked.

Officer Dixon thought the question was odd but acknowledged that he was at the Stock Island office, and then asked, "Why do you ask?"

Gil walked out back to the boat where Tyson was sitting on the deck cleaning a regulator. He climbed up the ladder and then onto the console of the flying bridge and asked the officer, "Which side of the building are you on?"

Carl indulged the man and answered, "I'm on the front side of the building."

Gil then asked, "Do you have a window office?"

Officer Dixon was losing his patience but answered, "Yes, I do. Why do you ask?"

"Take a look out your window and I'll show you."

Carl slid his chair back so hard it knocked a hole in the plaster. He turned around and scanned the parking lot below, then asked the stranger on the phone, "Where are you?"

"See that blue tile roof over on Key Haven Road?"

Carl looked beyond the Municipal Marina and the community college buildings toward Key Haven and saw that only one house had

blue roof. He looked closer and saw Gil standing on top of his boat holding his phone to his ear.

"Is that you?" he asked with a chuckle.

"No asshole, I'm down at Hog's Breath drinkin' a beer. That's my idiot twin brother and he better get off my boat." The two of them broke into a mutual level of laughter and they both knew that a friendship was soon to develop.

"It's one mile straight out there." Gil pointed toward the open waters of the Gulf of Mexico and the sand flats behind the Sheriff's Office.

"Come on over and I'll put you on top of it in less than fifteen minutes." Carl was thrilled with the idea of being able to put his eyes on the vehicle so quickly and possibly get the GPS coordinates. Time was the most important element in solving a missing person's case and if he didn't come up with Jill before 4:06 p.m., things might get dicey.

"How 'bout twenty minutes?" he asked his new friend.

"Come on, I'm burning fuel as we speak." Gil replied as he tossed the phone to Tyson and said, "I think you may have cracked open something when you found that yellow Bug."

He slid back down the ladder and explained the plan to his son as they gathered up the beer bottles and trash. "Go put this stuff in the shed and get your dive gear. We're heading back out to show off your catch to the C.O.P.S.

"Officer Dixon grabbed his notepad and headed out the door. At the front office, he called out, "Rita, I'll probably be out for the rest of the day. If any emergencies come up, call me on my cell or tell dispatch." He turned toward the exit door and came face to face with Tripp.

"Hey bud, what's up?" Tripp asked.

"Go get your pole pal, it's fishin' time." Carl held the door open and gestured for Tripp to join him. They had many times in the past collaborated unofficially on investigative work. This was nothing new to Tripp and Carl was happy that his friend was going to be able to break away.

They pulled up in front of the house on Key Haven Road and walked the stone path around the side to the backyard. Tyson greeted them with a friendly handshake as the two men climbed aboard. Gil was topside at the controls and shouted down the ladder, "If you gentlemen are ready, we'll be on our way.

Tyson coiled the stern line and pushed the boat free from the dock. "All clear, Dad!"

As they motored down the canal Carl climbed the ladder while Tyson gave Tripp a tour of the boat. It was a 1998 35-foot Hatteras with modified twin diesel Cummings engines. It was one sweet ride. Gil recounted the events of the day before and how excited Tyson had been over the find. They never imagined the car might be part of a crime.

Carl explained that they had no evidence of a crime and merely needed to check the car for a tag. The two men shared their history and knew that this would not be the last boat ride they took together. Gil explained that his wife and daughter were due to fly in on the following Tuesday afternoon and that they might all go out for dinner sometime. The seeds were set for what promised to be many interesting and mutually rewarding times to come. For now, there was work to do.

Tyson was at the bow with the anchor ready as they slipped closer and closer to the site.

"Got it!" he called out as he carefully lowered the anchor over the side. All four men gathered at the transom as the tide pulled the boat backwards from its mooring. A perfect landing! Directly below them was the hood of the little yellow Bug. Tyson was downing his dive gear and readying himself to get to work.

Gil sat down in the fighting chair and asked, "Tyson can get the tag, but do you want him to try to get in the trunk?"

"Ya know," Carl thought aloud, "we better not interfere with too much at this point. I'm pretty sure we'll run a salvage team out here this weekend."

Tyson offered a bit more information, "I'm not positive but I think there is a purse buried in the sand right in front of the passenger seat. I pulled on a strap but it popped off. I could probably dig it out pretty easily."

Tripp and Carl looked at each other and agreed that this would be a great idea. Tripp suggested Tyson take a dive bag down so no evidence was lost to the current.

"See if you can get in the glove box, too," Carl suggested.

Tyson descended downward while the three men watched from above. His feet hit the ocean floor, then he made his way to the back of the car. After a few minutes of fanning the sand with his hand, the tag emerged. Grabbing the stainless-steel pliers and screwdriver from his dive pouch, he removed the two retaining screws, then turned the tag toward the men on the boat so that they could read the plate. It was a Massachusetts tag! Carl gave a 'thumbs up' and the boy placed it in the bag.

Tyson moved to the passenger's side window. Reaching in, he rolled it down the rest of the way, then opened the glovebox door. Some papers started floating out and he gathered them as they drifted with the current. There was a small bottle of yellow VW touchup paint that popped out of the glovebox and immediately ascended to the surface above. Gil retrieved it with the fishnet that was hanging from the rod rack. Tyson shut the glove-box door and began fanning at the sand that had filled the floorboard. Soon, he saw the zipper of a blue leather purse. The outside pocket revealed a cell phone. He finished fanning the sand and put the purse in the dive bag as curious little fish darted in and out of the car windows.

Once Tyson was back on deck, the men examined the retrieved items. Things were not looking good for Ms. Jillian Bethany Dougherty. It was 12:47 p.m. Friday afternoon, and so far, it seemed she may be somewhere out there, out in the Gulf of Mexico, feeding the fishes. The big, hungry fishes.

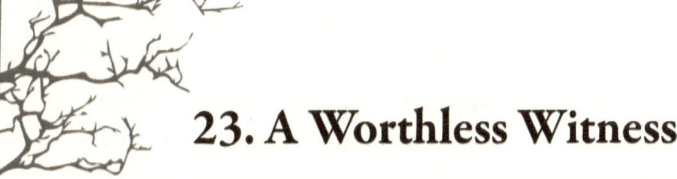

23. A Worthless Witness

On their way back to the station, Carl pulled off the road directly across the street from the hospital and stared at the entrance to the E.R. The late July temperature was a scalding 102 degrees and the air conditioner in his Crown Victoria was pumping a cold blast of air from the dashboard ports into the two men's faces. Carl turned to his friend Tripp and asked, "Why do you think her windows would have been down?"

"Maybe her A/C was broken," Tripp offered. This seemed like a good possibility and no surprise that it was Tripp's first idea. After all, he is the chief of the I.T. department and his focus is always on the "fix it or throw it out" way of doing things. Carl was scanning the building for surveillance cameras. There were two covering the helipad outside the E.R., three on the building, and two more mounted on light poles.

"You hungry?" he asked Tripp as he dropped the cruiser into drive and pulled across College Road and into the hospital parking lot.

"Am I never?" Tripp laughed as he answered. Carl parked the car in the "employee only" area that was just beyond the Trauma Star helicopter docked on its pad. The two men admired the hightech machine as they walked toward the entrance to the E.R. Carl stopped before going through the door and once again studied the orientation of the surveillance camera. He could see the tall buildings of the junior college across the street. Just below the roof line, at each corner of the building, he saw what he was looking for.

"I hear they have a mean pudding cup," he said to Tripp as he held the door open and slid his sunglasses into his shirt pocket.

They both laughed as they stepped into the air conditioning and headed for the elevator. They walked past the ATM machine in the hallway just outside the cafeteria. Carl gave it a look as if to tell it he knew about the $200 it had disbursed to Jill on Wednesday. Over a hot lunch of meatloaf, mashed potatoes, and steamed broccoli, the two friends went over the information they had thus far gathered.

Carl finished his lunch and as Tripp took his last swig of soda, he said, "I want to get a look at any surveillance cameras that might have caught her leaving here after she clocked out on Wednesday. You got time for this?" Tripp answered without reservation, "I'm on it man! Let's get it!"

They walked to the security office on the first floor and met with a man they both had met many times before. "Hey Casey, how's it going over here these days?" They shared some friendly catching up, and then got down to business. Casey scanned through the digital archives of the three cameras that might offer the greatest potential for viewing Jill's leaving on Wednesday, and minutes later they had two different angles of her car.

At 4:11 p.m., she had approached her car. She retrieved her keys from her pocket and opened the driver's door. She got into the front seat, and started the engine. She leaned over and rolled the passenger's window down halfway, got out of the car, rolled her window down while standing beside the door, she then turned toward the Trauma Star helicopter and ran between three rows of cars, then went off screen. A moment later, she got back in her car, turned left out of the parking lot, and headed slowly down College Road. "Can we get another angle and see what she did off-camera?" Tripp asked.

Casey pulled up the camera that covers the helipad and put in the date, then the time. Jill entered the screen from the upper left and ran to the front of the helicopter. She spread her arms out wide and with open palms said something to the front of the chopper. Then, to everyone's surprise, she hugged the front of the chopper and gave it a kiss. Tripp was the first to say it

."She's crazy! Ab-so-flunkin-lutly crazy!"

Casey and Tripp were laughing about the whole thing while Carl grabbed his chin with his hand and stared at the video.

"Look at this!" he said. "Go back!"

Casey moved the cursor to the left and the video showed her run off screen again toward her car. Then all they saw was the chopper, the first row of cars, and in the distance, in the upper left corner, they could see College Road and the corner of the parking lot on the college property.

"Keep watching!" Carl directed as he pointed into the mangrove trees that lined the perimeter of the college property and buffered the shared access road to the Municipal Marina and the sheriff's office.

"What? All I see is a bunch of trees." Tripp was getting impatient.

"There! Did you see that?" Carl excitedly pointed into the tiny cluster of bushes at the very top of the screen. "No! What?" Tripp responded.

"Hang on! Let me get in here for a second," Carl said as he slipped into the chair and put his hand on the mouse. He pulled the tracking bar back to the left once more and the video played forward. Again, there was nothing to see but the breeze moving through the mangrove leaves. Carl tapped on the pause button several times and the video crawled forward until all motion came to a full stop.

"There! You tell me this isn't the right door panel of a yellow VW."

He pulled his ink pen from his shirt pocket and pointed the tip toward a gap in the foliage.

"Ready?" he said slowly as the three men leaned into the screen.

"Watch this!" He triggered the play button and it was undeniable. A yellow door panel passed through the gap in the trees as it traveled up the approach toward the sheriff's office.

You would have thought the three were watching the Lakers beat the Rams as Tripp and Casey yelled with excitement and highfived each other.

"Get me copies of everything!" Carl told Casey. He dropped his business card on the desk and added, "There's my email address."

Casey gave the response Carl wanted to hear. "It's already on its way."

They drove slowly up the winding road. The mangroves on both sides blocked their view of everything except the tops of the highest buildings at the college. Carl hit the down buttons for all four windows. The car was instantly steaming from the humidity that rushed in. In seconds the powerful air conditioner of the police cruiser was rendered ineffective. The two men were drenched in sweat.

"You know what she was doing, don't you?" Carl asked Tripp.

"Oh yeah!" he answered with confidence. "She was cruisin'! Seein' the sights!"

"And what was she seeing at 4:30 p.m. on a hot July Wednesday afternoon?" Carl prompted his intuitive buddy, respectful of all the investigative experience that was packed in his head.

"Homeys! They're all dragging their nasty butts to the shelter to get a shower," he answered as he watched the white shelter tents come into view. They drove slowly past the tall chain link fence that encompassed the shelter compound. The heavy lock hung from a chain at the gate. Carl drove through the circle between the jail and their office and stopped the car.

"I've got a couple of errands to run.

"He looked off toward the shelter tents as he continued, "Can you get me the footage for Wednesday afternoon? I want to watch the rest of her little sightseeing cruise."

"You bet! It'll be on your system in less than thirty," said Tripp as the car door slammed shut.

Carl put the shifter in drive and left for the day. There was only one place he could think of that might allow a car to fall into the Cow Key Channel. That would be the Cow Key Bridge.

The traffic was light that time of day as he slowly drove across the bridge. He was looking for any sign that might indicate a car had hit the concrete railing and flipped over into the water below. There were no suspicious marks. He pulled off the road and stepped out of his car onto the lush green grass of the slope that leads down to the water's edge. He closed the door leaving the engine running and the air conditioner on full blast. It was hot! Damn hot!

He stood on the grassy knoll with his hands on his hips as he inspected the area. There were no apparent tire tracks that might confirm his suspicion, but, if there had been any, the heavy downpour on Wednesday night would have washed them away. He studied the trajectory from the road to the water. He concluded that Jill would have had to come off the pavement, take a 135degree right turn, and hit the granite boulders on the erosion bank at no less than twenty miles an hour in order for her car to be launched into the water.

He walked down the narrow footpath that the fishermen and homeless used to go under the bridge. Crouching by the water, he studied the leading edges of the rocks. It wasn't long before he came upon an area where several boulders had recently been impacted by something heavy. Closer inspection revealed at least five impact points where the granite chips had been knocked off.

He stood up and looked under the bridge. In the shadows, he could see two or three bodies curled up on cardboard beds used to insulate them from the sticky mud. He ducked his head as he walked into the dark cave and headed for the closest of the vagrants. He kicked the man's foot gently, then harder, and called out to him.

"Hey! Hey!" Then, "Get up!

"The man cussed angrily as he rolled into a seated position. When he realized, a police officer was awakening him, he pushed himself up from his cardboard bed and knocked the dust off of his pants.

"Get your buddies up and come with me," the huge officer ordered. He turned back toward the sunlit grass and waited for the threesome to present themselves for inspection. When they staggered into the light, he recognized all three of them and cordially addressed them by street names.

"You doin' all right, Bunkie?" Officer Dixon asked

."Oh, you know, considering all the heat and bugs, I guess I'm okay," he answered while squinting up at the officer.

Bunkie was a longtime resident of the bridges around town. He got arrested now and again for trespassing, but, he had never really been a problem. He always moved on when told. The other two were a different story though. Younger than Bunkie, and more ambitious, they each sported no less than two pages of arrests, mostly petty theft and disorderly public display. Still, their collective six eyeballs offered the possibility of seeing into corners that video surveillance cameras might miss.

"You guys know you're not supposed to be sleeping under these bridges. Isn't that, right?" Carl began his interrogation by putting them under the threat of being incarcerated, which, to them meant they might miss out on a night of drinking and probably lose ground in their battle against sobriety.

They hung their heads and studied each other's shoes like schoolchildren sent to the principal's office for misbehaving. They swayed as they stood there, bumping into one another, sweating the alcohol out through their pores under the torturous hot sun. They smelled like low tide.

"Listen, I don't want to keep you out here any longer than I have to. It's too hot for all of us. I need to ask you guys if you saw a yellow VW Bug hit the water two nights ago."

All three of them looked up as though he had told them they had been granted a reprieve by the governor.

"Oh, Yeah! I saw everything!" Bunkie insisted.

They fought over who was going to talk first. Officer Dixon took control and had them sit down in the shade of the bridge while he asked for specifics. Before long he realized that, yes, they saw the car floating in the water, but, no, they had been way, too inebriated to verify if the girl was in it.

"There was a guy on the bridge saw it, too!" one of them remarked. "We all started singing a song. A Beatles' song, '*Rocky Raccoon*'; no, it was; '*Let it Be*.'"

The three of them had fallen off into freefall. They were grabbing at each other's words like clowns at a circus, climbing up a ladder that goes nowhere. Officer Dixon had taken as much as he could and told them to clean up the trash under the bridge. As he leaned into the climb back up the steep hill, they were picking up the trash along the rocks and singing, "We all live in a yellow submarine, a yellow submarine, a . . ." The sergeant was chuckling as he listened to their tuneless voices. Sitting in the front seat of his cold cruiser, he wiped the sweat with his handkerchief and wrote some notes in his pad. He scanned his contact list on his cell phone and landed on Mark Ambrose's work number.

"Tow Boats U.S.! This is Mark."

"Hey Mark, this is Carl Dixon."

"Hey Buddy, don't tell me you're in need of a lift back from fishin' the Tortugas now."

Mark and Carl had been good working friends for many years. Some of Mark's best calls had started as referrals from Carl and Barb. He was always happy to get a call from the "Big D."

"What's up?" he asked.

"What's the chance of getting a car pulled out of some sand?" Carl smiled in expectation of Mark's response.

"Ooo, that sounds like a tall order for a boat like mine." He was trying to come up with a clever response that might make it into one of Carl's famous fish stories. He was going blank but ended up with the following reference to his hated competition. "So, what happened? Did Arnold's Towing drop a police car off the end of a pier?"

It was a nice attempt, but, Carl's scenario had already made the top ten for this year.

"No, it's not as simple as that. I need you to recover a VW Bug from the flats about a mile behind my office." The laughter was so loud he had to back his phone away from his ear.

"Is this a joke?" Mark asked.

"I wish it was. Can you get it this weekend?" Carl had full confidence that Mark would do the job.

"Yeah! Now that the races have been scrubbed, I'm ready to go," Mark answered. "What do you mean? I thought they were making the final runs today." Carl had hoped to be rid of the weeklong partiers before Sunday so he and Barb could knock down some fishing without having to brave the wake of the big speedboats.

"You need to get down to Mallory Square and look toward the southwest. There's one of the biggest waterspouts ever seen bearing down on the race field. They just pulled all the boats out of the water. It should be out of here by 4:30p.m., but that puts tomorrow as a set up day and Sunday is now the final race. I can get your bug and drop it off as soon as the waterspout passes."

When it came to business, Mark was always quick and impeccably thorough.

"You want it dropped at impound behind your office like the last one?" "Impound will be great. Here are the GPS coordinates. You can't miss it. It's the yellow one with the peace sign in the back window." They finished the call laughing, as they had always done.

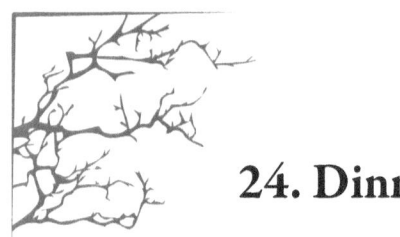

24. Dinner with Barb

Carl pulled up at the front door of the bank. He could see Barbara standing in the lobby talking to one of her tellers. He pushed the send button on his phone and watched as she scrambled back to her office.

"Hey Sugar, what's up?" she answered her phone in her usual loving way. She adored her husband. Since their only daughter, Kelly Ann, had married and moved to Oklahoma, the couple had found the kind of romance that others could only dream about.

"Let's get out of here!" Carl whispered seductively into the phone. Barb smiled and asked, "Who is this and how did you get my husband's phone?" She glanced out the window and waved toward the Crown Victoria with the blacked-out windows parked at the bottom of the stairs. She put her phone on speaker mode while she shut down her system and locked up her desk. She grabbed her bag and mouthed, "Bye, Bye!" to the tellers as she pushed through the glass door and into the afternoon sun.

They had both previously planned on being off all afternoon and driving up the Keys to do some early Christmas shopping at the Rain Barrel Craft Gallery on Islamorada. That plan had been shoved aside. Still, she loved spontaneity! It was romantic, intriguing, and wonderful, especially for someone so deeply in love with a superhero. She had no choice! Spontaneity is every caped crusader's modus operandi.

She gave him a juicy kiss and buckled her seat belt. "What's the plan?" Carl dropped the shifter into drive as he explained, "Oh, I just wanted to make up to you for putting off our little trip." Something was under his skin and he was hoping she would pull it out so he could move on without its' distraction. She reached her hand over and laid it on top of his. She began to gently massage his muscles with her thumb.

"Did you hear about the waterspout?" she asked as she stared out her window and across the shallow bay, hoping it had not yet dissipated.

"That's where we're going right now. Then, I'm taking you to Louie's for your favorite dinner." He smiled as he handed over his plan.

She spun her head to face him, "Macadamia encrusted seabass?" She squealed with excitement as she patted his huge strong hand.

It was early, just after 4 p.m. when they pulled into the parking lot and ran across the cobblestone wharf toward the overlook. A crowd of people had gathered to watch the monstrous tornado as it tore through the deep-water channel beyond the western out islands. Everyone was snapping pictures as it disappeared into the western sky.

Carl and Barb walked back to the cruiser hand in hand, talking about the impact that the boat race being postponed would have on their Sunday fishing plans.

Halfway across the promenade, Barbara asked, "Were you able to get in touch with Jillian Dougherty this afternoon?"

The seemingly innocent question was hiding a well stream of other curiosities, and Carl knew it. He stopped in his tracks, twenty feet from the car, turned, and looked her in the eye.

He tilted his head slightly and raised one side of his black mustache and asked, "You workin' me, girl?"

She threw him a hard-felt hip butt and pulled him closer to her side.

"Yeah! I'm workin' you with everything I got."

As he opened her door, he assured her that he would tell her the whole story.

On the drive over to Louie's Backyard Café, they talked about Kelly Ann and her husband, Don, and the baby. Don had started with T.S.A. as a baggage checker at the Marathon airport three years earlier and had been promoted to supervisor within his first nine months on the job. His new assignment had moved them to Oklahoma City where they had just closed on a little condo. Kelly Ann and their only grandchild, Celia, would be flying in for Carl's birthday in October and Barb couldn't stand the wait.

"Hey Carl, Barb! You guys trying to beat the crowd tonight?" Jimmy greeted them at the front door and led them to their favorite table out on the deck overlooking the dog beach and the ocean.

"Naw! I'm still working." Carl said as he pulled Barbara's chair out and scooted her up to the table.

"Well, I'm not working and I'm ready for one of my regulars," Barb eagerly announced as she looked up at him licking her freshly-glossed lips to signal her request.

Jimmy smiled and exclaimed, "Yes ma'am, one Bahama Mama for a Bahama Mama coming right up."

"So, tell me what's up with the girl." Barb couldn't wait any longer. Carl started from the beginning, with all the details. He described the videos with her and Paddy buying the liquor, the VW being found in the ocean, the kissing the helicopter, everything! Barbara pushed for all the details.

He finally said, "Listen, instead of you going home alone after dinner, how about you come with me to inspect her car? Then, I need to see if she checked into the shelter, and if these two things don't turn something up . . ." he leaned back in his chair and sighed deeply, then turned his head and looked out across the glassy ocean. After a short silence, he bit his bottom lip and said, "I'm gonna have to make a call to her folks." He dropped his head and rubbed his nose, then continued. "If they haven't heard from her, I just don't want to think about what could have happened."

He took a long swig from the glass of iced tea and wiped his mouth with his napkin. Barb could see his sorrow. She felt him buckling under the thought of facing the painful emotions that can't be avoided when losing someone you love. Her eyes welled up with tears as the two of them sat there, remembering the Saturday morning that they had received such a call. Carl's twentyyear old son, from his previous marriage, was hit and killed by a drunk driver while writing a speeding ticket on the shoulder of the Overseas Highway. It was May 16th, six years earlier. It hurt too much to think about right now. He was the, "spitting image", of his father.

Barbara reached across the table and took both his hands in hers, gently massaging as she comforted him and said, "I know, sweetheart! I know!" They relaxed on the deck sipping their drinks as they watched a man on the beach throwing a rubber dog toy over the waves for his golden retriever to chase. The dog would swim out and bring the toy only half the way back, then, when he returned to the shallows and could touch the bottom, he would drop the toy in the water and wait till the man came close to grab it. They played tug-of-war until the dog was ready to let go, then the man threw it once again over the breaking waves for the dog to chase. Carl and Barb laughed as they watched them play.

Finally, Carl raised his sunglasses, leaned toward Barb, and said emphatically, "We're getting a dog!

25. A Special Delivery

C arl held the elevator door button as Barbara stepped through the retracted doors and into the second-floor reception room. Rita had left for the weekend and the Plexiglas booth was empty. The funny shadowbox still hung on the wall behind her desk as a reminder that she had not yet finalized her resignation.

Carl liked being the only one in the building. He could accomplish so much more when the constant distractions weren't threatening to break his concentration at every breath. He keyed in his access code and held the door for his wife to enter.

He had grabbed his highpowered binoculars from the trunk of his cruiser when they parked under the building. Those, and his leather note-pad, were all he carried. Once behind the security doors, Barbara turned to the left, toward his office door. "No, honey, this way." He grabbed her arm and held it until she oriented herself to the change of plan. "I thought you had some phone calls to make," Barb remarked with a puzzled look on her face.

"First, I want to check and see how Mark is coming along with salvaging the car." They walked the quiet corridor toward the observation deck at the northern end of the building. Through the thick glass door, they could see the vast expanse of the Gulf of Mexico. The last light of the day was an hour away as they stepped out and took in the view. He wiped the eyepieces to the binoculars and held them to his eyes. As he made the necessary adjustments, and focused on the Bug, he said, "All my questions may be answered right here."

The towboat was making its way through the private channel that had been cut deep into the coral as an emergency police channel when the new buildings went up. Signs were posted at the entrance that identified it as a 'Sheriff's Emergency Egress Only' zone. It was a difficult maneuver for Mark, but, he had done it several times before. He was at the controls of his twentyseven foot Mako towboat. Two twentyfoot ropes pulled a small black barge with a heavy winch mounted on the front. The back of the barge folded downward, into the water. This was used as a ramp when pulling boats, heavy equipment, airplanes, submersibles, or yellow VW Bugs off the bottom. Mark pulled up to the boat ramp and untied the barge. The yellow Bug had been beaten up from tumbling across the sand.

"I can't believe the roof didn't cave in," Barbara remarked as she handed the binoculars back to Carl.

Two heavy concrete stanchions had been anchored on the pavement halfway between the impound lot gate and the ramp. Mark pulled the heavy cable from the winch and wrapped it around one stanchion.

"Lookin' good, Mark!" Carl called down as he handed the binoculars back to Barb for safekeeping. "Any problems I need to know about?" Mark was pulling his leather gloves off as he turned to look up.

"Oh, hey Carl, is that Barb up there with you?"

"Hey handsome!" she called down in response, "Looking good in those tighty-whities tonight, Mark!"

They all chuckled. Mark threw the lever on the winch into drive and looked back up at Carl.

"Naw, it was a clean pull. You got a lot of sand to blow out before you can check under the seats though."

The barge was equipped, on the bottom, with four large inset wheels. As the cable tightened, it pulled itself up the ramp and over the flat pavement. Mark shut off the winch and unhooked the cable.

"I'll fax you the work order first thing Monday," Carl called down to the young man.

Mark jumped into the boat and rummaged through his equipment chest for a set of heavy casters and a car jack.

"No problem!" he answered.

After setting the brake on the barge and dropping the chains from the fenders of the car, he used the winch cable and a pulley to slide the car down the ramp on the back of the barge and onto the pavement. He strapped one caster to each wheel and within seconds he was pushing the beat-up Bug toward the impound gate. After keying in the access code, he pushed the car to the center of the compound and then walked back to the open gate.

Carl called out, "You can leave it open, I'll lock up when I'm finished." He and Barb expressed their appreciation and headed back inside while Mark situated his equipment and motored out of the channel.

Carl's desk was loaded with pink notes. He didn't want to deal with anything right now that might pull him away from his mission. He was now past the 48-hour waiting period necessary before filing an MPR (Missing Person's Report). Two things to do before calling the parents in Gloucester: check the trunk of the Bug for a body and check the shelter roster for a nurse. He hit the power button to start his computer.

"Ready to take a walk?" he asked his wife as he grabbed his flashlight from the bookcase by the door.

They stopped off to get a crowbar from the utility closet on their way out.

Standing beneath the bright floodlights, they looked at the rumpled metal car.

"I think the trunk is in the front," Barbara said.

Carl slowly raised his eyes off the car and toward her. Her demeanor was so serious as she said it.

"What?" she defensively exclaimed. "I had a girlfriend that had one in college."

Carl laughed and stepped to the front of the pitiful little car. He took a deep breath and grabbed the trunk lever. He pushed the release button and pulled. The bends in the metal had folded over each other and the trunk would not release. Several more tugs and he decided to use the crowbar. He carefully situated it under the lip of the hatch and placed his huge black shoe squarely on the higher end. He leaned into it and the trunk popped open. They were both happily relieved to find only a spare tire, two empty wine cooler bottles, and a couple of soggy paper trash bags.

"Well, that's a relief!" he said as he moved to the driver's door. There wasn't much else to see. The sand was up to the edge of the seats as Travis had told him earlier that day.

"Maybe the guys can find something when they wash it down on Monday," he said as he locked the gate and headed back to the building.

Darkness had fully engulfed the island. The blazing security lights flooded the property from corner to corner. As they walked back under the office building, they watched the homeless people filing through the shelter gate across the parking lot. One lone police car idled under a light post out front.

"Come on," Carl said to Barbara. "I'm gonna save myself a phone call." The young officer was leaning against the door frame watching the names pop up on his computer screen. His radio was chattering away with the busy Friday night service calls for police assistance. He didn't hear Carl as he approached the open window.

"Billy Bones!" Carl called out as he bent down to the officer's line of view. Billy jumped, completely caught off-guard by his name being called out. "Oh, hey, sergeant," he said as he regained his composure and straightened up in the driver's seat. "Hey, Mrs. D."

Barbara was right behind Carl and greeted the young officer saying, "Hey Billy Bones. How are Jenna and the kids?"

Billy opened the door and stepped out into the light. He straightened his uniform and brushed off the pistachio shells that had missed the open window and landed in his lap.

Carl slapped him on the shoulder and asked, "Have you been on night shift all week?"

Billy had graduated from the academy in the class right behind Carl's son, Douglas. The two boys had played ball together in high school. Billy had always felt badly for their loss. He had many times been consoled by the couple when he came to them for help with his own problems.

This was nothing new. The Dixons were a goto kind of team that all the young rookies went to for help and advice. It's what made working in this quirky town worth putting up with. The people!

"Yeah! It's no fun for the family but I sure like being able to fish when I get off in the morning," he answered.

"Did you have shelter watch for the past two nights?" Carl asked. "Yes sir! I pull out when they close the gate," the young man said. "Can you check and see if a name shows up on your system for me?"

The young officer adjusted his belt and reentered the front seat. He was honored to be asked to assist Officer Dixon with anything he needed. Anytime!

"Hang on! OK, go ahead," he said once his system had clicked to the search screen for the 'unofficial' shelter roster.

Carl spelled out the name. "JILLIAN B. DOUGHERTY." "Nothing for Thursday," Billy reported.

He ran the name for Wednesday. "Nothing for Wednesday either."

They tried several variations of the spelling of the name and found no record that she had checked into the shelter.

"Thanks, Billy! I'll catch you later," said the senior officer.

"Where does she live?" Barbara asked as they headed back toward the building."

She shares an apartment with another girl about her age, Canyon Scaletee. I've been calling her phone number all day," Carl explained.

He pushed the up button and as they climbed into the elevator he continued, "They're in a third-floor flat over at the Casa Del Mar on Higgs Beach. Ocean view! One of Tripp's guys lives there and went over at lunch. He left a note on the door for them to call. Tripp said nobody answered the door."

They got off the elevator and turned left toward his office. His was the only one with the light on.

"I want to get a look at one thing before I call her folks."

He sat down in his chair and unbuttoned his shirt. His grey chest hair bulged over the edge of his V-neck tee. His Italian gold chain was the perfect length for displaying the gold 1622 Spanish escudo that Barb had given him on their twentyfirst wedding anniversary. She loved the way he smelled. Like a man! Her man! Barb moved behind him and massaged his broad shoulders as he opened his email from Tripp. They both watched as the attachment opened and loaded the video clip. Tripp had already edited it to the time when the little yellow car first came into view of the rooftop camera.

There she was. Her window was up and the passenger side window was halfway down. She drove slowly along the curved road. Her head was twisting left and right as she looked at the building to her left, and then at the homeless people on her right. She seemed unusually interested in studying every one of the people she passed. A patrol car pulled up behind her and turned under the jail. A homeless man on her right was screaming something into the sky. He was throwing his arms up wildly. She drove by him slowly and almost stopped. Carl and Barb could see her clearly through the windshield. She bent her head low as she passed the crazy man, probably to get a better view of him as she passed.

The car almost came to a stop as she looked to her left and, apparently, watched the zoo animals under the jail. Carl and Barb could see Jill laughing at something she had seen, perhaps one of the pigs, rolling in the mud hole. Her mouth was saying something as she laughed. She pulled by the gate to the shelter and stopped the car. The camera perspective was lost but they assumed she was reading the signs. A minute later, she finished driving the circle and headed back toward the main road.

"Look!" Carl said. Something had made her hit her brakes before disappearing around the last turn. They saw the hand of what appeared to be a police officer raised to stop her. A few seconds later, the front of a police cruiser came to a stop in the road, blocking her path. An officer approached her window and she rolled it down. The officer was looking toward something further beyond view up the road as he instructed Jill. It appeared he was more attentive to what was ahead of them than he was to Jill. Four minutes later and three police cars raced toward the building, then, the VW moved off the property toward College Road.

"I remember what that was about." Carl leaned back after stopping the clip.

"There was a shakedown call on two homeless guys that had beaten up a fisherman on Cow Key Bridge."

Barb moved over to the chair beside the desk and sat down.

"Yeah, it had nothing to do with this girl." He took a big yawn and stretched his arms as far out as he could. He shook his body as he centered himself and rubbed his eyes with his balled fists. Another deep breath, then he grabbed the desk phone receiver from its cradle. He opened his notepad and dialed the Massachusetts phone number. Leaning on his elbows, he looked over at Barb for support. She was sober and serious! Confidently supportive!

"Yes ma'am! This is Officer Carl Dixon with the Monroe County Sheriff's Office in Key West, Florida. By chance is this Jillian Dougherty I'm speaking with." He was so good on the phone. His solid confidence flowed through the lines riding on his deep masculine voice. Barbara had to sit back in the chair to avoid showing him that she was getting goosebumps as he talked. She felt her temperature rise as she watched him work his charm. No matter how difficult the situation, he was always in control. She loved her man!

Trina was surprised to be asked if she was Jill and responded with," No sir, I'm Trina, her sister. Jill's down there, in Key West, where you are. Do you want to talk to my mom?"

Trina was nervous already. She was waving her hand toward her mother who was standing at the kitchen sink, now as alert as a mother hawk protecting her nestlings. She took the phone from the younger daughter and took command.

"This is Mrs. Dougherty, is there something I can help you with?" She jerked the tie open on her apron and tossed it into the sink.

"Well, I hope so. This is Officer Carl Dixon down here in Key West. I was just hoping to get in touch with Ms. Jillian B. Dougherty to ask her about her car. Would you happen to know where I might be able to find her tonight?"

He winked at Barb who was glued now to the front of her chair. He knew just how to approach people without making them suspicious. It was one of his many gifts.

"Well, I can give you her cell phone number, but she hasn't returned my calls and her voicemail box is full. I do know though, that she was putting her phone in the shop to get it fixed." She paused briefly and asked, "Is there a problem with her car?"

"Yes ma'am, I have to say, her car was abandoned apparently on Wednesday night and I had it towed to my office until I can get her to come claim it. Is there anybody else you might know of that could help us make contact with her?"

He wanted to raise as few red flags as possible. If Jill walked through the door tomorrow morning after a three-night binge with some race team crew, the only thing he would have to deal with would be the paperwork.

"No one other than her father and I. Let me give you the store phone number so you can get hold of us if you need, too." Mrs. Dougherty gave the number to him and then asked, "Is there any reason for us to come down there?"

Carl didn't want them to overreact. The case was not even filed yet and it would be Monday before he would have time to write his report and turn it over to Missing Persons. Besides, he had a little detective work he wanted to explore that might turn up some information.

"Oh, I don't think you need to come down here right now. She'll probably call this weekend and by Monday, hopefully, everything will be back to normal." He gave her his office and cell numbers and hung up the phone.

"Man, I'm ready for a drink," he said as he slumped back in his chair and started gently rocking.

Barbara lifted her right leg across his lap and settled slowly down. Carl was completely caught off guard by her sexual aggression but willingly surrendered.

She pulled his face to hers and once they were eye to eye, she said, "You don't need no stinking drink, Officer Dixon! What you need, I've got right here!"

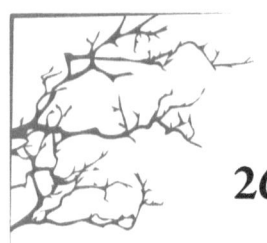

26. To Catch a Scamp

"**Carl!**" **she yelled.** "Carl!" again she yelled. "Carl!" He couldn't hear her calling to him. He was sprawled across the deck of the boat with everything waist up hanging down in the engine compartment. His tools were laid out on a dirty towel to his left where he could reach them as needed without coming up. Barbara was shouting down to him from the edge of the deck, fifteen feet above the pool.

"Caarrrr-lll!!!!" She tried one last time to get his attention to no avail. She put the phone back to her ear and said, "Hang on, he's working on the boat." She walked to the corner of the deck and grabbed the hose gun that was dangling over the railing next to her bougainvillea's. She pulled enough hose up onto the deck to reach the middle and adjusted the selector to the 'stream' tip. She stood there, middeck, in her best drop-dead *Sports Illustrated* bikini pose and pulled the trigger. Three quick blasts did the trick.

Poor Carl almost slipped into the engine compartment on his head. He was mad! She was hysterical!

"Hey, is this really necessary?" he asked as he shut off the CD player and stood looking up at her from the sundrenched deck of his second love, the *DONE-IT.* "It's the Watch Commander!" She held the wireless house phone receiver in the air by its antenna, as if she was going to drop it into the pool. Carl wiped the oil off his hands and climbed out of the boat. He crossed the pool deck and stood directly under her. He clapped his hands to signal her to drop the receiver. She faked a drop and he flinched. Once more, he was pissed!

"Come on!" he cried out.

She let it drop into his hands.

"Hey, Charlie, thanks for calling me back. Yeah! Well, personally I think they all need to be on medication."

Barbara hit him one more time with a squirt of water before returning to her vacuuming in the living room. The men talked for a minute or two, and then they heard her pick up the bedroom extension.

"Listen, Charlie, he's not coming in today. He's all mine, you got that?" She slammed the phone back on its cradle and stomped back to the living room where she cranked up a Brad Paisley CD and turned the Hoover back on.

She didn't see him sneak through the open French doors and pull the plug out of the wall. As the vacuum wound to a stop, he looked at her sternly and asked with crossed arms, "Does Barbie need another spanking?"

She threw a pillow, he caught it, and they collapsed laughing on the couch. After a couple of sweet kisses, he assured her that his plans were to spend the entire weekend with her. But, he wanted her to assist him in a little investigative scam first.

Charlie had returned Carl's earlier call to have the Street Division locate and maintain surveillance of one Patrick Oran Broslen, aka Paddy, whom, as they spoke, was sitting on a park bench, alone, at Higgs Beach. Barbara listened to the plan with wide felt anticipation over her role in the scam. He told her that time was wasting and for her to grab a throwover for the beach. She was ready to go in less than five minutes. They threw beach chairs, a cooler, and a quilt in the trunk of her white Saab, and then she drove them over to Higgs Beach. A squad car was parked across the street by the tennis courts and Carl signaled the officer that he could leave. Two flashes from his blue lights acknowledged the officer understood and the squad car pulled onto South Atlantic Boulevard and then disappeared around the corner. Carl and Barb carried the beach gear across the sidewalk and followed the shade along the brick wall of the West Martello fort,

then cut across the sand toward the water where they set up camp directly in front of Paddy, who was now sound asleep on the picnic table bench. They were less than fifty feet away from their clueless, drunken target.

Carl walked to the car and retrieved the ice chest, then carried it back and set it between the two chairs. Paddy had not moved, as of yet. They turned up their radio and spread out the blue quilt across the sand. Carl instructed Barb to pop her top off and lay on the quilt face down. She was happy to oblige. Carl began to rub lotion on her back and the stage was set. He sat down, pulled a can of beer from the cooler, slipped it into a coozie, and using his sunglasses as a mirror, he watched Paddy as he slept on the picnic table.

"He's moving!" Barbara was watching him through one squinted eye. "He's got whisky!" she said as Paddy took a long swig from a counterfeit Mountain Dew bottle.

"I can see him, honey," Carl whispered.

"He's looking over here," she said through closed lips.

"All right, do it now." Carl leaned his head back as if he had fallen asleep while Barb rolled over onto her back.

Paddy went crazy. He climbed up on the top of the concrete table and sat as upright as he possibly could to get a better view. He was as fidgety as a groundhog on the last winter's day. Carl fought the laughter as he watched the frail, little imp squirming, trying to take in as much as he could.

"Greedy little bastard," Carl said.

"What's he doing now?" Barb asked as she grabbed the lotion bottle and plastered her bare chest with oil.

"He's so drunk! He's trying to climb from the top of the picnic table to the limb of that Australian pine next to it," Carl said laughingly. Then he added, "Man, I wish I had my video camera."

After about fifteen minutes Paddy settled back down. He was worn out after the show. Barbara hooked her bikini top behind her back but left the shoulder straps dangling loose over the front cups. Carl directed her to return to the car for a towel and on the way back, if Paddy offered any attention at all, for her to go set the trap.

She played him like a radio. Carl watched the reflection in his glasses as she buttered the old man up. She offered him beer, then sashayed over to the cooler, swinging her hips as she dug her feet into the soft sand. She grabbed a four-pack by the plastic strap and swayed her gorgeous fortyoneyearold hips like a runway model back to the picnic table. Paddy was drooling like a thirsty Georgia hound dog on a six-mile hunt as she approached, more over the beer than over her.

They chatted and laughed, in the shade of the huge tree, like old friends. It took him all of another ten minutes to down all four of the beers. The seedy old boozer never even offered her a sip.

Carl was reaching his limit of hot sun and ready to initiate phase two. He grabbed a beer from the cooler and poured half of it into the sand. He set his sunglasses on top of his Yankees ball cap and grabbed a four-pack of cold wine coolers from the igloo. He turned toward the two at the table and slowly staggered like a drunk toward them.

"Paddy, oh man, is that you?" Paddy looked to the right to see if he had a clear getaway path but the officer fell over on the ground to nail his part down a little tighter. He over-animated every move as he pulled himself back to his feet and wrapped his huge arm around the little weasel and said, "I'm so sorry those sonsabitches treated you like shit. I just want to kick every one of their asses every time I see them." He fell against the tree then back against the table like a silver arcade ball hit by flipper pads. Barbara was having a great time watching his antics unfold. She grabbed one of the empty beer cans off the ground and joined the party.

Paddy fell right down the hole. They gave him the wine coolers, then invited him to go for a ride with them in Barb's new Saab. They left the gear on the beach and put Paddy in the front seat. Carl sat in the back, right behind him, the conductor of the orchestra, the writer of the script. He left the rest to Barb, who kept Paddy engaged with flirtatious chat. She was fabulous! They stopped for sandwiches to go, and more cold beer. When Paddy was far enough out to sea, they started working him for information about Jill.

"Hey! I ran into your girlfriend a couple of days ago," Carl started. "The cute little nurse you were dating."

Paddy was excited to hear about her even though he couldn't recall her name.

"She felt so bad about the misunderstanding that they had with the cards and all. She said if I saw you, to tell you 'Thank you' for all you did for her." Carl had no idea how easy this was going to be. Paddy's mouth started running like a runaway Kentucky coal train. He grabbed his pad and pen that he had already stashed in the map pocket behind Paddy's seat and took notes. Paddy told it all. From the E.R. meeting, to the skinny dipping, to losing her out at Boca Chica Beach, and to the ATM shopping for PIN numbers, he spilled all his little beans. One by one!

When Carl determined, they had enough information, they dropped him off in front of the AA meeting hall on Virginia Street and said goodbye like he was their oldest friend.

Halfway down the street, Barb looked up at Carl's reflection in the rear-view mirror and they both broke into uncontrollable laughter, amazed at how easily the plan had worked. After retrieving their beach gear they headed for Boca Chica Beach to look for Jill, or, evidence of Jill.

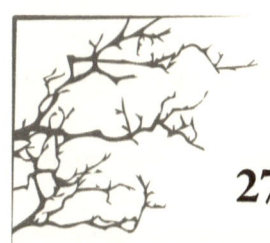

27. Boca Chica Beach

Carl's phone rang as Barb turned off the Overseas Highway and onto Boca Chica Road.

"Hey, Tripp!" Carl always checked his caller ID for a name before hitting the receive button.

"Are you on the greens?" Tripp was used to finding Carl playing golf or out in the boat on his days off when the weather was this good.

"Naw, I'm on a picnic with a beauty queen," Carl responded. "What's up?"

"You remember Lionel, the kid that lives in the same complex as your little nurse with the yellow Bug?" Tripp asked.

Carl had met the young man several times around the office. He was one of Tripp's newer technicians.

"Yeah, sure, why?" Carl asked.

"Well, guess who's on my other line sitting by the pool with her hot little roommate, Canyon?"

"You're kidding!" Carl exclaimed with amazement that his questions about the lost girl were all being answered so easily.

Tripp went on to explain, "She's saying that the girl came home Tuesday morning all cut up and covered in mud and that she slept all day at the apartment. Canyon told Lionel that your girl was sunburned all over and had met some guy with a boat. She thinks his name was Dillon. The last time she saw her was that night, Tuesday.

"Carl listened with interest as Tripp continued.

"Do you have any questions you want Lionel to ask her while I've got him on the line?"

Carl considered the new information and said, "Tell them both I appreciate their help and have him get me all her contact info, work number, etc. . . . Thanks Tripp, I owe you man!"

They were almost to the end of the road. Carl had turned on the speaker mode on his cell phone and had held it up high so Barb could listen in. She pulled onto the shoulder and turned off the Saab.

"I don't know how you do it," she said as the canvas roof snapped into place."

"Do what?" Carl asked as he grabbed the little igloo cooler, still full of ice and beer, from the back floorboard.

"Keep track of all that inutia," she said.

"Ooh, big word for little Barbie," he teased.

She pulled off her sandal and threw it at him. He tackled her from the side and ran to the water's edge with her in his arms. After twenty minutes of kicking and splashing, they wrapped themselves around each other like mating seahorses and fell in love all over again.

Lots of people were out on the beach that day. It was an out-of-the-way kind of spot that's popular with the working-class poor. Dozens of beat-up cars and trucks lined the sides of the dead-end road. The high fence to the back side of the naval airstrip left only the beach side of the road for recreation. Fishermen were standing knee-deep, casting out toward the coral heads, hoping to land something worth taking home. Hispanic kids were wading in the shallows tended by their cousins and sisters and pregnant mothers, while the men played checkers and drank beer under the hurricane-twisted cedar trees.

This was an unmaintained beach. No facilities, no beach cleanup crews, no contour equipment raking off the highs and lows of yesterday's sandcastles in preparation for the onslaught of a new crowd each morning, and no lifeguards to run to after being stung by the toxic tentacles of the dreaded manowar that drifted in the gentle current and washed ashore with the waves. No, this was an olddays kind of beach. A "swim at your own risk" kind of place, the way it used to be.

One 55gallon trash drum stood at the end of the road. It looked as though it was only emptied by the hurricanes that washed through each year. Overflowing with bait bags, food wrappers, bottles, dirty diapers, discarded clothing, and dead fish, every fly on the island knew how to find it. Beyond the trashcan was a footpath that followed westward along the shoreline.

Carl was keenly familiar with this isolated stretch of beach. He had coordinated many drug busts, in both day and night, out there over the years. He had also assisted with several murder and suicide investigations that had taken place there. On several occasions, gay men had sought to use this hard to get to beach as a place to end their pain after being jilted by lovers. They almost always left a note, sometimes hidden, sometimes not.

The young gay boys loved to roam this stretch of beach. Here, they could explore their fantasies without fear of being 'found out' by their mothers and girlfriends. They might be murdered, but maybe not 'found out'. You can only know which is worse once you've tried them both. It was part of the allure this beach held for them; some kind of dark seductive call to their souls.

"Well, you ready to see what we can come up with?" Carl was referring to the purpose behind their little Saturday afternoon excursion.

"Anything in particular we ought to be looking for?" Barb asked as she lay in the cool, shallow water.

"Yeah, a body might wrap this case up, but anything that corroborates Paddy's story will do for a start."

They pushed themselves up from the tidal pool and walked hand in hand to the spot where Carl had dropped the cooler. They shared a Corona on their climb back toward the trash barrel.

"Listen, you head on up the trail and look around in the sea grapes. I'm going to take a look at this trashcan," said Carl.

She dropped his hand and watched the sandy footpath for stickers as she headed up the trail.

"Don't get out of my sight!" he called out to her as she bent to pick up a shell.

"Yes, Papa!" she called back without turning around. He loved to watch that girl walk in the sand, and she loved for him to.

Carl should have been born Irish instead of Greek. It would have made his luck easier to explain. He really didn't want to go anywhere near that trashcan on this blisteringly hot afternoon.

He stood twenty feet back and surveyed the area at the end of the paved road. Against the chainlink fence on the other side of the broken pavement, he saw a pile of trash that sparked his curiosity. The recent storms had blown the debris into a spot between the fence and a cluster of mangroves. The heavy rains had beaten the trash down flat against the sand and rocks. Something seemed familiar in the color of the printing on the boxes. He picked up a broken, fiberglass fishing rod and approached to make a closer inspection.

Immediately, he knew that Jillian's car had been parked there five days earlier. When he had viewed the video of her and Paddy buying the alcohol from Roger, at Bone Island Liquors, and loading it into the trunk of the Bug on Monday, he had paid close attention to the products they had purchased. Red Bull: Salem 100's, corn chips, Miller Premium Gold, Bacardi Breezes, Absolut Swedish Vodka in gift boxes, wine and Slim Jims. All of them were represented except for the wine and Slim Jims. Someone had apparently unloaded the trunk of everything that wasn't smokeable, edible, or drinkable. The empty Salem carton and the two Absolut Vodka gift boxes were enough to support Carl's conclusion.

He pulled out his phone and snapped off some closeups, then headed down the sandy trail to join his wife.

"Find anything interesting?" he asked as he approached her from behind. "Some pretty flowers and some shells." She held them in her palm for him to look over. She poured the little periwinkles into the pocket of his bathing suit and said, "Don't you lose them."

Then she asked, "How 'bout you, anything in the trashcan that looked admissible in court?"

"Maybe!" he said. "Come on, I think you're going to get a kick out of what's up ahead."

They walked the same path that Jillian had walked with Paddy. Carl led the way and was keeping an eye out for anything that may lend assistance in his search. He was planning to turn all of the information over to Missing Persons on Monday.

"Wow! What a great piece of art!" Barb said as she looked up and saw the colorful wall of shoes and sandals that someone had woven into the chain link fence.

"This is the famous *Wall of Missing Soles*, or *Lost Soles* I think they call it," Carl told her.

She stood on the trail admiring the creative montage for a second and said, "I wouldn't mind seeing that on my lobby wall at the bank."

She was drawn to funky art like a backyard mosquito to a zap light. She started to push through the vines and sea grapes to get a closer look. "No wait Barb, let me go first." Carl still had the broken fishing rod and used it to beat down the tall grasses. Good thing he did! While clearing an area for her to stand directly in front of the display, he noticed that a keychain was tangled in the reeds. He bent down and pulled it from the dry straw. He held it up and turned so Barb could get a look at it. On the end of the chain was a little brown teddy bear.

"Cute!" she said as she reached to take it from his hand. He closed his fist around the trinket and grinned at her scornful reaction.

"Evidence, my dear!" he exclaimed.

"What evidence?" She ignored him and returned her focus to the 'Wall of Lost Soles'.

Carl remembered the image from the video of Jillian standing at the liquor store checkout counter, flipping a keychain in her fingers. This keychain! They proceeded down the trail along the beach. The path became more and more difficult as they reached the area where years before the hurricanes had eroded the sand from under the oceanfront road and made the area impassable by vehicles. Carl lifted Barb up and over the large crags and slabs of asphalt. They climbed up on a huge sandstone boulder that had been delivered to the beach from deep water. Looking across the ruins that must have once been a beautiful place to drive, Carl pointed at an upturned piece of a concrete slab and some pilings that were sticking out of the sand.

"What do you think that used to be?" he asked her as she scanned the beach from their lofty perch.

"Oh, I don't know, part of a bridge?" she guessed as she wrapped both hands around his upper arm for safety.

It was a good guess but wrong.

"That's what's left of an oceanfront house," he pointed up and down the beach in both directions as he continued.

"And there, and there, and that's another one. This road was the original Overseas Highway. People in 1901 started building little fishing shacks out here and by 1920 this road was finished. Houses lined the beach from way down there, to just before that marsh up there."

He jumped down from the rock and took her by the waist. She placed her hands on his shoulders and he set her down into a pool of shallow water between some sections of the broken highway. The cracked blacktop was now shoulder-high as they made their way through the washout and back up toward the dry sand.

"This is unbelievable!" she said as they waded across the last stretch of clear water. "How do you know all this?" she asked.

"We've got a research room at the office. It's full of boxes of old photographs and documents salvaged from attics of houses that were raided in the sixties and seventies during the square grouper days," Carl explained.

Barbara was familiar with the term 'square grouper'. It was the name of one of her favorite restaurants just a short drive up the Keys. The walls are decorated with pictures of the great Jewfish, better known in later years by its less offensive name, the Goliath Grouper. It was a highly sought-after member of the grouper family, well known to grow to be over six hundred pounds. Some have historically weighed in at over seven hundred. Now, it's a protected species and rarely is one seen that has made it to five hundred.

In the heyday of the 60's and 70's pot smuggling era, Florida shrimp boat captains, as well as boat owner entrepreneurs, and a few daring private plane pilots, built themselves lucrative businesses smuggling marijuana from South America and Jamaica. They used to transport the product baled with wire, like farm hay, then wrapped tightly with burlap or canvas. These bales weighed hundreds of pounds and were easily rolled overboard when the Coast Guard or DEA engaged them in chase and stopped them for a search. Later, the jettisoned bales would wash up on the beach and the local dopers would be out on the beach looking for them, pulling them from the surf and hauling them home. Those floating bales became known as 'square grouper'. The whole story is depicted on the walls of the restaurant, through its very tastefully displayed photo collection and artifacts.

Carl and Barb walked back up to the footpath and past the first marsh run. Soon, they were looking up at the driftwood castle that the local derelicts fondly christened, *The Driftwood Oceanfront Resort and Spa*. It was a collection of beach debris that if it weren't built on the edge of the Naval Air Station property, would have been bulldozed by the police department years ago.

"So, this is the Driftwood! I always wondered what it looked like." Barbara stood just behind Carl looking up into the weird and unusual-looking structure.

"Can we take a tour?" she asked.

"Do you value your life?" Carl jokingly asked.

"Not today!" she answered as she stood with her hands on her bikinied hips. She pushed him out of her way as she headed for the structure's entrance.

"Hey!" Carl grabbed her by the hand tightly. "Let me go first. It could be dangerous.

"She let him pass and followed close behind as they walked under the driftwood arch. They explored the stone and driftwood rooms and grottos on the ground floor first. The walls had been constructed by packing small rocks and bits of coral between the intertwined logs and branches of dead trees that had been washed up on the beach. People had decorated the walls with plastic buckets, lobster trap buoys, toys, shoes, and other colorful pieces of debris found on the beach, and coconut shells were everywhere. Carl was inspecting for evidence that the girl may have been there.

They climbed a spiral staircase that led to a crudelymade solarium on the roof. Whisky bottles, cans and broken glass lined the back wall of the area. Carl circled the portico and stretched to look over the sides of the wall.

"Hey!" he excitedly exclaimed. He had seen something.

They descended the rickety stairwell and pushed through the overgrowth behind the structure. He reached up into a buttonwood scrub, and withdrew his prize. Turning around to show it to Barb, he stretched the pink smock out and held it proudly in front of his chest.

"Oh honey, nice color but you'll never get it over your head," she joked.

"It's the girl's," he said. "This is what she was wearing in the video." He handed it to her to carry and headed back toward the beach.

"Come on," he said as he pushed aside the limb for her to pass under.

"Where're we going next?" she asked as they returned to the trail.

He let her lead the way and grinned as he answered, "To pick up my new dog!" Barb thought he was being funny. She had no idea that while she was vacuuming upstairs, he had been on his cell phone, making arrangements to have a rescued stray transported from the Key Largo Humane Society shelter to the Key West office. Rayla Sanchez and Carl were friends from way back. She had been hired to run the Sheriff's Zoo and stayed there until she was offered the directorship of the countywide humane society operations. When he had called her that morning, she had told him about a four-year-old red female golden retriever that had been left behind after a domestic abuse/drug arrest on Key Largo. Her description hooked him immediately. His decision had been made before his phone snapped closed. He was just waiting for the right name to come to mind.

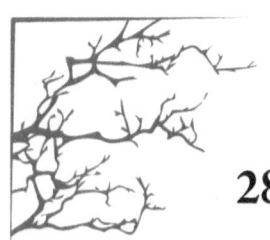

28. What's Her Name

Carl and Barb pulled into the animal shelter just as the red van from Key Largo arrived. They could see the beautiful smiling face of the excited dog standing on the front seat. The air conditioning was blowing her long ears back and her entire rear end was wagging so hard that the driver was getting whipped in the face. Rayla came out of the front entrance to the building just in time to see Barb open the passenger side door and wrap her arms around the ninetypound pup.

"Hey, baby!" Barb squealed while the dog gave her an ambitious face washing.

"You're gorgeous!"

Carl and Rayla hugged. They had not seen each other in over a year.

"Well, I think you've got a dog," she said to her old friend.

Carl had a tear in his eye as he approached the van. His last dog was the shepherd that had grown up with his son Douglas. He had resisted getting another one. They just don't last long enough. He didn't want the pain. Now, the time was right. He was ready to feel the trust you only get from a dog.

"Look Carl, she wants you!" Barb said.

The dog had turned her attention to the big man in the v-neck tee shirt that was approaching from just off to the side. Barb made room for him to move in closer, then stepped back to watch the introduction. It was a wonderful thing to see. The dog's green eyes lit up when she looked at him. Her heavy tail was pounding the back of the now-empty driver's seat like a bass drum. She cast two gentle yelps at him as he raised his hand for her approval. Her smiling eyes were beckoning him to come closer. Everything about this dog was saying, "I know you, and you're mine!"

She took his arm in her jaws and began gently chewing on his salty wrist as if he was a chew toy.

"She's bonding with you," Rayla told them.

"She didn't do that with me!" Barb said disappointedly.

"There's a reason," Rayla suggested. "It's a selective behavior. Dogs are pack animals. She parented over you by licking; she's flirting with Carl. She's finding her place in his pack."

Carl stood back and straightened his shoulders. The dog sat down precisely at the same time. Carl held his hand out toward her and said, "Shake!" Her paw hit his hand in less than a millisecond. "Speak!" she roared out her response, never taking her eyes off him.

"Well, she better like sleepin' out on the boat 'cuz I'm not rollin' over just because some stud tells me to," Barbara joked.

"It'll take her a few days to work through her insecurities, and then she should start to settle down," Rayla instructed.

"Shoot, you don't know her very well. I've been waitin' twentytwo years for her to settle down," Carl jokingly said as he glanced at Barb, then flinched as she landed her fist on his upper arm. The big red dog got excited over all of the laughter and tossed in a couple of friendly yelps as if to say, "That was a good one. I like you people." Carl led the dog over to the shrubs at the edge of the parking lot where she relieved herself, then he told Rayla to get her paperwork to him on Monday. He slipped a shelter donation check for two hundred dollars into her hand as he gave her a goodbye kiss on the cheek.

Back on the road, the big red dog sat in the middle of the rear seat with her head cast straight up to catch the wind with her chin as the family of three, in the white convertible, headed back toward town.

"Hungry?" Carl asked Barb.

"I could do with a snack, I guess. What have you got in mind?" He directed her to pull into the gravel parking lot at "The Hurricane Hole" and park over by the dock. The popular waterside pub/marina/dog park was a great place to see how their new little girl would handle being with other free-roaming critters. There usually were pelicans on the pilings and several pups playing on the dock. Oh, and the beer is always as cold as ice.

"Hey Carl, who's this little beauty?" Melissa Landrum and her husband Ben had owned the place since Hurricane Andrew and had developed the property into a great stop for the locals and the tourists.

"Baby!" Barb announced.

Carl leaned back and glared over his sunglasses at his presumptuous wife. "Oh, no! I'm not having a dog named Baby in my house," he insisted.

They scooted into their seats at a table beside the water. The dog sat quietly between them, attentively watching every move they made. Melissa offered them menus but they already knew what they wanted. She never needed to write down orders. She just repeated it once before heading to the kitchen. It never failed her.

"I'll have a turkey club and a Miller Light," Carl said as he reached over and stroked the dog's head.

Barb ordered a Miller and a platter of nachos and, as Melissa headed for the bar, Ben showed up with a large bucket of ice water and set it down by the dog. She lay down and played with the ice floating in the cold water while the two men exchanged greetings and caught up on the latest fishing reports.

There was a large party of raceboat team members sitting at the other end of the long dock.

"Aren't those guys supposed to be out racing today?" Carl asked as Melissa left for the kitchen.

"Oh, man!" Ben said sadly. "God, I feel so bad for these guys. This is the crew from the 'High Tide'. That's Colt Pouigdonavitch in the chair with his back to the water. His brother Shawn was the one that died in the crash on Monday afternoon. Fiberglas from the wreck sliced him in half. Colt was in a coma until Thursday night, snapped right out of it. He still can't remember a thing about the wreck."

Carl invited Ben to join them. Ben went over to the bar to get his beer, then returned and sat with them at the little table under the umbrella. Carl and Barb shared the story of how they had acquired their new dog.

"She was seized during the raid and Rayla said the officers told her that the dog obeyed every command they gave it while they arrested the people in the house. They found the registration papers in a desk drawer and are sending them to me on Monday. She's apparently a well-trained, pedigreed golden retriever."

Ben asked," What's her name?"

Barb started to say 'Baby' but Carl put his hand up to shush her and explained, "You can't just tag a name on a dog until you know something about the dog's personality. I knew a guy that named his dog 'Backup'." Ben laughed. Then asked, "Backup, was it a police dog that he trained to back him up?"

"No! He named it Backup, because when it was a puppy, it used to lie down and go to sleep against his closed bedroom door every night. In the morning, he just pushed on the door till it climbed back up on the chair that he had set up for it to sleep in. That was no problem, but, the dog grew up to be 140 lbs. and got lazy. He couldn't get out of his room till he yelled, '*back up*'. The name stuck." "Man, he loved that old dog." Carl lifted his beer and looked through the amber bottle at Barb's disapproving glare, then added, "Man, he loved that fat old dog."

Ben laughed so hard he almost fell out of his chair, and then jokingly said, "Jesus, Carl, and you're still on the county payroll? Somebody needs to get fired for that mistake."

He said goodbye as Melissa delivered the food. The big red dog sat back up and watched every move they made.

"She's really beautiful." Barb said.

Carl looked down at the dog and she snapped her stare to meet his. "You're a smart girl, aren't you?"

"Woof!" she answered with enthusiasm.

Carl then leaned closer and asked, "What's your name?"

She gave him her answer: "Woof!"

They laughed and prepared to enjoy their food.

"Woof!" The dog was trying to tell him something. Giving him the command!

"Throw her a nacho," Barb suggested.

Carl broke a chip in half and flipped it in the air. The dog sprang to her feet and the leash, which Carl had looped under the leg of his chair for safety, went taut, flipping him over onto the wooden dock. Barb was hysterical!

"Yeah, that's your dog alright. No dog of mine would ever treat me like that," she laughed.

After bowing to the clapping audience at the bar and reseating himself, Carl said, "Well, at least we know her name."

"Excuse me?" Barb looked up at him wondering if she had missed something.

"Her name is what, *Watch Me Jerk The Idiot Big Guy To The Ground Dixon*?"

"Nope!" Carl answered. "That's a good one but way to easy to confuse with, *Attack My Wife's Jugular Vein And Put Carl Out Of His Misery Dixon.*" Barbara sat back in her chair and waited. Carl dipped a chip in the bean sauce and loaded it into his mouth, then took a long swig of beer and released a gasp of satisfaction.

"OK, I give up. What's her name?"

Carl scooted back in his chair and took a nacho from the platter. The dog sat attentively watching the golden corn morsel as he held it between his fingers.

"What do you want?" he asked her.

"Woof!" she answered."

And what's your favorite snack?"

"Woof!" she proclaimed."

And what is Daddy's new dog's name?" he asked.

She gave the same answer, but this time with increased fervor: "Woof!"

"Good girl," he said as he tossed the treat in her waiting mouth and slid his chair back to the table.

"So, that's it? Woof?" Barb sarcastically asked.

Carl washed down another bite of the sandwich with his beer and said, "No, weren't you listening?"

He took another bite and after a little chewing he spoke the dogs name out of the side of his foodfilled mouth. "Nacho," he said.

"What?" Barb yelled laughingly. "Nacho, what the hell kind of name is that for a dog?"

He washed down the last of his sandwich and as he reached for his wallet to drop a tip on the table he smiled at her and said, "Yeah! 'Cuz she's 'notcho' dog, she's mine!" Then he left the table and took his dog with him. Barb sat shaking her head and finished her half of the turkey sandwich. She picked up the platter of remaining nachos and carried it over to the edge of the dock. She dumped them into the water and watched as the baby tarpon and mangrove snapper broke into a feeding frenzy below.

"Nacho dog, it's my dog," she snickered. It was a clever name and she liked it. She just didn't want Carl to know she liked it.

She left the second half of her beer in the bottle on the table and turned toward the bar at the other end of the dock. Carl and Nacho came out of the men's room and headed under the canopy where the crowd of patrons had gathered to avoid the heat of the afternoon sun. Ben and Melisa's dog, Sideline, was watching the tarpon from the end of the dock and ran over to meet the new kid when she came into view. Carl could tell they were going to be great together and unhooked Nacho's collar. The two dogs bounded along the edge of the dock jumping and playing like old friends. Carl tested her response to her new name and called out, "Nacho!"

She snapped back to his side and sat anxiously for his next command. He could have named her anything. She had already accepted him as her alpha and from here on, his wish was her command.

They were almost back at the house when Barb remembered that she had earlier in the day had an idea that she had not yet discussed with Carl.

"Hey, the guy who the nurse met, Dillon, wasn't that his name?" she asked.

"Yeah, that's the name that Tripp used. Why?"

"Well," she said, "I've got two customers at the bank that go by Dillon. One is about thirtyseven, married, has three little boys, and thumps his bible in the front row at the Fifth Street Baptist Church. The other is a retired engineer married to a photographer. They moved here a year ago from Colorado. It may not be one of them but whoever it is he has to bank somewhere. I can poke around and maybe we can find this Dillon guy and see if she's shacked up with him."

Carl agreed that the idea was well worth pursuing, and Barb planned to get to work on it first thing Monday morning.

They pulled up the pea rock driveway and parked under the house. Nacho sat on the back seat anxiously waiting for Carl to clear her to exit the car. They were amazed with her restraint.

"OK, girl!" Carl told her and motioned for her to exit the car. She carefully climbed out of the passenger's side door and began exploring her new surroundings. After peeing in the grass on the side of the house she headed for the backyard while Carl and Barbara unloaded the car.

A minute later they heard a splash and ran to find her in the pool, swimming from one side to the other, trying to get her mouth around the plastic duck chlorine dispenser.

"That's my Baby!" Barb said as she stepped into the water and sat on the top stair. Nacho swam over and climbed up in her lap with the duck in her mouth. Barb laid her head against her wet shoulder and massaged her thick red coat. Nacho was wagging her entire body, enjoying her newfound home. She didn't take her eyes off of Carl while he stood on the pool deck, enjoying the moment.

"Yeah, you got a nice dog lady," he said.

He dug his hand into his pocket and pulled out the little cluster of shells that Barb had placed in his charge and set them on the glass tabletop. He pulled his shirt off over his head and dove into the deep end of the pool. Upon breaking the surface and clearing his eyes, he treaded his way to the stairs where he leaned against the pool wall and asked, "What's her name again?"

Barbara lifted her head with tears in her eyes and struggled to make her answer audible.

"Baby!" she said as she tightened her hold around the dog's neck.

"Sounds perfect to me!" he said as he reached up and took the duck out of her mouth.

"I guess I better go see if I can find an old can of tennis balls in the shed." They were just sitting down for a late dinner under the stars. The tiki torches lent a nice touch to the tropical aura of the deck. Baby was curled up beside the barbeque grill. Carl's cell phone rang. He checked the ID and read the words out loud, "Out of state call."

"Hello!" He sat back in his chair and looked across the table to watch Barb's response to the interruption.

"Yes, this is Officer Dixon. No sir, that's perfectly all right. Well sir, I've got one last lead to run down but, as it stands right now, nothing."

Carl looked across the table at Barb and raised his eyebrows. "No sir, that sounds like it might be a good idea. That's absolutely correct, the sooner the better." A second more and he finished with, "Excellent, I'll see you then. Yes sir! You, too! Thank you!"

"He set down his phone and picked up his fork and knife.

"When does his plane get in?" Barb asked.

"Tomorrow night. Late! He'll meet me at the office first thing Monday."

Carl sliced the first bite from his porterhouse, and put work back in the box for Monday.

The rest of the weekend was made in heaven. Sunday, Carl finished tuning the carburetors on the old Shamrock, while Barb finished the house cleaning. They caught the last run of the boat race, then fished until sunset. They took Baby to the dog park to play and still had time to watch a couple of good movies on HBO. Baby was a perfect addition to the family.

A real, 'Nacho' dog!

Not his dog, nope, her dog.

Lost Souls of Paradise Photo Gallery

Soup Kitchen Entrance See Chapter 31

Thomas (Tom) Bozeman Shelter Director
See Chapter 18

In this picture is Sunshine, the homeless girl who was the inspiration for the story of Jillian. (See the girl in the orange hat!)

Bunkie's Breakfast cart under the Cow Key Bridge

This is what ripped the hole in Ethan's thigh. This one lived on the sea-wall behind my house for two years. I named him, "Narley Marley"!
See chapter 36

Barb's second favorite dish at Louie's, Grouper on Black Beans.
See Chapter 24

Louie's Backyard Café See Chapter 24 &33

Memorial to Ethan (RIP)

Bohemian Way (aka 'Lazy Way') Chapter 37

'Flamingo Crossing Ice Cream' See Chapter 32

Rollye
See Chapter 36

Krismas Chastity Hall See Chapter 38

29. A Curious Little Fellow

Carl turned left onto the access road to his office and passed the first group of homeless people parading slowly toward town after a night in the shelter. He was hoping to catch up on some of last week's avalanche of paperwork before his 7 a.m. briefing. As he turned under the building to park, he noticed a curious little man climbing out of the back seat of a taxicab wearing a cheap suit and a wide tie. After parking his cruiser, he met up with two other officers that were waiting at the elevator. Before stepping into the upbound car, he glanced toward the little man who was now exploring the parking garage looking for an access door.

"Here you go!" Carl called out, suspecting that the man might be Mr. Dougherty. The little man skipped awkwardly under the weight of the leg brace he wore hidden under his pants leg and hurried to join the officers who waited in the elevator. Upon entering the car, he turned around and faced the closing, polished doors. Struggling to catch his breath, he nervously clasped his hands in front of his chest and stared at the images of the three officers looming behind him. A lifetime of similar awkward situations had taught the man to be prepared for anything. Anything from rude jokes about little people, to being asked if his mother knew where he was. The battles in his past had forged him into a man with greater tenacity and fortitude than any champion mountain climber that had ever launched an assault against Mount Everest. Or, so he liked to think. As he scanned the three faces he asked, "Would you gentlemen know where I might find Officer Carl Dixon?"

Carl reached over the man to hold the door as they exited and responded with, "I'm Officer Dixon. Are you Mr. Dougherty?"

Offering his hand for shaking, the man said, "Bill Dougherty! Call me Bill." Carl directed the man to sign in with Rita, then after he had affixed his visitor's badge on his coat lapel Carl punched in the access code and led him down the corridor and into his office.

"Hang on just a minute," he said to the man as he picked up his desk phone and dialed three numbers.

"Hey Tripp! I'm here with Bill Dougherty, any chance you could join us in my office?"

Tripp was one of those get there before the hell breaks loose kinda guys, always on time, if not an hour early. He was on his way.

The officer sat in his chair and motioned for Mr. Dougherty to have a seat. "First, let me tell you, we have uncovered a lot of information with regard to where your daughter was, but not yet where she is." Carl moved some files on his desk as he talked. "I'm expecting a phone call before nine this morning that hopefully will answer that question."

He unhooked his utility belt and dropped it into his lower desk drawer and added, "Frankly, all I have is her car and a missed appointment. What I'd like to do is bring you up to speed with what we know so far, then, you can make a decision on which way you want to go."

Tripp stepped into the doorway with his U.S. Coast Guard Criminal Investigations coffee mug hanging from his trigger finger. He leaned against the doorframe flipping the mug like a Colt revolver as he listened to Carl's last few words, then said, "Come on boys, it's coffee time!"

The introductions were made as they headed down the hall. They gathered around the coffee pot and talked about the past week's development of events. Mr. Dougherty felt confident that he was in the right place, with the right people.

"I can't tell you gentlemen how thankful my wife and I are that you called," he said in hope of establishing a strong positive rapport with the men. He reached in his pocket, pulled out a handkerchief and removed his eyeglasses. As he cleaned the lenses, he tried to hide the moistness in his eyes.

Looking toward the blank wall he continued. "I don't know if you have ever had children, but my kids are my life. I'd fight to my last breath to keep them safe."

He turned to Officer Dixon and took a deep breath. "Can I ask you a question officer?" he asked.

Carl took a quick look at Tripp, then back to the man. "Go ahead!"

The veins in his forehead betrayed any coolness he hoped to portray. His heart pounded with fear as he asked, "Is my little girl dead?"

Carl gave him his answer without the least hesitation. "No sir," he answered. "She's just missing!"

Carl explained that he would be unavailable while he prepared for the upcoming briefing of his team of patrol officers. He asked Tripp to set up a laptop with a web feed in one of the empty offices. Tripp also offered to move the audio/visual cart for Mr. Dougherty to view the video from the liquor store. Tripp agreed to brief him on all the developments that he knew of and set up all the video clips. Carl told them of the discoveries he and Barb had made Saturday, out on Boca Chica Beach.

"Hopefully, we'll get in touch with this Dillon guy and close the case before it even gets opened," he speculated.

They walked back down the hall and as they came to an empty office, Carl turned around and gave them one other idea.

"The shelter can't help us without a court order, but even though her name didn't show up on our roster link, if she was there, maybe one of our surveillance cameras picked her up."

He paused for a second, then said, "Tripp, run the time periods for check-in and check-out from Wednesday afternoon on, and let Mr. Dougherty look 'em over for his daughter. Be sure to pull the best angle you can find." He knocked his knuckles against the wood door trim and added, "With a little luck, she'll be home for dinner."

Back at his desk he gathered Rita's pink callback notes and sorted through them pulling out the most important and throwing away any that he knew were already taken care of. Next, he set the unfinished time sheets under the call-back notes. He continued prioritizing the stacks of files and papers in his office until it was time for the briefing. As he left his office, he remembered that he needed to call Impound and order a cleanup on Jill's car. He pulled his cell phone from his belt and made the call. "Hey Nelson, this is Carl Dixon . . ." Nelson would have the car ready in one hour and all personal effects would be ready for inspection.

About thirty minutes into the briefing his phone vibrated across the podium. A quick glance was all it took to know Barb had info to deliver. When he finished issuing their assignments, he dismissed his men, gathered his papers, and returned her call as he walked back to his office.

"Hey, Sweetie," he greeted her. "Anything turn up on this Dillon character?" "I talked to Kitty, the wife of Dillon Maddox. She said they were out kayaking off Boca Chica Beach Monday morning and found Jill buried up to her waist in the salt marsh behind the N. A. S. landing strip. She told them she had gotten lost after a beach party and ended up stuck in the mud. They took her to her car on the front of Dillon's kayak. There was no boat! It wasn't a boating party with a lover named Dillon. She made it all up, probably to keep the roommate off her back!" Barb excitedly relayed the information.

"Thanks, honey! I gotta' go!"

He snapped his phone closed and slipped it into his top pocket. He stuck his head in to check on Mr. Dougherty who was attentively glued in amazement to the laptop screen.

"I'm on the video of her driving through your complex," he said without raising his eyes.

Carl tossed him an ink pen and said, "There should be a legal pad in the top drawer. You'd best take notes! Anything you see that fits into the puzzle, write it down. When you start looking at the lineup at the shelter gate, give everybody a number. We can cross reference the numbers later to our roster and maybe find something helpful. I'll be in my office if you need me." He started to leave then pulled back into the doorway and added, "The Dillon fellow was a hoax! It'll be in my report."

Mr. Dougherty tried to give Carl his thanks but he was already gone. Back at his desk, he started working on the time sheets. The deadline for submission was 11a.m. His phone rang and Nelson reported that the VW was ready to inspect. Several more calls came in, several others were returned. Rita brought more papers. Carl finished one stack and then returned a couple more calls. It was a masterful juggling act.

Just shy of 10 a.m., Mr. Dougherty tapped on his door and excitedly announced, "I found her!"

"I mean, on the video, the video of the line, at the shelter. She was in the line! She's number forty-seven. She was with a friend. An older lady with a big quilted bag." He entered the office and sat down in the side chair.

"What do we do next?" he asked.

Carl rocked in his big leather chair and searched his thoughts for the answer. He needed to prepare the man for what he was going to see when they entered the impound lot.

"This is good." He rocked to a stop and leaned forward. He opened his black leather binder that held his notes.

"Was she wet or dry?" Carl asked as he considered the implications of this new information.

"I think dry," Mr. Dougherty answered. He was obviously confused by the question!

"Did she walk up from the main road or drive up?"

Her dad answered quickly, "She walked, all the way up the road with the other woman."

"Was that on the video from Wednesday or Thursday?" Carl asked.

"Wednesday," Mr. Dougherty answered.

Carl asked, "What time?"

"5:32 p.m., that's when she first walked up," the man looked at his notes to confirm that his quote was correct.

"Well then, she lost her car sometime between 4:30 and 5 p.m," Carl said as he stood up behind his desk and reached to open the side drawer. "That left her just enough time to walk from the Cow Key Bridge to the shelter." He grabbed his gun belt out of the drawer and snapped the buckle closed. "This is good!" He stepped through the door and turned to Mr. Dougherty who was rising to his feet with a confused look on his face and said, "Let's get a look at her car." As they walked across the parking lot toward the impound gate, Mr. Dougherty asked several questions.

"Why did you say, 'this is good' when you found out she walked to the shelter on Wednesday?" he asked.

Nelson was standing in the shed and stepped out, into the morning sun, to greet the men. Before they entered the gate, Carl stopped in his tracks, which caused the little man who was almost running to keep up to pass him and then turn around to get the answer. While Mr. Dougherty caught his breath, his back was to the impound gate and he had not yet seen Jillian's crumpled car. Once his footing stabilized and he was looking at Carl's face, Carl explained, "Mr. Dougherty, when we found your daughter's car, it was a little more than just abandoned. It was abandoned one mile offshore. Now, we know that when it went into the water, your daughter didn't go with it."

Carl motioned for him to look through the gate. As Mr. Dougherty turned and saw his daughter's beat-up yellow Bug Carl said, "I'd say that's very good news!"

Carl allowed the dumbstruck man to approach the car and take in the scene on his own. Nelson led the officer into the shed to view the personal effects that had been buried on the floorboard. A purse, a cardboard box from Verizon Wireless with a new phone charger and ear plug still in their unopened plastic wrappers, a new cell phone, auto maintenance papers, her car owner's manual, and an assortment of other papers and personal items which one might have in a purse, were all clean of sand and lying on the insulated drying grid for inspection.

Mr. Dougherty joined the men in the shed and had noticeably lost what little color there had been in his face. He was not someone you might think of as being particularly 'accustomed' to the sun.

"Was this hers?" he asked as he slowly pulled himself up into the open doorway and looked at the display.

"It still is hers, as far as I'm concerned," Carl said as if he expected to be having lunch with the girl at noon.

"Mr. Dougherty, I don't know any better way to say this, but, I find no evidence that your daughter is dead. We just don't yet know where she is." He directed Nelson to bag up the items, then as he stepped back out of the shed, he slipped his sunglasses carefully in place and said, "I would suggest that you call your wife and have her fax you as current a picture as she has of your daughter, then you get it over to Office Max and print up some flyers."

Nelson handed over the bag and Carl headed back to the elevator with Mr. Dougherty trailing behind him. Under the building overhang, he dropped his glasses and added to his previous suggestion, "Give me an hour to put my notes together, then you can set up an appointment with our Missing Persons Department. Get the case filed then hit the streets. Talk to everybody you see. If you can't afford to rent a car or an electric cart, you might check out one of the scooter rental operations. They're on every corner around town.

"He shook the man's hand but didn't release it.

"Do you have a cell phone?" he asked as he closed his grip a little tighter.

"No!" the man answered.

"Go get one!" the officer directed.

He released his grip and turned his back toward the man as he walked away. He stopped at the elevator door and pushed the up button. Without looking back, he said, "A cab will pick you up in five minutes."

As he pushed through the security door he called out over his shoulder, "Rita, would you please call a cab for the little guy in the suit out front?" His tolerance was waning under the pressure of the mountain of work waiting on his desk. He was cool, but his magma was always kindled when around people who wanted to be coddled.

A man was a man no matter how tall he was, or wasn't. In Carl's experience, the daughter would probably turn up after some pretty boy from Texas was called home by his wife, and she got dropped off on his way out of town. Carl wanted to be through with the whole thing. He felt that he almost was.

.He finished typing up the sevenpage case discovery and stuffed it into an envelope with his business card stapled to the top left corner. He added the number of the Missing Persons Unit to the front of the card and wrote, 'Mr. William Dougherty' on the front of the envelope. He carried it to the front office and left it with Rita to hand over to him. He closed his office door, took a breath, picked up six bowling pins, and started juggling them in the air over his desk.

Well, maybe it was just five.

As far as he was concerned, the circus had left the building.

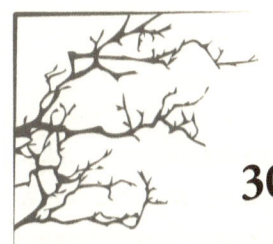

30. Ninety-Six Hours

S he had only stopped for a moment. The colors in the sky were so beautiful, the view of the Gulf so pristine this time of the morning. The sun was yawning from behind the clouds, stretching its golden arms across the starry universe, and over there was the moon, running toward the west, leading the way for all the stars to follow. It was the great celestial marathon and Jillian was watching in wonder, from her perch on the Cow Key Bridge.

"Hey, you better get moving, dingbat, or you'll miss the wagon."

Jill turned and watched Beni stomping off down the sidewalk toward town. She was always stomping, it was the way she kept people and roaches away from her. Who would want to walk with a skinny dried-up crackhead that walked like that?

"My, my", Jill thought. She smelled like a firefighter. She must have just gotten off work after battling a blazing house fire. Jill started to walk slowly in the same direction. The trail of smoke from Beni's recycled stogie followed her as she stomped away from the bridge.

"Thank you!" Jill yelled out toward the ghostlyframed woman.

Beni flipped her 'the bird' over her emaciated shoulder without a thought of turning around.

"Aren't you Chastity?" a woman's voice asked as a couple took her flanks, the tall lanky man on her left and the woman on her right.

"We met you in line last night at the shelter" the girl said with a suspiciously alluring smile.

Jill kept walking down the sidewalk as they adjusted their stride to match hers and smiled back as she looked at the woman and then at the man.

"I'm Laura, this is my boyfriend, Joe. Are you headed over to Higgs Beach to get breakfast at the Good Shepherd truck?" Laura asked.

Jill smiled and picked up her gait as she answered, "Oh yes, I always dine on their fabulous crepes. Aren't the blueberries delicious this year?"

Pastor Dan Haikus had bought the 1966 GMC concession truck from an old fellow that ran it as a mobile hotdog and slushy operation on the beach for over twenty years. It was a familiar landmark with its blue and green awning that rolled out over the sidewalk and shaded the bare-backed beachgoers while they waited to be served. Now, its claim to fame was as the roving outreach services vehicle for Pastor Dan's Ecclesiastical Holiness Church. The antiquated paintings of slushies and hotdogs had been sandblasted away and replaced with elaborate pictorial portrayals of Christ feeding the multitudes beside the sea, and huge unrolled scrolls of parchment proclaiming the entitlements of the meek, and their rights to inherit the earth.

As lofty and admirable as the endeavor was, it existed more by the grace of the city commissioners than the grace of God. At the monthly commission meetings, arguments from the public were regularly raised with regard to the effect such availability of free food had on the enabling of the homeless. Every seaside community in the world knows quite well that if on Thursday night you feed one seagull, by sunup Friday you could have six hundred more to feed. Many residents fought bitterly against the sanctioning of Pastor Dan's continuing with the practice of feeding the poor. Somehow though, their fury was quenched by some unforeseen power when taken to vote before the council.

Laura and Joe were charmed by her imagination and asked if she would like to walk with them to breakfast. She pulled up her baggy oversized blue-jeans and gamboled along between them. By the time they were halfway there, they were arm in arm like old friends.

Chastity was making up stories about working summers at Sundance, snow skiing the Utah slopes in winter, sitting in on preseason meetings, and movie screenings with Robert Redford treating everyone like family. She was being born again, right before their eyes.

She had overheard every word that Cheryl had said during Ronnie's in-take the night before. It stuck with her, a little too deeply. By the time they reached the line for breakfast, Jill no longer existed. She had been reinvented as Chastity A. Marrow. Born on December 14th, 1981 to the wonderful happy parents, James and Caroline Marrow of 3498 Paiute Dr., Provo, Utah, in the best little zip code in the world, 84604.

Bill Dougherty was only ninetysix hours behind her at that very moment. There she was, sitting beneath the tree by the beach enjoying the first bite of food she had eaten since the piece of pizza she had while watching the Letterman show on Tuesday night.

There he was, climbing from the back seat of the taxi cab at the black security gate in front of her apartment complex, not knowing if he would ever see her again, and her, not knowing that he was even looking. Less than a gentle 96-hour fold of time could have reunited this father with his little girl. From afar it looked so simple. Theories have a luxury in that respect.

He waited for a car to pull up. It didn't matter if it was coming in or going out. He just wanted to ask somebody if they had seen her. They came, they left. They pulled in, the gate closed behind. Not a single window lowered to his beckoning gestures. He must have looked like a door-to-door salesman. Drenched in sweat, tie pulled loose, coat draped over a black trash bag in the sand.

A girl on a bicycle punched in the gate code and was preparing to head out for a ride. He pushed off the curb and dragged himself over to the opening gate. "Please, I'm trying to find my daughter in apartment 302. She lives there with a girl named Canyon," he cried. His desperation was intense, and the girl on the bike saw it clearly.

"What's her name?" she asked.

"Jillian, Jill Dougherty. She's a nurse at the hospital. Do you know where she is?" he anxiously prayed.

"No! But you need to get out of the sun before you pass out. There's a hose behind the building." She reseated her ear buds as she took her first down-stroke against the pedal.

"Don't go in until I'm gone. I can't afford to get kicked out of here." She was out on the road when he grabbed his stuff and made his move.

There was no way to get into the building without the right access code for the keypad by the door. On a midafternoon Monday, there was not much activity when the 'humiture' was onehundred and six degrees. He lay low, in the back of the building, near the covered parking for a while. A few cars pulled in but the people appeared to be scared when they saw the strangely overdressed stranger on their property.

Soon, a police car pulled around the building and two officers stepped toward him. He started to approach and one held out his hand and ordered him to turn around and put his hands behind his head.

"Please, I'm just trying to find my daughter, she's missing," he said as he turned and complied with the order. One of the officers was patting him down when the little man said something that turned the whole dismal situation around.

"Please, call Officer Dixon, he'll verify . . ." he was cut off in mid-sentence. "Are you Mr. Dougherty?" one of the officers asked with concerned inflection.

"Yes, Bill Dougherty!" he answered.

"Mr. Dougherty, I am so sorry. Please, you can put your hands back down. We thought this call might be connected to you."

The two police officers stepped out of the sun and into the shade of the Royal Poinciana tree where Mr. Dougherty had been sitting.

"Sergeant Dixon has had all of us looking for your daughter since Friday morning. Here's her picture right here. He put these out at the Friday briefing." The officer said this as he held up a picture of Jillian that had been lifted from her Massachusetts driver's license. The other officer picked up Mr. Dougherty's belongings while the first led him over to the idling squad car and opened the back door. They went on to explain that every officer had been making routine checks on the apartment and that Jill's roommate was now dating one of their staff people and no one had seen or heard any news of his daughter's whereabouts.

In the car, Bill asked several questions and they advised him that Sergeant Dixon had prepared a report and a copy was waiting for him at the office. The officers drove toward the hotel district to drop Mr. Dougherty off at his room.

"Where are you staying?" the driver asked. There was a long silence in the back seat. "Sir, are you all right?" The officer on the passenger side looked over the seat to find that Mr. Dougherty was slumped forward with his face buried in his right hand. "Sir!" the young officer called out again.

Mr. Dougherty lifted his head out of his hand and mumbled, "Just drop me off at any park bench." Then, he sat back in the seat and hopelessly glared out the window toward the clouds.

It was an awkward situation. The two officers thought the man might be on the brink of an emotional cascade. They had no idea that he had spent almost all his money on the plane fare. He had come to save his daughter, but, he had to save himself first.

They pulled up at the side door of Anna's Cafe on South Street. The two officers climbed out of the patrol car and straightened their uniforms before climbing the stairs to the wraparound porch and the openair kitchen where Anna stood behind the counter waiting for her next customer to place an order.

"How's an ice, cold, lemon tea sound?" the officer called back to Mr. Dougherty before closing his door.

"That would be great, thanks!" Bill answered.

After retrieving the three cold drinks from the window, one of the officers sat at a table and waited while his partner took Mr. Dougherty his drink and returned.

"Man, this guy is in deep!"

"I don't know, Bud! I'd probably do the same thing if I was in his shoes. What do you think we ought to do with him?" The officers were ready to help to a point, but, there were calls going out on the radio all over the island, and they wanted to get back in the game as soon as possible.

"Let's get him back to the office so he can pick up the Sergeant's report before Rita leaves, and maybe he can check into the shelter when they open up."

The officers agreed on the plan and ordered three Cuban subs to go from Anna. Minutes later they were back on the road.

The officer in the side seat turned and handed Mr. Dougherty the third sandwich and explained the plan. They had no idea that the man had been hoping to find a way back to the shelter. After viewing the video of his daughter in the line, he thought that the shelter might be the place to meet someone who knew her. He already had the image of the older lady that was with her in the forefront of his mind. In reality, it was a futile hope. Nothing he might find at the shelter would help him "close the fold". He was still 96 hours behind her and the distance was growing by the minute. Sadly, it had more growing to do.

They dropped him off in the drive-through under the Sheriff's Office. He thanked them and then rode the elevator to the first stop. The doors opened in front of the Plexiglas booth where Rita sat protected from the threat of intrusion. She had to stand to see him and placed the envelope in the metal retractable drawer then pushed it through the airtight wall.

"Good luck, Mr. Dougherty," she sympathetically called through the intercom. "I'm sure you'll find her!"

He smiled but said nothing as he re-entered the elevator. The gate on the impound lot was locked. Jill's yellow VW was a sad reminder that she was somewhere out there, searching for her purse, her new phone, looking for her keys, wondering where she left her car.

He walked past the sheriff's helicopter landing pad and toward the concrete seawall. He sat there, dangling his tired legs over the water below. He opened the black trash bag and lifted the items one by one, laying them out on the seawall to his right. Next, he opened the envelope and began reading the sevenpage report.

When he finished, he turned and looked back through the fence at Jillian's car. It began to seem clear that she had suffered some emotional trauma or possibly just snapped. Maybe someone forced her to take a drug, or spiked her drink. Some wire came loose and just needed to be tightened down. If he could find her, he knew she could be fixed. It seemed no more complicated than when the equipment in his ice cream shop back home broke down. He either fixed it himself, or, he called someone else to do it. Simple as that!

The shelter gate opened and the cheers of the crowd awoke him from his thoughts. He slowly walked past the cavalcade of people that were making their way along the tall fence. Tired eyes, tortured bodies, and worn-out faces, none of which he recognized from the surveillance video. Perhaps the lady that he had seen with Jill was one of the first to go in and he had missed her. Perhaps he would find her already inside. He studied every face. He looked at nothing else, just faces. A few people walked up from behind him and joined the crawl. His advancement was slow and his legs were killing him.

By this time of night, he and Trina would be in full swing. The ice cream shop was always packed on hot July evenings. Kids would be screaming for their favorite flavors and then changing their minds about sprinkles or nuts. Trina's school friends would be there by now, keeping her distracted from her work. Now, his wife Dolores would carry the ball. The grueling fourteen-hour days would be tough on her, but she had done it before. Even while pregnant with the kids, she never complained.

As he shuffled forward, he considered the dilemma he had put himself in, and whether or not risking financial ruin to come here was the right thing to do. It was obvious that Officer Dixon and his men had gone far beyond their duties in their attempts to find his daughter. There seemed to be nothing he could do but get in their way.

Another shuffle brought him directly in front of the patrolman sitting in his squad car with the parking lights on. It was Billy Bones! Bones was a nickname that he had acquired in his junior high school days when he first learned to cast a fly for bonefish from his stepfather, Rocky Sandler, who was a pretty well-respected flats-fishing charter boat captain.

Billy was the boy to beat in the local junior men's division. If you strung up his stack of trophies you could anchor a cruise ship with them. Many of the patrolmen that work with Billy think that his name is actually Bones. But, not so! There he was now, monitoring the nightly shelter roster from his patrol car computer, tossing pistachio nut shells into a pile below his open window and thinking about fishing.

Mr. Dougherty was fighting a familiar old enemy that was climbing up the mountain behind him. He felt the grasp of the sinister specter as it wrapped its hand around his ankle, threatening to pull him down from his climb into a pool of defeat. Seeing nothing he could contribute to the investigation, he wondered if he shouldn't start looking for a way to get back home and just wait.

He moved his coat and the plastic bag one step closer to the shelter gate. Leaning against the fence to rest his sore left leg he gazed inside the compound and studied the strangers' faces as they loaded up their arms with their issue of linen and towels. Then, he had an epiphany. Maybe he could go places that the police couldn't. Maybe he could infiltrate the street people. Gather information, see things, clues that no policeman could find. Surreptitiously gather information, then feed it to the police. Maybe Jill was closer than he thought. He had a rejuvenation of purpose. Once again, he was a man with a mission.

"Oh man, this line moves too slow for me, how about you?" he complained to the man behind him.

"Yeah, I'll tell ya'one thing. I'd just as soon be back at my camp cep' the rain flooded it up last week and nothin' I ken do till it dries out good," the man said. Bill was intent in getting familiar with everyone he could. He wanted them to accept him as one of them and he felt that it wouldn't take long. Heck, he already was one of them. Just being broke, made him one of them.

That first night he laid a foundation that would hopefully serve to help him survive the endeavor that lay before him. He sat up with the smokers and told jokes, stories, lies, complained, spit, and laughed until the last one retired. He met Ronnie and her brother Tom, and Carter and Beni, and probably half of the night's guests before leaving the next morning. The one thing he purposely didn't do was ask if anyone had seen his daughter. He knew that if he was marked as someone trying to find someone they would cast him out, and the discovery of his purpose might be the downfall of his mission. This was not a trusting bunch of people, he could see that clearly.

The morning was still dark as he crossed the parking lot and passed by the pile of nutshells where Billy Bones had been parked the night before. He sat on the bench next to the elevator, waiting for the first of the Sheriff's Office staff to arrive. Shortly, cars started pulling underneath the building and people headed toward him. He recognized Officer Dixon and straightened his tie as he stood to greet him.

"Good morning!" he cheerfully announced to the officer as they met.

"Morning, Bill," the officer responded. "Any new developments?" Officer Dixon had successfully removed over half of the avalanche from his desk the day before and now felt a bit more available to the man.

"Well, I've got to tell you, I am so impressed with all the attention you and your wife and all your officers have given to my case, and I just want to tell you I absolutely will do my best to not become a burden on you or your department." He followed Carl onto the elevator and up to the reception room. The lights in the Plexiglas booth were not yet on and Officer Dixon held the security door for the man to enter. He reached into Rita's top desk drawer and pulled out a visitor's badge and handed it to the little man, who continued talking as they headed down the hallway. He sat in Carl's guest chair and continued his dissertation until all his intentions and plans were clearly put forth.

As Carl put his holster away he said, "You need to get the missing person's report filed as soon as you can. Then at least the detectives can pull in their tools. She may be right around the corner, but, if somebody doesn't get their eyes on her, she might as well be in Timbuktu."

He lifted a file on his desk and casually moved it to a stack of others, then added, "I understand you're staying at the shelter."

Mr. Dougherty was obviously embarrassed as he told the officer that he and his wife would be living off of the daily profits of the shop's ice cream sales, and that he would be getting a check each week for a small amount. Carl directed him to establish a general delivery address at the post office, then he suggested Bill see his wife Barb over at the bank for a local account. They talked about the need for having access to a phone. Carl advised him to take Jill's destroyed phone back over to Thomas at the Verizon Wireless store beside the bank to see if it was insured. He pulled a black and white copy of Jillian's driver's license from his notebook folder and slid it across the desk.

"Have you got a picture of her with you?" Mr. Dougherty advised that he did not and Carl left it on the desk for him to pick up.

"Have you got any money?" he asked. It was a direct question. Not one worth skirting. Bill knew the officer was only asking in his best interest. "Twentyeight dollars and about thirty cents," he humbly admitted.

"Well, you're not the first father who jumped in over his head to save his child from the jaws of an alligator, trust me on that." He then gave the man his final advice. "Pick up a monthly bus pass. It'll save you money. Get a cell phone. Eat at the soup kitchen; it's good food and it will free your money up for other things. Put out flyers everywhere and talk to everyone. Get hold of the detectives with anything you find out." He stood up and offered his handshake as goodbye, and added, "Don't get sick! Every handshake down here holds the potential to land you in the grave. It's just a tropics thing. You got to pay attention to it!"

Mr. Dougherty once again expressed his appreciation. They walked back to the lobby and Carl advised him to tell Rita, when she arrived, that he was there to file a missing person's report. He shook his hand one last time and said, "Good luck!" and then added, "She's a lucky little girl! I can't wait to meet her."

The little man sat down in the reception area to await Rita's arrival. It felt good to have a plan. He felt like hope had turned in his favor. He focused his eyes on the image of her face, staring up from the sheet of paper in his hands. In the silence of the waiting room, he whispered the thoughts from his heart, "Hang on baby, daddy's coming to find you."

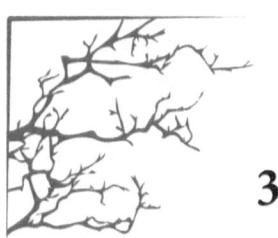

31. Gone in a Flash

"**Hey there Ms. Sundance,** let me get you some of our delicious banana pudding to top off your dinner today," Barry offered from behind the kitchen counter as he spooned a ladle full of the overly-processed gelatinous yellow mud onto her paper plate. It spilled into her meat pie and Caesar salad as it slopped down. He had met Jill the night before on her first visit to the soup kitchen. She was becoming known as 'Sundance', a nickname referencing her selffabricated imaginary life of working for Robert Redford at the famous film institution in the Utah Mountains.

Chastity looked up from under the brim of her newlyacquired used straw hat and smiled graciously at the cheerful fellow.

"And may God bless you, my dear friend," she said, then turned toward the old wooden social hall and proceeded to look for the perfect seat.

The day before, she had wandered over to the back door of the Salvation Army Thrift Center just a few blocks away, and, was allowed to pick out three charity items of clothing. She first chose a pink straw hat, decorated with green cellophane and two little Easter eggs. Next, she saw a yellow cotton skirt with a tiny colorful bird of paradise print. She pulled off her baggy jeans and tried on the skirt, right out in the open. It fit wonderfully! She folded her jeans and left them on the pavement.

Her eye caught a glimpse of a canvas bag with handles on top. She pulled it out from under the piles of other items and saw that it was lined with water-stained, white, nylon material. The outside was boldly painted with the words 'Florida's Best'. The words made a circle and in the middle of the circle was a beautiful full-color painting of three oranges. She held the bag up in the sun and squinted through the fibers to determine if it was waterproof.

"Yep, this will do just fine," she announced to a fly that happened to be passing by.

Talking to flies was becoming as natural to her as changing clothes anywhere the clothes determined to be in need of being changed.

"Hey, Missy Sundance! Looking good girl!"

It was Laura. She had met her the morning before with her boyfriend, Joe. They had walked to the breakfast wagon together, and then to Bay View Park, where they had spent the greater part of the morning laughing at the tourists as they stared at all the people sleeping the day away.

"Where's Joe?" Chastity asked.

"In jail where he belongs," Laura answered angrily. "He got caught with some other dirtbags doing a hit of coke and then tried to fight the cops. I didn't want anything to do with it and told the cops to just take him. That son of a bitch beat my ass too many times for me to put up with his crap."

None of this seemed to phase Chastity as she picked at her plate of food and kicked her leg in cadence to the ceiling fan above her head.

"Good riddance to Joe!" Chastity said. Then she added, "Typical dirtbag for me, I guess."

It seemed that the words didn't have to be appropriate. They didn't even have to make sense. Just a group of words somewhat sounding like they might support a consensus was all it took to align the two women against Joe and create the necessary bond to make it through the next few hours.

Laura picked through the plate of food and tasted one thing, spit it out, then another, and spit it out. She looked up and shouted at her friends as they took seats along the line up of cafeteria tables. She tasted the banana pudding, spit it out, turned to Chastity and said, "Let's go out to Christmas Tree Island and get some good food. Ya' wanna?"

Chastity was all over anything glazed in Christmas. Her expectations were sky high as images of Rudolf, Santa, chimneys and falling snow flew through her head. With a, wide open mouth and eyelids lifting the edge of her hat, she excitedly took a deep breath and shouted like a six-year-old, "Yeah, count me in for that!"

They darted from the hall hand in hand, like school girls heading out to recess. Three blocks away Laura was still tightly holding on to Chastity's wrist. Chastity was a step behind, trying to keep up. Her body was weak. She was still running on less than two hours of sleep per day. Like a welfare mother dragging someone else's child to the food stamp office, Laura pushed on, jerking Chastity by the wrist each time she slowed down.

"Almost there!" Laura announced as they walked down a dark alley to the edge of the water. Several small beat-up boats were pulled up on the sandy beach. Chains were wrapped around their engines to deter the motor thieves and most looked like they were a hundred years old. There were several people standing in the water loading guitar cases and bags of food into a couple of the boats. Three or four more people were sitting in their kayaks beside them waiting for the signal to depart.

"Who are these people?" Chastity asked as she and Laura approached two young men with long woven dreads standing on the sand passing a marijuana joint from one to another.

"These guys are rainbow children and those out there are boat people. They live on the houseboats and sailboats that are moored off the back side of the island," she explained confidently.

Laura walked over to the two boys as if she knew them and after taking a long toke from their joint she asked if the Saturday night jam was still on. Chastity walked out on the concrete dock and looked toward the western sky as the last orange rays of sun turned purple, and then faded into darkness.

"Come on, Sundance!" Laura called out for her to join them. The two boys unlocked their dinghy and pushed it out into the glassy water. Minutes later the three little boats were slowly idling across the deep channel, followed closely behind by a string of kayakers. As they pulled farther away from shore, they met with an armada of similar microvessels. Up ahead, across the dark water, was the ghostly silhouette of their destination, Christmas Tree Island.

Some of the boats had red and green navigation lights on their bows. Those without lights left their operators vulnerable to citation if caught by the harbor police and subject to being arrested. To Jill, they looked like water sleighs, pulled by swimming reindeer, with Christmas light noses. They motored toward the eastern end of the island and then followed the dark shoreline around to the back side, where each boat found a place to pull up onto the beach, hidden from view of Key West.

People were unloading their instruments and supplies, dogs, kids, pots, pans, beer, walking sticks, flashlights, and everything imaginable. One guy even carried his drum set. There was a trail that led from the beach into the forest of trees. People were disappearing into the darkness with their flashlights blinking in all directions, shooting beams of white light through the treetops.

"Is this Christmas Tree Island?" Chastity asked Laura as they climbed from the boat and into the shallow water. Laura turned around quickly and gritted her teeth at Chastity.

"Shut up! Just shut up!" she said angrily, then grabbed one of the boys by the arm and disappeared down the trail. The second young man overheard Laura's rude lashing and came over to Chastity to console her.

"She's just a burnout stoner. Don't let her get to ya," he said.

He was a handsome though unusually skinny boy, probably nineteen or twenty years old. He wore cutoff jeans that hung so low that they showed his striped underwear, and a white tank top. He pulled two bottles of wine out of the front of the boat and said with a grin, "Come on, let's go see if Santa Claus is home."

They walked the trail into the darkness of the tall Australian pines. A light breeze was whispering across their tops sounding a faint and gentle whistle as the highest cones lost their seeds and launched them toward the ground. The tiny pods fluttered and twirled all around them as the couple made their way up the trail.

"What kind of bugs are these?" Chastity asked as she followed the boy through the shadows toward the firelight up the trail.

"No, they're not bugs!" he laughed as he explained; "They're seeds. You can make tea out of them. Or you can eat them. I'll show you tomorrow. Come on, we're almost there."

He was holding her hand as they made their way through the last stretch of the trees. They emerged into a broad clearing where people were busy preparing for the Saturday night festival. The growing bonfire was casting everyone's shadows high up the wall of the tree trunks that stood guard over the secret village. Several tents had been erected at the perimeter of the camp. The ground was covered in a mesh of pine needles, and fallen logs circled the fire pit.

A blue tarp had been hung over the kitchen area. Several girls were preparing salads and bread, almost ready to be served. There were lots of musicians tuning their guitars, mandolins, banjos, and fiddles. The drummer had almost completed his setup and was making his last-minute adjustments before sitting down and striking up a rhythm. Lots of dogs ran freely through the camp, and there were children, beautiful children, running and playing through the shadows and sparks. Blond-headed boys with beads in their long hair were chased by redheaded girls, the sons and daughters of the boat people. Homeschooled boys and girls that were growing up free to explore their creative souls by making up poems, painting on shells, and keeping count of the stars that fall. Everyone knew each other. No one was a stranger. It was Christmas! Christmas Tree Island!

Chastity followed the boy as he reunited with old friends and acquainted himself with new ones. She shyly stood to his side and held his hand with her fingers as they moved through the camp. He went to the kitchen to open his wine and Chastity joined a group of girls, dancing to the music of some of the guitar players that had begun a song. The smell of burning pot was thick in the air. They passed it freely from one to another. No attempt was made to hide it from the children and several of the older kids were allowed to take drags from their mothers' own hands.

Chastity joined in with great enthusiasm. She danced, she smoked, she sang, she drank; she ran, jumped, fell, rolled, spit, ate, listened, and then passed out in the pine needles behind a log. Sometime in the night she woke up to find everyone except two men had either fallen asleep or left. She walked to the edge of the encampment and crouched in the needles to relieve herself, then returned to the kitchen and poured a glass of wine from a bottle that was half empty.

One of the men that was still there was a guitar player who had caught her eye earlier. He approached the kitchen and poured a glass of wine. He drank the dark juice like water, then wiped his lips. Chastity stood closely in front of him, watching his every move. Their eyes locked in the fading firelight. He reached up and without a word stroked her hair. She leaned slightly forward into his arms and closed her eyes. Their lips gently washed over each other's like waves breaking over a jetty. They dropped to the ground and kissed deeper and deeper until the tastes in their mouths merged into one.

"Good morning!" he called down through the open hatch above. She squinted as she tried to see what this charming, shirtless fellow looked like in the daylight. His curly hair and blue eyes were the first attributes she noted. He climbed down into the cabin and sat on the edge of the narrow bunk.

"Someone said your name was Sundance." She rubbed her eyes and smiled.

"I'm Ethan," he said, "Ethan Hall." He reached up and gently brushed some sand off of her shoulder, then handed her a damp washcloth to wipe her face.

"Are you hungry?" he asked as he climbed back out of the tiny cabin to check on the snapper filets that were waiting to be turned on the grill. He ducked his head back in and pointed to the door on the right. "This is the bathroom if you want to freshen up. Just be sure to turn off all the switches or it will drain the batteries."

Chastity felt completely comfortable with her new surroundings, like-wise with her newfound boyfriend.

"Don't put any salt on mine, I hate salt," she called out as she folded the sheets and climbed into the head to pee. She left her skirt on the couch and joined the handsome fellow on the deck. She stretched and yawned as she looked at the vessel she had been swept away to.

"Nice boat!" she said with approval, as if she was a connoisseur of nice boats. "You like it? I built it from scratch. Every bit of it! It's a trimaran, *The Canadian Soul*!" Ethan said as he slipped the fish onto two paper plates and poured coffee. "After we finish eating, I'll take you on a tour." He took his first bite and began to shed his thoughts.

"You've got everything you ever need right here. All the food you could want, rainwater to drink, cover from the sun, and sails to take you away from the storms; there is very little beyond this boat that we need."

He finished his breakfast and as he began his morning inspection he continued, "I've lived like this for fourteen years. This is my third boat."

He had claimed his cabinmate, and was now ready to return to St. John. She seemed a perfect catch. Completely malleable, easy prey! This was why he had sailed back to the miserable little tourist town at the end of the road. He had grown disillusioned and impatient. He was tired of too many nights of playing catch and release. Their first words after waking were always, "I need to get back . . ." This one seemed like a keeper.

She sat there in the morning sun, smiling at him, eating fish with her fingers, listening as he talked of his bold and cavalier ideologies.

"I've had enough of this stuff," he said as he looked toward the million-dollar yachts tied up one on top of another dockside at the bight. He went on with his rant.

"Here, you've got too many people! There's the clubbers on Duval Street, the tourists, the money makers, then the boat people, the rainbows, and the criminals; they're all on the take, tripping over each other while they try to fill their cups. Their all missing it! This is the only thing anybody needs," he explained as he held both of his hands out toward the ocean. "If you don't need it, leave it for the next guy. It's all gotten so complicated."

He kept talking as he climbed through the guy wires and around the mast making his preparations. He pulled on the rope until the anchor released its grip on the sand below. The craft bobbed and yielded to the current, swinging its bow into the outflowing tide. He hooked the boom into the eyebolt and inserted the cotter pin, then began hoisting the heavy sail toward the sun. It hung there flapping in the gentle breeze and when he returned to the helm and cinched the ropes tight, she flew like a great gull, off toward the southern horizon. Gone in a flash.

32. Flamingo Crossing

It was **Mr. Dougherty's** second night at the shelter. All the faces he had seen the night before, he was seeing once again, plus a few new ones. Unfortunately, the one he was hoping to find had widened her gap from ninetysix hours and one mile, to ninetysix hours and onehundred and seventy-eight nautical miles. While he waited for the nightly shuffle to begin, Jill and Ethan were dropping anchor on a rock pile behind the south Bimini Island lighthouse.

He had moved to the halfway point in the line. He stood with his back to the fence while he watched the young officer sitting in his police cruiser, scanning the roster for suspect information. The sun had dropped behind the jail and soon the bright security lights would flash into night mode, blitzing the compound like a war zone.

Mr. Dougherty was mentally reviewing the details of his case. He realized he was standing at about the same place in line that he had seen on the surveillance video where Jill had turned around and said something to the man behind her. She had seemed familiar with the fellow. He strained to recall the image of the man's face, but could not quite bring it into focus.

Jill had been number fortyseven in line when the gate opened on that Wednesday night. Two people ahead of her had turned and left before going through the gate. That meant that she would have moved up to be the fortyfifth person checking in. The woman that she had arrived with would have been the fortyfourth person. He had been told by Officer Dixon that the information could, later, be checked by the missing person's detective. He picked up his coat and the black trash bag and headed toward the officer in the parked police car.

Billy Bones looked up and saw him approaching then intentionally locked his stare back on his computer screen.

"Yes sir, how can I help you?" he asked without looking up as Mr. Dougherty set his bag on the pavement. The officer's left shoulder was leaning against the open window as he continued to scan the computer.

"Yes sir," he began, "my name is William Dougherty and I was just wondering if . . .

"Billy cut him off and asked him, "What's the number?"

Mr. Dougherty was taken aback by the officer's astoundingly intuitive question. He answered the officer with a tone of surprise. "My daughter was number fortyfive and the woman she was with was forty-four. Is it possible to check . . ." Billy broke him off again. "Was that on Wednesday?" he asked as he accessed the roster information for the previous week.

"Yes sir!" the little man answered.

Billy took a second to count through the list, then printed two pages of data. In the top right corners, he wrote the appropriate corresponding numbers and passed the pages inconspicuously through the open window.

"Don't ever approach a police car when it's parked over here. We don't want these people to think that we sit here for their benefit. Understand?" Billy admonished him. Mr. Dougherty appreciatively acknowledged that he understood and bent to pick up his coat and bag. When he stood back up the officer was still watching the screen and asked, "Did you get the MPR filed upstairs yet?"

"Yes, I did," Bill responded.

"Did you get a phone?" The officer asked.

"No, but I'm checking back with the guy at the phone store tomorrow," he answered. He was amazed that so many officers were so knowledgeable of his problems. He stood there waiting to see if there were other questions that the officer wanted answered. Instead, Billy said, "Have a nice day," and then tossed a fist full of nutshells out the open window.

Mr. Dougherty backed away from the car as he thanked the officer and turned to return to the line which had progressed without him. Over the next thirty minutes, he watched several others break line and attempt to persuade the officer to give them information or assist with their problems. After the first two men were denied, Billy Bones moved his patrol car to the next lane back and resumed his previous posture. Mr. Dougherty soon discovered that he had somewhat alienated himself from the population of shelter guests with this earlier contact. The same fellows that he had worked so hard building trust with the night before now gave him a cold shoulder. He had betrayed solidarity. It was easy to see that with this one seemingly innocent move, he had marked himself, possibly forever, as an outsider, or even worse, an infiltrator.

That night before the lights were turned out, he reviewed the information he had received from the police officer. Number 45, Chastity A. Marrow! Where did this name come from? He had never heard of a James or Caroline Marrow, Chastity A. Marrow, or anything that sounded like these names. He began to wonder if he had counted the numbers in the line correctly. If he had been off by one number, Jill might be the next one on the officer's list. He decided that, if needed, he would seek to review the video again and renumber the people in the line more carefully. Until then, he had to trust that this was the name she had used when she registered.

He waited till the lights were turned out. He watched the shadows of the smokers outside as they put out their cigarettes and retired for the night. He listened for the storeroom window to be closed and locked, then likewise, the door. He could faintly hear Ronnie and her brother talking inside the office. The hum of the concession machines blocked him from making out their words. He laid waiting for hours, till there was no human noise beyond the roar of snoring men, then he ventured through the tent flap and up to the closed glass window at the office.

He tapped on the wall beneath the counter. Ronnie frowned through the glass and cleared the safety bar. She pulled the window up only halfway and asked, "What do you need?" He held up the picture of Jillian that Officer Dixon had given him for her to see and asked, "My daughter, she was here last Wednesday night. Do you know where she is?"

Ronnie opened the window and snatched the paper from his hand. "Hey, Tom," she called to the back office.

She handed the picture to her brother and, after they both had examined the image, Tom explained, "Look Bud, we can't verify that kind of information. People in these shelters are here for all kinds of reasons. There is no way we can be sure that you're not an ex-boyfriend trying to track some girl down to cut her throat. So, I'm sorry but, it's a confidentiality thing. One slip and we shut down. *Comprende?*"

Bill held up his own driver's license to show that the last names were the same but Tom handed the picture of Jill back through the window and apologized as he closed it and walked away.

Bill finally fell asleep just minutes before the morning lights came on. After turning in his linen, he turned to pick up his coat and bag and almost fell into Ronnie's breasts as he turned to leave. She was reaching over him to toss some towels into the laundry room.

"Sometimes life bites you in the ass, and sometimes it cuts you to the bone, but sometimes," she paused as she bent to pick up two more towels that she had dropped at her feet intentionally and continued with, "it hits the *Marrow*, and that's when it hurts the most."

She turned and walked toward tent #2 without looking at him. He dried his eyes as he walked through the open gate. Before he rounded the corner of the compound his glance caught hers through the fence.

"Thank you!" He mouthed silently. She offered no acknowledgement to his gesture. She just coolly eyed him as he walked away. He could have sworn that he saw her lip turn slightly upward in one corner. Maybe, that was too much to expect.

By the time he walked the mile it took to reach McDonald's, the morning sun was already burning through the clouds. He sat outside and ate his Egg McMuffin and drank his cup of black coffee. He was in no hurry. The Verizon Wireless store would not open for two more hours. He looked out across the bay as a jet skier sped across the glassy water. Halfway between his seat on the bench and the bay, a red Dodge Durango passed by on the highway, then pulled abruptly into the motel parking lot that adjoined the McDonald's. The driver circled back across the pavement and pulled into the vacant space directly in front of him and stopped.

"Mr. Dougherty!" The driver called out after lowering his window. It was Thomas, the manager of the phone store. Bill left his coat on the bench and carefully traversed the steep grassy decline to the truck.

"I got through to our business office and was able to get them to approve me setting you up with a new phone. I just need to fax them a copy of your driver's license and a missing person's report, and then call someone in Massachusetts that can verify that you are who you say you are."

"My God! That's great news," Bill exclaimed.

Thomas went on to explain, "Your daughter purchased insurance on the new phone last Monday and caught up on her bill so you could probably use it for maybe three months without having to make a payment."

"Oh, that will be no problem. The bill can be sent to my home in Gloucester. My wife pays all our bills on the third each month," he proclaimed with pride.

The young man explained, "I've just got to run over to Publix, and then if you want, I can open up early and get you fixed up." Thomas seemed genuinely anxious to help him in his quest to find his daughter.

"Oh, I can't tell you how great this is," Mr. Dougherty told him.

Later, at the store, all the requirements were met and his first call was to Officer Dixon. He left his new phone number on the officer's voicemail and headed to the post office to arrange for his mail delivery. By three p.m. he was on his way to the soup kitchen feeling like a real human being again.

He now had a phone, a place to receive his mail, had located the Western Union office, got the prices of fliers and cards at Office Max, found a small electric scooter at a pawnshop that he could purchase for $85.00, a perfectly reasonably priced place to sleep 'free', and an almost all you can eat for free feeding hole that opened at 4 p.m. seven days a week. He would call his wife Dolores that night, after the ice cream shop closed, to fill her in on his progress and arrange for a $200.00 cash transfer. By lunch tomorrow he would be scooting around town with a hammer on his belt and every telephone pole, park bench and tourist turnstile would be posted with his daughter's picture. It was a well laid campaign and his expectations were sky high.

He was just about to walk through the gate to the Good Shepherd soup kitchen. The line at the door was building fast and his belly was growling for lack of food. The energy from the morning's McMuffin had long ago been spent on walking in the hot sun. His phone rang for the first time. He scrambled to find the right button to push, then answered, "Hello, this is Mr. Dougherty!" It was detective Anthony Rivera calling from the sheriff's missing person's division.

"Oh, yes sir, can you tell me anything about my daughter?" he asked anxiously. The detective explained that he and Officer Dixon had been looking at the case together since the previous Friday morning and that he had been waiting until it was formally filed before he could act officially on the information that they had gathered. He said that he had already contacted Ms. James, the lady who had brought Jillian to the shelter, and had discovered that the Marrow name had been made up and now considered to be Jillian's alias.

Every question asked by the hopeful father was answered thoroughly and it appeared that the sheriff's office was at a dead-end. The detective explored the possibilities of criminal activity or abduction and asked if Jill had any individuals in her past who might want to do her harm. Bill assured him no one had ever expressed anything less than the best of feelings for her. The conversation ended with the detective admonishing him to refrain from any activity that might be best explored by the police, and to report any pertinent information directly to him. Mr. Dougherty acknowledged that he understood and that he intended to comply with the instructions. It was all too clear that their road had come to an end. If anything was to be turned up, he would be the one to do the turning.

Almost six months passed. It was two days before Christmas. The posters of Jill had twice been replaced. His heart was no lighter nor less determined than it had been when he had first landed on the island. His electric scooter had served him well on its daily motoring from the Stock Island Shelter to town and back. Several hurricanes had come and passed, and still no sign of his little girl.

He had taken a part-time job at the Flamingo Crossing ice cream shop on Virginia Street. The owners also owned the wine club next door and had turned over most of the ice cream shop duties to Bill while they enjoyed serving a higher class of clientele, sitting on the front porch smoking cigars, drinking wine, and hobnobbing with their guests. The regulars trusted him and the tourists pushed him around. People tend to be more arrogant and demanding when they're on vacation. With nobody of hometown familiarity to call them out as they misbehave and no reputation to protect, they seem to take liberties beyond their usual character and explore their limits. Bill was used to it. He handled them well!

Officer Dixon and his wife Barb would bring Baby by after their evening trips to the dog park. Bill had come up with the idea that if all dogs that visit were given a free doggy cone, their owners would feel obligated to purchase a regular cone for themselves. The idea became a tremendous hit with the local dog crowd. Bret and Tequila, the shop owners, loved the idea and watched the dollars mount as the promotion became more and more popular. Hot nights brought a steady parade of fancifully dressed mutts and their paying parents to the little ice cream shop on the corner. Bill had begun offering Liver Snap Crunch dip as a topping and Chicken and Gravy Sundaes in a cup. It was pure genius!

"Hey Bill, how are you doing?" Carl offered his usual congenial greeting to the little man who he had come to know so well. They regularly ran into each other around town. Barb likewise had become quite familiar with him. He had opened a savings account with her help and she saw him all around the island. This 'particular' night, Bill looked as if he had not slept in days. As he scooped their order and handed the cones across the counter, he shared his dilemma.

"My wife and I have been trying to decide how much longer we should go on like this. We can't make up our minds if I should hold out for the whole year or call it quits. I think that every day I stay is one more chance to meet someone that knows where she is. I really don't want to go back yet. I just feel like she's close, so close, and ready for me to wrap my arms around her and take her back home. I think we should hold out longer." His eyes were swollen and red as he confided his misery.

Carl passed him a twenty and stuffed two ones in the tip jar. Bill went on to ask, "What do you think?" He handed Carl his change then continued, "You think I'll ever be able take her back home?"

Carl and Barb both felt sympathetic to his story. Barb wasted no time at all with her answer. "Bill, you just have to do what you feel in your heart is right. If you believe, anything could happen."

Carl took a lick off his spumoni and turned to look down into Baby's expectant green eyes. "What's the good dog think?" he asked the big red golden.

"Woof," she answered as if she knew exactly what to say.

"I think so, too, Baby!" he agreed.

Carl looked over at Bill as he held the cup low for the dog to get a lick and said, "Yeah, I can't wait to meet her!"

Carl had always made his opinion on the matter clear. If he could bet on the worst of odds that his own son could return from his grave, he would be the most penniless pauper in the betting line. Unfortunately, the hinges on death's door swing in only one direction.

33. Delivered, Devoured & Delectable

D r. Colburn drifted off to sleep as the little puddle jumper passed over Florida City and flew south toward Key Largo. The roar of the engines was a much-needed sedative. His last night in Chicago had been more than draining. After years of advising clients to submit to their primal instincts and allow laughter to ease their worries, to howl when frustration threatened to break them, to hug when they needed a touch, and to cry often, his advice had fallen deaf to his own ears, until last night. He was drained! Only sleep would salve his open wounds and it came easily tonight. Unfortunately, his respite would be short-lived.

The bell chimed and the pilot announced, "Ladies and gentlemen, please bring your seats into the upright position and assure that your seatbelts are properly locked in place as we begin our descent. The temperature is currently seventyseven wonderful degrees at sea level on this July evening and we at Gulfstream International Airlines wish you a safe and enjoyable stay in the beautiful city of Key West."

The doctor straightened himself and buckled his seat belt. His only baggage, a magazine and the clothes he wore. He struggled to get comfortable as he adjusted the envelopes of money bulging in his pockets. He gazed out the window as the plane rumbled along the landing strip then turned toward the terminal and rocked forward as it came to a stop. The crew began their preparations for unloading the waiting passengers. The weary doctor turned his eyes away from the window and fought to avoid remembering the last time he had landed there. He was not ready! Not yet!

He paused on the tarmac before entering the terminal. He turned and looked back at the plane and for a moment he thought he saw himself in the window, preparing to disembark with a beautiful woman at his side, laughing, smiling, and happy. But, the plane was now empty. He could see the attendant walking through the fuselage straightening up for the next passengers to board for their return to the mainland.

He dropped his eyes to his feet and hoped that they would turn him around and lead him back to Chicago, but no, not this time. Not a chance! He had decided to face his demon and it lived on this island, this 'Island of Bones'.

He turned back toward the terminal and proceeded straight through the lobby without stopping. He exited the front of the building where the cab drivers were waiting to carry the travelers the two miles into the city. He looked out across the parking lot toward the Atlantic Ocean and took in a full dose of the tropical air as he stepped into the crosswalk and over to the sidewalk that would lead him into Key West.

"Excuse me!" a man called out as he approached on a green electric scooter and pulled to a stop by the curb.

"Listen, I'm leaving to go back to my home in Massachusetts and if you want to have this scooter, it's yours," he said as he climbed off of the machine and leaned it toward the apprehensive stranger.

The odd little man seemed quite genuine in his offer but the doctor gratefully declined.

"No! Really!" the fellow continued. "I've had it for a year and just put new bushings in the motor a week ago; it's electric and runs great. I absolutely insist! It's yours! You can use these bungee cords to strap your bags on the handlebars, what do you say?"

Dr. Colburn was taken by his persistence and finally accepted the gift with the stipulation that as soon as he found someone that needed it more than he it would become theirs. The men happily shook on the agreement and Mr. Dougherty handed him the key to the lock on the chain that was wrapped around the seat post, then he headed into the terminal.

The July night was breezy but, at seventyseven degrees, completely acceptable without complaint, compared to Chicago. He pushed the scooter slowly along the sidewalk at a casual speed; he was in no hurry. The night was dark but the streetlights and moon adequately illuminated the way.

Passing along Smathers Beach where the summertime vacationers would soon be rallying in their revelries, he saw the Hobie Cats sitting in rows on the sand, waiting for the tourists and the next day's sun. The breeze beat the sail lines gently against the aluminum masts. He could hear the brass snaps tapping metal to metal as he approached on the sidewalk. It was a clatter not easily avoided in the night air.

He found himself in a surprisingly pleasant state of mind. Looking at his watch he was happy to see that the time was just before nine p.m., earlier than he thought it might be. There was more than one good reason to get into town before it got too late. As he slipped his right hand into his jacket pocket for assurance that his finances were still intact, he picked up his pace.

Now was a good time to consider what he wanted to do when he got into the city. Actually, he could hardly believe that he had made it this far. Ever since he left Chicago, he had been sure that something would come up to knock him back into reality and cause him to turn and go home. He had fully expected for that to have happened before he even got into that Chicago cab and hired Leo to take care of the birthday present for his grandson. But, when he let his phone drop into the fountain at the airport, well, that was when he heard the crack, and when the rubber band goes snap, nothing is ever the same. He rounded the corner at Atlantic and First Street and followed the ocean toward Higgs Beach. He started making mental notes as he pushed the scooter along. First, a good meal, and a beer! I haven't had a cold beer in way too long. And a hotel room, maybe a little mom-and-pop Key West kind of operation. Must find a bank! Local! No big chains! Keep it simple for a while. Maybe give this scooter to a kid and rent one of those electric carts. This thing is far too dangerous for an old man!

The beautiful, historic Casa Marina Hotel was being remodeled after suffering extensive damage from Hurricane Wilma's surges. Construction equipment and trucks blocked the sidewalk along Seminole Street. He moved to the middle of the road and pushed the scooter for another block and a half. At the end of the road, he came upon a small oceanside park.

It appeared to be a commemorative park with the entrance flanked by two bronze plaques. The light was not quite bright enough to read the relief but he determined to make it back and read it at some later date. He passed the beautiful Coconut Beach Resort, turned the corner and felt lucky to find Louis's Backyard Café still serving.

"Good evening, sir, welcome to Louis's Backyard Café," the gentleman greeted.

"Will you be dining alone?" he asked.

"Yes, thank you." Dr. Colburn answered.

"Do I remember reading that you have dining outside by the water?" Dr. C. asked the man as they turned into the main dining room of the beautifully converted old Key West two-story oceanfront home.

"Absolutely sir, it is a beautiful evening for dining on the deck," he answered. "I believe the moon is almost full tonight."

They made their way down the back stairs to the broad wooden dining deck and the outside bar over the water. He handed the doctor a menu and advised him that his waiter would be with him in a moment, then turned and returned to the house through the open glass doors.

The doctor relaxed and took in the view for a moment. What a wonderfully romantic place to dine. He imagined his wife's gentle voice, reading the wine list aloud. He slowed his breathing to the lowest possible flow and searched for even the slightest hint of her perfume.

"Good evening, sir, my name is Sebastian. Have you had a chance to review our wine list?" The waiter's voice drew him back from his fantasy. 'Sebastian', he thought! Sounds like a name that someone would choose for themselves as an escape alias. A name one might use to hide a lifetime of disappointments, failed expectations, brutal relationships, and possibly unacceptable behavior practices behind. Sometimes the eye of a highflying eagle sees the tiniest of movement that a lesser hawk would miss. Such is the way when flying through the canyons of psychiatry. It was so hard to turn off the radar.

"No, if you don't mind, I'll have a bottle of beer, please," he told the lanky young man as he handed him back the wine list.

"May I recommend a nice Irish Kells Lager we have just added to our selection? It has a very smooth mellow flavor with a crisp apple finish. It is considered to be an excellent accompaniment to seafood and poultry."

Dr. Colburn was delighted with the waiter's presentation and accepted his recommendation instantly. The menu offered an eclectic selection of Caribbean, European and modern American dishes. Reading it was as enjoyable and entertaining as everything else about the restaurant had proven to be. When Sebastian delivered the ale, he was well prepared to place his order.

"I'll start with the Arugula salad and the Bohemian conch chowder. Oh, and bring me some of the crabstuffed Portobello mushrooms, too." He was already salivating as he imagined the feast that would soon be laid before him. This was going to be the first formal meal he would be sitting down to in over a week.

"And the fish and shellfish Garganelli pasta with roasted garlic sounds great," he ordered as he handed the menu back to the man.

"Very nice choices sir," Sebastian commented. "If by chance the gentleman is partial to a touch more 'fiery' cuisine, may I offer that we have a delicious roasted jalapeno butter sauce that might lift his pleasure to a slightly more desirable height, if you know what I mean," Sebastian suggested with a devilish grin.

The doctor was amused by the man's obvious sexual connotation but had no intention of acknowledging that he, 'knew what he meant'. It was far more obvious from his flamboyant gestures and his hesitation of tongue that Sebastian probably rode his Harley from the sissy seat. Still, no amount of discretion could hide the good doctor's appreciation for the unprecedented service. The boy was looking for a tip, and he need not stretch his luck.

Dinner was delivered, devoured, and delectable. There was absolutely no question about it. He topped it off with a key lime tart and a hand-rolled Cuban cigar. The moon made friends with everyone it cast its smile upon as they relaxed and talked on the tiki-torched deck. He knew now that he had made the right decision.

Yet, it was no decision. He had not considered any consequences that might result from turning his back on his responsibilities. He merely answered a calling, yielded to a force, submitted to his destiny, and ended up here.

Finally, he understood what had happened. He had fought his need to confront the loss of his wife for almost one full year. He could go no further until it was over. He knew all the answers, all the processes, all the stages, but he had not asked the questions, taken the steps, or walked through any of the doors. Now, he was on the end of the plank, and ready to jump. He had no choice, no excuse, and no reason to say 'no'.

Sebastian calculated the bill and offered to take it when he was ready. Dr. C. put two onehundred dollar bills in the folder and headed for the front of the house. Sebastian passed him in the main dining room as he was leaving and they exchanged a friendly goodnight.

He stepped out the front door and down the stairs to the sidewalk where his scooter awaited his return. The doctor was now growing quite tired and anxious to check into the nearest hotel. He climbed onto the seat and flipped the power switch to 'on'. After a couple of test circles under the streetlight, he disappeared into the darkness down Vernon Street in search of a suitable place to sleep.

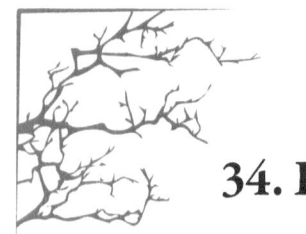

34. Earthbound Deities

"**G**ood morning, Mr. Colburn!" the lanky fellow at the desk greeted him as he stepped through the open office door.

"I have a message for you that may be of some importance," he added as he held out a business card for the doctor to take. Then, as Dr. C. read the card and flipped it over to search for further information, the clerk explained.

"Two officers were inquiring as to the owner of the green scooter. They asked that I have you call them as soon as I saw you. I hope there is no problem!" He waited as the doctor finished studying the card and then offered him the use of the desk phone. He spun it around and pushed it directly in front of him, anticipating an opportunity to listen in.

"Stookerelly," the voice on the other end of the phone answered.

"Yes sir, I just received a note that you wanted me to call you regarding a green scooter," Dr. C. said. He imagined that perhaps the little man that had given him the scooter had stolen it and he would have to explain how he came to have it in his possession. Not exactly what he had planned as his first duty of the day on his first morning in town.

"Where are you now?" the officer asked.

"I'm in the motel office to check out," he replied.

"Stay there, I'll be right over."

Two minutes later three police cars pulled into the parking lot from two different directions. Five police officers crowded into the office as the doctor stood with his back to the counter. His adrenalin instantly began pumping through his brain, and as would be expected, his stomach wrapped into a half hitch and cinched up tight.

"Are you Walter Colburn?" the first officer asked.

"Yes, Doctor Walter Arlin Colburn," he answered, hoping that there may have been a mistake of identity, and he would be allowed to show them his driver's license, and then be free to go on his way without further delay. But, no! These five officers of the law were not that easily dissuaded. There seemed to be some universal curiosity that was waiting for its immediate satisfaction and only he held the prescription for its cure. "How can I help you?" he added.

"Mr. Colburn," the first officer began, dismissing his attempt to establish recognition of his professional stature, "Could you please tell us how you came to be in the possession of the green scooter parked in front of your room?"

All five of the officers pushed closer through the doorway as if to assure not missing a word of his response.

"Well," he stammered slightly as he began his explanation, "I was at the airport, just standing, last night, looking across at the ocean. A man, a short man, rode it up and stopped in front of me. He said he was going home to Massachusetts. He insisted I take the scooter but I declined his offer. Finally, we agreed that I would pass it on to someone else who might need it. I assure you, I am in no need for a scooter as small and dangerous as this."

Halfway into his explanation two of the officers in the rear returned to their cars and were talking amongst themselves. Radio transmissions were snapping from all of their walkie-talkies throughout his explanation and the officers were constantly making adjustments to their volume as he talked.

By the time the doctor completed his story all but one officer had left the tiny office to join the others out front. His name plate read 'D. Stookerelly'. He appeared to be the youngest of the officers and was a huge, intimidating figure of a man. He relaxed his stance as he thanked the doctor and offered his appreciation for his assistance. There appeared to be no further questions and Dr. C. felt relieved as he followed the young officer through the door and into the bright morning sunlight.

As Officer Stookerelly seated his sunglasses on the bridge of his nose, he turned toward the doctor and casually asked, "By chance did he tell you why he was returning to Gloucester?"

The doctor had not known Gloucester to be the destination of the little man and replied, "I'm sorry, officer, but he didn't give me his name, and he only told me Massachusetts. No city was mentioned."

The officer turned and looked toward the sky, then turned back and asked, "Dr. Colburn," he dropped his glasses lower on his nose, and with an inviting smile, looked eye to eye at the doctor and continued, "What say you join us for a nice big breakfast and we can explain the whole thing?"

This seemed an intriguing proposition! How could he resist! "Oh, yes! That would be great. Let me just drop off my key and I'll follow you . . ."

The officer interrupted him and said, "No sir, the scooter will be fine right here. Just drop the key off and ride with me. Do you have any bags?" he asked as he opened the door to his cruiser and grabbed his radio mike. Dr. C. slapped the key on the desk and bid farewell to the clerk as he hurried toward the police car.

"No, I'm traveling light," he said as he buckled his seatbelt and waited while the officer finished his call. "I'll be 108 at 1202 Simonton Street."

"Well, where to begin?" the officer sighed aloud as he dropped the car into drive and considered his attack on the story. He reached his open hand toward the doctor and offered, "As you apparently picked up, I'm Officer Stookerelly, but everybody calls me Stookey."

The three police cars converged at Camille's Restaurant. After gathering at the front door and exchanging introductions, Dr. Colburn and his new friends filed in one by one. The entire staff greeted the officers by their first names. It was like hanging with five hometown heroes, champs from the local football team. Any apprehension Dr. C. had earlier felt had disappeared once he saw how much respect the men commanded. Regular patrons were calling out their greetings while several of the officers made rounds through the dining room to personally receive hugs and handshakes. Once they were all seated and handed menus, the staff began pouring coffee and tending to their ritual of making room for the five gladiators to move about. Chairs from other tables were taken away, and paths were made wider between their table and the ones next to them, typical accommodations necessary to facilitating five earthbound deities such as these.

"Well, let's see," one of the officers exclaimed as he opened his menu. They respectively made their selections, according to their rank, and passed their orders to the two attending waitresses. Stookey ordered the yellow corn cashew waffles topped with fresh mango/passion fruit and coconut milk sauce while several others ordered the French toast with Godiva white chocolate and fresh strawberries topped with Capt. Morgan Spiced Rum Bananas Foster sauce.

The doctor was amazed at the lack of restraint these obviously overweight titans exhibited when the very next entry offered a much less calorically charged and equally filling selection.

"I'll have the eggs galore omelet with fresh lobster, asparagus, tomatoes, onions, and brie topped with your Caribbean hollandaise sauce, please," he ordered, "oh, and a small orange juice, thank you!"

Once all orders were filed, one of the senior officers asked, "Well Dr. Colburn, are you here on vacation or scouting out the island for real estate?" The doctor considered the importance of establishing his reason for being there not only for their benefit, but for his own. He knew the reason, but he had not yet pronounced the words that might officially establish it. He thought, perhaps, this was the right time.

"Well, gentlemen, without elaboration, I'm here to say goodbye to my wife," he said.

There was stillness across the entire table. In the minds of these law enforcement professionals, this was the kind of statement that could lead to anything from the description of a marriage gone bad, a divorce gone good, a murder gone undiscovered, or the death of a loved one. Two of them had experienced the divorce gone good and another was caught up in a marriage going bad. They waited silently for him to qualify his statement.

He continued, "We were on vacation here, one year ago next Thursday. She suffered a brain aneurysm and passed away. To be honest, I just want to back up and deal with some of the feelings that I couldn't face then."

The support and understanding bounced around the table like a ping pong ball as the officers brought up their personal losses in hope that the doctor might appreciate their fraternal alliance when one from their brotherhood was impacted by such bereavement. Once established, his purpose was accepted by all, but, best of all, by himself. As the feast was laid before them, Officer Stookerelly suggested to the other officers that Dr. Colburn might appreciate being told of the history behind his scooter and why so many of them reported to the motel to find out why it was there.

Stookey began the story. "I saw the girl! She was sleeping on the seawall," he said as he dripped the last of his coconut sauce across the stack of waffles.

"Her yellow VW was parked in the No Parking Zone at Spotswood Park on a Monday, about seven in the morning, a year ago."

Then he went on, "I wrote her a ticket and stuck it under the driver-side wiper blade."

It took him almost an hour to finish the story. The other officers left the table to answer their cell phones or report in on their radio calls. There were many interruptions, but Stookey got it finished. Right down to how everybody in town was inspired by her father's relentless dedication to his search. That was why they were so puzzled to find his scooter at a motel. They worried that something criminal may have befallen him and his scooter stolen. They didn't know of his decision to leave and return home. He had apparently kept it private. They were glad to have the information.

It was clear to Dr. C. that the man had built a respected reputation in the community. Owning the scooter now had a relevancy that the doctor could not deny. The story offered him a reason to keep it, as a tribute to a cause that was yet to be completed. Now, it would serve to represent two causes, one man's search for his lost daughter and another's search for his lost wife.

The party disbanded and Officer Stookey dropped the doctor off at the motel where he mounted his little green steed and headed down the street toward the other side of the island.

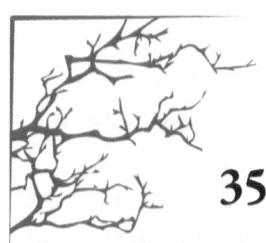

35. The Galleon Resort

"**G**ood morning, sir, may I help you?" he was greeted at the front desk of The Galleon Resort by a most charming girl with an East European accent.

"Yes, thank you! My wife and I stayed in your resort one year ago and I wondered if I might be able to occupy the same room again this week," he explained.

The girl stepped to her computer and asked which room they had stayed in.

517," he answered.

She searched her reservations screens and said, "I'm sorry, sir, but that room is leased until Wednesday, July nineteenth, and then it is only vacant for two nights. If you like I can see if another room is available."

She was efficient and polished in her attendance to her duties, certainly someone who could be counted on to give solid information. He felt no reason to doubt her report and asked, "Could you reserve #517 for the two vacant nights and perhaps find me a room on the same floor with a similar view until the nineteenth?"

After a moment of diligent searching she smiled and asked, "Will you be placing this on your Master Card, Dr. Colburn?"

She had already searched the room's history for July the year before and had all his registration information before her.

"Cash, thank you," he answered as he opened one of his envelopes and began peeling off hundred-dollar bills.

"And will your lovely wife be joining you, Dr. Colburn?" she asked. "Yes, she will, but not until Thursday the twentieth," he answered without looking up.

The girl completed the transaction and, as she handed him his access card and a resort directory, she offered that for his convenience there was a safe in his room or he could utilize the larger office safe if needed. He thanked her for her assistance and proceeded toward the elevator door.

It was as though someone hit him across the chest with a metal baseball bat. He was so struck that he fell against the door as he lost his breath. It was the same upholstery, the same curtains, the same view as he looked across the room and out the glass door overlooking Christmas Tree Island; it was all the same. He had not been prepared for this. He checked the numbers on the door to make sure it was correct-'516'. He was one thin wall from the bed where he last made love to her. It was completely overwhelming. His knees buckled under and he fell to the floor crying like a baby. He had no will to resist. It was time! He was back! She had been waiting for him to arrive, and now, she could begin.

"Sir, are you all right?" A lady and her little boy were standing in the hall looking in at him balled up on the floor.

"Do you need help?" The lady was holding her son tightly against her huge hip, looking in through the open door.

"No!" the doctor answered. "I'll be fine in a minute. It's just a condition I have." Then, as he rolled from his position against the wall and sat on the floor in a pool of his own tears, he said, "Really, I'll be fine. I've got some medication to take if it happens again. Thank you, though, for your concern!" He pulled himself to his feet and extended further gratitude as he gently closed the door.

He emptied his coat pockets on the nightstand beside the bed. He set the five envelopes in a stack next to the clock. Then he drove his hands deep into his pants pockets. One hand retrieved his change and keys, the other, the photo memory card. It dropped to the tabletop and bounced to the edge, stopping just before falling to the carpet below. It hung there, fortuitously positioning itself to capture his attention.

"What about that openair place we passed around the corner?" she called out through the bathroom door as she brushed her hair and misted it with her favorite hairspray.

"It looked like a fun place." Then she added, "Maybe they'll have that Mojito drink you like so much."

"Amelia," he stammered. "Yeah, that sounds great," he called out as he closed the glass door to the deck and pulled the curtains shut.

She stepped into the room holding a bottle of White Linen and sprayed a wisp into the air, then, with the grace of a Hollywood starlet, she stepped through the fragrance as it rained down upon her bare shoulders and across her freckled chest.

"What do you think?" she asked as she spun around so he could watch her new tropical print skirt spring to life, then cascade over her sultry figure.

"Absolutely ravishing as usual, my dear," he answered with sincerity that welled up from his soul. He loved his wife. She loved her husband. They knew what it took to keep love alive and they met that charge with matched fervor. After thirty years of marriage, there was no loss of words when opportunity for a carefully placed compliment arose.

"Shall we?" he said as he offered his arm and led her through the door. He made his way along the wooden dock toward the Conch Republic Bar and Restaurant. He was in no hurry. Plenty of time to admire the beautiful boats and look over the photographs of captured fish hanging from the catch racks behind them. He casually read the signs that were posted on the dock behind each boat, spelling out their terms of contract and prices. Everything he saw confirmed what he had always heard about this place. It really was the fishing capital of the world.

Looking down into the water he watched as the tarpon sailed in and out between and under the docked boats, scooping up the scraps of fish being washed into the water as the mates cut up the day's catch at the cleaning stations. The smell of barnacles left bare by the low tide permeated the air. Sea birds screamed in the sky above. Dr. Colburn slowly made his way past the dock master's office and the Tommy Hilfiger store, then, on to the open dining room of the Conch Republic Restaurant.

"Good evening, Sir! Will you be dining alone tonight?" the maître d' asked.

"Yes!" the doctor answered, and then requested, "Could I take a table by the water?"

"Oh, yes sir. Please feel free to take your pick."

She handed him a menu and the doctor slipped into a table for two overlooking a commercial lobster boat that was being cleaned by its crew. The menu looked familiar but the dish he was hoping to find was no longer listed.

"Hi, my name is Claudia," the waitress greeted him cheerfully, and then announced, "I'll be your waitress this evening. May I bring you something from the bar?"

"Yes, please, could you bring me a Mojito?" he requested as he laid the open menu out on the table.

"Yes sir, one of our new bartenders just moved here from Cuba. Everybody is raving about his Melon Mojito. Would you like to try one?" she asked.

"Yes, thank you! And, the last time I was here I had a fabulous dish but I don't see it on the menu."

"Yes sir, our menu offers lots of our chefs' specials and when they move on, unfortunately, they take some of their best dishes with them. What was the dish?" She was obviously interested in taking the time to hear the description, so he gave it.

"It was a baked bell pepper stuffed with tuna and shrimp. There was a delicious mango sauce and yellow rice on the side with steamed vegetables. Is there any chance that it might still be available?" His mouth was watering as he described it to her.

"Give me just a minute and I'll check on that for you," she said, and then headed toward the back of the dining room and through the swinging kitchen doors. Minutes later she arrived and set his drink on the table. With her was a gentleman in a chef's hat and uniform. Food stains confirmed that this was a working chef and not some disguised marketing person in costume.

"Sir, this is our head chef, Chef David. He would like to discuss the dish you asked about, if you don't mind." The girl disappeared toward the kitchen, leaving the two men to the business of food. The doctor stood and shook the chef's hand and after a casual introduction, Chef David offered the following explanation. The dish had been one of his chef's specials and it had been very well received, but, determined to be a little pricy by the new manager and cut from the menu. He further explained that he was trying to have the dish re-introduced and that he would consider it a personal honor to prepare it for him. Dr. Colburn was thrilled and the chef returned to the kitchen.

"You always do that!" she said.

"What?" he asked with a grin.

"Get exactly what you want without even trying."

"No I don't!" he defended.

He picked up the tall icy glass and took a sip. The mint and melon was a match made in Cuba. He held the glass up and looked through the frost and liquor. There she was, smiling back at him. Amelia!

She slipped her foot out of her shoe and rubbed her toes against his leg. He felt his heart begin to race. She was stunning! Radiant! Alive!

Claudia arrived with his dinner and set the hot plate on the table. "Be careful," she warned. Then asked, "Can I get you another Mojito?"

"Oh thanks, please. It was delicious," he answered. "I thought you'd like it!" she said with a smile as she headed back to the bar.

"You are such a stud!" she proclaimed as she returned to her previous below table antics.

"Leave me alone!" He grinned as he prepared to taste the tuna. The steam was still rising from the morsel on his fork as he slowly positioned it onto his tongue.

"Well, is it as good as it was a year ago?" she asked.

"Exactly!" he happily exclaimed.

"No difference at all?" he heard her ask.

"None!" he answered as he took a second bite.

"Did you realize that this is the same table?" she continued prodding his memory.

He grabbed the edge of the table with his left hand and felt the hard urethane finish. His fingers reached to the unsanded area, underneath, where the wood and the glassy coating came together. He looked off across the bight at a solid white pelican that was roosting on a dock piling. It was all the same: the boats, the fish, the table, the drink, the smell, the tuna, and the bird; it all seemed to be the same.

Later, he strolled along the docks as they had one year before. He looked in the same store windows, laughed at the same funny people, stepped over the same sidewalk drunks, and listened to the same bands playing inside the same bars. When the last door closed, and the last drunk staggered home, he was still walking. When the last cop stopped for his last cup of coffee and the first garbage truck turned the first corner, that's when he turned around and called it enough for one day.

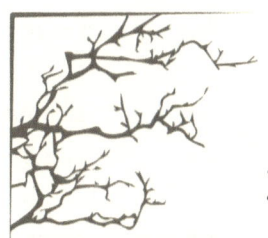

36. Cinnamon Bay

"**A** nother day in Cinnamon Bay, my friend," Rollye greeted his pal of twenty years with a burly man-hug, and then squared off in the sand as if his next move would be to sucker punch him and knock his other front tooth out.

"Well, I am so sad to hear that you and the missus will be takin' my baby girl and pullin' anchor for Key West. I always don't want to see this day on my beach when you leave," he added as he leaned back and studied his friend's smile.

Rollye, a native of Trinidad, born in the coastal town of Lower Manzanilla, had relocated as a child with his family to Guyana. His father had been hired by the minister of agriculture to oversee the introduction of the larger, and less vulnerable to disease, African Cameroon strain of banana to the nation's roster of exportable crops.

His father was an agriculturist and economist trained in both disciplines at York University in Toronto, Canada. In the late seventies, his father's graduate studies had led him to explore possible cures to the devastating fungal disease 'Sigotoka' that had destroyed 40% of the banana crops in Uganda, and threatened to be the undoing to the world's entire banana industry.

At that time, the threat was due to the continued practice of genetically altering the banana toward a more flavorful and thus more marketable product. The mutant 'Worlds Favorite Fruit' was becoming seedless, and eventually would become completely sterile, leaving it to fade into botanical extinction if not rescued by such farseeing scientists. If not for Rollye's father's work, the banana we enjoy today would taste like a Macintosh apple. Rollye's father and Ethan's father had studied together at York University, and it was through their friendship and visits to Rollye's home in Guyana, that Ethan and he had come to be the brothers that they are today.

"Yeah, I guess Melinda told you about the bleeding," Ethan offered as the reason for his deciding to return to Key West.

Melinda, Rollye's wife, had assisted Miss Lucy Jenkins, the islands mid-wife/taxi cab driver, in the delivery of Baby Krismas five weeks earlier. There seemed to be no problem until the fourth week after the birth when Chastity began bleeding again and had not stopped since. Ethan was worried that the clinic on St. John would deny treatment for her since he was a Canadian citizen and had never applied for a U.S. visa. Without identification for Chastity, they would probably assume she was also an illegal. The threeday sail to Key West seemed to be a good solution, besides, after being away for a year, it would give him a chance to show off his new baby girl to all his friends.

"Yes!" Rollye answered. "She told me all about it. You need to just do the best thing and get her seen by a real doctor. Most of these island hacks don't know a breadfruit from a bedpan."

Rollye and Ethan walked up the sandy path through the red mangrove and toward the steep stairway that led to the campground. They cleaned the bathrooms and showers, then moved to the cabin area where, one by one, they readied each cabin for the next night's guests.

To avoid immigration complications, Ethan worked as an independent under his friend's contract with the U.S. Department of Interior. Rollye and his wife Melinda had bid the contract in 1992 and somehow had been able to keep it going ever since. He always had room for Ethan on his team, and paid him cash at the end of each day.

After lunch, they left Melinda to run the laundry and walked to Rollye's rusty, chopped up Jeep. Twelveyear old Mica had not been seen since they had arrived that day and was probably on the trail headed for Watermelon Cay to dive with the tourist girls.

They tallied Ethan's pay for the last time. Rollye threw in a substantial chunk and referred to it as 'Baby Money', then climbed in for the final ride back to Cruz Bay where the Canadian Soul was moored.

"What about supplies?" Rollye was prepared to stop at the market and wait if Ethan needed to pick up diapers or food.

"I've already loaded up with the basics," Ethan told him. "We're gonna' sail over to Ginger Island and spear enough fish to last us for the trip. Maybe I'll grab a few bugs if I see any."

He was referring to the Caribbean spiny lobster. Though still out of season in all U.S. waters, Ginger Island was just outside the line of their jurisdiction. Even if it weren't, Ethan would grab them anyway, just to show his contempt for anyone trying to tell him what he could or couldn't have for dinner.

The two men embraced and said farewell, then Ethan jogged down to the pier where his inflatable was tethered to a mooring buoy. Rollye stood on the pavement leaning against the front of his jeep waving goodbye to his friend, unknowingly, for the last time.

"Almost there!" Ethan called out to Chastity who was too weak to climb up from the cabin below.

He had no idea just how weak she was, or how serious her condition had become. She and the baby were lying on the starboard bunk. She had a fever and her sweat had soaked through the cotton bedding and into the wooden frame that supported it above the outer pontoon. The small round hatch above her head was braced open and two battery-powered fans blew across their uncovered bodies. Krismas slept soundly beside her mother.

Ethan dropped anchor fifty yards off of the outcropping of rocks that marked the beginning of shallow water. The limestone cliffs were a familiar landmark that he had used for years when coming here to spear fish. The sandy bottom rose slowly into the rocky crags and fingered between the coral ledges at a depth of no more than twenty feet. It was a perfect spot to shoot lane and black grouper. Sticking his head in the cabin one last time to check on the girls, he called out gently, "You gonna be alright while I go down for a bit?"

Chastity nodded her head then dropped it back toward the wall. It was hot! Too hot to be sick, sick and nursing a newborn baby.

Ethan hurried to grab his mask and flippers from the floor hatch on the upper deck. He reached above the capstan and unhooked his spear gun. Seconds later, he took his first aim at a twentyinch black grouper. At the surface, he hurled it over the rail, and descended back to the sand below.

He nailed a lane grouper, then a yellowtail snapper, one hogfish, and another black weighing about fourteen pounds. He climbed up the ladder and slid the catch into the fish hold and threw the refrigeration switch to 'on'. Grabbing his tickle stick and hand net, he jumped back in to hunt for lobster.

Ethan had lived like this for years. The Bohemian lifestyle had become second nature to him. Catching fish was easy, lobster, somewhat more difficult. He held his breath and followed the rock line looking for their long antennae, poking out from under the coral, feeling the currents for morsels of falling food. He saw a cluster of the thorny spines all gathered in one brood and went for them. As he hung upside down, working the crustaceans into his net with the tickle stick, he was hit on his left thigh by what he imagined was a reef shark. Instantly, the water was cloudy with blood. His blood! He screamed as his mask flew off. Whatever had a hold on him would not let go. He pushed on the rock ledge with his feet to get away from the fish, but its grasp was still tight and he could feel it chewing deeper and deeper into his muscle. Through the blood and the stinging pain, he caught a glimpse of the mouth that was attempting to devour him. It was a moray eel!

He dug his thumbs into its eyes until he felt the eye sockets crush inward. Then, his thumbnails pierced through the mush that was its brain. Finally, the monster's jaw went slack and he pulled it from its cavernous lair.

Back on deck he added it to his catch in the cooler and blotted the wound with towels. An eightinch flap of bloody flesh hung on his side. He folded it back into the hole from where it had fallen, and slid down the stairs where he sat on the galley floor and packed it with ointment, then taped it closed. He leaned against the cabinet and clenched his teeth as the pain began to grow. He knew he would have to endure it for at least three days. He tried to convince himself that this would be no problem. Besides, he had suffered accidents before. One time he had fallen from his boat's mast and broken his shoulder as it hit the gunwale on his way to the water. Another time, he was shot by another diver's spear gun. This was just going to be some more pain and another scar to prove to the world that he could survive anything. It was the Canadian in him. It served him well!

He gritted his teeth and checked on Chastity and Krismas. Both were still sleeping as he climbed through to the forward hatch and retrieved the anchor. Luckily there was a prevailing east wind and they should make good time before dropping anchor, hopefully off Vega Baja for the night.

He doused his pain with the last of his cheap vodka and went through half an ounce of ganja before he realized he had overshot his destination of the little Puerto Rican town. The next morning, as the sun launched its first threatening blades of fire toward the Canadian Soul, Ethan was nipping at his fingernails, fearful that he had underestimated the seriousness of his predicament. In fifteen hours, he had gone from confident captain to shivering fool. Luckily, the winds were still blowing favorably and he was still on course.

He tied off the wheel and stumbled down the stairs to check on Chastity and the baby. The stench of human waste permeated the cabin. He soaked towels in fresh water stored in the tank below the galley floor and cleaned up as quickly as he could. Chastity was mumbling as he wiped her blood away from the baby. Another clean towel, then he positioned the baby where she could easily nurse when she awoke. He lifted Chastity's head and poured water down her throat, then across her body to keep her cool. He sliced a mango and set the plate on the shelf above her head where she could reach it when she awoke. Then he climbed back up to the helm, wincing under the excruciating pain. A fever was setting in.

By late afternoon he was fighting to remain conscious. Perhaps, if the wind didn't give out, and he stayed on course, they might make Key West by late the following night. At dusk, he recognized the coastline of the Turks and Caicos Island. He was pleased that his deadreckoning skills had not failed him during his battle to survive. Again, he checked his compass and set the lines on the wheel. He grabbed a fish from the cooler and slapped it on the stove below without scaling or cleaning it. He knew that if he and Chastity were to survive the last leg of the trip, they would need protein to fuel the fight. Once again, he cleaned the body fluids from the bed and wrapped the baby's diaper tightly in a plastic bag. She had awakened several times through the day and nursed from her mother's breast while Chastity struggled to keep breathing on the hot and fetid bunk. Ethan dug his hand into the side of the fish and dropped a fist full of the steaming flesh on the mattress beside Chastity's face. The pain and delirium caused every thought and every movement to burn deeper inside of him.

He tossed the remaining fish carcass into the pilot house then turned off the gas and climbed back up the stairs. All that night he held fast, screaming at the stars, cussing at the gods, hoping for the best, but heading toward the worst.

The third night had almost finished its sheltering reprieve. One last brush with consciousness would assure him that the Canadian Soul was dead on course for Key West.

Ahead, the silent island city slept comfortably beneath the cycloptic watch of its southernmost lighthouse. He was one mile out when he tied off the wheel for the last time and dragged himself below to kiss them both goodbye.

He knew he was about to die. He didn't want to be found like that, collapsed at the helm in a pool of his own blood, next to a charred carcass of a fish. No, not by anyone! Not by Chastity, not by the police, not by his friends, no one!

He wrapped a line around his wrist and dragged himself over the railing. The Canadian Soul silently sliced through the dark water toward its destination. Ethan considered his options one last time, and then let go. He had faced his destiny and embraced its salutation.

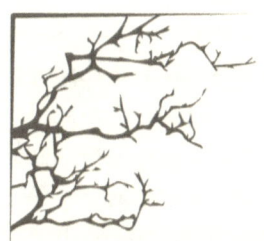

37. Island Muse

"**J**ust one, please!" Doctor C. said to the girl behind the ticket counter of the Mel Fisher Nautical Museum and Historical Conservatory.

She peeled off his ticket and held it against a shiny pamphlet. As she handed them over to him, she announced to the meandering crowd, "Ladies and gentlemen, our twenty-minute movie presentation will begin in five minutes through the door to the left of the cannon."

The smell of sulfur and rusty metal hung heavily in the crowded gift shop. People that were coming in were bumping into people going out. There was not much that he found interesting in the front room. With any luck, he'd be able to push his way through when half the crowd filed into the movie room. He stood in the hallway with his back to the elevators and read the life history of the late Mel Fisher. The photographs and dive suit in the corner made the man seem more than just a legend. "Just another lucky hillbilly!" he heard Amelia's voice sarcastically resound in his ear.

"No, he wasn't! It wasn't luck at all. This guy chased his dream till it couldn't run anymore. He was relentless, a man of commitment who in spite of anybody that ever called him a fool, never gave up," he argued. "Yeah, he was a hero!"

"Yeah, maybe a drunken hero who got real lucky," she said as if she believed it. She was just trying to push a button. Get his goat! She had always been good at it. She was the sauce on his barbeque.

"Hey, why don't you ride the next elevator," he suggested as he turned around and pushed her back out the door and into the hall.

He stepped out on the secondfloor landing and was greeted by the same wall of dioramas and display cases he and Amelia had wandered through one year earlier. Now, he was free to let his imagination drift, undistracted, with the presentation of life as it was in the seventeenth century. The dank museum did well to mimic the era famed by pirates and privateers. He wandered between the artifacts and reconstructed ship parts, read all the literature, studied the maps and diagrams of warfare and maritime travel, then proceeded to the next level where the treasure was on display.

He viewed the mounds of encrusted silver coins, stood in amazement at the elaborate gold and emerald jewelry, and reached his hand through a hole in a clear thick plastic display case to feel the weight of an authentic gold bar minted nearly four hundred years ago. Back on the first floor he drifted down the narrow corridor, past the stairs, and into the purchase room.

"Oh, hey! If I remember right, you were here with a gorgeous blond last year! I hope she didn't take off with those earrings you bought." The salesman was just trying to be funny. He had no way of knowing that Amelia had died three days after walking out his door. It was an unavoidable faux pas! Sooner or later, this kind of thing was bound to cross his path. It's not that the widowed doctor was ready for it; no, you can never be ready for something like that. You just take the hit and try not to fall on the floor.

Doctor C. was not surprised that the lanky fellow behind the counter recognized him. After all, it was only one year to the day since he had handed him the check for $30,000 dollars and dazzled Amelia with the stunning little bobbles from antiquity. It was just another long-forgotten commission, probably spent on three nights of partying, one month's rent and a new Vespa moped, straight from the factory in Italy.

"David, isn't it?" the doctor pressed his memory for the name. The man smiled as he nodded a pleasing confirmation and shook the doctor's hand.

"Well, Dave," he said as he began looking down into the brightly lit display case, "They come and they go!"

There was no need to engage with the man. Acknowledgment of the truth would just lead to discomfort for both of them. He made his way around the room, enjoying the beautiful artifacts and amazed that many were still being offered at, what seemed to him to be, reasonable prices. He stopped at the end of the first case and stared at the collection of gold coins that filled the space where her earrings once lay. He stood there, captive in a moment of unexpected déjà vu.

"Oh, aren't these exquisite!" He felt her breath on his neck as it left her mouth, carrying the words, and delivering them softly into his ear. He couldn't deny it! Yes, they were beautiful, simple, yet absolutely elegant from every angle. David had attended to his queue like the pro that he was, and opened the door to the case, then laid the emerald and gold earrings on a garnet-colored pad.

"Yes, they certainly are fantastic!" he commented. "These were found on January sixteenth of this year by Mitch Sorenson, one of the divers on the Dauntless. Mitch has been diving with us for over twenty years. He just came in a few minutes ago and is in the back with our investor relations coordinator. Let him tell you about them while the lady tries them on."

David had trustingly left the room and walked around the corner to where they had heard the diver talking with another man, then returned followed by Mr. Sorenson. He was a rough, outdoorsy sunburned fellow, no-nonsense kind of guy. As he stepped into the room and saw the emerald earrings hanging from Amelia's ears he said, "Oh yeah, those little babies were one of my all-time favorite finds!" He then proceeded to tell them the lengthy yet interesting story of the day's dive and how he had come across the items hidden inside a silver salt shaker.

"Obviously, someone's contraband," he had speculated.

"See what I mean?" she said as they walked past the security guard and out into the sunlight.

"What?" he asked her as the door shut behind.

"You always get what I want," she said with a coy grin.

"You mean, you, you want. You always get what you want," he corrected her.

"OK, if that's the way you want it," she slyly accepted the correction. After stepping down the stone stairway to the cobblestone street, she stopped and held her face toward the sun and asked him, "Don't they turn my blue eyes green?"

He unlocked the chain and climbed back on his little scooter, then sped off to his next stop, leaving the image of her standing there, in the sun, to dissolve away, back into his memory.

"Good afternoon, sir, how many in your party?" the young man asked from inside the stone booth by the gate to the Ernest Hemingway house.

"Just one, thank you!" he answered as he handed over the twelve-dollar fee and took the brochure from the boy.

He sauntered up the brick walkway past lazy, lounging cats on cast-iron benches, toward the beautiful old twostory mansion where the man known as 'Papa' had once lived. A crowd of people were blocking the main entrance, gathering in the front room, waiting for the tour guide to begin his dissertation. Dr. C. never was one for tour groups. He always designed his approach to things according to his own interests. Having been an avid reader all his life, there were few places he ever visited that he didn't research before beginning his trip. This was an example of that very trait.

Since childhood, Hemingway had been one of his favorite authors. *The Old Man in the Sea, A Farewell to Arms, For Whom the Bell Tolls*, and *Death in the Afternoon*, were favorites of anyone that happened to get hooked on this highly acclaimed, yet egocentric, journalist's writings. But Dr. C. was much more than a fan of Hemingway. He had been waiting all his life for his hair to turn white, his beard to grow out and his belly to bulge so he could join hundreds of other devotees and compete in the annual Ernest Hemingway lookalike celebration. Hell, if bull running was made legal in the states, he'd be ready to give it a whirl, just for the bragging rights, and maybe the sake of posterity.

"You would not," she said as she reached around and tugged on his beard.

"You just stand there and watch me," he defiantly commanded.

"You wouldn't even climb down out of the stands, and you know it!" she fanned his flame with every word.

"I'll tell you what I know! I know I've just about had enough of you! Now light me another cigar and back up while I reel this black marlin in! Things are gonna' start flyin' around here any minute."

His thoughts were in a Hemingway-induced freefall, carried away by the memories of the last time they had explored the old man's island home and tropical gardens. It was sacred ground, full of inspiration and ghostly presence. He was almost to the top of the rickety stairs that led to the writer's studio over the garage. Nothing had changed. Everything was just as Papa had left it. The only thing missing was the man himself, and the sounds of his typewriter chattering out his next prize-winning creation. The doctor exited the grounds and climbed back on his little green scooter. As he pushed away from the sidewalk he looked up and saw a sixtoed cat walking along the top of the stone wall above him. Funny, some folks say that the Hemingway family never had a single cat while living in Key West.

"How are you today, sir?" The ranger asked as the stranger let off the throttle and cruised to a stop by the open door of the Fort Zachery Taylor State Park guard gate. Then, puzzled, he continued, "Isn't this Bill's scooter?"

"That's right!" the doctor answered. "He went back to Gloucester. I think he reached as far as he could go. I don't know if you knew it, but in a couple more days it will be a year since his daughter disappeared."

"Oh, yes sir!" the ranger said. "I knew that. I used to date, Canyon, her roommate. We all figured that after they found her car a mile out in the Gulf, that she had probably been washed out to sea. I'm surprised he stayed this long. I guess that's the power of hope."

The doctor nodded his head to the ranger's sympathetic presumption and then suggested, "Well, hope is a powerful thing, but I think in this case, it might be more appropriate to recognize the power of denial over hope." The young ranger raised his eyebrow as he considered the comment and offered his hand to the doctor.

"I'm Robert," he said.

"I'm Walter," the doctor said as their hands met.

He reached into his pocket for the fee and Robert stopped him and said, "Oh, no charge Walter. It's a pleasure to meet you." Friends were just that easy to make on this little island where the fabric that held society together was strongest in the middle and wet around the edges.

He wound his way through the park until he saw the walls of the old fort hidden behind the buttonwood scrub that grew up from the polluted green waters that lay stagnant in the surrounding moat. It was an enormous fortress of brick-and-mortar construction. The toxic water wrapped around it from the front gate to the ocean side. Only a third of the original bastion remained.

Two great wars had seen its demise as a fort and reinvented it as a burial site for military wastes such as used grease and oil. Some wise conservationists and a couple of history buffs launched a campaign to have it partially restored and opened as a tourist attraction, and then the State of Florida laid its claim and adopted the project. Now, it's the most visited toxic dump site in the state.

Dr. C. locked his scooter to the bike rack and walked up the sidewalk to the glass display case to read the history of *Fort Zachery Taylor*. Construction began in 1845. Five years later, it was named after the U.S. president Zachery Ta . . .

"Hey, you, you with the white beard," he ignored her taunt. She was standing behind him, in the shade of a large mahogany tree just thirty feet away.

"You know you read that stuff last year. Nothing's changed! They don't rewrite the history every year hoping you'll show up to stand in the hot sun and check it for mistakes." She was looking for just the right button to push.

He kept reading in spite of her heckling. Her voice grew louder as she shouted out over the tall Australian pines, toward the people on the beach, "Hey! Somebody come help this old guy before he loses his . . . Agg!"

She took off running, through the entrance to the fort and across the open courtyard like a colt cut loose on the first day of spring. He was right on her heels. He slowed as his breath ran out, just in time for her to escape up the spiral stone staircase. Her laughter echoed down through the cracks in the bricks and ricocheted through the old ruins like cannon fire. As he turned and walked back to his scooter, he thought he heard her snarl, "Nice try!"

That evening he enjoyed sipping wine on the balcony while the breezes blew over Christmas Tree Island and across the Gulf. Amelia left him alone that night. Left him to sort through his memories and savor the moments.

"Good morning, are you traveling alone today?" the first mate asked as he took the doctor's ticket.

"That's right," he answered.

After tearing off the stub he handed it back to the doctor and said, "If you would like to make your way inside we are just about to begin serving breakfast." Dr. C. stepped through the sliding door and made his way to the counter at the front of the huge catamaran's observation lounge. The windows offered a panoramic view of the docks and the array of yachts tied to them. Shortly, the engines would rumble and they would be jetting across the waves toward their destination, sixty miles to the west of town.

"Don't eat that!" she barked as if she was speaking to a sixyear old. He grabbed two more mini-donuts and put them on his plate, defiant over her futile effort to control him.

"No! No! No!" he told her. "This is my vacation and I'll eat, drink, and do whatever I want!"

She laughed and leaned close as he spoke the words, then grabbed his ears and kissed his sunburned nose, leaving lipstick behind as her mark of possession.

"You can eat whatever you want," she exclaimed as she sat down and tucked her feet under her thighs and yawned.

He sat on the bench under the portside observation window and stuffed his mouth with the powdery delights, then washed them down with a sip of coffee from a white Styrofoam cup.

"Are you going to try snorkeling this time or just watch everybody else while they have all the fun?" she asked.

"You'll see," he answered as he took the first sip from his coffee cup.

"When are you going to call the kids, and let them know you're OK?" she asked as she picked up a magazine from the seat next to her.

"Don't you mind, I'll take care of that when the time comes."

The huge boat idled away from the dock, and once it cleared the breakwater, rose up and flew across the waves on its way toward the Dry Tortugas National Park and Fort Jefferson.

"I don't remember going this fast," he commented.

"No, it's no faster than it was before. It's exactly the same," she asserted.

A minute later he was right back on it. "I'm telling you, this thing is moving a lot faster than it did last year."

She set her magazine on her lap and looked at him before giving him her answer. "You ever notice that when you take a trip out of town it always takes longer to get there than it does to get home?" she asked him.

"Yeah, of course I've noticed that. I've always known that," he answered. "You know I know that. I even know why."

"Well," she said, "how is this any different?"

He was confused but willing to search for an answer that might leave him with his dignity intact. Unfortunately, no answer made sense and he was forced to ask, "OK, how is this different?

"Her answer glued his feet to the floor and his eyes wide open.

"Maybe, you're finally on your way home!" She dropped the magazine on the seat and walked to the front window. Looking toward the horizon, she slipped her hands in her jeans back pockets and announced, "Almost there!" He wrapped one arm around a pole and leaned forward as the ship rose, then slowly came on plane. He was reminded of the longest twohour ride of his life, one year earlier, on that same boat. He pushed that memory aside, as quickly as it arrived.

"Good evening, Dr. Colburn! Right this way to your table." He had made the reservation the night before while relaxing on the balcony. This would be his last night before moving to room # 517.

"You certainly surprised me today," she said as he studied the wine list.

"How so?" he asked without looking up.

"The way you took to snorkeling, along the dock and around the coral." He heard her shoe drop to the floor then felt her toes begin stroking the front of his leg.

"Well, you know what they say about old dogs and new tricks." He smiled as he conjured up a clever answer.

"No, what do they say about old dogs and new tricks?" She poised herself for his best response.

He set the wine list on the table and looked into her loving, blue eyes. He saw sunrises and sunsets, hurricanes and fluffy white clouds, birds of all colors, and oceans of tropical fish, sails on horizons, children laughing, and flowers and rainbows. He saw puppy dogs, and ten million smiles, and the hands of God. And then he saw it all again. He leaned closer and gave her his answer, "If the old tricks brought the old dog everything his old heart desired, he doesn't need new tricks."

The walk from the A&B Lobster House back to the Galleon Resort was less than two blocks. By the time that he finished his dinner, a summer storm had rolled over the island and set in for the night. He walked back in the rain and, after a hot shower, decided to watch TV and turn in early.

"Good morning!" he said as he walked up to the counter and slapped his electronic room key on the polished pink granite counter.

"Yes sir, checking out of room #516?" the desk clerk asked.

"Yes, and then checking into #517 if it's ready."

The man reviewed his computer screen and announced, "I'm sorry, sir! It appears as though housekeeping will need a little longer to finish up with #517. If this would be of too great an inconvenience, perhaps I could locate another room," the man offered.

"No, I'll take a walk and check back with you later."

Two days earlier he had purchased three Hawaiian print shirts and three pairs of shorts at the clothing shop across the street. He had dropped his dress clothes off at the cleaners on Southard Street and everything he owned was in one bag which he left with the desk clerk. He took three-hundred-dollars out of one of his envelopes and deposited the rest in the house vault. With the receipt in hand, he walked out the front door and toward the waterfront.

"Remember this?" he heard Amelia's voice ask as he stepped off the curb in front of Kermit's Key Lime Pie Shop and crossed the street under the shade of a Royal Poinciana tree. The little orange petals from the blooms in its canopy had fallen to the pavement, and carpeted the walkway. They approached the stop sign at the end of the oneway alley and looked up to read the name, 'Lazy Bohemian Way'.

"Oh yeah," he remarked with fondness. "I remember this well!" "Didn't someone say that this island was built the Bohemian way?" she asked.

"No sweetheart, the man said it was built 'On Bohemian Whey'," he laughed as he added, "That's Caribbean for, 'built by drunken island carpenters after they polished off too much fermented coconut milk'."

She wrapped her arms around him and together they strolled down the shady lane, kicking up a trail through the carpet of orange flower petals beneath their feet.

"What can I get for you this morning?" the waitress asked.

"Just a black coffee, thanks," he said with a smile.

He was one of only three customers in the cozy little dockside café. As he scanned the bar and the umbrellashaded courtyard he counted five staffers. The wooden bandstand and the driftwood bar, with the forest of lady's undergarments hanging from the ceiling, implied that by the time the sun goes down the ratio of customers to staff would dramatically swing in favor of the night shift over the day. The girl set his coffee on the table and walked back to the kitchen.

"So, figured out why you're here yet?" Amelia asked as she squinted to read the sign that hung in the air over the entrance to the quaint little hideaway, '*Hang With The Big Dogs*.'

"I think I have," he answered as he tasted his brew. "I want to find a purpose."

"You have lots of purpose," she emphatically exclaimed. "More than anyone!"

"No, you were my purpose," he said.

"No, I was never your purpose! I was your pleasure, your reward, your desire, your inspiration, your lover, and, I was a part of you. I was never a purpose for you." She sat back in her chair and approached the issue again. "So, figured out why you're here yet?"

He dropped his sunglasses over his eyes and turned his head toward a sailboat motoring out of the bight.

"I'm here," he paused to consider how deeply he was willing to go with this challenge to discover, and then he continued, "To resolve some unresolved issues that got left here a long time ago."

"Sorry, Charlie!" she cut him off short. "If you're talking about feelings of loss and abandonment, and calling them issues never resolved, that won't cut it. All of that stuff was resolvable in Chicago." She knew what she was talking about and pushed him a little bit closer to his edge. "So, why are you here?"

"I'm searching," he answered, "searching for a reason to get up every morning; for a reason to breathe, to go to work, that's all there is to it."

She was growing impatient with him. He was making her do all the work. He was refusing to exercise insight, skirting the question, dodging the answer like one of those spoiled country club wives that he always complained about, and she was not interested in evasive chatter.

Then he followed up with, "You were always my reason."

"Oh, please," she scoffed.

"Did you get up this morning? Did you get up on Saturday morning fifty-five years ago? Why? I'll tell you why, because you were scared. That's right, scared that if you didn't, you might miss something. Fifty-five years ago, you were scared that you might miss an episode of 'The Jetsons', and today because you were scared you might miss an episode of 'Walter'."

She sat back in her chair and twirled the ends of her hair as she continued. "Reasons are just things we tell ourselves we need to keep us from climbing back into our self-indulgent beds. You want a reason to open your eyes every morning, a reason for stepping off the bus? Well, here it is. How about fear? That's a perfect reason. Fear, that if you don't, you might miss an episode, an episode of life, your life!"

She took a deep breath and stretched her arms. She readjusted her posture and asked again, "Now, why are you here?"

He wanted to find a simple answer, but he realized her question was really his own, and if he shorted the answer he was only cheating himself out of finding the real reason he had returned to the island. In hope of discovering something easily missed before, he offered his last response.

"What about love?" he asked with reservation, fully expecting his answer to be chewed up and swallowed right behind reason.

"That's a nice one," she said, "but you know better. Love is everywhere you look. Once you know love you can't shade your eyes from it. No, you didn't come here for love, not love lost, and not loves yet to be found. No! You're here to wrap your hands around something that is far more terrifying than love, something that you have feared all your life, something that no one has ever been able to explain away to your satisfaction." She stood up and slid the chair under the table and stepped behind him. She bent over as he sat there, dumbfounded by the bluntness of the conversation. She slid her hands over his shoulders and down his chest and as her lips met his ear she whispered, "I heard you that night. As I took my last breath, I listened to you cry. Your voice was the last voice that ever spoke in my ear. Your tear was the last taste on my tongue. I took the smell of you with me to my grave. I felt your heart stop beating when mine stopped. No, you're not here for love! You have all the love you need!"

The doctor never finished his cup of coffee. He sat at the little table and rearranged the napkin and plastic spoon several times, then stared out across the Key West Bight, beyond the rows of dinghies tied to the dock, beyond the sailboats with their whirring wind generators spinning in the breeze that blew over the tin roofed turtle cannery, across the deepwater channel beyond the breakwater, and out toward Christmas Tree Island.

He left the Schooner's Wharf bar and strolled slowly back down *Lazy Way Lane*, between the wedding chapel and the backside of Jimmy Buffett's recording studio. A mother chicken with fifteen little babies scrambling to keep up darted out from under the rotten corner of a shed and ran across his path, then halted in the dirt on the other side, where they began kicking and pecking in the scattered mulch. He followed the trail he had made earlier, through the carpet of fallen Royal Poinciana flowers, back to the Galleon Resort.

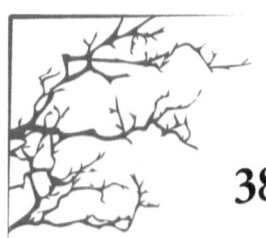

38. The Return of the Canadian Soul

"**O**h yes, Dr. Colburn,** perfect timing. I just received confirmation that unit #517 is ready for you to move in."

He retrieved his bag of clothes and headed to the room on the fifth floor. This time he was prepared for the blow. The door opened slowly. He stood there, taking in the scene. There was nothing to fear, there was no reason to refrain, no hidden purpose, but he loved what he saw.

"What took you so long?" she asked as she crossed the room and sat down on the leather sofa.

"Come look at this!" she directed him. He entered the apartment and closed the door. He tossed the bag of clothes on the table and slid into position beside her on the couch.

"What?" he asked.

She nodded toward the coffee table where a real estate sales brochure lay. The photograph on the cover was a shot of the Galleon Resort, taken from a boat across the channel.

"You need to take a look at the blue page," she said as he reached to pick it up.

He opened the folder and removed the page. The column on the left listed apartment numbers, the second column listed the description of the unit, the third column listed the seller's asking price, and the last column stated the status of the property relative to its sale.

"What do you think?" she asked with a smile. "A little getaway so to speak, with summers in Chicago, winters in Key West and a Sailboat in the marina?"

"Why do I get the feeling that the choice has already been made?" he asked her.

"That's probably because it has," she said as she got up and walked into the master bedroom.

He sat on the sofa reviewing the material and then picked up the phone to call the realty number on the card. Thirty minutes later there was a knock at the door. By five p.m. the offer was formalized and a deposit check for eighty thousand dollars was clipped to the top of the contract, and Dr. Colburn became a resident of the State of Florida.

"How did that feel?" she called to him from the bedroom.

"It felt like it should have been done a year ago." He filled a glass with water from the doorfront of his new refrigerator and walked into the other room.

"It comes furnished, you know," she said as she turned for him to zip up her dress. "The people who owned it had it painted and completely remodeled just six months ago." Then she asked, "You like it?"

He finished zipping her up and walked over to the sliding glass doors to admire the view of his new front yard. He watched the Sunset Key ferry boat break away from its dock and head back across the channel.

"Oh yeah, I like it fine," he approvingly answered.

"That's good, because I picked out the colors." They were still laughing as they stepped into the elevator and pressed the 'down' button.

The setting sun was gracing the sky with its last brilliant display of pastel as he rounded the corner of Sunset Pier and entered Mallory Square. The street lamps flickered to life above the gathering crowd and the nightly show was about to begin. The beautiful gypsy smiled as he slipped into the empty chair and set his hands on top of her linen-covered table. She said nothing, just explored his face with her eyes. The tightrope walkers and the magicians, and the jugglers and the carneys faded away as he became mesmerized by her charm.

She was French-Canadian he remembered. She had given a reading to his wife the night before she suffered the aneurysm. "She was right about the long journey you know." He ignored Amelia's toying whisper.

"So, nice to see you again," the gypsy lady said.

Her voice had an old European flavor that assisted her as she created a certain, mystical ambiance. The little candle sitting next to the stack of cards flickered in the soft summer breeze.

"In case you don't remember, my name is Jazelle." She reached across the table and met his hands midway.

"Walter," he said, and nothing more.

She frowned as she picked up her tarot cards and began setting them one by one in a sweeping pattern across the table as she asked, "Did your wife ever take that journey?" She peeled a card from the top of the deck, and set it on the table.

"Yes! She died, two days after the reading."

"Oh, I am so sorry to hear that," she said as she stood up and beckoned him to allow her to hug him. She held him firmly and read his energy, then said, "You loved her so very, very much. She knew how much. She still knows how much you love her. Her energy is in you. She is waiting for you, always, waiting."

She released him and straightened herself as she dried her eyes and sat back down.

"Be patient, there are many good things coming to you as we speak." She returned to her cards and began interpreting her findings. The card was an armored knight on his steed.

"Death will no longer be a stranger for you to fear. He will be close to you many more times in your life. He will pass by you at his discretion, denying he knows you, but he knows you, and, he knows that you know him. He is relaxed with you. There is a trust that bonds the two of you together."

She silently laid two more cards out, then one more.

Pointing to the image of the peasant girl she said, "Very soon you will receive a calling from a girl. She will bring you more love than your chalice can hold." She pointed to the picture. Her finger landed on the clay pitcher held by the girl's hand. "You see, here, the pitcher is in her right hand. The wine is spilling on the ground. The wine is life. There is lots of wine still in the pitcher. This speaks of long life, maybe yours, maybe hers!"

Jazelle turned over one last card and slowly placed it face up on the pile of others. Dr. C. looked down to see the image of a castle tower, on a mountain top, with goats and laughing people all around. Jazelle folded her hands and laid them over the cards. This would be her final card. She looked into the doctor's eyes and smiled as she gave the following interpretation.

"There are changes rising in your life, big changes. Embrace them with your heart, and they will prove to hold you up." She stood and offered her two hands across the table with a smile. He thanked her and set a twenty-dollar bill in her jar.

"Well, maybe if you had tipped her like that a year ago I'd still be alive." Amelia just couldn't resist dropping the little quip as they made their way through the crowd and back toward the main esplanade, then up the cobblestone road to Kelly's Restaurant for dinner.

"Good evening, sir, a table for one?" The answer was becoming more comfortable for him to give. "Yes, thank you!"

Kelly's, a charming converted 'Old Town' home, bar upstairs, court yard dining. They had so enjoyed it last year. The little iron table fought to stabilize its footing against the bricks underneath. Wedged beneath a gigantic bird of paradise, and a monstrous ponytail palm, it was like dining in the Amazon. He ordered the broiled Mahi and drank two melon martinis.

After dinner, he walked over to the Cuban cigar factory on Green Street and chose a Quai d'Orsay Corona as his night's second vice. He sat on the same park bench that he had sat on the year before, waiting while she explored the shops inside Clinton Square. This time, she would wait for him. Until the day he dies, she would be sitting on a park bench beside the gates of Heaven, waiting for him.

"Good morning, Dr. Colburn, you're up awfully early today." The night auditor called out across the lobby as the Galleon's newest resident came down from his apartment and pulled a copy of the newspaper from its box.

"Yes, I thought I'd scoot over to the pier and catch the sunrise before I start the day," he said as he walked past the desk and through the front door. Out in the parking garage, his scooter was locked in the #517 parking space. He unplugged the charger and stowed it in the pouch under the seat, then flipped the switch to 'on' and quietly sped down the driveway and off to the South Beach Pier on the other side of the island.

There were very few people on Duval Street at fourthirty a.m. that morning. A couple of truck drivers were busy dropping off bundles of newspapers, a few drunken tourists were making their way, arm in arm, back to their motel rooms after surviving a night of festive debauchery, the Key West Cat Lady was struggling to pedal her squeaky threewheel bicycle home after her early morning rounds of feeding strays, but not much else was to be found moving at that time of the morning.

The doctor hit the scooter's kill switch as he approached the end of the road and glided to a stop directly under the lone streetlight. He stood motionless for a second and listened to the lapping of the waves as they broke gently against the concrete pilings under the pier, then he set the machine on its kickstand and walked up the ramp toward the dark expanse of the Atlantic Ocean. A sticky breeze was blowing in from Cuba across the Florida Straits and the stars seemed to be as bright as candles. He walked to the end of the pier and looked out across the sea. For a moment, he thought that he saw a sailboat in the distance, probably moored a half mile or so offshore. He turned his head toward the east and waited for the first rays of the sun to announce the arrival of the new day. He kicked off his sandals, then sat down on the edge of the pier and dangled his feet inches above the rippling water. Leaning back on his elbows, he gazed blissfully into the Milky Way, taking in as much of the great expanse as he could. Dr. Walter Colburn had finally found paradise, and it was as perfect as perfect could be.

Looking again toward the horizon he caught a clearer view of the sailboat that he had noticed just moments earlier. Now, it was much closer, and he could see that the sails were up and that it was making way directly toward the pier. He was puzzled to see that there were no running lights displayed and expected the captain to tack to the west and follow the deep-water channel safely around the island. A moment later, he could see that it was too late to make the turn and apparent that the vessel was destined to hit the pier. It was coming toward shore at a fast clip. The doctor quickly moved back from the edge, out of harm's way and off the pier. As the sail-boat came closer he recognized it to be a multi-hull and knew that it could go much shallower than other designs. One more minute and it would be on top of the pier. Standing safely under the streetlight by his scooter, he braced himself and prepared for the impact.

Lucky for anyone on board, the boat hit bottom fifteen feet from the end of the pier. It lurched forward under the impact and the tiller snapped into pieces as it planted itself in the sand. The sounds of loose gear and kitchen implements hitting the walls inside the cabin crashed through the silent morning air as the boat turned on one side under the pressure of the breeze against its sail. As it fell back from the inertia and settled into the knee-deep water, the clamor died. Then he heard a sound that shook him to the bone. It was Krismas, crying.

"Catch a dream! Don't let go

39. Epilogue

That **morning the** South Beach Pier was a beehive of activity. Everyone on the island made their way down to the end of Duval Street to take a look at the Canadian Soul and cast their speculations as to how Jillian had disappeared. She was hanging on to life by a breath when the EMS truck rushed her and the baby away. The questions left unanswered by the bloody mess at the helm and the open first aid kit in the galley would be satisfied later that day when a purser on the Carnival Cruise Line ship, *Imagination,* exited the bridge on the portside and spotted Ethan's lifeless body floating face down twelve miles offshore in the Florida Straits. Luckily, the Coast Guard retrieved him before being lost to sharks.

It's been a year and six months since Jillian washed ashore. Doctor Colburn now works as the staff psychiatrist in charge of the Mental Health Services to the Homeless division of the Lower Keys Medical Center at the De Poo Hospital on Kennedy Avenue. Jillian is working as a part-time office assistant to Dr. Colburn at the hospital. Her duties are limited to cleaning the offices and preparing the therapy rooms for sessions. She had refused to return home to Gloucester so her folks are supporting her and baby Krismas while she struggles to reestablish herself in Key West. She continues to do volunteer work at the soup kitchen.

The Canadian Soul was released by the sheriff to Ethan's dad in Montreal and, after several trips to Key West to visit his new granddaughter, he signed the boat over to Jillian's parents as a second home for all to use. He stays on the boat when he is in town and continues to contribute generously to Jillian's monthly financial needs. He pays all the medical bills for her and Krismas and picks up her monthly rent payment as well. Without his help the Dougherty's could never have covered the expenses.

Bill and Dolores recently purchased the Flamingo Crossing Ice Cream store from Bert and Tequila, who are keeping the wine club next door. They now run the shop in both Gloucester and Key West. They hope to sell the Massachusetts operation and move permanently to the island where they can offer better support for Jillian and the baby. In the meantime, Bill sleeps on the boat and rides a scooter to the Crossing every day of the week while Dolores and Trina run the shop back home in Gloucester.

Bo is planning on moving to the island this May when he graduates from high school. He wants to attend classes at the Florida Keys Community College to study in its marine propulsion department while working with his dad. He plans to get his associate degree under his belt and then try out for the Navy SEAL program in San Diego. He is turning out to be quite the pride of the family.

Evenings, Jillian scoops ice cream at the Crossing with her dad while Krismas plays with the patron's dogs on the porch. As long as she stays on her medication and doesn't miss her psych appointments with Dr. C., her condition continues to improve and she seems to function reasonably well. All in all, things are working out just fine.

I got a call from Barb last Tuesday night. She gave me the update on everybody and said that my stuff is still safe in storage in their downstairs storage shed/guest house. My desktop computer, my dive equipment and fishing poles, my Fender amplifier and 1967 Gibson SG guitar, and my kayak are waiting for my return. Unfortunately, I am still here at my father's home in Deltona waiting for the neurosurgeon at the Tampa Veterans Administration Hospital to schedule my neck surgery. Hopefully, I can soon get this behind me and return to the friends and life I left behind in Key West. Till then, may all our boats stay afloat and our losses manageable. Hopefully soon, I'll see you on the beach!

The End

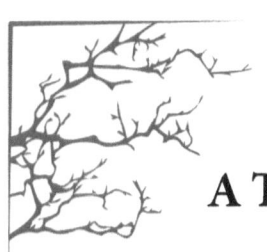

A Tribute to a Lost Soul

Unconfirmed Report

Paddy was found in the woods on Stock Island last month, beaten to death. Rumor has it that two local teens in a white pickup truck had been seen leaving the area in a hurry the night before the body was discovered. The story has been kept hushed by city officials, leaving all of us that knew Paddy wondering what had happened to him. This kind of brutal crime is always suppressed in the news down here. It's bad for "business" you know! Tourism business that is!

I always kept a glass of Chardonnay by the printer for Paddy while I wrote this book. Kind of a toast to Paddy's lost and tormented soul.

Here's to you, old buddy! I hope you found your pot of gold on the other side of the rainbow! You were such a mess over here!

Authors Note

Sonny was a friend to me and though his troubled and tormented last years were full of episodes well worth depicting in a novel, the portrayal of Paddy in this work of literature is in no way intended to represent any action or behavior known to be engaged in by Charles W. Rosen Jr. (aka Sonny).

May this novel stand as a memorial to a lost soul who lived the life he chose with remarkable courage and adapted to its challenges with uncommon resilience!

Thank you, Sonny, for the inspiration of Paddy!

Charles W. Rosen Jr.

VIRGINIA BEACH – Charles W. "Sonny" Rosen Jr., son of the late XXXXXXXXX, and the late XXXXXXXXXXX, died in Key West, Fla., March 25, 2007. Sonny was born in Norfolk. Sonny served his country in the United States Marine Corps and was honorably discharged in 1963. Sonny is survived by his children, XXXXXXX. XXXXXX, XXXXX, XXXXXXX; four grandchildren; his siblings, XXXXXXXXX, XXXXXXXX, and XXXXXXX; as well as cousins, nieces and nephews. An informal graveside service will be held at Forest Lawn Cemetery, Norfolk, November 3, at 11 a.m. The family requests in lieu of flowers, memorial donations should be made to Alcoholics Anonymous.

Rosen, Charles William (aka: Sonny)
Monroe County Florida Arrest Record
DoB: 04/04/1942 **Age:** 63 **Sex:** M **Race:** W
Arrest Date: 02/04/2006
Arrest #: MCSO06ARR001090
Offense #: KWPD06OFF000773
Address: 881876 O/S HWY, TAVENIER, FL
Occupation: MCSO00MNI402809 in RETIRED
Arrest Location: DUVAL STREET KEY WEST, 218
Charges
1 Felony Count(s) of 784.021.1a
AGGRAV ASSLT – W DEADLY WEAPON WITHOUT INTENT TO KILL
1 Misdemeanor Count(s) of 790.1.
WEAPON OFFENSE – IMPROPER EXHIBIT FIREARM OR DANGEROUS WEAPON
1 Misdemeanor Count(s) of 827.04.2

CHILD ABUSE – DEPRIVES – PHYSICAL/MENTAL INJURY
1 Misdemeanor Count(s) of 877.03.
DISORD CONDUCT – BREACH OF PEACE
Officer/Agency: KWPD – KWPD
Bond Amount: $0
Arrest Date: 05/16/2006
CAD #: MCSO06CAD047866
Arrest #: MCSO06ARR004484
Offense #: MCSO06OFF004581
Address: 881876 O/S HWY, TAVENIER, FL
Occupation: MCSO00MNI402809 in RETIRED
Arrest Location: OVERSEAS HWY MARATHON, 5407
Charges:1 Misdemeanor Count(s) of 812.015.
RETAIL THEFT/SHOPLIFTING
Officer/Agency: 4118 – MCSO\ROAD PATROL – SECTOR 4
Bond Amount: $0
Arrest Date: 12/03/2006
Arrest #: MCSO06ARR010719
Offense #: KWPD06OFF7310
Address: 881876 O/S HWY, TAVENIER, FL
Occupation: MCSO00MNI402809 in RETIRED
Arrest Location: #B DUVAL STR./REAR PARKING LOT KEY WEST, 419
Charges
1 Misdemeanor Count(s) of 810.09.1A1
TRESPASSING UNAUTH PERSONS ENTERING UPON OR
REMAINS ON PROPERTY
Officer/Agency: KWPD – KWPD
Bond Amount: $0
Arrest Date: 02/17/2007
Arrest #: MCSO07ARR001574
Offense #: KWPD07-000701
Address: 881876 O/S HWY, TAVENIER, FL
Occupation: MCSO00MNI402809 in RETIRED
Arrest Location: N. ROOSEVELT BLVD KEY WEST, 2900

Charges
1 Misdemeanor Count(s) of 810.09.1A1
TRESPASSING UNAUTH PERSONS ENTERING UPON OR
REMAINS ON PROPERTY
Officer/Agency: KWPD – KWPD
Bond Amount: $0

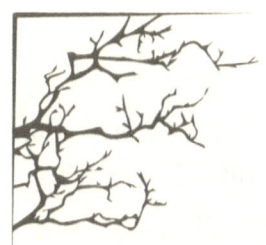

News Articles

10 Men Wanted in Killing of Guyana's Agriculture Minister
Tuesday, July 18, 2006

GEORGETOWN, Guyana (AFP): Ten men are being sought in connection with the April killing of Guyanese agriculture minister Satyadeow Sawh, police said Friday.

Assistant Police Commissioner Ivelaw Whittaker said police were offering a $10,000dollar reward for information leading to each man's arrest. Among those wanted is Troy Dick, who escaped from prison along with four others in 2002.

Four of the men are known only by aliases.

Police linked the wanted men to the criminal havens of Buxton Village, about 12 miles (19 kilometers) east of Georgetown, and Agricola, Greater Georgetown, about five miles (eight kilometers) from the heart of the city.

Sawh, 50, was gunned down by heavilyarmed men on April 22 at his home near Buxton Village, along with his brother Rajpatri Sawh, 62, and sister Phulmattie Persaud, 54. All three were Guyaneseborn naturalized Canadian citizens.

The Indianbacked Guyanese government had called the killings politically motivated but had stopped short of directly blaming anyone in the South American country that is racially divided almost evenly between descendants of indentured laborers from India and descendants of African slaves.

Sawh served as Guyana's ambassador to Venezuela, Colombia and Ecuador from 1993 to 1996.

Prior to that, he lived in Canada, where he earned a degree in economics from York University and headed a support group for Guyana's ruling MarxistLeninist People's Progressive Party.

Found bodies were Cubans

Case epitomizes human drama

When he was called to attend a Cuban migrant landing, a mostly routine assignment while on road patrol, Monroe County sheriff's Detective Terry Smith said it was like babysitting until the federal agents arrived.

But when four mostly decomposed bodies washed ashore in the Upper Keys over two days in August, Smith began to see the human side of Cuban dissidents and the suffering of their families when they go missing at sea.

The four Cubans whose remains were found between Ocean Reef Club and Lower Matecumbe on Aug. 21 and 22 launched a special investigation that lasted eight months, until all four were identified.

But they were only four of eight who left Cuba in a homemade raft just as Tropical Storm Fay was skirting the underbelly of Cuba, soon to turn north and roil the Florida Straits, according to Ramon Saul Sanchez, a citizen activist who works with the Cuban Democracy Movement in Miami. They knew it was a time when the Cuban government would not be looking for them, he said.

"These men were dissidents and the Cuban government was watching them," Sanchez said during a sheriff's press conference Wednesday at the Murray E. Nelson Government and Cultural Center. "They are among the many thousands of dissidents who have perished in the ocean, fleeing suppression."

The tedious process of identifying the bodies and then telling their families was outlined for the TV, radio and print media by Smith, Sanchez, Sheriff Bob Peryam and Monroe County Medical Examiner Dr. Hunt Scheuerman.

"I had to give the relatives the news," said Sanchez. "Osmani SeguraGarcia was a Cuban journalist, one of those we were able to identify through DNA. When I went to his mother's house in Miami, the first thing she said was, 'Please don't bring me bad news.' Of course, I did. She started crying.

This is very sad, but we were able to get some closure for these families," he said.

After media reports began appearing in South Florida, Garcia's mother contacted the authorities. She, as did other family members, provided a DNA sample for comparison. The sample was sent to the FBI's Mitochondrial Missing and Unidentified DNA Data Base in Quantico, Va. Her son's remains were identified.

Two brothers, Rolando and Raul Alberna, were on the raft with the six others. Their sister lives in the Miami area.

"She heard about the bodies and knew her brothers had left Cuba and had not arrived in the United States. She submitted a DNA sample . . . and it was confirmed that one of the bodies was one of the brothers, but there was no way to tell which one," according to a sheriff's press release.

Scheuerman said the brothers did not look alike, that one was taller than the other. After being at sea so long the only identifying factor was a shoe on one foot. Wave action apparently had stripped their bodies of clothing.

"After determining that the shoe size would match the taller of the brothers, we determined that Rolando's body was the one we found."

His brother's body, along with men known only by their first names, never was found.

"The families were frantic," Smith said. "Miami family members began receiving DNA samples from relatives in Cuba in plastic bags. They were not sterile and not secure samples so the FBI was not able to use them. There is nothing now in place for us to get supervised samples from Cuba."

As a result, Sanchez in December sent a letter to U.S. Sen. Robert Menendez asking for help in setting up supervised DNA sampling in Cuba.

"This was a tough case," Peryam said. "In some cases, there will never be closure."

Smith said the case personalized the Cuban dilemma for him. "I saw their concern for their loved ones," he said. "It's tough on the families."

Authorities initially thought the men could have been murdered, so they put forth a great effort, Peryam said.

"What if these men were our own families?" he reasoned. "This is a prime example of desperate people taking desperate measures."

"I hope I don't have to do this again," Smith added.

Don't miss out!

Visit the website below and you can sign up to receive emails whenever Ian Ritchie Stewart publishes a new book. There's no charge and no obligation.

https://books2read.com/r/B-A-HHQCB-TSXYC

BOOKS 2 READ

Connecting independent readers to independent writers.

About the Author

Florida native, Ian Ritchie Stewart delivers a unique perspective on living life at the "End of tha Road". As a Community-Based Care Social Worker, Family Services Coordinator, and long-time resident of the Florida Keys, Mr. Stewart is profoundly familiar with the hidden pitfalls and challenges that lie in wait, ready to swallow the dreams of ill-prepared seekers of Paradise! Welcome to Lost Souls of Paradise!

Read more at https://www.lostsoulsofparadise.com.